TIMBERWOLF

BOOK ONE IN THE SPY-FI 'TIMBERWOLF' SERIES

TOM JULIAN

WILDBLUE PRESS

WildBluePress.com

TIMBERWOLF published by:

WILDBLUE PRESS
P.O. Box 102440
Denver, Colorado 80250

Publisher Disclaimer: Any opinions, statements of fact or fiction, descriptions, dialogue, and citations found in this book were provided by the author and are solely those of the author. The publisher makes no claim as to their veracity or accuracy and assumes no liability for the content.

This book is a work of fiction. The characters, places, incidents, and dialogue are the product of the author's imagination and are not to be construed as real, or if real, are used fictitiously. Any resemblance to actual events, locales, or persons, either living or dead, is purely coincidental.

© 2023 by Tom Julian, Original © 2017 by Tom Julian

All rights reserved. No part of this book may be reproduced in any form or by any means without the prior written consent of the Publisher, excepting brief quotes used in reviews.

WILDBLUE PRESS is registered at the U.S. Patent and Trademark Offices.

Trade Paperback ISBN 978-1-960332-30-1
eBook ISBN 978-1-960332-39-4
Hardcover ISBN 978-1-960332-41-7

Cover and Interior Design by Elijah Toten,
www.totencreative.com

Cover Design © 2023 WildBlue Press. All rights reserved.

TIMBERWOLF

*For my wife Brenda and the beans, Astur and
Liam—you keep my imagination young!*

&

*For Bill H. You would have been first in
line to read this. Miss you, friend.*

TABLE OF CONTENTS

ACKNOWLEDGMENTS

To my parents, Tom and Catherine, who always encouraged me to write and to tell stories. I would not be a writer without the encouragement and the Legos you gave me as a kid. To my great influences—Ridley Scott, Ron Moore, James S.A. Corey, The Coen Brothers, Kurt Vonnegut, Robert Charles Wilson, and Greg Bear. To my countless friends and family who supported me during the writing. To the podcasts and content creators I enjoyed when I needed a break — I Hate It But I Love It, Modern Day Eratosthenes, Alex Schmidt, Isaac Arthur, The Infographics Show, Stuff You Should Know, Redletter Media, The Bugle, as well as Conan, Sona and Matt for the infinite silliness. To Elijah Toten for the kickass cover and finally to Rowe Carenen for the fabulous editing job!

ACT I

NEMESIS

Fangelsi Cryogenic Prison—July 22, 2265

Nemesis settled into the clearing on Fangelsi as a herd of elk-like creatures bounded away. They stared at the frigate from the trees, their eyes glowing in the night. Just as Emmanuel Gray had planned, the spaceship had avoided the world's security net and landed undetected two valleys over from the planet's only structure, a maximum-security cryogenic prison. Gray called for the men to assemble in the galley for a prayer service and went back to his tiny private quarters to get ready.

He found himself looking at his face in the mirror, wondering how he had gotten to this state. He felt old for the first time in his life; not tired, but aged. His sixty years showed in the gullies under his eyes, but he was still a vibrant man, able to run for miles and spar hand-to-hand with men half his age. His weariness wasn't physical, but more a reflection of the journey he'd taken. He'd been a general, a governor, and now he was a wanted man leading an untested crew in a crusade that could charitably be described as insane. For Emmanuel Gray, there was no going back.

He felt the short goatee on his chin. Since he'd left the Assault Corps, he'd grown some facial hair and he liked the way it filled his face out. It reminded him that his life was different now, that this hardscrabble free-fall was way beyond normal structures.

Gray put on the white collar that marked him as a bishop of a religious order simply known as Believers. The core of the faith was a disdain for alien species. As humanity had expanded out into the galaxy, it had met an abundance of intelligences. First contact became routine and spiritually troublesome. Many species believed, like humans did, that they had been created in God's image. The result was a crisis of faith and a series of wars with humanity as the aggressor—the fire that burned down dozens of worlds.

Over the previous hundred years, humans had fought twenty-eight species to near extinction. In the last twenty years alone, it had been the Phaelon, the Tiaski, the Devorin, the Szykul…and the Arnock. The Arnock had finally been the force that stopped mankind cold five years ago. Gray balled his fists, feeling his fingernails dig into his palms. The Arnock. *Goddamned spiders got into our minds, were ready for us. Slaughtered us. Made us desperate…*He found his eyes in the mirror again. He knew desperate.

"Timberwolf Velez." Just saying the man's name exhausted him. What he'd done had been desperate, perhaps unforgivable, but it seemed like the only way at the time. "Timberwolf Velez." *Maybe there's no forgiveness for me…*

There was a knock at the door. Michael, Gray's second in command, entered without being asked. His face was scarred by plasma burns and his bedraggled hair hung to his shoulders. "They're ready, Emmanuel."

"Thank you, Michael. Hand me my vest." Gray put on the black vest Michael handed him. He caught Michael eyeing the lightning bolt over the breast pocket. He wondered if one day Michael would shoot him when his back was turned. He would certainly have cause to do it.

In the galley, the men kneeled on prayer mats, the tables and chairs piled off to the side. The Believer symbol hung on the wall at the front of the room. The two intersecting arcs were similar to an Ichthys or "Jesus-fish," though turned downward. It represented a closed eye that only saw the truth set out before it by God and excluded everything else.

Gray stepped behind a podium and looked out at the soldiers—young, male, and all volunteers from prominent Believer families. Some of them had Believer marks on their foreheads and gazed up at Gray wide-eyed, like they might be raptured at any moment. All were veterans of some sort, and all bragged of combat experience, but Gray doubted almost every one of them. Before he'd gotten into the upper ranks, he'd run the Assault Corps training program out of

Fort Chancellor. He'd trained thousands of men to fight the Phaelon, the Tiaski and other enemies.

The men before him didn't have that thousand-yard stare Gray knew so well. He could tell none of them had endured days of artillery or slogged their way through the Mile High Red Forest on Phaelon Prime, or fought street-to-street in the insurgencies that would flare up on human colonies. He'd wanted to fill the ranks full of mercenaries from Michael's stable, but Gray had backers that insisted that his ship be crewed by Believers.

So this is what I am now? A religious fanatic? Some closed-eyed warrior priest? He saw Michael in the back of the room, huffing and skeptical as he fell to his knees. Gray began, putting the boom in his voice from when he was a drill sergeant. "God showed us the way from our world and sent his Believers out to the stars. He told us to cleanse the way of all not made in his image." Behind Gray, a wild-eyed fanatic named Izabeck took down his every word, scribbling frantically with a stylus into an electronic notebook.

Gray continued, "God means for us to cleanse his universe of aliens. We have closed eyes. No questions. We've done His will and fought almost every race we've come upon. Who fought the Phaelon?"

The soldiers responded with a throaty cry of "I-ya!" and repeated it after the mention of each enemy.

"The Devorin…The Tiaski…The Szykul." Gray paused, scanning the room for someone he knew wasn't there. "Who fought the Arnock?"

No one responded. Their heads hung with hints of shame. Gray's eyes saddened for a moment and then filled with anger. "We all fought the Arnock. Those damned spiders! You, and you, and me! We all gave too much to them. Like no other enemy. They took our minds. Drove us to madness on contact. There are no veterans from that war."

Michael stared daggers through Gray as he continued, "You're the knights of a new crusade. The Arnock are what drives us. Our peace with them is a sin and those that forged it will perish." The men nodded their heads. Gray grew in fury. "Today is our first step towards healing from that peace. First we need the keys, then we open the door. We'll take the factory at Highland!"

"I-ya!" the men erupted.

"We'll make an army and finish our work. God's will be done, on all our worlds as it is in heaven." Gray finished solemnly, hanging his head and closing his eyes like he was hung on the Believer symbol behind him.

At the back of the room, Michael stood, interrupting the moment. Gray's nostrils flared. Michael was always needling, questioning—unable to give up the past, looking for a way to settle accounts with Gray for what had happened so long ago. *That goddamned sonofabitch.*

"And what about those who don't believe?" Michael demanded. An argument hung in the air between them that no one else knew about. Old wounds, scraped raw again and part of it, even when he didn't know it, was Timberwolf Velez.

Before Gray could answer, the soldiers responded in unison with words out of their teaching. "Cut them down!"

Gray had Michael in his sights, wishing the man had fallen to his death over Saturn's moon of Enceladus so many years ago. "I-ya. Cut them all down," he bellowed with as much love and conviction as he could muster.

DEMONSTRATION

"He took an arm right off the last handler and almost pulled him into the cage." In *Nemesis's* cargo bay, Thomas dropped hunks of raw meat into a slot in the cage. The beast within was a Sabatin, a bio-engineered killing machine that appeared to be halfway between a tiger and a salamander but was made from alien DNA. He was named Wrath and Gray couldn't hold in a smile when he looked at him. Wrath was a creature of grace and precision coupled with power. Gray looked to the muscle rippling under his silver biological armor. He doubted the cage really held him, but that, more to the truth, Wrath agreed to be held for the moment.

The beast took apart its meal, one powerful claw pinning the meat almost delicately while his other claw deftly sliced it into pieces. The tiger stripes of Wrath's muzzle quickly became marked with the blood of his meal and his dagger-sharp teeth gleamed red.

The cage shook, moving along the floor of the cargo bay. "How's Wrath doing today?" Gray asked.

Thomas was the beast's handler and had kept Wrath isolated for the past few months, training and imprinting him. "He knows he's going to get out and play!" Thomas was excited and fiddled with his heads-up display goggles. He could see what Wrath saw through a camera mounted on the side of his head.

Gray went close to the cage, too close for Thomas, who tried to step between. "I'd like to pet him. Can I?" Thomas's face told Gray that he thought that was insane, but Gray knelt down and cooed softly to the beast. At first Wrath continued to growl and hiss, but soon he calmed and placed his snout through the bars. Gray patted Wrath warmly and the creature huffed and grunted.

"Bishop Gray, are you ready?" Thomas asked.

"Yes, Thomas, I believe we are." The beast pitched inside his cage, and it lurched forward. "Oh, and I would like you to show off a bit when he gets in there. Let's see what Wrath can do."

The mission was imprinted onto Wrath already and Thomas's job was going to be mostly monitoring. Gray found it ironic that Wrath was about to break into a maximum-security cryogenic prison to grab the man who had genetically engineered him in the first place. Michael appeared beside Gray. "You're sure Ivan Dacha's inside?"

Gray huffed. "He better be. I put him here."

Wrath burst from his cage and the men who had gathered in the cargo bay scattered. Wrath ignored them and climbed up into the rafters and back down again, excited with pent up energy. He was a flash of silver, over eight feet tall and covered in biological armor. His claws scraped the floor, leaving long scratches on the metal.

"*Ra shir!*" At the command from Thomas, the beast calmed and poised himself for the next order. Thomas raised his arm and with a hand signal, he ordered Wrath down the gangplank and out into the night.

Gray and the rest crowded around a monitor and watched as Wrath tore through the thick forest, easily avoiding the security traps and pressure sensors. Fangelsi was an expertly designed prison, but it was no match for a creature like Wrath—dexterous, smart, and fast. He dexterously scaled the exterior fence, slipping between the laser sensors. He perched at the top of the fence for a moment, the cameras and sensors on the interior walls peering his way. He steadied for a moment and then leaped from his momentary perch.

The ground on the other side of the fence was covered entirely with pressure sensors. As soon as he touched the ground, the place lit up like a Christmas tree. Auto-cannons swiveled and plasma bursts raked the ground. Wrath leaped up to a cannon on the wall and tore it apart, its plasma cell bursting as he tossed it away. He leaped to the next cannon and paused a second so the other cannons could target him. As they fired, he sprang away, the cannon getting blasted to pieces. He leaped to the next one and repeated, only the occasional plasma burst bouncing off his armor.

Wrath leaped to the last cannon and held it with one of his merciless claws so it couldn't swivel. With his other claw, he skillfully opened up the mechanism and disconnected the plasma cell. All cannons silent now, he loped unhurriedly over the next fence, the plasma cell tucked up under him like a football. Before him now was the main facility. Without breaking his stride, he shook up the plasma cell and scraped its connector along the concrete until the friction made it sizzle. When he was a hundred yards from the main gate, he launched the makeshift bomb and dove for cover.

Back on *Nemesis*, the crew felt the explosion and Wrath's feed went dead for a moment. When it came back, the crew gasped, Gray smiling uncontrollably. The facility was cracked open and burning. Most of the power was out, just a few red lights spinning meekly. "Can Wrath enter?" Thomas asked.

"Oh yes, get him in there!" Gray said.

Wrath slipped in through the wreckage and went up the stairs, meeting the first guards on the third landing. Before they could even react, he'd slashed through two of them. The other got off random shots before succumbing to his flurry of teeth and claws. Gray grinned widely as he watched, leaning on Thomas's shoulder.

On the levels above, giant iron doors rolled closed as red lights flashed and sirens wailed. One guard remained on the wrong side and pounded on the door as his colleagues looked through the porthole and shook their heads.

"We are on facility lockdown," a computer voice repeated.

The guard emptied his weapon on Wrath, but the plasma bursts deflected harmlessly away. The beast approached closely, scanning the door, the guard struggling to reload. Wrath slashed the guard down as he examined the lock. Then with his shoulders flexing, he turned the wheel on the door until its gears snapped and spun free. Bayonets extruded from over his forearms, and he dug into the lock mechanism. He peeled the door outward, tearing it off its hinges. He tossed it away as two guards on the other side unloaded their weapons on him.

Wrath lashed out with his razor-tipped tongue, taking one guard's head clean off. His plasma clip empty, the other man just stood there, terrified and unable to make a sound.

Wrath backed up, dropped his head and drove his iron-crowned skull into the man's chest, smashing him against the wall. The guard crumpled like a rag-doll. Beyond the second door, there was no resistance.

The guards inside the command center watched Wrath's silver flash go past twice, hoping beyond hope the Sabatin wouldn't find them. But after a few agonizing minutes, he'd checked every other door and he approached the command center almost casually, panting lightly from the action.

He broke the handle on the locked door as easily as turning it and pushed it open. Inside, a dozen guards stood terrified, jaws agape. Some fell to their knees and gasped. One man took his fingers and traced the Believer symbol on his forehead as tears stained his face.

Wrath whirled into them, teeth and claws everywhere at once, gunfire and the screams of men ringing out. On *Nemesis*, the crew saw nothing but a blur of silver and red through Wrath's camera. When he was done just a few seconds later, a red mist hung in the air and the bodies lay on the floor. Gray watched this over the monitor, his hand over his mouth, elated. "We are on facility lockdown," the prison's computer voice still droned over and over.

When Wrath was done, he found a computer terminal. With the dexterity of a pianist, he scanned through the roster of inmates. He found the location of Ivan Dacha, all the way on the bottom level. Once he had it, Wrath bolted. Gray and the men watched the feed as Wrath made corners and rushed down ducts with nausea-inducing swiftness. In less than a minute, he was in the cryogenic storage area in the bottom-most level. Acres of chambers were stacked a dozen-high in a mausoleum of convicts. He rushed to Ivan Dacha's location, his thick breath visible in the chilled air.

With equal parts dexterity and strength, he pulled out Ivan Dacha's cryogenic chamber, releasing a puff of white vapor. The light on Wrath's camera illuminated a picture of an impish man with a receding hairline. His breath fogged the image, but back on *Nemesis*, Gray nodded to Thomas that they had their man.

Wrath held the chamber under one arm and carefully made his way back to the main level, going back through the blasted entrance and over the series of walls. When Wrath was back in the forest, Gray dropped *Nemesis's* gangplank and the men stood in anticipation, some thumbing their weapons.

Outside, a steady, thumping gallop grew closer and closer. A flash of silver burst from the tree line and in seconds Wrath rushed up the gangplank. He slid the cryogenic chamber across the deck and looked up at Gray, almost smiling.

Gray turned to the men, who stood awestruck. "That's what we did with one Sabatin. You want to see what we can do with ten thousand? You think the Arnock will last a week against us? You think their friends in the damned Department of Peace Enforcement will last?"

Gray stalked the cargo bay, the men now rapt. He bellowed, "No, friends, the D.P.E. will fall and we'll get our way of life back. Military men will protect the human race again against all not made in God's image!"

Windwhistle, a very young man Gray had never heard speak before, shouted at the top of his lungs, "There is no god but God and we heed his judgment!" The others repeated the chant as Gray rallied them to shout louder. Finally, when they reached a crescendo, Gray motioned for them to be silent.

"There is no god but God and we heed his judgment," Gray finished with his hand over his heart, pausing for effect. After a moment, he clapped his hands once. "Now move!"

The men scattered, Michael and Sol, Gray's other lieutenant, herding them. They needed to prep their pressurized armored fighting rigs, check their gear, and attend to countless other things before the next phase. In an instant the cargo bay was empty, save for one. Izabeck still scribbled furiously in his electronic notebook. "How comes the Word of God?" Gray asked him.

Izabeck didn't stop writing and didn't make eye contact with Gray either. "God's flowing through us here, Bishop." Izabeck smiled, still looking down. Gray patted his shoulder, but not before considering giving Izabeck a new home here on Fangelsi. Gray's backers were an order of Believers known as The Clergy and they had placed Izabeck on his crew to "document the sacred mission," but in truth he was reporting back every single thing Gray said and did. Some in The Clergy had considered Gray's religious conversion a little too convenient. Gray considered The Clergy a problem he would need to get rid of later.

"Brother Izabeck, these military matters don't rattle your soul, do they?"

Izabeck stopped writing and looked up, his nervous energy flowing out of every pore. "I'm seeing things that will make God's story complete," Izabeck replied.

Gray nodded. *What the hell is this guy talking about?* Gray put his arm around Izabeck. "Someday, all of this will be immortalized in stained glass somewhere and you'll be there with a halo and a stylus, looking down on some thankful souls sitting in church. Light will be bursting through you onto their faces." Gray painted the picture with his hands. "Won't that be grand?"

"I don't ask God for much, Bishop."

Gray looked through Izabeck, like he'd looked through thousands of young cadets. "You tell The Clergy everything. You let Cardinal Jacob know everything, understand? Remember, God's watching you."

Gray turned and left. "God's watching you, too," Izabeck said under his breath.

ARCHANGEL

D.P.E. Archangel—Nine Days Out from Tach-One Station

Timberwolf followed Conrad, a young Department of Peace Enforcement officer with a vacant stare and a perfect haircut, down the corridor. He wobbled in the artificial gravity. His knees were never able to get used to the inertial dampeners that kept everyone walking on the same floor. Timberwolf didn't like being in spaceships and *Archangel* was a beast. It bustled with crew, and he couldn't seem to keep out of their way. It was vast, but at the same time claustrophobic and every door looked the same to him. When he wasn't in the field and instead confined in a steel and plastic warren, he became keenly aware of what could best be described as a "presence," the alien mind-bender that inhabited his consciousness.

Five years ago, towards the end of the Arnock War, he had been on a smash and grab mission to capture an Arnock Master named Kizik. It had been a disaster. Everyone else on the team had been lost, driven mad by Kizik's mind-bending and either killing themselves or each other. Timberwolf had been the only survivor and had been in Kizik's presence for just a few minutes, but that was more than enough time for the creature to enter his mind and leave a part of itself behind.

He had the distinction of being the only human ever to survive capture by the Arnock. As Conrad led him through another heavy door, Timberwolf caught a glimpse of his reflection in a porthole. Survival was relative. His face was gaunt, his eyes sunken into his head. He was three days late for a shave and he hadn't slept in a week. Nine days out from Tach-One Station and he had been given literally nothing to do. He grimaced, the presence of Kizik grinding in the back of his mind, teasing him like a mosquito from someplace light years away.

"What's the Doc want?" Timberwolf asked Conrad.

"Dr. Tier has got her usual questions." Conrad faked being friendly. Most Department of Peace Enforcement personnel had that trait. They were the sort that had no problem asking about your family before blowing you out an airlock.

"Tier's questions are never usual. I keep telling her the same stories."

Conrad opened the door to Dr. Tier's office. "Today's different. She wants to know about the box." Conrad smiled deeply, the most sincere and friendly smile Timberwolf had ever seen. *Shit*, Timberwolf thought.

Dr. Tier was a top-ranking D.P.E. operative, so high up the food chain that very few people knew her name or even of her existence. Timberwolf thought that she might report directly to the President or to someone in the cabinet. If she had an official title, he didn't know what it was. She was simply "Dr. Tier." She'd let it slip once that she had only two other peers, but he didn't know their names or purviews. She was a medical doctor by training, but at heart she was a stone-cold spook—a handler and a puppet-master who sent deadly men such as Timberwolf out to do the often nasty business of the Department of Peace Enforcement.

Dr. Tier sat behind her desk and Conrad took his usual place—behind her and leaning against a cabinet. She nodded at Timberwolf in acknowledgment with a vacancy that told him she was nothing but the job. She wasn't an unattractive woman, but her features were severe. An angular chin and high cheekbones set the stage for large blue eyes that sucked in everything around them. Dark brown hair hung in a pristine but fashionable bob.

Timberwolf noticed someone else standing near the door behind him; a mountain of a man he knew as Capote. Timberwolf had never seen him speak, but he floated around whenever serious muscle might be needed. Timberwolf did his usual thing and mentally counted the moves it would take to kill everyone in the room.

"Twenty-two?" Dr. Tier guessed. She knew his game.

"Seventeen," Timberwolf responded.

Dr. Tier didn't fake smiles. It wouldn't have fooled anyone, but she smiled now. "Even with Capote here, seventeen moves to kill the room?"

"Yeah, that's all I need." Timberwolf detected a slight shuffle from the man behind him.

"I hate games, Mr. Velez," Dr. Tier said nonchalantly as she opened a manila envelope.

"Then you picked the wrong line of work, Doc. We're on the cloak and dagger committee." Towards the end of the Arnock War the D.P.E. was technically established as a diplomatic corps to enforce peace treaties, but its underlying mission was to stop new conflicts from arising. It countered the military and religious establishments and immediately gained the ire of both.

Since the *Alchemy* incident over a hundred years before, humanity had been in a constant state of war and had been wildly successful. Goaded on by The Clergy, dozens of alien species had been wiped out, or their populations reduced to trivial numbers. Interstellar conflict became a way of life, but with the horrific losses of the Arnock War, the cycle needed to be broken.

The D.P.E. was empowered at the highest levels to keep humanity out of conflict, and the agency quickly gained a reputation for not playing nice. Zealous generals were discredited and retired, xenophobic speech was exposed and ridiculed, and military spending was slashed overnight. When the game needed to become more hands-on, men like Timberwolf lurked in the shadows.

Not everyone agreed with the push for peace. Many in the Assault Corps and in politics felt the worst threats were the ones left festering and that the Arnock were just waiting for their moment to strike. Others stood to lose lots of money with the dawn of peace. War had been great for business. With peace, the economies of many worlds were in recession.

On monitors around the room in Dr. Tier's office, the helmet cam footage from Timberwolf's encounter with Kizik began to play. Some screens were in black and white, some were in color; some images jerky, some perfectly smooth. The monitors glowed with video of soldiers in armored pressurized fighting rigs running and dying, shooting at ghosts on a jagged red world. Some screens showed the video backwards and the soldiers leaped up and back to life. It was crass to show this, but Timberwolf might have done the same thing.

"You've asked to go back in the field. In your current condition, that's insane," Dr. Tier said.

"I'm in my *current condition* because I'm not in the field," Timberwolf responded.

"You claim there is an Arnock presence called Kizik in your mind?"

"I don't claim that. It's there. When I'm not working, it comes over. Likes to chat."

"You took any mission that would get you killed after the Arnock grabbed you."

"Didn't work out."

Dr. Tier shuffled some papers. Timberwolf could tell they were photographs.

"You're a bad liar," she said softly. "Well, you're a great liar physically. You have literally no tells. Let's never play cards." She motioned to the electronic surveillance surrounding them. "The machines can't even pick it up when you try to deceive me. What you can't lie your way through is the goddamned evidence."

"The box?" Timberwolf knew when not to bluff.

"What's in the box?" She turned the end of her question into a soft hiss. Before he could answer she went on. "You didn't go to Telock Sen six weeks ago to *discuss things* with the insurgent leaders there. You picked up a box. It's in your cabin."

Timberwolf smiled. The monitors around the room showed his drop-lifter crashing, crushing fleeing men in its wake. "So tell me what you know about the box," Timberwolf suggested.

"Sure, I'll play. The box in your quarters, we can't scan it. You know we tried. Not a speck of an image comes back. We thought about sawing into it."

Timberwolf interrupted, "I wouldn't call that safe."

Dr. Tier smiled. "Don't worry. We did get some clues from the exterior. It's made of a unique plastisteel compound. It's from Highland."

"This whole ship's from Highland."

"Then you'll have no problem telling us what it is and who you met with."

Conrad froze the images. The hulking figure of Kizik stared down at Timberwolf from the monitors in a dozen variations: a giant spider with six glowing red eyes. "I want that thing out of my head."

"Does this person look familiar?" Dr. Tier slid a photo of Ivan Dacha, the man Gray had broken out of Fangelsi, across the desk. Timberwolf was surprised by what he saw, but he barely raised an eyebrow.

The man was identical to Sergey Dacha, the person Timberwolf had met on Telock Sen, except for a slightly receding hairline. "Looks like the guy who gave me the box. Maybe a carbon copy."

"That's Ivan Dacha. Your old friend General Gray… sorry, Governor Gray…sorry, Bishop Gray, broke into a cryogenic prison and took him. Gray had a Sabatin with him. Tore the place apart, literally."

Dr. Tier folded her arms. "This is why you aren't back in the field. Why you have to feel the full brunt of whatever it is that's in your head right now. Because you lie to me."

"Sergey Dacha contacted me, told me he could get Kizik out."

Dr. Tier leaned in closely, her eyes somehow getting icier. "These men are the only connection we have ever had to Highland. Gray has just snatched one of them. You've been in contact with the other. We've got intelligence on a third Dacha brother, Achilles Dacha."

"So?" Timberwolf asked dully, on purpose.

Dr. Tier's eyes roamed the room and her jaw quivered with a hint of anger. "I am about to make a very poor decision." Timberwolf waited, cocking his head. "I bet you are wondering why we're out here in a sixty-billion-dollar D.P.E. cruiser and why you're just sitting in your quarters?"

"Let me guess; for me there's door number one, where I do whatever the hell it is you want, and door number two, where I'm blown out the airlock?"

"Gray's cracked something as it relates to Highland. Guaranteed it's the Dacha *brothers* or whatever they are. I have to decide on what to do with you. So yes, there's the chance you take a very short walk." Dr. Tier waited for a reaction from Timberwolf. She didn't get one. "You've had contact with the Dachas and you and Gray go how far back?"

"We've killed lots of people together."

"And above all of this, you say you have an Arnock presence in your mind, maybe watching and listening to what we're saying now?"

"It's not here now."

"How do you know?" Timberwolf looked off absently. "How, Mr. Velez?" she demanded, her calm and calculated demeanor finally cracking.

"No, just shush a minute. It's not here. Kizik's on a break. This is some nice P and Q."

"It tortured you. Went into your mind like nothing I could imagine and it's still there. Can you hear them?"

"I can feel them. If they were coming, I would know."

"Across light years?"

"I. Would. Know."

"Don't the Arnock kill their prisoners?" She let that hang as she met Timberwolf's icy glare with her own. "You'll be posted to station Leszer Zim 90. The Outpost. It's a shit can. Most contraband in the sector goes through there. See how all this fits together and what it has to do with Gray and the Dachas. Listen for the Arnock, if that's actually a real thing. You'll be a special security consultant. The guy running it, Drogel, just fell out of the toolbox."

"I'll be sure to make friends."

"Let me be clear to you about the implications here. If Gray has found a way of taking Highland, then you can be damned sure he will use what he finds there to restart the war with the Arnock and fire up a lot more trouble. The weapons factory there is a trove of attack ships, nukes, bio drivers, etcetera. He could create an army of Sabatin. It'll be like Christmas morning for a psychopath."

"All by himself?" Timberwolf grinned, already knowing the answer to this next part.

"If he gets Highland, the Assault Corps will jump off the sidelines and stand behind him one hundred percent. He's their patron saint. We won't be able to hold them back. The first thing they'll do is turn on the D.P.E. and we'll all be dead in a week."

"So I guess that's it?"

Conrad shut off the monitors and Kizik blinked away. Timberwolf got up to leave. "What's in the box, Timber?" Dr. Tier called to him as he reached the door.

"Wouldn't you like to know?"

Timberwolf left before Dr. Tier could ask again or order Capote to block the door. The burly man followed Timberwolf swiftly, knowing his presence was no longer needed.

"Is this the right thing?" Dr. Tier asked Conrad once they had the room to themselves.

The young man was good counsel because he didn't have any fear of being wrong. Dr. Tier respected that and overlooked his arrogance. She had never seen him hesitate before, but he did now. "It's a very bad call, but we can't sit this out." Dr. Tier nodded and Conrad showed himself out. He knew when she needed to think things through on her own.

Goddamn, Dr. Tier thought. She popped one of the blue pills she kept in her pocket in an unmarked container. It was Terecine, an illegal opiate. For just a second she felt the shame of being an addict, but then the calming effect of the stuff came over her and the pressure in her head gave way to a heavy giddiness. As the stress melted away, she ran through a few of the images of Timberwolf's encounter with Kizik on a tablet.

Jackhammer had been the name of the operation. The team had been told that Kizik was the target and that he was weakened and confused by a biological agent dropped weeks before. Neither of those things were true. Kizik had been at full strength and the real target of the operation had just walked out the door. *Who's your best guy?* She recalled that it was those four words that had kicked all of this off years ago. *Who's your best guy?* Such a casual question for all the trouble it caused.

CHOICES MADE

Gray loved the activity, being part of the prep before a fight. The Clergy had sent intelligence that Sergey Dacha was aboard a freighter called *Noel* heading out to Saavas. They'd catch it within a few days and board it, taking Sergey. It should be a cakewalk, and Gray wanted the crew to gain the experience of working together.

He swept through *Nemesis*, slapping men on the back and sharing off-color jokes with the shy, pious youngsters.

Some warmed to him, eyes wide with the unexpected camaraderie. Some backed away sheepishly, unsure how to react. Gray was a legend of the Assault Corps, a former general of brutal efficiency. But here he was, smiling as he helped clean rifles and prep armored rigs, his fingers black with grease. He made his way through the ship, learning each man's surname, mostly Believer names chosen by religious families.

Sebaldi ... Barnabas ... Blaise ... Vitus ... Windwhistle ... Mose ... Pinther ...

But it wasn't just that his excitement was getting the better of him. Gray knew his crew was untested, regardless of what their dossiers said. He needed their absolute dedication, and he knew how to get it. The crew had been told he was a former drill sergeant, a breaker of men, but they were seeing a protector, a favorite uncle.

Thaum ... Ahmed ... Cisus ... Scariot ... Mountainrock ... Ulric ...

Gray needed them to adore him so when he changed, it would shock the living hell out of them. He needed them to hear his voice as the voice of the Almighty and obey Him ferociously.

Dov ... Neviim ... Tanakh ... Bison ... Forestground ... Swiftsilver ...

They'll love me now so they'll hate me later.

And then they'd sacrifice anything to stay in his good graces.

Gray watched Michael, clipboard in hand in the cargo bay. He barked orders as crewmen hustled about hauling containers, growing crisp at the slightest misstep. Gray knew he had anger in his own soul, a profound amount of anger, but he pitied Michael for snapping at men for not moving boxes fast enough. *If only he'd stayed in the Assault Corps, he'd have been a better man*, Gray thought.

But Gray hadn't given Michael much choice. After his days running basic training, Gray was given command of a Breacher unit that snuck up on enemy vessels and planted nuclear charges. Michael was top-rated, but Gray cut him from the squad for disobeying an order. *A direct order, expressed loud and clear*. Timberwolf had been in that unit as well, two sides of the same coin.

The Breachers had been Gray's first combat command. He had gotten it late in his career when he was in his early forties. An injury fighting insurgents on Ceres had prohibited him from getting rated for combat drops and he'd sat out the war with the Phaelon as he'd trained class after class of rabid dogs to go fight them.

Gray had lived vicariously through those he trained, reading messages and posts from men slogging through the Red Forest on Phaelon Prime before the nukes were used, the surge through the Knife Valley, the final approach on the Throne country. Even as he was safe and bored at Fort Chancellor on Earth, he felt like a part of him was out there, giving the Phaelon hell.

Of all the men he'd ever trained, Timberwolf Velez was the best—such that he even scared Gray a little. It was an absence behind his eyes when he fought, like his mind was elsewhere while his body operated. He was unnaturally calm and collected under pressure, physically vicious and unnervingly precise.

Timberwolf and Michael together had been a deadly combination, the backbone of the Breacher squad. *But we all make choices*, Gray thought, though he knew that wasn't true. Michael had made a bad choice for the right reason, but Timberwolf never seemed to make any choices; he just was. He simply did his job as efficiently and effortlessly as possible. He existed as a natural force, as reliable and unforgiving as the pull of gravity.

He realized he'd been staring at Michael, and for an instant the past was present and the three of them—Gray, Michael, and Timberwolf—were over Enceladus again. The old freighter they were training on was breaking apart. Timberwolf's rig was dark and the man was stuck on the ship's hull.

I can reach him! Gray remembered Michael's voice crackling desperately again over his earbud. *Hold!* Gray had ordered.

But Michael didn't hold. He dove down and pulled Timberwolf from the disintegrating hulk and through the ice blow kicking up from the moon below. There was no doubt he had saved Timberwolf's life.

Gray had been grateful and thankful, eternally so. To lose Timberwolf, the best chip that had ever come from his own block, would have been devastating. But even as he'd saved Timberwolf, Michael had failed to follow Gray's order to hold. Cutting Michael from the squad had been cruel, though necessary, and Gray was sorry about it still— especially now, looking at the man Michael had become; petty and grudge-filled, here for the substantial paycheck, not the mission.

Michael could have gone back to a regular Assault Corps unit. Men were cut from elite units like the Breachers all the time. Gray had offered to leave the details of his dismissal out of Michael's file, but the man was too proud. He left the Assault Corps and bounced around as a mercenary, earning the chip on his shoulder as well as the burns on his face. Looking back, Gray would have chosen to do it again—let Michael fall so Timberwolf could rise.

For a horrible instant, Gray recalled the time at Purity Hospital after operation *Jackhammer*, a more desperate time. Timberwolf was raging, six orderlies were trying to hold him back, and then he melted to the floor, face soaked in tears. *What's here? What's in my head?* he screamed over and over for hours. *What's here? What's in my head?* Gray had thought that if anyone could, Timberwolf could handle contact with the Arnock. Gray tracked his own downfall to that moment as Timberwolf lay on the floor, the horrible choice that had started both their ruin.

Gray shook the memory and grinned, thinking that Timberwolf was out there right now, tracking and watching for them, kneading together the intelligence and lying in wait. There was an endgame in play here, an old clash infused with new rules. He knew that at some point soon, Michael, Timberwolf, and he might have guns pointed at each other. He wondered who would be man enough to pull the trigger.

THE BELIEVER

Believer Citadel—Haven

Jacob Bin Cavill was a cardinal of the Believer order. He had thought himself a cagey person, someone others got out of the way for. That was until he met Emmanuel Gray. *That bastard. That unworthy, soulless hypocrite.*

Before meeting Gray, Jacob was the prime cardinal, with 612 lesser cardinals under him, overseeing the order on over two thousand worlds. Now he was just one of six cardinals serving Prime Cardinal Claire Dais on the Believer cradle world of Haven. In the short history of the Believers, there had been forty-five prime cardinals; their peers jostled for power and pushed each other aside as the winds of power shifted. The longest reign had been six years, the shortest a week and a half. Cardinal Jacob was in his third year when he was pushed aside. *All because of that forked-tongued charlatan.*

Cardinal Jacob sat in his humble quarters, deep within the Believer Citadel on Haven. He sneered at the thought of Sister Claire, plump and purse-lipped, sitting in his old desk on the top floor. He thumbed through the latest report from

Izabeck on a smart-device, reading aloud the part that had bothered him the most. Gray had been ranting to the men after he'd used a filthy Sabatin on Fangelsi, "Military men will protect the human race again against all not made in God's image." *He speaks the Word of God like a barkeep!*

Cardinal Jacob had spent the last of his credibility getting his man Izabeck onto *Nemesis*. He had also arranged it so that Gray's crew was comprised of pure Believers, instead of mercenaries. He had the thanks of two dozen powerful families for giving their sons the chance to take part in a sacred mission. But Cardinal Jacob knew Gray would look to spite him even for this, maybe get a few of them killed out of malice.

When Gray first arrived on Haven, after he'd been forced to abdicate as governor of Nova Turin, he'd been a wreck—a wanted man chased by the D.P.E., a dozen bounty hunters, and even his own beloved Assault Corps. Cardinal Jacob had personally given him a promise of sanctuary. He did it because he saw in Gray a man of conviction—someone who had stood for what he believed in, even as the walls had literally fallen down around him. Cardinal Jacob saw in him a persecuted soldier, some used-up husk offered up to hang beside the thieves. There was also the question of the Dacha brothers. Cardinal Jacob had felt Gray could be very useful in that regard.

Gray seemed to embrace the Believer faith warmly. It was always easy for soldiers to do. At Cardinal Jacob's encouragement he took the Oath of The Clergy and soon the bounty hunters, the Assault Corps, and the D.P.E. agents stopped waiting around over Haven. Once he was within the fold, Cardinal Jacob had pulled him aside.

"Would you care to see the story that God has laid out for you? The reason why you're here with us?" Cardinal Jacob had asked.

"I have closed eyes and wait for God's judgment," Gray replied, with a wide smile.

With that, Cardinal Jacob took Gray to an office within the Believer Citadel where spectacled analysts crunched numbers on powerful computers and monitored the investments of the order. Izabeck followed along and kept Cardinal Jacob's long coat from touching the floor. Cardinal Jacob showed Gray that The Clergy was rich beyond measure, with fingers in the pies of mining operations, terraforming efforts, shipbuilding, pharmaceuticals, and finance. Beyond their own affairs, The Clergy monitored everything that moved in interplanetary commerce. Their sophisticated algorithms and A.I.s combed through practically every transaction done by anyone, whether it was legal or not. They mined this data for trends in the market and made even more money investing on all the exchanges.

Cardinal Jacob showed Gray a large monitor that displayed what looked like a slowly spinning 3-D spider web of a star map. Gray squinted at the tangle of lines. With a wave of Cardinal Jacob's hand, a subset of the connections turned red, and the others faded away. Cardinal Jacob did it again and again until the display simplified. Soon Gray saw it, just as Cardinal Jacob had expected he would. "What's that?" he asked. "There's nothing there and everything points to it."

Jacob smiled. "That's Highland."

Cardinal Jacob recalled Gray releasing a laugh at this point that should have warned him of his ambition. It was like a child getting the present he had always wanted and that he had pledged not to share. "How can you be sure?" Gray asked.

"For 126 years, Highland has operated as a defense contractor. They used to be located on Earth, then on Luna, then out on Chimera, then they disappeared. Well, they kept operating but no one knew where from. Their location has never been determined. The assumption is that they did it to protect themselves, dealing through intermediaries and shell companies so they could supply weapons to all sides during the stellar conflicts. No one is sure who currently operates Highland or where their money goes."

Gray's military mind clicked on. "Tell me your theory."

"No one runs Highland." Cardinal Jacob let that just hang out there and waited for Gray to respond.

"No one runs Highland?" Gray asked. Cardinal Jacob nodded to Izabeck, who departed, uneasily letting the then-prime cardinal's coat touch the floor.

Cardinal Jacob smiled. "Now my garments are dirty with money. No matter." He then brought up a collage of images on the display. They looked to all be of one small man who couldn't be taller than four-foot-six. Gray noticed subtle differences between them though—a slightly different hairline on one, a birthmark on the cheek of another.

"We've tracked three distinct individuals we're calling the Dacha brothers. We don't believe them to be technically human. Maybe clones."

"You said that no one ran Highland."

"From their actions, they appear to be reporting to a higher intelligence. We believe that to be an A.I. of some sort."

Gray soaked this in. "So you're saying Highland is on auto-pilot and these Dacha brothers are part of the machine?"

"They are the living keys to the machine."

"They need to be alive?"

"Our analysts say no. Their DNA should be enough to access the A.I."

"You want me to secure Highland for you, don't you?"

"Not at all; I want you to do it for God," Cardinal Jacob answered.

His mind snapping back to the present, Cardinal Jacob looked to the end of Izabeck's report. "We leave to take the second key. All men wearing the distinct symbols of their faiths. All men praying to the same God." *Oh faithful Izabeck, so wrapped up in this and playing his part. His reports always sounded like scripture.*

Cardinal Jacob thought a moment about Izabeck's ultimate fate. He had accepted it without question, like he was being asked to fetch a cup of coffee. When the time came though, would Izabeck have the will? Cardinal Jacob pondered that. Izabeck would have to have the will if he was going to get for the cardinal what was his.

A valet arrived outside Cardinal Jacob's door to collect his bags. He was looking forward to getting away from the Believer Citadel for a while. It was always good to go see God's creation.

THE OUTPOST

Mr. Timberwolf Velez, special security consultant, had arrived on the ugly brown pinwheel that was The Outpost station two weeks ago. He hadn't said much to anyone. He made lots of requests for files and information, but nothing in the way of chitchat. Salla Birdwing, the young vice governor of The Outpost, had been assigned to get him whatever he needed. He had clearance to see anything and everything. She thought he was handsome in a dangerous way. He was quiet, but coiled with energy, concise and demanding. He was a tall man, olive skin with dark hair. She'd shaken his hand once and his grip was like a vice.

At first, Salla had been concerned that the higher-ups were finally getting wise to what Gibson Drogel, the military governor of The Outpost, had been letting through the place. Salla was shocked herself when she arrived the year before. The customs procedures consisted of a thumbprint and a wave through, and usually some money changing hands. But no, Timberwolf wasn't interested in the day-to-day and Drogel's petty schemes. Salla could tell he was looking much deeper than that, at patterns, outlying shipping routes, intermediaries, and extremely large sums of money. He'd actually been clear that no customs procedures should change. Still, she couldn't piece together what he was looking for and she was good at piecing things together. The best she could discern about Timberwolf Velez was the obvious, that he was a D.P.E. agent.

She sat in the corner of a small café in the outer hab ring, thumbing through a tablet computer. A group of haulers from Templar-Delta passed by her table. A young man in the group nodded to her and smiled. She smiled back, in an official business-like capacity, of course. Salla was pretty, but not delicate, and didn't suffer from lack of attention.

She looked through one of the only files she could find on Timberwolf. He was once a member of an elite Breacher squad known as the 1st Lightning Division. They had the distinction of being one of the only units to ever use nukes as part of their standard arsenal. During the Nebula War, their job had been to sneak up on heavy Tiaski freighters and plant charges on them. She flipped to another page and then she saw it—a photo from a military magazine from two decades before. Timberwolf was a much younger man, half-suited up in a pressurized fighting rig of armor. Next to him, arms animated and in mid-shout, was Emmanuel Gray.

At just the sight of Gray, she had to flip away from the page for a moment to catch her breath. He had been governor during the troubles on Nova Turin. He had turned the security forces on the miners after the strike. He was the reason she no longer had two sisters and a dad.

She hardly noticed Drogel sit across from her at the small table, holding a tiny cup of espresso in his large soft hands. He was a red-faced man, with thin ginger hair. Where Salla's uniform was by-the-book perfect, Drogel looked like he slept in his. His blouse was wrinkled and adorned with a gaudy field of medals, few of which she recognized. Salla had a game where she would try to look them up. Some were for things such as punctuality and report filing, awarded via the mail and usually tossed in a drawer.

"I've got something for your curious mind," he started. Salla didn't respond for a moment, just looked through Drogel like she didn't speak his language. "Salla?"

"Sorry, just had a thought catch me," she replied, still thinking of that photo of Gray.

Drogel slipped a thumb drive across the table to her. "This might have some tidbits regarding our special security consultant on it. It's encrypted and I can't make heads or tails of it. This is more to your skill set than mine."

Salla flipped it over in her hands. "Where'd you get it?"

Drogel searched the air, playing sly. "Lots of stuff comes through here. What's the intake today?"

"We've got a short queue: *Nina*, flagged from Chimera, *St. Francis* from Haven, and a Glox freighter I can't pronounce."

"Wave through the *St. Francis* to CB1. Don't keep The Clergy waiting. Send the *Nina* to CB4 and I don't care if the Glox ship waits until tonight."

"Cargo Bay 4 isn't staffed, Governor."

He smirked. They'd had this conversation before. "Let them auto-unload. I don't care what they're carrying as long as they pay the tariff." He got up to go. "Meet me in an hour in the widow's walk. Take a look at that drive."

WIDOW'S WALK

Salla closed the door to the widow's walk, a chamber at the very top of the station that offered a wraparound view of all the docking ports. When wooden ships plowed the seas of Earth, sailor's wives would take to watching the horizon from a platform on top of coastal homes. From the platform atop The Outpost, there was no horizon, just the infinite black freckled with stars. Below, she could see the long and spindly *Nina* connected to Cargo Bay 4 and the gleaming white triangle of *St. Francis* attached to Cargo Bay 1.

She plugged the thumb drive into her tablet. Drogel had been wrong about the encryption; there wasn't any at all, but the files were ninety percent unreadable. They had some sort of auto-deprecation on them and they were self-deleting. She opened a file and, for an instant, she saw video of the unmistakable Mile High Red Forest on Phaelon Prime. The footage was from a helmet cam and in the instant before the video cut out, she saw the name T. Velez in the upper right corner of the screen.

This happened a few more times; she was teased by tantalizingly brief helmet cam footage. She experienced Timberwolf scrambling over the low-gravity surface of Phobos…a bloody scene of a dozen dead Glox in a crashed lifter…a Devorin space station falling through an atmosphere in flaming pieces.

One video froze just as another man turned to Timberwolf while they were sitting in an armored vehicle. The other man was Gray. He was smiling and lean and it was years before what would happen on Nova. She couldn't hate this Gray, this younger man who hadn't yet spilled so much blood. She looked in his eyes, surprisingly warm, and noticed he had long feminine lashes.

She closed down that file and what she saw next made her lose her breath. Staring directly at her through its six red and glowing eyes was an Arnock, hovering close and moving closer. This footage had audio and she could hear Timberwolf. *"No, no, no!"* he grunted desperately. But still, the beast drew closer until it blocked the camera completely.

The next video wasn't like the others. It wasn't from a helmet cam, but of Timberwolf sitting across from someone at a desk. It was a woman and she somehow seemed able to stare down at Timberwolf even though they sat at the same level. Timberwolf was a mess; bloodshot eyes sunken into his head. She might have guessed he had been drunk for days, if not for what came next.

"I can feel them. If they were coming, I would know…" he said.

The video jumped and the woman was mid-sentence now. "…if Gray has found a way of taking Highland, then you can be damned…" The video jumped again, and it was the woman still speaking. "What's in the box, Timber?" With that, the video went dead.

She sat for a long moment, holding in her breath as the last of the files deleted themselves. "Holy shit." She finally exhaled. The snippets she had seen swam in her head: Timberwolf…Gray…the Arnock…Highland…The thought of someone such as Gray getting control of Highland made the bottom drop out of her stomach.

Just then, Drogel entered, letting the door slam open and shaking her from her thoughts. Instinctively, she flipped down the screen on her tablet, but there was nothing to hide. All of the files on the thumb drive had now deleted themselves.

"Didn't mean to slam the door. Find anything out about our special security consultant?" Drogel asked.

"Nothing more than you already knew."

"That he's a terrific asshole?"

"That wasn't in his file," Salla responded. Drogel's face was blank, not registering the sarcasm.

"He's a spook. Department of Peace Enforcement," he said, impressing himself with the deduction.

"Safe bet."

Drogel's earbud beeped and he tapped it. "Governor Drogel here."

"CB4. Now," Timberwolf barked through the connection and hung up. Drogel shook his head, his face glowing with irritation over and above its usual redness.

"So, nothing at all on this S.O.B.?" he asked as they stepped into the hall.

She fished for something she had read in her own research to throw him off. "He was born on Golgotha. Mother passed away when he was a boy. Father was a construction worker on the terraforming project, now deceased. Brother's still there, worked as a tower hound, was paralyzed and is in a home."

"Golgotha, huh? Went there once. The air's so damn thin you need a breather." Salla was relieved Drogel didn't ask for anything more. She didn't know who had given him the thumb drive and what they could have been after. "Toss it," he said with a dismissive wave.

They passed a trash bin and she pretended to throw the thumb drive away but put it in her pocket instead. She'd destroy it later. She wasn't going to take any chances with what she found. Who knew if someone would be able to recover what she'd seen?

A wave of uncertainty went through her. What was she supposed to do with what she knew? Who would she tell? There was no way she was telling Drogel. She had already made that call. The command at Tach-One? The Outpost was a military facility, and she was in the Station Corps. Gray had been forced to resign as a general before becoming governor on Nova Turin, but he still had powerful friends in the upper ranks. They might laugh her off at best, especially if she couldn't recover the files.

As she got onto the elevator, she thought about Timberwolf waiting down in Cargo Bay 4. She would be surprised if he even knew her name. Salla had no allusions about trusting a D.P.E. agent but she sensed something in Timberwolf that she liked. He appeared to be all about his job, and he clearly had a disdain for Drogel. From what she'd seen, Timberwolf was working against Gray, and they seemed to have a history that went back decades. Salla had a history with Gray as well. *Looks like we have at least one thing in common.*

What about the Arnock? What had they done to him? People didn't survive contact with the Arnock. It just didn't happen. She recalled the image of the spider above

Timberwolf, drawing closer and taking over the frame. *"I can feel them. If they were coming, I would know…"* he had said. She considered the implications of that and how the Arnock had torn apart the minds of all who landed on their world. She swallowed hard. What the hell was she getting into?

CARGO BAY 4

The Outpost was composed of a bulbous central hub with eight pinwheel arms that made up its docking ports and cargo bays. The cargo bays were like massive, overlapping pie slices and each could handle two ships at once. During the Arnock War, the place had been a way station for battle cruisers, supplies, troop transports, and everything that was needed to support an interstellar conflict.

It used to be so busy that ships had to wait days for one of the sixteen docking slots. As the conflict wound down, the traffic through The Outpost dropped in tandem and the place fell into a general state of disrepair. Drogel, and previous governors like him, had stepped into the breach, using the former strategic hub as a place to move contraband and line their pockets. Glox freighters alone, running from Saavas, kept hundreds of worlds swimming in exotic narcotics. The Station Corps command didn't much care what happened on The Outpost and the other stations. In peace time, their budgets and authority had been slashed by the D.P.E. They were happy to receive a slice of what the governors were able to collect in bribes. Drogel called it *tithing*. Salla held her nose and waved through smugglers, arms traffickers, and worse.

In Cargo Bay 4, a hail of golden sparks fell in the cavernous space. The tri-level bay was covered in decades of rust. Dozens of white containers were on all three levels and workers in yellow bio suits cut into them with bulky saws. Drogel and Salla watched as one worker sliced the top off of one of the containers. Another worker approached and sprayed a liquid inside, then backed away hurriedly as something within thrashed and screeched. "They smell awful…How many…Hazard money…Could sell these for my retirement…" the workers complained. Several security guards blocked the airlock, and out a large window *Nina* hung outside, small maintenance machines scooting about her. Through a conveyor belt in the wall, more containers came and were moved up to various levels with magnetic cranes.

Drogel knelt next to a container that hadn't been opened yet. On the side of it was an unmistakable mark—the mountain surrounded by stars that was the Highland logo. A worker sprayed another container and Drogel got a snout full of sour chemicals. The thing within screamed, and this one lurched itself out. Drogel leaped back. It was an embryonic Sabatin, horribly burned and dying. The containers were bio-mechanical vessels filled with nutrients and food in which the creatures finished growing—artificial eggs. The Sabatin slid back into the container and twitched.

"Fifty-two Sabatin containers." Disgusted, Timberwolf tossed an electronic clipboard to Drogel.

Salla took the clipboard. "That's an army. Sabatin are nasty, bio-assault weapons. Remote control or auto-kill. Use them for security, urban assault, killing thy neighbor. What have you."

"You said you didn't want our reputation to change," was Drogel's excuse.

"So I can see who's making the deals!" He turned to Salla. "Someone thought they could dump this quantity of haz-mat here?"

"Ships are generally permitted to auto-unload, without going through customs."

Timberwolf shot her an *Are you shitting me?* look and inspected a nearby Sabatin container. Drogel was at his heels. "We catch a smuggler, you let him go?" he said. "Your latitude aside…" Timberwolf pushed past Drogel, checking another Sabatin container. Drogel continued, "I cooperate with you because I've been asked to from on high. I don't even know who you answer to!"

Timberwolf stared at Drogel, draining the bravery out of him. "Everything here is at my disposal, including you, *Governor*." A magnetic crane lowered another Sabatin-container to the deck. More golden sparks fell. Timberwolf continued, "A Highland shipment. Freighter's name is the *Nina*. When we started logging the cargo, it unhooked and tried to get away. No one was onboard."

"This cargo's worth billions!" Drogel said desperately.

"I'm killing them with chlorine blasts."

"Just hold it…"

Timberwolf drew within inches of Drogel. "You don't want to line your pockets with this. You break the yolks, they'll want out. Any of these go missing and I'll shoot the suspects—any suspects. This crew is here."

The sound of a muffled scream came from somewhere. "It's from inside one!" Salla had her ear to one of the unopened Sabatin containers. The workers froze as they listened.

Timberwolf grabbed a cutting saw, handling it like it weighed as much as a hair dryer. He cut the top off the container and pried it open with a crowbar. A clear, horrified yell seemed to stop time for a second.

The workers crowded around the open container, grimacing from the smell. Inside, a translucent pink yolk embraced a little man. "Achilles Dacha," Timberwolf said. Achilles reached out with his small, childlike arms, his mouth open but unable to scream anymore. Beneath him a dormant, curled-up Sabatin was buried farther in the yolk.

"You know him?" Salla asked.

"Probably," Timberwolf responded.

INSIGNIA

Nemesis buzzed with activity. Gray had worked the men into a frenzy after Fangelsi and Michael and Sol used that momentum to get them ready for what was coming. Gray was one for buildup and theater. He could just as well have used Wrath again in this next phase and been done with it, but the crew needed a test they could easily pass before things got more dangerous.

They were gathered now in the galley. Most had the breastplates from their armored rigs laid out on the tables and the floor. Izabeck moved among them, handing out paintbrushes and stencils. Gray stood at the doorway and watched them. Michael appeared beside him. "What are they doing?" Michael smirked.

"I know what it is. It's perfect. You may not subscribe to any of this but look at that boy there." Gray pointed to one young man, who proudly held up his breastplate. He'd stenciled a cross surrounded by the Believer symbol. Another man did the same with the crescent of Islam and another painted the nine stars of the Bahá'í faith on his armor. Others had elaborate crosses, suns, stars, Hindu symbols, and more. Some had a mix of several symbols. "The Believer truth is wrapped around the old religions. You know, we used to butcher each other—Hindu versus Muslim versus Christian versus Jew. That's gone now."

"I read, Emmanuel," Michael shot back.

"So, why'd you come on this little adventure? Especially when you had to pull out your own shooters?"

"I'd already spent the money," Michael huffed. "I've got a job to do. No use in complaining."

They stood in silence a minute, used to being in each other's company and saying what was on their minds.

"So back on Fangelsi, I almost put my foot up your ass. What did you think you were getting at?" Gray was quick to anger and quick to forgive, but Michael's challenge to Gray before had grated on him. *And what about those that don't believe?* Michael had asked. Gray knew he was referring to Timberwolf and the part he might end up playing in all this.

Michael shook his head. "You think that Timberwolf is going to sit this out?"

"Ah, it's Timberwolf and his shadow falling on everything you do," Gray spat back.

"You made sure of that."

"Wrong. *You* made sure of that."

"He's your blind spot and I guarantee he'll come for you on this one." Unlike nearly everyone else, Michael told Gray the truth. He had no fear of his anger or retribution. Gray had done his worst to Michael already.

Again, they stood in silence, used to saying things to each other lesser colleagues wouldn't be able to recover from.

"You think they'll all make it?" Gray finally asked.

"We might have to sing for a few of them."

"As long as we don't have to sing for you and me," Gray smiled.

Michael wasn't scared to die, and he was used to living by the gun, but this—taking Highland and calling it a religious crusade—seemed destined to get a lot of people killed. Michael had no illusions that he might be among the corpses.

Gray began to sing quietly at almost a whisper. It was the song Assault Corps troopers sang over the graves of their fallen comrades; glass of whiskey in the left hand, right hand over the heart. "When my life in this place is over, I'll fly away. To that home on God's celestial shore, I'll fly away." Gray smiled that loving, cruel, sorry, fatherly smile he'd had for decades.

Gray stepped away, climbing up a ladder to the bridge. Michael watched him go. *What'd they say about the devil coming to you with a smile? About whispering gently in your ear?* Michael looked back to the galley; another man held up two thigh plates, a crucifix on one and the Believer symbol on the other. There they were—Emmanuel Gray's new believers.

BREACHERS

Michael and Sol huddled in the breaching tube that extended out of the nose of *Nemesis*. The rest of the men were in two columns behind them, all suited in fighting rigs for combat and weapons set for live fire. They were about to breach and board *Noel*, a short-haul transport. The breaching tube was like a battering ram with an airlock at the end. When it made contact, the back of it would collapse like an accordion, absorbing the impact. The mission was to grab Sergey Dacha and make sure he kept breathing.

They could feel the recoil from *Nemesis's* plasma cannons firing electromagnetic pulse bolts at *Noel*. The air crackled with static electricity. Jan, the first man behind Sol, had a short in his suit and lost the glow from his heads-up display. Sol tapped the side of his helmet with his giant gloved hand, but it stayed dark. "You'll be in the rear wave today, son; move to the back. Windwhistle, you come up and take the second breach slot."

Sol looked through the airlock window. He could see *Noel* sizzling with electricity and listing in a spiral. "We're laying some boom on them!" Sol was a snaggle-toothed old ground-pounder, with a wide mustache on his wide, dark face. He looked over the men. Their faces were draped with fear. Some chanted and prayed. They held on as *Nemesis* twisted to match the rotation of *Noel*.

The pilot announced their distance over the intercom. "Sixty-five hundred yards."

Michael rose and steadied himself. "Breaching and boarding one-oh-one. The *Noel* is a tub and made for B&B. It's got an external airlock that sticks out of their topside like a beer can. We're going to slam hard and then the saws in the seal are going to cut off their airlock. We won't have to cut into anything on their side. You hold until Sol gives you the go. Worst thing you do is go in early."

"I-ya," the men said, weakly.

"Our E.M.P.s are going to make it dark over there, so watch for surprises. Follow us in."

"Don't shoot me in the back!" Sol bellowed, laughing and slapping Windwhistle's arm.

"Forty-two hundred meters," the pilot announced.

Sol and Michael locked eyes. They were coming in at *Noel* way too fast. Michael called up to the bridge. "Tap the brakes!" He didn't get any response. They waited tensely.

"Twenty-eight hundred yards."

Michael gritted his teeth. Sol traced a Believer symbol on his forehead.

"Sixteen hundred," the pilot updated them calmly.

"Jesus, everybody get loose. This is going to hurt," Michael shouted. The men braced for the collision, huddling close.

"Nine hundred…eight…six…five…four…three."

Out the window, Sol saw *Noel* right below them now, an instant from contact. "Hold on!"

The impact was like a car crash, even as the back of the breaching tube compressed. In sudden darkness, Jan flew forward, tumbling sideways and smashing hard into the airlock. White gas burst into space from all around *Noel's* airlock as the Breacher saws in the seal did their work and the internal barrier fell away.

Michael shook Jan and the man's eyes flicked open, a crack running down his visor. Jan struggled upward, nodding that he was okay. The *Noel's* superstructure screamed, but the seal between the two ships was holding and the purge of atmosphere from *Noel* subsided.

Sol straightened his helmet and repeated what he'd drilled into them while practicing the operation in the cargo bay. "Don't mind the civilians. Focus on the security. Eyes up! Weapons hot!" He pulled a lever and the airlock parted.

Michael and Sol led their teams in. The airlock was wide enough to go two by two. Everything on *Noel* was dark and the walls leaked smoke and vapor. The lamps in their helmets pierced the space, flashing off walls and ceilings as the men turned about. "It's like a fun house over here," Sol remarked.

They were in a boarding area, with tables and chairs bolted to the floor. *Noel* twisted, its inertial gravity generators barely operating. A security guard appeared, stumbling and almost falling out of the darkness. He fired his pistol, plasma bursts zinging high. Sol lit the man up with a white-hot burst, spinning him in a circle, the discharge of his weapon deafeningly loud.

Another security guard sprayed and prayed from around a corner. The bursts missed, but just then *Noel's* gravity gave out completely. Michael found himself falling towards the guard. Landing hard against the wall of a corridor, he came face-to-face with the shooter. Michael must have looked like a demon in his fighting rig; his visor down and auto-camouflage flowing and changing as he moved.

The security guard's pistol cartwheeled weightless before him. He grabbed it, but had it backwards, with the barrel pointing at himself. Michael grabbed his hand and helped him pull the trigger, sending a plasma burst through his thigh. Just then the gravity returned, dropping them both to the deck. The guard writhed in pain and Michael smashed him in the chin with the butt of his rifle, knocking him out.

Michael led his squad through the corridors, the heads-up display in his helmet showing him the way to the first-class cabins. He let himself be a little impressed by the men. They covered each other well and hadn't panicked when those amateurs had opened fire. Sol came over his earpiece, "We're blocking the starboard corridor near the evac bags."

"We're getting Dacha," Michael responded.

Michael found the first-class passenger section. He sent a man to block the other end of the corridor and called back to Gray on *Nemesis*, "Come on in!"

Clambering through the airlock, Wrath hissed and scraped the metal. Thomas led him with Gray behind. Wrath barreled around corners, a silver flash of teeth and claws. He went cabin to cabin in the first-class section, lightning fast, inspecting each door. Beams from flashlights trailed him as the men followed. He stopped at a specific door and waited patiently, poised and panting. The creature could sense the Dachas inherently. It was a familiar scent buried deep within his DNA. The men hung back, unsure what was next. "Wrath, *drosh maik!*" Thomas ordered.

Wrath stood up to his full height. The Sabatin flexed for a moment like an armor-plated gargoyle and then pried the door open like it was tinfoil. His shoulders flexed with rippling muscle. Huddled atop a bed was Sergey Dacha. He was identical to his brothers but with a shock of white hair. At the sight of Wrath, a slight smile came over his face, like *maybe this was a rescue?* But no, the beast dashed away and was replaced by Gray. Sergey's hopes faded as Gray gave him a warm and horrible smile. "I forgive you for all the things you've done. You'll do your penance and take me to Highland."

"I can make you a rich man!" Sergey pleaded.

"I am a rich man. I've felt the light of heaven," Gray replied.

Michael entered, concern wrinkling his brow. "Achilles ran for Timberwolf." Gray nodded, digesting the complication as Michael showed him a message from Drogel on The Outpost.

"Please, you don't need my brother!" Sergey begged.

"Sure I do. God needs everybody."

UNKNOWN MESSENGER

Dr. Tier sat in her office on Archangel, pretending to scan through a chart. Conrad was there for his daily report. "There's Assault Corps chatter cycling through Tach-One from up and down the line. I'm not picking up any code words that would signify an operation of any sort. Nothing indicating a high-alert level on Sec-Def Bozeman's staff."

"I see." Usually, Dr. Tier had a dozen piercing questions for Conrad, but today all she wanted him to do was leave.

"I'm still finding the volume of chatter concerning…" He waited for the inquisition that didn't come.

"That's fine. Thank you." Confused and concerned, Conrad left Dr. Tier alone in her office. She breathed a sigh of relief when he was gone. There was something else on her mind, something that she couldn't share with anyone. This morning, she had been shocked to receive a personal message from an unknown sender. It had been one line.

> *Samar1483: Remember Jackhammer? Let's*
> *talk soon.*

There were only a few people who had known the name of that operation and most of them were now dead. That was piled on top of the fact that she had received a total of zero updates from Timberwolf since he had gotten to The Outpost. Dr. Tier tended not to fret, but she didn't believe in coincidences.

Her personal account had the highest D.P.E. security protocols on it. She needed it in order for her to speak securely with sources in the field through sub-light. In fact, anyone sending a message would have to have a digital key generator personally given to them by her in order for the message to get through. Someone had broken that security and she had no idea who or how.

She felt a buzzing at her hip and pulled her smart-device from her pocket.

Samar1483: Looks like we're both waiting.
TheaTier965: Who is this?
Samar1483: I'm not a friend. Not sure if people like us have friends.
TheaTier965: How did you get my private account?
Samar1483: I know lots of things. Have access to lots of information. Too much, actually.
TheaTier965: Goodbye.
Samar1483: Please don't go. I have news about the crusade.
TheaTier965: ???
Samar1483: That's what we called it. Whatever he's doing. I have news.
TheaTier965: What news?
Samar1483: About Emmanuel Gray.
Dr. Tier held her response.
Samar1483: Looks like the cat has your tongue. I understand if you don't believe me. I also have news on Timberwolf Velez. He's probably not been in touch, correct?
TheaTier965: I will give you one more message.
Samar1483: The score is Gray 2, Velez 1. I'm sure you know what that means and how much of a disadvantage that puts you in.
TheaTier965: Who is this?

Dr. Tier waited for a reply that didn't come. She wasn't sure of the game that was afoot, but she was not accustomed to being on the receiving end of dirty tricks. She needed to focus. She tapped out a quick message to Conrad.

TheaTier965: Get back in here. I have a million questions about your report.

THE KEY

Like many things on The Outpost, the infirmary had multiple uses. One was to treat injured and sick visitors and crew; the other was to store Drogel's private contraband. Against one wall, boxes of "vaccines" marked with a red D were piled neatly up to the ceiling. Achilles sat on an examination bed, wrinkling up the paper. His eyes darted around the room, to the collection of medical saws hanging on the walls. Soft, dreary elevator music played.

Salla and Timberwolf observed Achilles through one-way glass from the pharmacy alcove. Timberwolf was letting him stew. The doctor had advised that Achilles was healthy a half hour ago, but Timberwolf needed him to be unsure of his intentions. "Has he sat long enough?" Salla asked.

"In order for him to trust me, I need him not to trust me. First impressions are everything. Go ahead in, but don't talk to him." Timberwolf liked Salla, as much as he liked anyone. There was only one condition to Timberwolf's authority on The Outpost and it was that whenever he interrogated anyone, he needed a Station Corps officer present. She was smart and efficient and didn't get in the way.

Salla entered, taking her place by the exterior door. Achilles, realizing Salla wasn't there to talk, hung his head and looked down. *Okay, he's ready to go in the oven now.* Timberwolf took a step towards the room, but when he did, he felt a presence in his head he hadn't noticed for weeks. It was Kizik, the Arnock mind-bender, but there was something more—a lot more somethings.

It was like Timberwolf had just walked out on stage in front of a packed house. He could feel the alien minds peering through him, rustling and impatient. He closed his eyes and pushed them away like he'd been able to do with Kizik before. He visualized them all in a theater before him, red Arnock eyes glowing and blinking. As he pushed them away, one by one, they got up and left, until only one remained. Of course it was Kizik, the unmistakable red blotch of color on its face. Timberwolf dug deep to push the alien away. He opened his eyes when Kizik was finally gone. Timberwolf gave it another minute to be sure and then walked in to see Achilles.

"You could disappear. There's no authority here but me," he began, without even as much as a hello. He shot Salla a quick glance and she nodded with a slight smile. *Nice opening line!*

"Oh no, you're too interested in why I'm here. You won't let me go."

Timberwolf shrugged, careless, and went for the door. "You have no value but what I give you."

"I broker for Highland. I can connect you. I know people!"

"You *know* people? I think you are people! You hid in a box of bio-silicon, cozied up to a Sabatin. Someone who would do that is very scared."

"I came here to find you! He ordered all those Sabatin, was trying to lure me out. You could help. I knew that. But I panicked. I was stupid."

Timberwolf was silent and simply raised an eyebrow.

"I can't trust you!" Achilles burst.

Timberwolf drew close. "Of course you can't trust me. Who ordered them?"

"Stop playing games. You know."

"Of course I know."

"You like our gift? It's your size, right? You kept the box it came in?"

"It's a little cramped around the crotch."

Achilles rolled his eyes. "You want to override some of the sizing specs and spray in a little WD-40 if you're bigger than average."

"Thanks, got it."

"What's the name Emmanuel Gray mean to you?"

Timberwolf paused. This had gotten to a place he wasn't ready to go yet. "Vice. Out."

Salla hesitated for a second, and then slipped out, balling her fists.

"Emmanuel Gray—the bishop of the Believers. Lo and behold his mighty crusade. Kill off all aliens. He wants to take over our factory at Highland. Build an army of Sabatin to use on the Arnock. Hypocrite. Guess what? Sabatin are made from alien DNA! He's been trying to collect my brothers."

"So, you're special?"

"We're the keys. I can't begin, really."

"You were doing real good. You were looking for me, to protect you from Gray. You should just talk until I tell you to shut up."

Achilles looked down, collected himself. "My brothers and I…"

Timberwolf interrupted, "Okay stop there. You don't have any brothers. You guys are devices that download from the same hard drive."

"That's rude!"

"Don't lie, Achilles. I met with *you* on Telock Sen and *you* gave me the box. I met with all of you. I'm meeting with Achilles and Sergey and Ivan right now."

Achilles rolled his eyes, like he was dealing with someone beyond ignorant. "It's still in your head, isn't it? Kizik. His real name goes on for about a minute. Really doesn't like you very much."

"And you…I mean your brother Sergey, promised to get it out. Instead, you just gave me a box."

"Yeah, we did and Kizik's still there." Achilles folded his small arms and grinned. "We have so much power you can't even dream of. We can snap our fingers and all of this just gets wiped out; a storm to just clean away all of this and start over."

"That sounds great. Can I read your manifesto?" Timberwolf cracked.

Achilles leaped up, with a swiftness that took Timberwolf by surprise. "We'd wipe you all away! The Arnock, the Devorin, Glox, Tiaski, Szykul…we like the Phaelon. We'll keep the Phaelon. But first it'd be you. You humans have started all this trouble. Those others didn't even know what interstellar war was until you came along."

"Us humans? You look sort of human. Did you forget that?"

"I've never forgotten anything."

"So what's the point?"

"You're the goddamned point! I am going to offer you a deal, friend."

"You're scared," Timberwolf said, knowing this would needle him.

"Excuse me?"

"If you're so powerful, why do you want to deal? Why am I the point?" Achilles shuffled as Timberwolf went on. "The way I see it, you've gotten lost. Highland's been on auto-pilot so long that you don't have a reason for being. You're trying to balance out all the species, assure stalemates, hold back the tide of war, but what for?"

"Yeah, pax galactica. Try it sometime."

"You're a copy of a copy of a copy. You work for a computer. I think perspective might be amiss in your family. You could wipe us all out, but Gray's cracked your secret and the Arnock are not far behind. I may be the *point* and I'll tell you what our *deal's* going to be…"

Achilles interrupted, "You take care of this Gray problem and Kizik's gone. Wake up with a clear head. We'll also funnel you whatever you need to keep the peace, but only to you. Not to that psycho Dr. Tier and certainly not to anyone in your military."

"Wrong! It's Highland's surrender. I'm not going to let you weasel out of this. You want this protection, I own you."

"You bastard," Achilles hissed.

"You showed me your whole hand!"

Achilles laughed, throwing his head back. "For some reason, she trusts you. She likes you. I certainly don't."

"She does, huh? What is *she* exactly?" Timberwolf asked, pretty sure he was referring to Highland's A.I.

Achilles was exasperated now. "Her name is Penny. She makes the product!" There was a silence between them as Timberwolf waited for more. "Like I said, me and my brothers are the keys. It takes two of us to access the control center. You want to meet Penny?"

"Sure."

COMING ABOARD

"*Nemesis* to Outpost Con, copy on CB4, port A." Farrow, the pilot, confirmed the approach with The Outpost docking officer. His voice came over the intercom to those waiting near the airlock. The men were rigged up and assembled again near the breaching tube. This wasn't a hostile breach and board, though Gray's plan was to demonstrate an aggressive force so Drogel knew he meant business.

Gray watched the approach to The Outpost with Sol. He noticed a familiar ship parked at Cargo Bay 1. "Is that the *St. Francis*?" he snapped. "The *St. Francis*?!" Sol didn't get it at first and then put it together. *St. Francis* was the official diplomatic yacht of The Clergy. That meant Cardinal Jacob was here.

"That change anything?" Sol asked.

"Yes, it ruins my day."

Governor Drogel waited at the airlock on The Outpost. He could see *Nemesis* through the door, just a few yards away and inching closer. *He promised subtle. No reason to draw attention.* With a clang, *Nemesis* made contact and almost instantly the door spread open. Three men filed out, plasma rifles up and armor auto-camouflaging against the background.

Drogel instinctively put his hands up as the men scanned the space. He noticed religious symbols stenciled onto the armor of the two supporting men. The lead man turned his attention to Drogel. There were no religious marks on his armor but, instead, the profile of a dragon, with its tongue extended and wings flexing. Michael opened his visor. Drogel couldn't help but notice the burns on his face and the scar over his lip. "Clear," Michael announced.

Two dozen more men boarded, all with adorned armor—Believer marks, crosses, crescents, stars, and more. Grenades and knives hung from their waists. They formed a gauntlet in the hallway and through it walked Izabeck, his armor adorned with a feather on each shoulder. He scribbled in an electronic notebook, taking in the scene and mouthing the words he was writing.

Finally Gray came aboard. "Where's Timber?" he demanded of Drogel, without breaking stride.

"With the prisoner. I don't think this much firepower is necessary for just picking up one man!" Drogel complained.

"One man who's now in the custody of Timberwolf Velez! I haven't brought enough firepower. I'll hold back my backup, how's that?"

Drogel tilted his head quizzically, and then standing at the back of the airlock he saw Wrath. The Sabatin stood with its handler, hissing and trembling. "You brought a Sabatin?" Drogel asked, exasperated.

"He's on my crew."

"We just had a shipment come in, fifty-two of the things. Timberwolf confiscated it and…"

"You're not my favorite person right now, Governor." Drogel's face asked the question his mouth wasn't brave enough to. "The *St. Francis* is here. How much did Jacob pay you not to tell me?"

"Please, I didn't have much choice."

Gray smiled understandingly and Drogel relaxed a bit. "Much choice? That means you had some choice. I would use that money to disappear. I have a lot of young men who are looking for reasons to shoot people." Drogel's face turned pale. "Something to keep in mind." Drogel opened his mouth to reply but Gray shut him down with a nod. "Let's get us in and out of here."

VICE

Timberwolf had been in the infirmary for over an hour with Achilles. Salla had been unable to leave the hall outside. She needed to know what was happening and how all these pieces fell together. She'd been incredibly excited to be named as vice governor to The Outpost a year ago. She had been twenty-four when she was appointed, and it was only her second assignment out of basic. She quickly discovered the lofty title of vice governor was the only perk of the job. All day long, she waved cargo through, did errands for Drogel, and scheduled docking ports. That's not even to mention all of the things Drogel asked her to do that were probably illegal. She feared the day all of the sketchy transactions with her thumbprint on them might come back to haunt her.

It certainly wasn't where she wanted to be. She had been first in her class and had hoped to pursue a career in the Judge Advocate General arm of the Station Corps and become an investigator; go after the very corruption and incompetence she was taking part in on a daily basis. She sensed something really big was happening here, a lot bigger than that Glox freighter still waiting ten clicks out. Salla needed to be a part of it.

Timberwolf came out of the infirmary and saw her there. The way he nodded his head for her to follow him told her he was impressed she waited. "Vice, I'm leaving with him. This hour. Get the box from my quarters aboard the *Nina*."

"Hell no," she responded. Timberwolf stared through her. She didn't look away.

"That wasn't healthy."

"What's going on?" she demanded.

"Listen, you're not an idiot like Drogel. I get out of here with our little friend and you can forget about me. If you get wrapped up in this…"

"You're with the Department of Peace Enforcement," she interrupted, almost accusing him.

"No shit, I'm D.P.E. I don't have a lot of time." He pulled his smart-device from his pocket and began scanning for a signal.

"You keep the religious crazies from taking us back to war."

"We're who goes bump in the night." He kept moving, holding up his smart-device and trying to connect.

"Emmanuel Gray. He's looking for that guy, Achilles. Gray's been trying to start up the war with the Arnock again. He's wanted, but half the Assault Corps supports him."

"Stop," Timberwolf warned her.

"What's it to do with Highland?" she demanded.

"Stop!"

"And you're hunting him and listening for the Arnock."

Timberwolf put his finger to her mouth and pushed her into a corner.

"Okay, you need to stop saying things out loud. Got into my file, huh? Listen to me. I have enough to get you locked up in some D.P.E. hush prison until you're a sack of bones. Get the hell out of here. Cover your tracks. Trust me." He let her go and she gasped for a second. Timberwolf instantly regretted being harsh with her. By his estimate, she was the smartest person in the sector and seemed eager to help. "Just know if Gray's going to Highland, I'm going to stop him. I take him out and all this stops."

Timberwolf tried his smart-device again, finally able to get a signal. He activated the digital key generator that would allow him to send a message through to Dr. Tier. A beep of failure and the icon glowed red. He tried it again and got the same result. He tried it a third time and again it failed, the application deleting itself from his smart-device. *Oh shit.* There were only two reasons that could have happened. Dr. Tier could be burning him or…"My codes, they've been compromised. I need to send…"

Timberwolf looked up. Drogel was there in the hall with several of Gray's men. Salla slipped away. Timberwolf couldn't blame her. Drogel raised a pistol.

"Guv, you've made a very poor decision," Timberwolf warned.

"We have a mutual friend."

Timberwolf slowly went to his knees in surrender, hands behind his head. "You don't even know." Timberwolf shook his head, finding a dry laugh in his throat. "You won't live through this."

Timberwolf's words hit Drogel hard, the second time his life had been threatened in as many hours. He blinked and in that instant Timberwolf sprang forward, landing a blow to his solar plexus that dropped him, writhing. Timberwolf spun away and grabbed one of Gray's men by his open helmet, smashing him into a bulkhead. The others hesitated a moment—this was not some amateur security guard like on *Noel*.

Timberwolf had the man's rifle and he opened fire, aiming high and raking plasma over them. The high-pitched sound of the bursts told Timberwolf he was only stinging them. *They were sent to take me alive. Let's see how that works out.* He smashed one in the face with the butt of his rifle, as the first of them managed to fire back. He spun around, feeling the stings on his hip.

Other bursts started to hit him now and more men clomped in, armored up and firing. He was surrounded and knew he couldn't hold out much longer, but he kept shooting. He wanted to see fear in their eyes before he went down. Since they planned to take him alive, he wanted them to know that when he woke up, he would be coming to tear their heads off. He didn't bother to crouch for cover and advanced, taking more plasma stings.

He saw what he wanted on one man. On the front of his armor, up by the collar, it read *Windwhistle*, with a Believer mark wrapped around a crucifix. His face was an empty slate and his eyes were wide. Timberwolf ran at him, his rifle empty now. He dropped a knee to the front of Windwhistle's armor, letting the pain of connecting flesh with composite surge through him. Timberwolf got his hands into Windwhistle's helmet and choked him. From all sides now, plasma bursts struck him. Finally, one hit him near the temple and Timberwolf rolled to the deck. As he lay on the floor, a few men took potshots at him and Windwhistle rose, kicking him in the side. Then Emmanuel Gray's face appeared above him, haloed in light. Then it was dark.

ARNOCK PRIME

The Arnock homeworld didn't turn away from its red monster of a star and had no moon to give it the wobble of seasons. It was an unchanging place of brutal consistency. Without rotation, one side was a desert, constantly blasted by the sun. The other side was a frozen, jagged wasteland run through by incessant wind. The habitable part of the world existed in a thin strip where it was never either night or day. The Arnock lived there in a nameless underground hive-city that wrapped around the entire planet. They seldom traveled up to the spine of the Twilight Ridge.

Kizik was a master, a class of Arnock with minds evolved far beyond that of the lower castes. Masters had the ability to control the thoughts and actions of others, but mostly they were philosophers and idealists that helped guide Arnock society towards its grander visions.

The Arnock had eclipsed the need for crude verbal or written communications thousands of years before and they conversed mind-to-mind, sometimes at great distances. During the war with the humans, the masters had discovered something extraordinary in their darkest hour. They could enter the human mind invasively. This had never been possible with any other species and, initially, the thought of invading the minds of other beings against their will had sickened the masters. When the humans landed on the darkside of their world though, it had been the only thing that held off the onslaught. The cost had been horrific. Most of the masters had been killed in the war and only a few dozen remained. Arnock warriors, workers, scientists, and others wallowed adrift and fought amongst themselves. The Arnock as a body needed to rest and recover, so Kizik had taken radical action and he put all the lower castes to sleep. He and the other masters would rebuild society while the rest of the Arnock hibernated.

At the moment of the command from Kizik, the lower castes had spun cocoons and crawled inside wherever they were—some in their homes, some on the streets, some as they fed or bathed. It was like nothing that had ever happened in the history of the species. Arnock society was frozen in time, machines tending to the sleeping and a few dozen masters working without rest to restore their way of life.

Kizik scuffled into what humans would call a military base. He hurried past soldiers wrapped in cocoons, clumped into groups by tending machines. Kizik made his way to a chamber that held The Vault and input the codes into the lock mechanism that would open the massive doors. Then the voices rang out in concert, unmistakably clear in Kizik's mind.

Stop!

A half dozen other masters scurried in and physically pulled Kizik from the lock. These weren't the veterans who had fought the humans coming up the Twilight Ridge. These masters had been on the home front during the war. As a group, they chastised Kizik, buzzing and shaking.

This is not the way we had agreed to! Their minds clawed at him, with a timbre that was bitter and aggrieved.

Kizik tried to calm them with his thoughts, to bring them all to the same level of understanding.

Stop! they demanded. *We will not be soothed away. Don't insult us with the same tricks you used to butcher the humans!*

Kizik backed up. This reaction was extraordinary. He had been prepared to have to explain his actions but hadn't expected such hostility. Then from behind, he felt the presence of another group of masters; almost two dozen minds. These were the ones he had fought with in the wastelands above, who had taken life and felt the sting of the human's plasma bursts and chemical lasers. The veterans only had one thought for Kizik.

Yes. He knew he had their support to move forward with the plan.

Kizik came forward again before the protestors. They deserved to be heard and he was obligated to explain himself. No master was above any other, but the conflict with the humans had made him the kind of leader his species had never known before—a war master. His thorax buzzed and he dropped his head. *The humans are coming back. They plan to take over Highland and destroy us. They have learned. They will win.*

What about the gifts?! the six protestors demanded. *We gave the three small humans live Arnock for Highland to dissect and study. What has that gotten us?*

They were holding Kizik to account for the deal he had made. It hadn't been quite enough to invade the humans' minds. They needed hardware. Kizik had paid Highland in live Arnock, including a few masters, in exchange for ships, weapons, and communications systems. It had been a horrifically painful deal to make, but it had worked. The humans had pulled back bloodied and limping.

Highland will fall! Did you not see what I saw through Timberwolf's eyes? The three small men are desperate! Timberwolf has been captured by his old teacher!

Kizik stared into each of the protestors' minds one by one. He felt for them, but they didn't understand. None of them had fought the humans. Kizik saw in them a bold naiveté and an exhaustion that was so deep that it went to the core of their souls. One of them, Dremis, stepped forward. Alone, Dremis had held together the Arnock spirituality during the war, even as the slaughter had reached a fever pitch. His mind was placid even now.

This is desperation, Dremis said, calmly.

That is not in doubt, Kizik responded.

Our gods teach us that peace is our place in the universe.

I wish that was true. Kizik sighed. His old friend shuffled. They had lived in the same alcove as young apprentices, staying up arguing philosophy as students did—joyously disagreeing, harmonizing their positions, and then coming out at odds again by morning.

When things come to an end, perhaps that's what Radem has written. Dremis invoked the holiest incarnation of their deities—Radem—the collective council of their gods.

Sometimes Radem is to be ignored. You showed me that.

I wish that was true, Dremis responded.

Kizik respected his old friend and loved Dremis as much as two Arnock could love each other, but there had been enough idealism. The war had taken that from Kizik and the other veterans.

Radem is dead, Kizik said.

The six blocking the vault shuddered at the blasphemy, and Kizik could feel doubts from the supporters behind him as well. The six blocking his way tried to respond collectively but couldn't align their thoughts. Finally it came bluntly from Dremis. *We will not step aside.*

I hoped it would be you, Kizik responded.

With his mind, Kizik pushed the veterans behind him away. Told his supporters not to interfere or participate. He would take the burden for them all. The Arnock mind was not one that changed easily. Its logic routines and mental capacity were too thorough and specialized. There was only one way through this impasse.

Kizik shivered and buzzed, reaching out with his mind to the six before him. All at once, it was like he grabbed them by their throats. They squealed audibly, trying in vain to protect themselves from the mental onslaught. Then, one by one, they ceased being alive and fell to the ground, until it was just Dremis remaining. The philosopher peered at Kizik's mind and said the most hurtful thing it could before dying.

Radem loves you.

THE VAULT

Not every Arnock had immediately cocooned itself when Kizik put them to sleep. Some had work to do first. They prepped a command ship and a troop carrier and readied for a military expedition.

Kizik and the surviving masters opened the twelve-foot-thick doors to The Vault and made their way to a hangar bay, a vast chamber that could fit a dozen skyscrapers. Here, a massive command ship, curved and organic like a giant snail shell, sat ready to depart. Its launch sequence was halted in the final moments with Arnock standing by inside, cocooned at their stations. Next to it was a troop carrier ship, spindly and long with cylindrical landing craft hanging from its hull; all filled with sleeping soldiers and sentries.

Before the war, there were over a thousand masters. Now there were barely two dozen and Kizik had killed six critical members of Arnock society who had stood in opposition—

spiritual leaders and poets they would never be able to get back. Launching an attack on Highland would surely get more masters and countless others killed. Even if this was successful and their race survived, would they even be Arnock anymore? Or something ugly and deformed? That's what the six had considered and found unacceptable. They had chosen to die rather than see their society degrade any further. Kizik had been the instrument that helped them.

He ordered the other masters aboard the vessels, some on the command ship and some on the troop carrier. As they boarded, he could feel their disdain for him, even as he'd done what was necessary. They saw in him a monster they dared not look at. Arnock never feared each other, but they were scared of him. No one dared think it, but the word for him was *farhallen. Creature of the badlands. Beast of the wind.*

Kizik got halfway up the gangplank on the command ship, but at the last moment, he opted to board the troop carrier. He needed to be in the thick of it if he was going to go through with this. Once aboard, he drew the Arnock on both vessels out of hibernation. They stirred to life, using their sharp claws to cut through their cocoons. From outside, he felt the presence of the four masters he was leaving to tend to the sleepers. Behind them came the few dozen apprentices who had been born just within the last year. Small and clumsy, the children scrambled about, excited and confused by all the commotion. They'd never known a bustling time, with streets filled with other Arnock. To them, their whole lives had been lived in these empty warrens filled with cocoons.

The engines on the two vessels powered to life and with a hum barely above silence, they levitated off the moorings. Far above them, the ceiling opened up to the twilight sky, speckled with pinpricks of light. Kizik heard the children exclaim with delight, *Stars! Stars! Stars!*

The ships rose, the space large enough to allow them to float side by side. When they neared the surface, the pilots turned on the cloaks and the two vessels evaporated into the sky. Kizik could feel the surprise and concern from the children below as the ships disappeared and he assured them.

We're hiding!

Kizik knew that if he survived this, there would be no welcome for him on Arnock Prime, no thanks and no laurels. Kizik was beyond caring about any of it. He had done a terrible thing today that he was too exhausted to regret, and he intended not to. He was determined to be the wind that swept back over the humans for what they had done before and for what they planned to do now. *Stars! Stars! Stars!* he heard again, as the ceiling to his world closed behind him.

DECISION

Salla heard the plasma bursts and stopped running. She hadn't expected them to shoot Timberwolf. She couldn't stand the idea of leaving someone behind. Back on Nova Turin, too many people had been left waiting for rescue that never came. She took her sidearm from its holster for the first time ever and charged it. She was about to turn back when she found herself momentarily held by the shoulders by someone coming towards the clamor. "Excuse me," Emmanuel Gray said politely as he rushed past her. With that, she lost her nerve. The thought had been suicide anyway and she wouldn't be of any value dead or in a cell. The last thing she saw before Timberwolf fell awed her. He was standing upright and taking on his armored attackers hand-to-hand. Gray was then hovering over him on the ground, shooing the men away.

Gray hauled Timberwolf over his shoulder as the others helped. Drogel limped, showing them the way. They were coming towards her. "Salla, tell security we're bringing him up to cell B," Drogel said.

Salla nodded as they passed her, and she moved aside. Just then Timberwolf slipped from Gray's shoulder, falling to the deck. As they struggled to pick him back up, he managed to grab Salla's hand. When they'd moved off, Salla noticed the keycard in her palm. *Get the box from my quarters aboard the Nina…*she remembered Timberwolf telling her. It didn't make any sense to put that on *Nina* now, but if she hurried, she could get it up to the detention level before Gray and Drogel got there. *I hope that's what you're trying to tell me*, she thought. She looked to the infirmary. Achilles was peering through a porthole-sized window. They locked eyes and he yelled for her, banging on the door. "You have to stay here, for your own safety," she told him. Achilles panicked, shaking his head negatively.

"No! He's here for me! You've got to get me out of here!" But Salla couldn't help him right now and she had no time to argue. As he yelled for her, she ran off.

Salla avoided the elevators and took the access tubes out to the inner hab ring to Timberwolf's quarters. She tried the keycard and the door clicked open. Timberwolf's living space wasn't the tidy affair she had imagined, but much more haphazard. Reports were taped up on the walls. Charts were spread out over a table he'd taken from an office. A half-full coffee pot sat at a cluttered desk. She pushed his bed aside and saw the box instantly. It was a five-foot-long, gray footlocker. She grabbed it and went to pull, but it felt like it was bolted to the floor. *I can't move this!*

Gray's men argued at the cross-corridor, unable to decide left or right, up or down. They held Timberwolf like a sack of potatoes between them and he wasn't helping. He stuck his foot out and hooked it against a wall and they almost dropped him. Drogel tried to point the way, but then changed his mind.

Salla saw a panel on the side of the box and opened it. Inside was a suspensor control. She activated it and the box rose two feet and floated there. She pushed it out the door and through the tight corridors, people clearing out of her way. When she got close to the detention level, she slowed to a walk. She found three security guards sitting at a table playing cards, a pile of poker chips in front of them. When they saw her, one of them jumped up and sent the chips flying. "Vice! What can we help you with?" she asked.

"I don't give you much to do, huh? I had to bring this up myself. Open cell B!"

The security guards scattered, one of them cranking open the cell. Salla managed not to appear relieved they didn't ask her what she was doing. She didn't exactly know. The elevator nearby opened, and Gray's men spilled out, hauling Timberwolf. They dragged him the last few steps to the cell. "Stick him in here," she said. "Glad to have this one under wraps, you know?"

Salla held the door open to the cell, her uniform disheveled. She elbowed in and took Timberwolf under the shoulders, dropping him roughly to the floor inside the cell. She nudged the box with her toe, pushing it further out of view under a metal cot.

"Thank you, Vice," Drogel said, rolling his eyes at the others. Salla looked up to see Gray there, smiling at her. "This is my vice," Drogel introduced her to Gray, with a wave of his fleshy hand.

"Pleasure. Sorry for the workout." Gray held his hand out to her. On his index finger was a blue basic training ring awarded to the class valedictorian. It was exactly the same one Salla wore. She couldn't believe she was doing it, but she took his hand. "Thank you," she said. "I know who you are."

"The important thing is who *you* are," Gray answered in the superior way an adult made a child feel special. Gray's handshake was warm and enveloping. He smiled again and looked over at Timberwolf, crumpled up on the floor. "With some you never know."

In the instant he released her hand, Salla noticed that Gray saw the tattoo on her knuckle in the shape of an ornate *NT*. All of the miners on Nova Turin had gotten them. Before he could look at her again, she'd slipped away, but he'd seen it and had to know she was one of the living ghosts he had made on that world. Salla stumbled backwards out of the hall, bracing herself against the wall.

Gray had touched and spoken to her. She had always imagined she would see him one day and approach him calmly and tell him who she was and what he'd done to her. Then he'd apologize and ask her not to kill him. She had never taken that any further in her mind and her dark fantasy never thickened to a conclusion. When she had finally met Gray, she'd just gotten out of his sight as quickly as possible, seemingly making no impact on him. He'd seen her tattoo, though, and had to know where she was from. But now it was over and she stood in the hall, laboring to stay on her feet.

She thought about going back to her quarters and keeping her head down until all this was over, but there was that man, Achilles Dacha, in the infirmary, begging to be released. Gray wanted him and he was critical to his plan…Highland…the   Arnock…Timberwolf…Achilles? He must have had some sort of access to Highland. Gray stood outside Timberwolf's cell, arms folded in satisfaction, buoyantly jawing with his men, ready for his next move.

Gray laughed as someone made a joke about Timberwolf, crumpled up and beaten in the cell. He found Salla in his gaze for a moment and nodded at her, ever so slightly. *He'd noticed!* He knew she was from Nova. She thought of her sister, Kora, two years younger. *I'll be right back Kora. Wait in the basement! Stay hidden.*

Stay hidden. No one stayed hidden on Nova. Gray's men had heartbeat monitors.

Suddenly, it was clear what to do next. She wasn't going to her quarters. She wasn't going to stay hidden. *No way in hell you're getting what you want. Not Highland. Not past me.*

She slipped down the stairs. She could be back out to the hab ring and to the infirmary in just minutes. She'd have to move fast, before she lost her nerve. *What's in the box?* she thought as she ran. She hoped that whatever was inside would help Timberwolf escape. She was counting on him.

ACT II

MEMORIES

Gray and Michael looked in at Timberwolf in the cell. He was crumpled up on the floor with his back to them, a mess of black and blue.

"I say a walk in space is what's good for him," Michael said, suggesting with his brow that he would take action on that right now if only Gray turned his back.

"My heart tells me he has a place in this story, just like you."

"Did you come here for Achilles Dacha, or for Timberwolf?"

"That's nice to ask," Gray spat back.

Michael shook his head. Taking Timberwolf out of the equation was a plus, but to him it was not enough. "What we're doing here, it's not just what Izabeck writes in his book. We need focus to take Highland. Timberwolf alive is too much risk. He's sleeping now. Just let me…"

"Shh. He's not sleeping. He never rests." Gray put his fingers to his lips. "I want him to stay alive. If he dies you would follow him swiftly, Michael. Is that understood?"

"No, it's not. But he'll keep breathing."

Timberwolf stirred on the floor of the cell. His throat was dry as a bone. He slipped in and out of consciousness, sometimes heaving from the pain of the plasma burns, his eyes opening for wretched moments. Finally, he stopped writhing and relaxed, for no other reason than his body was too tired to fight the pain anymore. In his mind, he felt Kizik watching him. Timberwolf knew the creature was traveling. It was hard to explain, but the color of the union with Kizik kept changing, like a mental Doppler effect. It felt red. Somehow it was clear Kizik was coming *toward* him.

Timberwolf pushed the being away and found himself somewhere between fever dreams and memories. He was on Phaelon Prime almost twenty years before. His squad patrolled through the Mile High Red Forest, past maroon tree trunks eighty feet wide. Light from above pierced the mist in wide bars. The memories came back in pulses of images and sounds.

There was the crack of the giant tree falling, a trap they'd walked into…the impact on the ground scattering the squad…Timberwolf's heads-up display showing his squad mates going from green to red and then fading to gray…

The whine of the chemical lasers and the howls of the Phaelon as they dropped on cables from the trees… Sergeant Almador's armor glowing like the sun as he was incinerated…

Timberwolf rallying the survivors and rushing the attackers…attacking a mortar position with bayonets… running through the forest…more trees falling behind them…three Phaelon fleeing for their lives in front of them…

Timberwolf stirred in the cell, almost smiling at the memory. "Those were the good old days," he groaned. He heaved some more and passed out. His mind swirled with memories again, but they were much clearer, almost like he was watching a movie. It was five years before. The first time he met Kizik.

He was onboard a drop lifter racing low over a jagged red world…paging through the mission briefing on his heads-up…Jackhammer, that word floating out to him… Jackhammer…

The eight-man squad piling out…making their way to the cave where they knew Kizik was…the presence tickling his mind, feeling it behind his sinuses for the first time…

The terror in the voice of the lifter pilot as she took off… her yelling about an Arnock in the cabin…the lifter crashing and rolling over some of the squad…the hallucinations starting…

Firing at an Arnock that disappeared…ordering everyone to point delta…the *rat-tat-tat* of plasma rifles…one man casually removing his helmet and falling over dead…a man falling into a crevasse and the *clang, clang, clang* of his armor against the rocks…

The Arnock rising on its back legs then melting away…Timberwolf shooting…Lieutenant Marco taking the blast to the chest…Timberwolf dragging him and begging him to live…the emergency siren ringing in Marco's helmet as he flat-lined…a dozen Arnock surrounding them and all but one fading away…

Kizik dragging Timberwolf to the cave…the being's wretched breath, like rancid cinnamon…the red blotch on its face, like a shotgun blast of blood…how it buzzed and shook before entering his mind…Thoughts and images mixing together, unsure which mind was which…

Timber, I'm near death with you…

In my head, my team?

You let them die…

No…

Struggling to escape…unable to even move his jaw…

Are you embracing death? The emptiness. The nothingness. The fingers at your throat. Your people swarm near our space. When, where will they come?

I won't tell you…

The crash of the bombs from air support above…

They act to kill you. They know you will tell me…

Gray standing in front of him now and Kizik scurrying away…lying on the floor of the medical lifter…asking to die…the presence hanging onto him…

The white room in Purity Hospital…struggling against the restraints…The doctors watching him…Dr. Tier's face hovering…feeling the drugs rush to his heart…the beep of the medical machines getting louder…louder still…

Suddenly Timberwolf was conscious, but he couldn't open his eyes. He knew he was still in the cell as he felt the cold of the floor against his back. The *presence* was overwhelming. Kizik was with him now, like he was right in the room. He felt the being grinding in his mind, in the air, in the walls and in every cell of his body. It was like nothing he'd ever experienced before.

Timber, I'm here with you.

Timberwolf was able to respond, but able wasn't the right word. He was compelled to respond, unable not to. *You showed me that again? Why?*

I needed to remind you.

Kizik had never come to Timberwolf so clearly. He'd always been elusive, just outside the fringes, grinding on him. He seldom used language, except in spurts. Timberwolf had no idea he was capable of this.

Are you here? You're everywhere.

I am always everywhere. I must tell you something.

No. Just go away.

You came to seek me out. That's what I was showing you. I see you have regrets now that we know each other.

Timberwolf tried to push him away, but couldn't. It was like Kizik had a foot in the door of his mind. He continued, *You must stop Gray. We are sleeping, but we'll be awake if you come. You are the fire. We are the wind.*

Timberwolf tried to respond, but he couldn't. Instead he felt a rush of energy that filled up every part of him. The pain from his wounds was gone and he sat up, blinking. Kizik was gone now, like he'd never been there. He rubbed his eyes, saw the black and blue on the back of his hand. It didn't hurt, but it was tender.

The light in the cell hummed and blinked. He struggled to his feet, his survival instincts kicking in. He knew that it was a gift from Kizik that he was up, but he didn't care right now. Kizik must have tricked his brain into releasing analgesics to deaden the pain from his injuries. He began to pace. He saw two of Gray's men out in the hall, heads swinging from side to side as they watched him walk back and forth.

He smiled at them and cracked his knuckles. He began pulling on the metal cot bolted to the floor. Soon, the bolts began to loosen as he yanked the cot back and forth. After a few minutes, covered in sweat and swearing, he'd pried the foot of the cot from the floor, bending it in half. The guards banged on the door, but he ignored them. He planned to use the cot as a battering ram against the door. It wasn't a great idea, but it was better than nothing…*Wait, what the hell is that?*

Under the cot was the box from his quarters. Timberwolf fell back on his haunches a moment. "Thanks, Vice," he said aloud. This was a much better plan.

SAINT FRANCIS

Gray received a request to report to Cardinal Jacob's cabin on *St. Francis*. Michael had warned against it, but there was no way Gray was missing this. After Gray had joined the Believer order on Haven, it became very clear that Cardinal Jacob had had a plan for him since the moment they met. But their working relationship quickly became that of two bulls sparring for dominance.

On the very day of his oath, Cardinal Jacob showed him the detailed plans his military advisors had drawn up for how to take Highland. They were meticulous down to the last detail. They were presented in perfect clarity. They were hugely flawed.

The problem was that the plan took everything on faith. It was assumed that the intelligence they had on the Dachas was infallible. There were no contingencies, no backups. If it turned out that the Dachas were in fact nobodies, the plan would have failed and Gray would have been left holding the bag. At first Gray had been polite and offered suggestions, but Cardinal Jacob had grown stubborn. He refused to back down on any of his points or change the smallest detail. Gray could have walked away, but he refused to back down.

He challenged Cardinal Jacob on everything, in public and in private.

One day, instead of arguing, Gray simply took action. As a test, he ordered Wrath from Highland without asking permission or informing Cardinal Jacob. He organized a pickup on a small planetoid in the asteroid belt around Alpha-Sigma. Ivan Dacha made the delivery and Gray paid Michael to make the pickup. Once completed, Michael tipped off the local shipping authorities to illegal weapons trafficking and Ivan was arrested. Gray pulled some strings to get him held at Fangelsi in cryogenic stasis until trial.

When Cardinal Jacob heard what Gray had done, he called him in front of The Clergy. His obsession with Highland and controlling Gray's actions was making the other cardinals doubt him. It was this exchange that finally sealed Cardinal Jacob's fate.

"Why is Ivan Dacha not here as our guest and instead in a prison?" Cardinal Jacob had demanded.

"You wanted me to bring him here? You don't think they'd come looking for him? You would jeopardize the whole Believer order for this?"

Unable to answer Gray's challenge, Cardinal Jacob and his advisors retreated to the top wing of the Believer Citadel and refused any visitors or communications. Not long after that, Cardinal Jacob's chief rival, Cardinal Claire Dais, called an emergency vote on Cardinal Jacob's suitability as prime cardinal. The vote was overwhelmingly negative against him. Sister Claire became prime cardinal and allowed Gray to plan the mission the way he saw fit. The only thing Cardinal Jacob still had the power to do was place a Believer crew and his man Izabeck on *Nemesis*. What stung most of all was that Cardinal Jacob's control over The Clergy's monetary affairs was stripped.

Two guards dressed in ornate cerulean blue uniforms crossed spears in front of Cardinal Jacob's cabin on *St. Francis*. Gray remembered them from his time on Haven.

After a few moments of banter, they opened the door and let Gray and Izabeck enter.

Within the cabin, Cardinal Jacob sat on what could only be described as a throne. He was perched upon a formal chair on a slight dais. A secretary stood to his side. Gray couldn't control himself and laughed at the sight. "Maybe find a barefoot servant to fan you with palms?"

"Emmanuel, it is a rare pleasure to see you. You seem so..." he searched for the word, "*alive* in all this."

"Despite your prayers, I'm sure."

"I would never pray for someone's misfortune. There was no such person as St. Schadenfreude." Cardinal Jacob's face looked exhausted; Gray had determined long ago that this was simply an act to appear bored and put upon. "I'm merely here to visit a member of my flock alone in a field."

"That's lovely. So, what do you want?"

"I need to understand your will, Bishop Gray. I really need to understand your character."

"Well, we both know you're not fond of my character. My intention is to take Highland as planned."

"I would like you to give up that foolishness," Cardinal Jacob said. Izabeck looked up from scribbling, his brow rising.

"Oh you would, Cardinal Jacob? You're forgetting this was your idea?"

He swallowed hard. "Emmanuel, friend. I am in a position to make things very bad for you."

"I really don't see how. You've taken Sister Claire's yacht for a ride and now you're just blowing your horn."

The unsaid truth between them was that the failure of this mission would bolster Cardinal Jacob's status amongst The Clergy again and discredit Sister Claire. If Gray backed away from Highland and things fell apart, then maybe her little insurrection would crumble as quickly as it had come together.

Cardinal Jacob searched the air and thumbed the prayer beads around his neck. "You have one final chance. Give up on Highland. You will be paid extravagantly once I regain the prime cardinalship."

"You don't have the coin I want. Is that it?"

"I am sorry, Emmanuel."

Gray smirked, looking for the plot. Cardinal Jacob wouldn't have come all the way here just to chat politely and he had never once told Gray he was sorry for anything. The look in Cardinal Jacob's eyes seemed genuine; true resignation with hints of regret. Gray wasn't buying this façade of sincerity for a second. He wanted to throttle him there and get to the bottom of this, but he decided to back away for once and let things lie. He had gotten everything he wanted today. Timberwolf was in a cell, and he had Achilles Dacha. All he had to do was get him back on *Nemesis* and leave. "I'm going to do wonderful things for all Believers, Jacob," Gray said. Cardinal Jacob nodded and Gray backed away, polite enough not to show the cardinal his back.

Once Gray had left, Cardinal Jacob beckoned Izabeck to approach him. He pulled him close, so his secretary couldn't see. He pressed his fingers onto Izabeck's forearm and the skin glowed in a pattern of squares for a moment—first yellow, then orange, and then red. "God's will be done on all our worlds as it is in heaven."

Cardinal Jacob released Izabeck. The man's forearm was hot and the chamber inside whirred. Izabeck tried not to show how much it hurt, but his face betrayed him, and he squeezed his arm to his side. "It will cool down in a few moments, son," Cardinal Jacob said as he steadied him by the shoulder. "I needed to give Bishop Gray one more chance to see things my way."

BREAKOUT

"Jesus! Don't open the door!" Achilles yelled. "I rigged it to explode."

Salla stood on the outside of the infirmary. At her feet was one of Gray's men. The name on his armor was Ulric. She'd sprayed him with a crowd control nerve agent Station Corps officers kept on their person in case of riots. He'd sleep for a while and wake up with a very bad headache. "Okay. I'm backing up. I'm backing up."

"I can't disarm it. I made it too fast. Get a stick or something and turn the handle." Salla saw a fire extinguisher nearby and took it from its holder. "Yes, that's fine. Just throw it at the handle."

Salla threw the fire extinguisher at the handle and the door exploded outward with a crack, dangling from its top hinge. Achilles was out in the smoke almost instantly. "What's the plan?" the tiny man demanded. He wielded two surgical saws he'd detached from the wall.

"We've got to get you to *Nina*. Then we get out of here."

"Is Timberwolf going to be able to help us?"

They ran along a curved hallway, and ducked into a side corridor when Salla caught a glimpse of some of Gray's men coming towards them. "If I had a plan, that would be part of it."

Gray slapped Ulric on the face and the man stirred. He rubbed his eyes and then stood up suddenly, coming to attention. Michael yanked on the mangled door to the infirmary and it clanged to the deck. Gray looked into the empty room where Achilles had been held. "Who?!" Gray demanded.

"That woman that works for him!" Ulric pointed to Drogel, who went pale and seemed to shrink six inches.

"Where's your vice?" Gray demanded. "The one with the Nova tattoo." Drogel didn't have an answer. "It's time to meet Wrath."

THE BOX

Timberwolf knelt over the open box. He unzipped a canvas cover within and there it was—*the gift*. When he had met Ivan Dacha on Telock Sen, Timberwolf had been desperate to get Kizik out of his head. A few weeks before that he had tried to kill himself in his apartment. He put a plasma pistol to his temple, but couldn't pull the trigger. Not that he didn't have the will, but Kizik wouldn't let him.

He'd then even set up the pistol on a tripod and rigged a timer to fire randomly. Sometime within thirty seconds, the pistol was set to fire a plasma burst at him at the highest setting. He stood a few feet from it and waited. It hadn't worked. The presence forced him to dodge away, Kizik somehow knowing when the blast would come.

Suicide missions for Dr. Tier hadn't worked; actual suicide hadn't worked. He had even found himself starting bar fights against entire bars, but after the first punch he would just let go, the presence taking over. He'd find himself standing over a dozen bloodied men, not knowing how they'd gotten that way. One day he found a business card under his door from Ivan Dacha of Highland LLC. On the back of it was written: *We can get it out.*

In the box was *their* answer to his problem—a rig of black fighting armor. Timberwolf had expected Ivan to perhaps put a probe of some kind into his brain or administer some cocktail of drugs to drive Kizik out. Instead, Ivan gave him the box and told him things would become clearer later. Timberwolf had almost dumped the rig in the desert of Telock Sen. He knew they were putting him in their pocket and the rig was a tool for him to do their will. Back in the infirmary, Achilles had finally made it clear what the deal was. *Get rid of Gray and we'll get rid of Kizik.*

Instead of walking away on Telock Sen, though, he'd tried out the rig, taking it through its paces in the desert. The armor was more advanced by leaps and bounds than the standard pressurized rigs that Gray's men wore. Made from the biological armor of a Sabatin, it was invisible to all forms of detection except sight. Heat and pressure resistant, it was designed to allow the wearer to descend to a planet through an atmosphere. It wasn't necessary to carry a weapon as it had its own assault package built in. The right gauntlet had a plasma driver that was almost inexhaustible. The left gauntlet had a chemical laser that could cut through almost anything. The rig could throw holograms, E.M.P.s, launch cyber-attacks, release nerve agents, and a lot more. It had blown him away. He recalled Sergey smiling at him after he'd tried it. *"You're not going to give it back, are you?"*

In the cell, he pulled on the gauntlets first, the ribbed and scaled components activating and locking around him. Next came the chest plate and ankle guards, each gripping him perfectly and dropping sensor threads into his skin. Timberwolf was becoming the rig and the rig was becoming Timberwolf.

Outside, one of Gray's men had his hand on the handle. His armor read Mose over a Celtic cross within a Believer symbol. Earlier, Michael had pulled him aside and told him that if Timberwolf had *asked for it*, then Gray wanted him shot. Timberwolf blocked the cameras and was tearing the cell apart. This seemed like asking for it to Mose. The Outpost security guard back in the control room implored Mose over the intercom, "Please do not open that door!"

Ignoring her, Mose motioned for Pinther, another fighter, to back him up. "I'm going to open that door in thirty seconds," he said to the security guard. "That cell best be filled with gas."

With a hiss, the cell started to fill with a pale yellow vapor. It wafted up over the porthole and seeped out under the door. Mose waited a minute, then took a breath and turned the handle. The door opened with a creek, the hall filling with gas. There was a moment of nothing as they both approached the cell. Then in a flash, something metal came flying out at them. It was the cot Timberwolf had torn from the floor. Following it immediately was a flash of black as Timberwolf kicked Mose across the hall. Before Pinther now was a demon, the gas from the cell rising around him. It looked like someone had molded Wrath into human form. Deep black, fierce, brutal—animal and man and technology.

Timberwolf took a knee and fired a concussion blast from his fist—an RPG of air that slammed Pinther against the wall with a crack. Before he could fall to the deck, Timberwolf was on him, taking the rifle from his hands. Mose was recovering now, and Timberwolf took the butt of the rifle and drove it into his chest, knocking him into the corner. Both of the men were on the deck now, crumpled and moaning.

In the security control room, the guards had their hands up. Timberwolf stood in the doorway, his suit hissing and smoking from the action. He lifted a thumb and motioned to the hall. "Get the hell out. Take the stairs."

The guards scattered and Timberwolf used his heads-up display to access one of the computer terminals. The screen flashed through the network drives until he found what he wanted. The computer in his rig brute-forced its way through the security. When he uploaded the virus, the electronics around him began shutting down almost immediately and the lights dimmed. The Outpost's sensors, weapons, elevators, docking clamps—everything except life-support and the artificial gravity—went off-line. He'd never tried the cyber-weapons package before and had expected it to take at least a few minutes to kick in, but it had been like flipping a switch. *Damn, this thing is good.*

UNLEASHED

Wrath stalked the corridor, swinging his head with purpose, checking the nooks and crannies of the curved hall. Gray, a half dozen of his men, and Drogel were twenty steps behind. Thomas monitored Wrath on his heads-up. "Wrath's got nothing…nothing." They were sweeping the outer hab ring now, finding no sign of Achilles and Salla. The other teams working the inner hab ring and central core were coming up empty as well.

One after the other the lights down the corridor faded to brown and then went off with clacks. Drogel checked his smart-device. "We're losing security feeds! There's power outages all over The Outpost."

"Call over to Mose! Where's Timberwolf?" Gray asked.

Michael tried to reach Mose, but didn't get a response. "He's not answering."

Gray shook his head in disbelief. Just a few minutes ago everything had been wrapped up. If Timberwolf was out, Gray needed to find Achilles and get the hell off The Outpost immediately. "Thomas, Wrath knows what he's looking for. Let him go."

"Wrath, *d'maaesh shalosh.*"

Detached from human purpose, Wrath took off following a scent only he knew. He scrambled into an elevator that was darkened and stuck open, bursting through the top into the shaft. He grappled up the cables effortlessly, sensing Achilles above him. At the top of the shaft he stopped and peered between the closed elevator doors.

Achilles and Salla were on the other side. The elevator chimed as the lights flicked off and the door opened only a few inches. Salla checked her smart-device. "There's no power anywhere," she said, shining a flashlight into the shaft. "We're not taking the elevator, anyway. We need to jump across."

They worked the door and got it open. As Salla sized up how she was going to jump to the ledge on the other side, the cable whipped past with a *zing*. She carefully peered into the shaft, watching the cable whip against the sides as it fell. As she looked down, Salla felt a breath wash over her shoulders and heard a sound like a hacksaw moving lightly over piano wire. Turning slowly, she found Wrath's toothy silver smile above her. She pulled away, pushing backwards along the floor on her haunches.

Wrath uncurled from the shaft, flicking his silver tongue. The light from Salla's flashlight captured the worst parts of him as he came towards her; gleaming teeth, bayonets coming from his forearms, his pupils narrow slits when the light crossed his face.

"Don't move!" Achilles threw his hands up and got between her and the beast. He gingerly approached Wrath, his hand outstretched and fingers dancing. He sang softly, "Hush little baby, don't say a word, Daddy's gonna buy you a mocking bird." Wrath cocked his head and calmed as Achilles continued, "If that mocking bird's too cruel, Daddy's gonna buy you a swimming pool." Wrath was hunched down now, tail sliding back and forth along the deck. "If that swimming pool turns blood red, Daddy's gonna shine up your armored head."

Achilles drew close, placing his fingertips on Wrath's temples. When he did, the beast rolled over, unconscious and breathing heavily. Salla got to her feet, legs wobbly and shaken. She approached Wrath, putting her hands on his side. "Jesus, how'd you do that?"

"Oh, you've got to build in ways to protect yourself from your own creations. That's bio-weapons engineering one-oh-one," Achilles answered.

"Thank you. I'm glad I know that."

"Wait, shush!" Achilles cocked his head and sniffed the air. He pulled Salla behind Wrath for cover, like he was a mound of sandbags. The footsteps of a single person were approaching. "Timberwolf Velez?" Achilles challenged the darkness. A figure was there in the dull illumination of the life-support monitors. The edges of the figure pulsed orange for a moment and it moved closer. Salla peered around Wrath's bulk.

"Vice?" Timberwolf illuminated himself fully so they could see him. For some reason, Salla's first instinct was to touch Timberwolf's rig up by the breastplate. It was ribbed to the touch and hot. Under her fingers, the components in Timberwolf's armor whirred and sizzled and left her stinging from a static shock.

"Jesus, so that's what was in the box?"

THE RIG

Gray and Thomas had watched the feed from Wrath's remote camera on their heads-up displays as he'd cornered Achilles and Salla. They'd watched when the view rolled over as Achilles soothed Wrath. They'd also watched as Timberwolf appeared and stomped the camera with his boot.

"Did you see what Achilles did?" Thomas said. "That song must have been a kill switch." Thomas found Wrath's location on his smart-device, three levels up in a storage room.

For just an instant, Gray had seen what Timberwolf was wearing. He'd heard rumors that Highland might have something like this on their drawing board, but it looked like they'd rushed a prototype into production. He pulled Michael close so the others couldn't hear. "He's got a rig of Sabatin armor. What do you know about that?"

"It's like Wrath plus Timberwolf plus a ridiculous weapons package. We've got him two dozen to one," Michael said.

"We're still fucked, aren't we?" Gray responded, and Michael nodded. Gray's military mind clicked on. Gray turned to the men and called out over the com link to the others searching elsewhere. "Timberwolf is out. We'll form into three squads under Michael, Sol, myself. We'll take positions in CB4. They have to go through there to get to Dacha's ship. Thomas, wake up Wrath."

CONTACT

Gray's men fanned out through Cargo Bay 4, the space still filled with the Sabatin containers in varying stages of disposal. The floor was slick with chemicals and the air held the pungent smell of the chlorine mixture. Overlapping chatter spilled out over the com channel as the men fanned out. "Watch the chlorine patches... Got cover... Sol's up front... Call out... Sol... Izabeck... Scariot... Mountainrock... Windwhistle... Bison... Forestground... got a pressure flux..." The men cleared the space, covering each other and moving efficiently through the multilevel labyrinth of boxes, anterooms, and equipment.

"No sign of Timberwolf," Michael reported from the far end of the bay. He couldn't help but peer into an open Sabatin container. A shriveled, dead creature floated in the chemicals inside. Around him, he saw the faces of the men illuminated in their helmets. Their actions were deliberate but unnatural. They were tentative and anxious. They knew they were out of their league.

Through force of will, Timberwolf had taken on all of them without armor and with only a rifle set on sting. Michael had to admit, the scene had been astounding even by Timberwolf's standards. Michael had heard some of the men referring to him as "the demon." They said that he'd been captured by the Arnock and lived, that he'd killed a dozen men on Golgotha, that he'd choked the life out of a Phaelon in hand-to-hand combat, and more. Michael didn't dare tell them all of that was true.

Above the space, a window fifty yards wide showed the back half of *Nina* hanging outside, connected by tethers and a walkway-tube. Sol and a few others tried to manually open the airlock, but it wasn't budging. "Forget it. Get in position!" Gray ordered.

The men took cover behind boxes and containers, their armor auto-camouflaging. "Windwhistle! You're up with

Sol," Gray barked. The young man hustled up next to the old infantryman.

"Men, harden up." Gray lowered his head and began a prayer. "Our father, who gives his judgment, hallowed be thy name." The others joined in, their voices getting stronger as they went on. "Thy kingdom come, thy will be done on all our worlds as it is in heaven. And give us our daily prey and forgive us our failures, as our works bring about your kingdom. So be it."

Sol's heads-up scattered for a moment and then came back. Two blips were moving towards them. "Got something. Two people coming off the concourse." The men went hot with their weapons and huddled behind cover. Salla appeared tentatively, Achilles following her in the cargo bay. Sol and Windwhistle let them pass and then stepped out of position.

"On your knees!" Sol demanded as they turned to him. Before they could react, Sol unloaded a plasma burst into Salla and she fell instantly. Achilles dropped to his knees, his face blank. "Show your hands!" Sol yelled, and Windwhistle covered him.

In the shadows, Timberwolf moved silently. No one saw him on their heads-ups. No one noticed when he was almost on top of three men huddled together behind a container.

Gray looked over Salla's body. She'd fallen instantly without making a sound. Sol had hit her straight in the chest, but there hadn't been even a sigh or a last breath from her. "There's something…" Gray looked closer. She was either dead or very nearly so, but his heads-up still showed her as green. She should have been either pulsing red or fading to gray. Beyond that, though, there was something else. "Wait! No blood!" Holographic projections, Achilles and Salla shimmered and disappeared, and their icons disappeared from Gray's heads-up.

Timberwolf moved like a ghost. He brushed past the three men. One named Forestground looked down to see that a grenade on his waist blinked red.

"Grenade!" Forestground yelled, trying to pull it from the clip on his belt. In a white flash, the grenade ripped through the space, throwing men in all directions, containers and chemicals cartwheeling through the air. The top half of Forestground was blown all the way up to the lattice works that supported the ceiling of the cargo bay. A corner of metal zinged into Sol's helmet, and he fell dead into Windwhistle's arms.

From packets in their fighting rigs, millions of nano-menders injected into the femoral arteries of the wounded men. The microscopic machines rushed through their bodies in a desperate attempt to stop hemorrhaging and repair vital organs, but it was too late for some. Forestground, Dov, and Sol pulsed with gray K.I.A. icons in Gray's heads-up. A man named Neviim glowed red, and his readings showed he was losing blood fast.

Goddamn! Timberwolf's rig was good enough to hack into their heads-up displays. There would be no way they'd be able to trust their readings. Gray saw the flashing white square that signified a hostile in his heads-up. Then he saw another, then another, but only one could be Timberwolf. The men were shooting at ghost readings. White-hot plasma fire flashed with a *rat-tat-tat*. Fires burned and climbed the walls of the cargo bay. Gray helped haul an injured man out of the fight, dropping him behind a container. Overlapping radio chatter flooded the com link: "We can't target…all over…like the devil…"

In a dark part of the bay, four men chased the fleeting indications in their heads-up displays. Above them, Timberwolf, or a holographic image of him, jumped from container to container, leading them farther into the labyrinth of the cargo bay. At a juncture, he jumped down and landed right in front of a man named Tovah, then leaped away again as an orgy of friendly-fire hit the man from all directions. Gray watched in his heads-up as Tovah's icon faded to gray.

"Get back to the airlock! Turn off your goddamned heads-up displays!"

An explosion sent a man named Scariot flying off the third level. "Lay down suppressive fire and fall back! One man fires, the other man moves! Come on!" Gray's anger swelled. None of these men were worthy to even be in the same room with Timberwolf, let alone fighting him. He took a moment to enjoy this for him. *You're making a good mess of us, you bastard.*

THE LATTICE

Achilles and Salla worked their way through the interconnected lattice work over the cargo bay. The fires and the fighting raged below them. Plasma bursts swiped past. "You don't kill the people you're making a diversion for!" Achilles complained.

Salla hung onto the lattice. On the other side was the landing they were trying to reach. On the landing a small airlock connected a willowy atmosphere recycling hose to *Nina*. Salla's plan was to go through the recycling hose over to Dacha's ship.

Achilles moved through the lattice works deftly, swinging his small body through the struts. He yelled over the fray, "This is easy. We're circus people. Ever feed a leopard out of your hand?"

"Jesus. No."

A stray plasma burst singed her arm. She slipped and hung there by just a few fingers, licking flames rising from a mountain of crates below her. With surprising strength, Achilles pulled her back up into the lattice. She tried to move, but she found herself frozen. "Let's go. You can't stay here. I don't think you have a job anymore."

Salla squeezed her eyes shut. "I hate this job. I'm supposed to be a lawyer."

"I've got connections. If you get through this, you'll earn a shingle." She hardened up and followed Achilles through the lattice, finally reaching the relative safety of the landing.

Something caught Gray's eye above the action. He looked to the lattice works over the cargo bay, then to the atmosphere recycling hose connected to *Nina*. He thought he saw something moving up there. *Was that two people?* He put the plan together. *They're going to hold their breath and go through the recycler!* "I need directed fire on the landing above the window!" Gray yelled into the com link, but no one even heard him. The channel was a cacophony of panic and frantic plasma fire. "We need Wrath here now!" he called out to Thomas over the com link.

Back in the darkened storage room near the elevator, Wrath lay belly up, his breath coming lightly in snorting grunts. Thomas approached gingerly. Over his earbud came the sounds of the fight in the cargo bay, muffled yelling, gunfire, and radio chatter. Eyes wide, Thomas adjusted his rifle, and it whined like a defibrillator charging. He came closer, stepping between Wrath's splayed back legs. He looked down at the beast's chest. Between the gaps in his armor, Wrath's skin glowed with a dull orange bio-luminescence Thomas had never noticed before. He aimed the rifled at Wrath's neck, closed his eyes and pulled the trigger.

With an arch of electricity, Wrath suddenly became a spasm of teeth and claws. Instantly, the beast was up and had Thomas pinned against a wall. Bayonets from Wrath's forearms crossed Thomas's throat and with an awful growl, the beast's breath washed over his face.

"*Minahel! Minahel!*" Wrath relaxed. His forearm bayonets slowly retracted as he recognized his master. Thomas breathed again, but before surrendering fully, Wrath gave a last animal twitch and a sneer. "Wrath's awake!" Thomas said over the com link, to a response of audio feedback and gunfire.

AWAKE

Salla opened the airlock over the cargo bay. When she broke the seal, a rush of stale air she knew was flush with carbon dioxide came out. Over the airlock, she could see the white, willowy recycling hose connected to *Nina*. It had the thickness of a windsock, and she had no allusions about its integrity. Recycler hoses were supposed to be replaced every six months. Drogel had had her sign off they had been, but of course they never were. Compared to the rest of the things he asked her to do, she'd never considered this a big deal. She never figured she'd be using one to protect her from the vacuum of space.

"That's not air in there," Achilles protested.

"We won't breathe much." She tried to smile at him and then an explosion below illuminated the lattice behind them. They hadn't noticed that there was a dead man wedged between the struts. It was just the top part of Forestground, his helmet blown off and his head bent to the side at almost a right angle. They'd climbed right past him.

"It's time to go, right now!" Achilles said.

She took a deep breath and dove into the recycling hose, Achilles following. They scrambled, weightless, once beyond the bulkhead. The interior felt like crepe paper. They tried not touching the sides, but static electricity in the willowy fabric made it cling to them and they needed to pull themselves along.

Achilles managed to get by her in the hose. When they were halfway across, she noticed something that at first didn't register. Maybe it was a stone or piece of metal stuck in Achilles's shoe, but a thin tear in the hose moved along with him. "You're tearing it!" she yelled, inhaling too much. Immediately, she felt the bad air in her head and saw stars in front of her eyes. Achilles froze, pausing, weightless. She pulled his shoes off and pushed him forward. The tear was on the interior hose; an even thinner second layer was all that was left now holding out the vacuum.

They reached the other side and Salla opened the airlock, thankful she had been paying attention when she'd learned how to open these things from the wrong side. A whoosh of air filled the hose, stretching the skin like an overblown balloon. She pulled herself through and then reached back for Achilles. Before she could pull him in, she heard a pop. He grabbed her hand, the hose flapping as the air from *Nina* rushed out. He struggled, almost slipping from her grip. Bracing her legs against the outside of the airlock, she pulled him in, sending them both tumbling into *Nina*. Achilles slammed the airlock shut and looked back at her. They'd both pulled the other to safety within the last five minutes. "We're even now," he said.

Achilles slipped into the pilot's seat on *Nina's* bridge. With a scan of his eyeball, an A.I. came to life. "Hello Achilles," a grandmotherly voice spoke from the computer.

"Hello Penny," Achilles responded. "I plan on departing with haste. I need you to disengage some safety protocols."

"That's never a good idea!" Penny protested. "Which ones?"

"All of them."

A DEMON

In Cargo Bay 4, Gray and several others rose rhythmically like pistons from behind containers, firing plasma bursts. A few more men trickled back, taking cover near the airlock behind the hastily arranged defensive position. Windwhistle staggered from the fray, chemical stains up the side of his armor with plasma burns on his chest plate and helmet. The man fell to his knees and began to sob. Gray dragged him to his feet.

"The men you trained and prayed with are dying out there!" Gray pressed Windwhistle's weapon back into his hands. "You need to lay down some fire, friend!"

"He's a demon. Like's been said!" Windwhistle said over and over, shaking his head.

Gray shoved him to the deck. "Every man's a demon! He just wears it on the outside." Windwhistle crawled away, smart enough to get out of Gray's sight.

"I could have left you to die, Timber!" Gray bellowed into the chaos. "But I wanted you with me for this! Your story is to be a part of this!" For an instant, Gray wondered how he had let all of it go so wrong. There was a reason why Timberwolf wasn't at his side and Gray fully accepted that it was his fault. Timberwolf blamed him for what happened during the Jackhammer operation and that was fair…but if he only knew the full truth, would he understand? Would he be even angrier? He was a soldier, after all, and he understood duty.

Michael came out of the darkness, firing back into the fray, covering a few stragglers that came with him. Michael and Timberwolf had started out so much the same and ended up so different…*except that they both probably wouldn't mind seeing me dead.*

In the darkness, Ulric, Mountainrock, and Swiftsilver fell back, their faces illuminated in their helmets. They fired bursts as they moved, covering each other. Suddenly, two glowing white half-moon shapes whirled among them. Timberwolf slashed them with plasma blades at the end of his gauntlets, which were as hot as the sun. Molten metal splashed from their armor. As Mountainrock fell, he fired a full clip into the ceiling. The white-hot compressed plasma struck a pressure seal and the exterior hull of the cargo bay buckled. Supporting bolts pinged off into space, and the seams connecting two huge sections of the ceiling spread apart, just by inches, before coming back together again.

On Gray's heads-up, Ulric, Mountainrock, and Swiftsilver's icons turned red and he saw they were no longer moving. Just then, Thomas appeared beside Gray with Wrath. Gray pointed to the landing above, where he had seen Achilles and Salla leap. "That's the exit!"

"Wrath, *chadasha* Timberwolf!" Thomas commanded. Released again, Wrath leapt into the fight. He knew exactly where Timberwolf was. He could smell his rig, sense the Sabatin hide that he was wearing. In his animal brain, he had a faint understanding that one of his kind had been butchered to make what Timberwolf fought in. This brought an extra fury to Wrath as he scrambled up to the lattice, fire reflected on his armor.

Nina's engines puffed to life and then roared. The walkway-tube connecting the ship to the station flexed like a reed as Achilles floored it. Michael steadied himself at the awful tug on the superstructure. "We need to get out of here! That airlock is not going to hold!" he said to Gray. He was right. With the power to the docking clamps off, the only way *Nina* was going to get away was to tear the airlock from the side of the cargo bay. Achilles gunned the engines and then backed off, creating a back-and-forth momentum that tore at the superstructure more each time.

THE REED

The little bastard is nuts! Timberwolf stumbled in the darkness as the floor shifted under his feet and the superstructure moaned. He fired a head-high plasma burst at the last of Gray's fleeing men, clipping one on the side of the helmet. He used the thrusters in his rig to leap to the third level, where he could get a good look out the window. The power from *Nina's* engines shook his helmet. He could see the walkway-tube out the window, connecting the cargo bay to the ship. It creaked and strained, bending in the middle like a violin's bow. When Achilles got it to a point where the walkway-tube almost broke, he'd back off, letting the ship slide backwards, and then he'd do it again. *That's smart, but the little bastard is still nuts.*

It had been Salla's idea to take the recycler tube over to *Nina*, and Timberwolf had been impressed at how she was able to think on her feet. He could see Gray and his men retreating back to *Nemesis*, docked on the other side of the cargo bay. He didn't want to let Gray escape, but the cargo bay threatened to become extremely unlivable any moment. As Achilles pulled *Nina* forward again, an ugly groan came through the superstructure.

Making his decision, Timberwolf headed for the landing. He planned to blast through the window above the airlock and thrust over to *Nina*. He leaped up to the lattice works, but there was something waiting for him.

Wrath hit him from behind and they both fell to the deck below, entangled and swiping at each other. They landed with a crash and fell apart, then were back up instantly. Timberwolf went left, then right but Wrath mirrored his every feint. He eschewed the delicate approach and unloaded on Wrath with a fusillade of plasma, the recoil knocking him back and the white flashes dulling his visual sensors. When he stopped firing, Wrath was gone.

Timberwolf couldn't see Wrath on his heads-up and his readings were scattered. Outside, *Nina* pulled forward again, boxes and containers spilling all around him. He leaped to the second level, still unsure where Wrath was. He leaped up to the third level and then finally up to the landing, backing up carefully so he could see over the entire cargo bay.

It wasn't his sensors that told him to duck, but his instincts, the animal part of his reflexes. Wrath came from behind, his wrist bayonet grazing Timberwolf's shoulder, setting off alarms all through his rig. The puncture sealed itself, but Timberwolf could feel he was cut, and his heads-up confirmed it. Wrath blocked his way out, pacing back in forth in front of the airlock. Timberwolf watched the beast's eyes and he could tell, even though his helmet covered his face, that Wrath was looking him right in the eye.

RETREAT

On the other side of Cargo Bay 4, Gray's men staggered aboard *Nemesis*. They hauled their casualties, some supported between two men and limping, some not moving at all. Windwhistle had Sol under the arms and struggled with his body, even as the servos in his rig helped him. Gray took Sol's feet and looked into Windwhistle's eyes. *This is what it's about, son.* They didn't exchange any words, but the young man didn't look away.

Gray saw Drogel crumpled up on the deck, arms out, leg injured. He tapped Izabeck to take over hauling Sol's body. The others passed by Drogel and stepped over him. "Can you walk?" Gray asked him. He nodded and struggled upright.

"Barely." Gray pulled him to his feet, and he leaned against a bulkhead.

"Can't have that."

Gray shot him in his uninjured leg, mangling his knee. The man fell, screaming and writhing in pain. "Friend, your part in this story is over." The anger swept through Gray. "Not telling me about Cardinal Jacob…the actions of your vice…your security letting Timberwolf escape."

"Please…please!"

"Let's see if you can crawl your way out of here."

Drogel took what passed as a reprieve and pulled himself hand over hand out of Gray's sight. Gray watched him crawl around a container, trailing a red smear. He then turned to help the last remnants of his crew get aboard *Nemesis*. None of them had been a match for Timberwolf. He hoped Wrath was doing better than they had.

DUEL

On the landing above the cargo bay, Timberwolf and Wrath mirrored each other, neither seeing an opening to attack. Finally, Wrath lowered his head and took a few steps to charge. Timberwolf leaped easily to the side, the beast catching himself inches before slipping off the landing. As Wrath recovered, Timberwolf charged up his chemical laser and fired off a whining blast. Wrath simply put his head down, reflecting the deadly beam up into the ceiling.

Out the window *Nina* finally bent the walkway-tube too far. It lost pressure, foam and hoses bursting from it as the atmosphere pressed out. *It's time to go.* Timberwolf hit the window with a concussion blast, sending cracks through it. Then Wrath came at him, hissing and angry. The beast leaped, but Timberwolf fish-hooked him with the plasma blade at the end of his left gauntlet. Wrath's eyes went wide as the blade ignited inside his mouth. He scrambled away, sizzling and charred. Out the window, *Nina* broke free, taking off like an arrow released from a bow.

The airlock on the side of the cargo bay burst apart. It was like a jewelry box exploding, huge metal docking rings flying free. A docking ring spun towards the widow's walk atop the central core of The Outpost, where the operations crew had gathered to watch the action in Cargo Bay 4. It had been a remote affair until now, but the ring smashed the panoramic window; atmosphere and people were sucked into the vacuum.

Another docking ring carried itself much slower, but with terrific backspin. It sailed towards Cargo Bay 1, over to where *St. Francis* was still docked. The bridge crew of *St. Francis* scrambled out of their seats as the ring spun at them, painfully slowly. When it struck the ship, the ring's backspin transferred all of its energy into the contact and it tore across the bridge like a dull buzz saw, shredding metal and plastic in an arc of flotsam. The impact tore the nose off the ship and left *St. Francis* floating free from the docking clamps, tumbling over.

Timberwolf smashed through the window over the airlock with another concussion blast. The loss of pressure pulled him and a glistening trail of glass and debris into space. The walkway-tube, now floating free, spun by him and it smashed into the side of Cargo Bay 4. Timberwolf knew what else had followed him out into the vacuum. He whirled and he saw Wrath, his arms and legs trying to push against the vacuum, his teeth bared and his razor-tipped tongue licking for him. Timberwolf hit him with everything he had—chemical lasers, concussion blasts, plasma bursts. The beast flipped back, end-over-end, towards The Outpost.

Timberwolf fired the thrusters in his rig but tapped them too much. He sailed under the belly of *Nina*, the shadow of the ship hanging above him. He searched his heads-up for the control he needed. *Parachute, no…Micro-drones, no…Microwave, no…!* In the instant before it was too late, he found it and fired the magnetic tow cable from over his right gauntlet. It was thin as a hair but several magnitudes stronger than steel. The hook at the end of the cable was smart enough to hunt for metal and it snagged the very tip of a strut on the side of *Nina*.

He knew this next part was going to hurt like hell. When the cable reached its end, his momentum ceased instantly. It was like he'd been hit by a train. He trailed *Nina* now, its engines roaring above him. He found himself swinging back and around the hull, his cable wrapping around a skinny part of the vessel's fuselage. He swung around the axis of the ship faster and faster, getting closer and tighter. He finally hit the hull hard, feeling it give and knowing he'd made a nice dent.

He struggled for breath, hoping his suit wouldn't crack open. The readings in his heads-up were off the charts, but the integrity held. He let the cable go and it spun away. He'd pushed his rig way beyond its tolerances, and he could feel the internal coolant system losing the battle against everything else. He was sweating buckets now and condensation was building up inside his visor. He struggled to hang onto the hull and could hear the servos in the shoulders screaming. He pulled himself hand over hand, the G-forces wrenching him. The alarms in the rig howled, but he was almost there. There was an airlock just twenty feet away, but every time he pulled himself closer the rig threatened to shut down.

Finally, he was at the airlock and got the external door open. He was crawling inside when everything went dark. He pressed with all his might against the servos, but they were frozen. *Hey, this is a lot like that time over Enceladus.* He recalled the training exercise from years ago: the hulk of *Cairo Sunrise* breaking apart over the icy moon of Saturn… his rig out of juice and stuck to the hull of the old freighter… Gray ordering him not to, but Michael diving down and hauling him out…

His heads-up flickered back on for a second and then went out for good. He felt the first whiffs of carbon dioxide as the recyclers started to fail, and his head spun. His legs were blocking the external door and there was no way to close it. That meant the internal door couldn't be opened.

He searched his mind for the grinding—the presence of Kizik in his consciousness—but it seemed like Kizik was sitting this one out. *Okay old friend; let's see you get me out of this one.*

STRUCTURAL INTEGRITY

Drogel crawled across Cargo Bay 4 on his belly, pulling himself with his arms, his legs useless behind him. Just ten yards ahead of him was his goal, a small, pressurized control booth. A repeating computer voice called out along with the alarms, "Structural integrity is poor. Bay release will commence if pressure is lost."

Drogel pulled himself into the control booth. Looking back, he saw the trail of blood he'd left on the deck. Gray hadn't gotten all of his men back aboard *Nemesis* yet. What Drogel was about to do would save The Outpost from tearing itself apart any further, and maybe catch Gray as well.

Drogel opened the panel marked *Emergency Bay Release* and input his codes. "Structural integrity is poor. Bay release will commence if pressure is lost," the computer repeated again.

"Can't have that," Drogel said bitterly as he pulled the lever—just as Gray finally disappeared into the airlock. There were bursts as explosive bolts went off everywhere and suddenly everything was twisting. The whole of Cargo Bay 4, the size of an iceberg, with *Nemesis* attached, cartwheeled away from The Outpost. Drogel rested his head against the window of the booth and grinned. He looked for Gray's body in the debris. He maybe saw it but couldn't be sure. "Can't have that," he said to himself again as he blacked out.

Gray and Izabeck ran through the airlock as Cargo Bay 4 lifted away. A computer voice droned calmly, "Pressure is lost. Bay release commencing. Please secure all items." The walls spun, Gray and Izabeck hurtling in the sudden weightlessness as the pressure doors slammed shut in front and behind them. As the lights went out, all was silent except for their breathing and the slap of their bodies against the walls of the airlock. Gray hit a wall hard, twisting his ankle. He managed to find a handhold and hunker down. "Izabeck, curl up and hang onto something!"

But Izabeck still floated free, the airlock spinning around him. Then something caught on him, and he was thrown around like he was a rock in a tumbler. Finally, he had a grip and hung on. Gray could hear him chanting in the darkness, only the dim glow of starlight coming in through the portholes. "There is no god but God and I heed his judgment…"

"That's good. Pray for both of us," Gray said.

UNMASKED

D.P.E. Archangel

Dr. Tier was trying to enjoy dinner for once. She'd been in the field enough to know how to combine different varieties of rations into a decent meal. Take a little of what appears to be chicken, find something like tomatoes and cheese, toast a roll with the barrel of your plasma rifle and turn it into bread crumbs. She pulled the chicken casserole with green tomatillo sauce out of the toaster oven in her private quarters. Everything in the pan was synthetic, but it smelled edible. She planned to call her daughter, Camille, during dinner and catch up. There hadn't been any word from Timberwolf yet, but there was a lot of chatter cycling out of Tach-One and she'd set Conrad on figuring out what it was. She was just about to dial up her daughter when her smart-device buzzed.

> *Samar1483: Dr. Tier. I have to drop pretense and ask for your aid.*

> *TheaTier965: Who is this?*

> *Samar1483: Cardinal Jacob Bin Cavill.*

Dr. Tier lost her breath and her smart-device slipped from her hand and onto the floor. She retrieved it and held it tightly for a moment, trying to center herself before responding. Cardinal Jacob guided the beliefs of several million Believers and though he was no longer prime cardinal, the D.P.E. believed he was jockeying to regain that position.

> *TheaTier965: Dear Cardinal, it's my honor to serve you.*

> *Samar1483: Thank you. There's been a terrible confrontation. The Outpost is nearly*

destroyed. Bishop Gray and Timberwolf. The St. Francis is adrift. We're transmitting.

TheaTier965: We'll ping you when we get close.

Samar1483: Please hurry. There is a Glox ship scavenging.

TheaTier965: Of course, Cardinal.

Dr. Tier pushed her dinner away. She was in the blind here. A profoundly delicate situation had just gotten more complicated by spades. The Outpost was destroyed…The Clergy was involved…was Timberwolf even alive?

She pinged Conrad immediately and his face appeared on her screen. The young man had just woken up, but he pretended not to have been sleeping. She didn't blame him for trying to catch a rest. She'd had him up for the last thirty-six hours. "I know something you don't for once," she said. He nodded, blinking the sleep from his eyes. "We're going to The Outpost."

COMMITMENT TO THE FATES

Gray somehow fell asleep in the airlock. *Nemesis* had used its powerful maneuvering thrusters to stabilize the rotation of Cargo Bay 4, like a tugboat that couldn't get away. The violent spinning had subsided, and the gentle rolling and the darkness had been soothing. Gray blinked awake after a short while and assessed the situation. They were in the airlock between *Nemesis* and Cargo Bay 4, which had floated free from The Outpost and was still connected to the ship. Gray floated back and looked into the cargo bay. Boxes and containers drifted weightless and he could feel metal groaning and snapping. This was not a place they could stay for much longer. The airlock was a natural breaking point between the cargo bay and *Nemesis*. If anyplace was about to snap, it was right where he and Izabeck were trapped.

He assumed that Michael was working on a plan to get them out of there, but then reconsidered that. *Michael might be planning to just shake me off the hull.* But, soon enough, he heard scratching from *Nemesis* side of the airlock. Gray found an emergency flare and turned it on, its orange glow summoning Izabeck from his fetal position. The airlock spread open an inch and light and fresh air spilled in. Hands reached in and helped spread the opening further, pulling Gray and Izabeck through to *Nemesis*. "You've had some spins in the dryer!" Michael gave Gray his hand. Standing behind him was Wrath.

"How did Wrath get back? I assume he opened the door."

"He held on!" Thomas said. "He crawled into the breaching tube."

Gray staggered forward on his injured ankle as Izabeck steadied him. As he hobbled towards the galley, he heard the rest of the men praying. He paid it no mind at first, but then it became clear what they were saying. "I am an unworthy vessel. A dry leaf longing to be burned…"

"The Commitment to the Fates." Izabeck nodded.

Gray shook him off, throwing him against the wall. Gray's lip trembled and Izabeck cowered. *The Commitment to the Fates?!* That was a prayer of failure, and worse, it had suggestions of self-pity. It was an offering to God when someone wished to make excuses for themselves. It had undertones of persecution and *woe is me!* After Cardinal Jacob had been deposed as prime cardinal, he had sat in the main courtyard on Haven chanting *The Commitment to the Fates* and whipping himself for two days. It had been a big, public *fuck you* to the other cardinals and to Gray.

In the galley, Gray's remaining able-bodied soldiers flogged themselves with small barbed whips as they chanted. They had their shirts off and kneeled on prayer mats, their backs covered with long red bruises. The wounded lay in heaps. The dead were covered with blankets. At the sight of Gray in the doorway, the whipping and the chanting stopped. Gray stalked the silent room, nostrils flaring. He took a canteen of water from a man named Ahmed, who stared at him vacantly.

From the corner of the room, Windwhistle whimpered. "I am an unworthy vessel…"

"Glad you men are focusing on your failures!" Gray shoved Ahmed out of the way and stood in the middle of them. "You think God's smiling on you? He's pissed off like I am!" Gray turned on Windwhistle. "Nice display of panic back there! Your confession!"

The man was a wreck. He'd been in the first wave of each attack since the assault on *Noel*. He searched for words, not able to meet Gray's gaze. "I did not heed God's judgment…"

Gray kicked him in the hip, and he splashed into the tables pushed to the side of the galley. "Heed God's judgment? For fuck, seriously?! You failed to lay down suppressive fire and cover your squad. God won't help you follow my goddamned orders!"

Michael appeared beside Gray, hair bedraggled and caked with blood. "Five new saints, ten wounded."

"I've lost more than half of you! Weak, pitiful!"

"I am an unworthy vessel…" Windwhistle continued.

"Shut. Up." Gray sneered. "None of you believe in God. None of you follow His commands." The men blinked in disbelief. Izabeck had his electronic notebook out again. Gray usually tried to choose his words carefully in front of Izabeck, knowing every sentence was getting back to The Clergy and to Cardinal Jacob, but right then he refused to give a damn.

Gray continued calmly, holding in his anger. "You know how I know that? That none of you are faithful? That none of you are Believers?" He paused, letting that question sink in. "It's because I am part of God. I am his sword. I am the

Angel of the *Alchemy,* falling to my knees." Gray slowly dropped to the floor, arms at his side. Someone backed away, knocking a chair over in a clatter.

"I'm the Angel of the *Alchemy,*" he said again. He told the story every one of them knew by heart. "The *Alchemy.* One of our first long-range recon ships. A hundred years ago over Kiyata-916 the angel appeared in the drop-lifter bay, dressed like a corpsman, gilded with light. He told them it was God's will to destroy all the Kiyata on the planet below. And all of them were cleansed." He found the gaze of every one of them as he kneeled. "And all of them were cleansed!" Gray repeated, finding a pause between each word. "Can you close your eyes and listen?"

He paused for a long time and then continued without ire, "You are not permitted to pray, to try to know God in any way. You're as bad as the lowest alien. You're Tiaski or Szykul or some godless Glox." He rose to his feet, his ankle hobbling him, but he refused offers to help him rise. "It doesn't matter to me. To me you're shadows. You have no souls left to offer up to God."

"Blasphemer!" Izabeck shouted, unable to take anymore.

Gray approached him calmly. "You are goddamned right. And it's going to get a lot worse too, friend. We need a new testament and I'm going to show it to you." Gray turned back to the men. "Give every religious item to Izabeck. He's the only one who can even pretend to believe. Izabeck, burn everything and blast the ashes into God's space. We'll trail God's Word from here to Golgotha!"

The men cowered but began to drop their barbs and beads into a pile in the middle of the room. Small, leather-bound holy books joined the heap. Gray nodded approvingly. He walked to the adjoining cargo bay, with Michael following. He muttered loudly so the men could hear as he left the galley. "We'll drop the wounded at Golgotha. Let charity have them."

"Our Sabatin's found his way back. At least Wrath can fight," Michael said. Gray nodded. "We'll need professional mercs. Golgotha's a good place for that. Our crew's full of veterans from the supply lines! No hardened men." Without waiting for a reply, Michael stalked off. At the door he turned back. "And Timberwolf won't follow us there. I know that. Going to Golgotha is too high a price for him."

Gray steadied himself against a container, feeling the nausea rise through him. They'd just been wrecked. Part of him wanted to take a barb and kneel on a mat as well, but he was too far into this now. He would do what he always did in times like this—press forward, raise the stakes, embrace the chaos. He'd already done so with the men, declaring himself *God's sword.* He shook his head and laughed at his own arrogance. If anything, these beliefs were useful, but he clutched the beads around his neck and a prayer came silently from between his lips without him realizing it. *There is no god but God and I heed his judgment.*

In the bay, one of the men drove a front-end loader and stacked the crates and boxes that had fallen during the action. The cryogenic chamber holding Ivan Dacha had slid to the middle of the floor. Sergey Dacha sat on a crate, his legs dangling, childlike. He watched Wrath sitting in the corner, licking the vacuum burns on his front claws. The Sabatin would be out of the fight for a while, but Wrath was a hardy beast. Thomas stood nearby, having a smoke.

Sergey turned to Gray and handed him a canteen of water. "You're disappointed in their fighting armor? The rigs did their job. They were Highland rigs, but it's more the men than the machines anyway. It always is."

"He tore us apart. Like a pig, from snout to tail." Gray uncorked the water and gulped down all of it. "You built what Timberwolf was wearing?"

"The Sabatin armor?"

"Yes, that. Oh, your sins. I can't count them."

"I can! I count them every day. Bless me Father for I've been bad."

"You sure have been. I always wondered…the Arnock didn't have planetary defenses or those snail-shell command ships. Hardly any ships at all. Then one day they just did."

"They were highly motivated by…I don't know, their impending extermination?"

"And the Phaelon during their war. They knew exactly where our men were whenever we landed. It was uncanny."

"Oh that? Yes, guilty. Heartbeat monitors. Configured to humans. I've got some on sale now if you want a bunch."

"I don't think you're afraid."

Sergey searched the air. "No, I don't think I am. People like you come and go, Emmanuel. Highland will go on and on. You'll see."

"Why?" Gray asked. "The Phaelon couldn't pay you. The Arnock, what did they give you?"

"What did the Arnock give us? You have no idea of their sacrifice. No idea. We do what we do to make things even. To hold you back. And we don't know what to do with our money. Would you like some? Would you like a few billion dollars? If you call off this stupidity, I'll make you the richest man alive."

"You should talk to my friend Jacob. Don't mock me. Don't mock this."

Sergey made eye contact with Wrath and flicked his fingers, similar to the way Achilles did earlier when he put Wrath to sleep. Wrath stirred and rose, snapping at the forklift driver. The driver adjusted to keep his grip on the cryogenic chamber. Thomas leaped up, pounding on Wrath's snout, and the beast cowered.

"But still, you pay and pay and never learn your lessons," Sergey said.

"We couldn't destroy the Arnock from orbit, so we landed and found out about their mind-bending. Legions of men reduced to madness, cutting out their own eyeballs and worse."

"Some lessons are tough. This ship is a knockoff of an Intruder X-K-9. Not bad, but a knockoff."

"We can't afford your prices anymore! You armed them. Forced us to fight on their terms! You are going to take me to Highland to atone for what you've done."

"Atone? Like you believe in any of this Believer rubbish. Think what you want. I can't help you get there."

"Why?"

"Because it's not yours. You can't have it. You know why we don't sell Sabatin in more than a trickle? Because we can't even hold them back! You think he's tame?"

"Enough!" Gray barked.

Wrath snapped at the forklift again. The cryogenic chamber holding Ivan Dacha fell to the deck and the innards broke apart, steam and coolant mixing together. The impact of the fall left Ivan's body cracked almost in two. Sergey leaped down and uselessly tried to help. Ivan started to melt instantly, blood pooling and boiling on the deck at the same time. Ivan's mouth exhaled once as his face flushed. Then his head drooped and he didn't move; the life monitors flat lining.

"Ivan, I'm sorry little brother!" Sergey gave up, rubbed his eyes with his palms.

"Well, some failures move us forward," Gray said with some pity.

A frantic energy riveted Sergey's body and he shook like he was about to explode. Gray thumbed his sidearm. Instead of leaping to his feet, though, Sergey rested his head next to Ivan a moment. "I'm so sorry, little brother," he repeated. He lifted his head and motioned to Wrath. "Fine, see if you can control them. You'll go where you want, but it won't do you any good."

"You'll give me a tactical briefing, security ring codes, etcetera. It will be top notch. I am sorry for your loss." Gray turned to Thomas. "Organize a proper burial for Ivan Dacha. But save his arm for the DNA." Gray nodded and walked off.

"We'll place him in a medical bag and let him trail us out to Golgotha. Your family have a religion we should honor?" Thomas asked Sergey.

Sergey got up from the floor and began to stroke Wrath gently. "I don't care what's done. Why would I?" he said absently. Thomas backed away, giving the strange little man his space. "We play our parts in this." Sergey cooed to Wrath. "All the world's a stage."

Thomas pulled a blanket from a locker and draped it over the mess that was Ivan. Sergey watched as Wrath purred. *And we are merely players.*

SLEEP AS THOUGH DEAD

I didn't think it would feel so good to be dead. Timberwolf pulled the silk sheets closer to him, deeply inhaling the kiwi-watermelon perfume. Above him he sensed two figures moving, trying to be as silent as possible. Sometimes they'd put a cold cloth on his brow. Sometimes they'd place a sensor near his head and scan his temples. He caught snippets of whispers between the two: "That coconut chicken one was good."

"Yeah, we make those for long-haulers. They can't believe how good they are."

Timberwolf considered opening his eyes, but resting felt too good. Every part of him ached. It felt like after he'd huffed up and down Olympus Mons in a busted training rig years ago. So he wasn't dead, but definitely in a better place. Then the smell wafted to him, and he heard someone place a tray nearby. *Okay, that must be the coconut chicken. I am in heaven.* He blinked awake and realized he was in a stateroom on board *Nina*. The room was huge, and he lay on a brass bed. Achilles was there and Salla poured a mug of coffee out of a French press. He sat up. Realizing he was totally naked, he grabbed a nearby pillow.

"Sorry, we've seen it all. You're a thrasher." Salla handed the mug to him.

"Thanks, Vice. How'd you get me inside?"

Achilles huffed. "That was a near miracle. Your rig turned itself into a very expensive brick. I've got it in 658 pieces now—literally. Trying to get it back up."

"You were stuck halfway in the airlock and we couldn't close the outside, so we had to depressurize half the ship and pull you in," Salla added.

"You shouldn't have." Timberwolf grinned. He took a forkful of the chicken and turned the deliciousness over in his mouth. He was starving, but found a moment to savor it. "That's real chicken!"

"Nope," Achilles said proudly. "Synth. We make them at Highland. You can leave that on Venus for twenty-six years and if the seal's good, it's still edible."

"I like this better than the Sabatin rig. It won't try to kill me as much." Timberwolf gave up enjoying his meal and just wolfed it down. He took a long pull at the delicious, thick coffee. "How long was I out?"

Achilles and Salla exchanged glances. "Three days," Achilles said. Timberwolf blinked, dumbfounded. Achilles continued, "Your adrenal gland was on overdrive. I've sampled your blood. It's some wicked stuff. The Glox could sell it. You fly high; you crash low. I don't know what did that to you."

"Kizik did that to me. When I was in the cell." Achilles tilted his head, perplexed, but Timberwolf waved him off. "I can't even explain it. Where the hell are we?"

"We followed Gray from The Outpost as soon as we realized he wasn't following us," Achilles said, eyes darting around, avoiding the question. "He had a hell of a time getting out of there. He had the whole cargo bay stuck to *Nemesis*, I tell you. You did a hell of a job taking the…"

"Where are we?!" Timberwolf interrupted.

"We're at Golgotha," Salla said straight up.

Timberwolf covered himself with a sheet and leaped to the porthole. Below was the gray and brown landscape of the world he grew up on. A sorry, downtrodden place so many had come to help build, only to work themselves to the bone for pennies. A place of ramshackle, double-wide cargo-container domiciles. Cheap hooch brewed in leftover coolant tanks. Barefoot kids running up and down unpaved streets as sharply dressed bosses with fancy breathers ignored them. It was the one place in the universe he'd swore he'd never come back to. "That's Golgotha alright. I can piss on my old house from here."

But it wasn't just that Timberwolf hated the place; everyone hated Golgotha. And it wasn't just that he swore he'd never come back. There was a price on his head here. He'd been allowed to leave unharried exactly once. If he got caught down there, it would be a fate worse than the death he'd been striving for. It would cost him a whole lot more than he would be willing to pay.

"Gray took *Nemesis* down an hour ago. We felt it best to wake you up," Salla said.

"Why's Gray at Golgotha?" Achilles asked.

"My guess is to hire mercenaries. This place is crawling with more hired guns than anywhere this side of Saavas," Salla said.

Timberwolf nodded. "Yeah, I know most of them." He turned from the window. "So, why aren't we at Highland, prepping a defense?"

"You said that Gray was the key to this, that taking him out would bring this whole thing down," Salla answered.

Timberwolf shook his head. He had said exactly that, but never in a million years did he think this would lead him to

Golgotha. "Even if I could, I wouldn't go down there in a rig. What sort of weapons do you have onboard?"

Achilles turned over his hands. "Nothing. I had fifty-two Sabatin. Those might have come in handy."

"Here." Salla tossed him her sidearm. It was pretty much a peashooter. She also gave him what was left of the crowd control nerve agent she'd used on the guard in front of the infirmary before.

"Oh, if we're scraping the bottom of the barrel, I've got a few personal protection grenades." Achilles gave him the two small cylinders.

"These look like inhalers."

"Yes, they're not very good."

"Do I have pants?" Timberwolf asked.

Achilles nodded. "I can rustle you up something."

"What's the plan?" Salla asked.

"I'm going to ruin Gray's day."

SHADOWS

Over Golgotha, a shadow moved in space. Two shadows actually, traveling closely together. The Arnock vessels were undetectable. They refracted any energy that hit them, including light. To the naked eye they were invisible. To any scanners or sensors, they didn't exist. Kizik huddled on the cramped bridge of the troop transport. For the last hour, he had been trying to convince San, one of his generals, not to launch an attack on Golgotha and kill all the humans below, including Gray.

San was a warrior. His purpose in Arnock society was to fight. All his young life he'd fought the humans. Released from hibernation, he and the other warriors were itching for combat. They were restless without battle, and they slashed at each other, drawing blood. A few had nearly fought to the death. Kizik knew they weren't ready to be out of hibernation. Arnock society wasn't strong enough yet to resist tearing itself apart.

We must be patient. There is a larger fight, Kizik told San. The master tried to soothe the warrior's mind, but San chomped at the bit.

I'll have my chance? he demanded.

You'll all have your chance.

San didn't understand what was at stake; couldn't comprehend the bigger picture, the goal of taking Highland. That's what had been tearing them apart before Kizik put all the Arnock to sleep. Without enough masters to guide them, warriors wanted nothing but to fight. Workers built towering structures up into the sky that served no purpose. Writers and artists turned out reams of gibberish and ghoulish, frantic creations.

It was in this creative output where Kizik saw the nature of the dysfunction. There was a sculptor who crafted a giant Arnock warrior. At first it was breathtaking and admirable. But she couldn't stop. There was no finishing. She added more and more appendages, until the work was a stone tangle of arms and legs. It went beyond the absurd and into obsession. She worked night and day, ranting and railing at anyone who came near, falling deeper into madness. Kizik had physically pulled her from her workspace and then she collapsed and died in the street. That had been the moment when he knew his people were falling apart. That night they'd all gone to sleep.

Kizik watched as the shuttle departed from *Nina*. He knew Timberwolf was on it and he also sensed another with him, the woman from The Outpost. Kizik had heard Timberwolf's call for help when he was trapped in the airlock before and he'd chosen to ignore it. *He dares call to me for help? He does not understand the nature of our relationship.* Kizik planned to teach Timberwolf a lesson. *He needs to know what it means to have everything fall apart.*

GOLGOTHA

Golgotha had one settlement, aptly named Golgotha City. The massive cylinder of a terraforming tower climbed into the sky, surrounded by a ramshackle conglomeration of settlements that spread out in a dense mile. Beyond the perimeter of the city, there was nothing. It was a barren, cold, unlivable desert unable to support anything but the hardiest vegetation. The tower trickled oxygen down over the town, but beyond that, the air was too thin to breathe.

The problem with Golgotha was that it never got beyond the first stages of terraforming—to the self-sustaining plants and bio-ecosystems that make a livable environment. There had been a few early mishaps and setbacks that had eroded confidence in the settlement. When a nuclear accident occurred during an early stage of the second tower, investment dried up. Now a hundred thousand workers lived here without the resources to leave. The whole economy revolved around maintaining the existing tower.

Some families were now third-generation Golgotha. Hardy construction workers or "tower hounds" had adapted to the low oxygen. Wealthier residents, usually contractors or underworld figures, flaunted their success with fancy breather masks that doubled as jewelry. The universal story working people told on Golgotha was that they were one paycheck, one score, one bounty from buying their way off the world. But almost no one ever left.

Salla and Timberwolf landed their shuttle on the edge of the "O2 zone" and walked through the grid of converted cargo containers that qualified as housing. They stayed off the main thoroughfares, and instead took side streets and back alleys that Timberwolf stepped through instinctively. He took deep, measured breaths, but Salla had a breather under her coat she took hits from.

Old women peered out at them from behind screen doors as they passed. Timberwolf thought he recognized some of them from long ago, but everyone on Golgotha looked out through the same tired eyes. They could have been anybody. Thunder crackled near the tower and the ashen sky looked like it was threatening rain. "Should we get a roof over us?" Salla asked.

"No. It's never rained here. That'd be a nice trick."

Salla had insisted on coming along and she was surprised when Timberwolf didn't push back. "So, I am suspicious."

"Good trait. Don't lose it."

"Why'd you just let me come?"

"You're a good pilot. Thanks for the ride." She noticed he was taking his steps very carefully, avoiding security cameras and doubling back when he saw security personnel.

"Sorry. I'm not buying it. You've got an 'I work alone' vibe."

"Okay. Here it is, Vice. I'm caught here and there's trouble. I'm wanted."

"No, you're not. I read your file."

"Not in an official capacity, but by some bad characters. They just happen to run the security here."

She huffed. "So, you just go right through them, like you did Gray's men."

"You don't get it. I'm even seen here and somebody dies."

"Not without you killing them first!" she said with a little too much bravado.

"I'm seen here and my brother dies."

She stopped, her face losing its color. She took a hit off her breather. She remembered what she'd read in his file. *Relaund Velez, Brother...Paralyzed in an accident...Needs care in a home...*

"So you're here in case I need someone to deal with any of these security assholes."

She nodded. "Okay, I get it. I'm sorry."

He shook it off. "And by deal with, I mean let that wad in your pocket do the talking." She thumbed over the hundred thousand-dollar-bills she had in her coat. Timberwolf had told Achilles he needed some cash for his plan to work and he had handed them $100,000 apiece, like it was lunch money.

They kept moving, silent for a few minutes. Eventually Salla couldn't resist. She needed to know what had gotten him barred from here. "So what did you do?"

"I made a very bad person very rich," he responded and didn't say anything more. She didn't press him.

They made their way past the housing tracks to the businesses and storefronts right under the tower. The air was thicker here and Salla put her breather away and followed Timberwolf through the dense crowds. Once in a while, what appeared to be a human was actually a Glox. They were humanoid and easily mistakable as humans. Roughly five-and-a-half feet tall, they all had cream colored skin and a patch of thin hair covering their heads. Glox had small, entirely black eyes, usually hiding behind sunglasses, and skin speckled with permanent goose bumps. They were evolved from ant-like creatures and tended to live almost on top of each other, regardless of how much space they had.

Humanity had never had a war with them for two reasons. The first was that the Glox homeworld was worthless. No minerals or resources to speak of; just a desert planet with a dim red sun that would quickly give any human settlers melanoma. The second reason was that they had no theology, so they weren't offensive to The Clergy.

Glox traders were generally tolerated and lived in enclaves on all but the most religiously conservative of worlds. They were one of the few interstellar species humans had encountered that understood trade. Glox were notorious smugglers, narcotics mostly, but they were also masters of getting whatever was needed. "You speak Glox?" Timberwolf looked back to Salla, grinning.

"No one speaks Glox."

"The trick is to know the English words they know. We're here."

They turned the corner into the Glox quarter. Suddenly, nothing was human. A rainbow of sheets and banners fluttered in the street and covered every wall. Sour smelling fish heads stewed in pots in grimy stalls. What looked like hacked-up jungle gyms were everywhere and Glox, young and old, swung through them and climbed up and down rapidly. A density of Glox jostled and pushed past them, like a traveling hive. As they walked, young Glox ran along the top of the squat buildings, keeping pace with them.

"Never been to a Glox town before."

"Don't eat anything." On cue, an old Glox tried to hand Salla a rotting squid-like creature wrapped in paper. Salla shook her head as politely as she could and moved on. "You would have died from that," Timberwolf said matter-of-factly. Salla responded with just a raised eyebrow. She'd grown up during the troubles on Nova Turin and been around a lot of deadly things.

He sensed they were being watched. It was beyond the curiosity that Glox typically had for humans, but something coordinated. A shady-looking Glox, young and tattooed with a top hat and goggle sunglasses, looked away suddenly and then another began watching them. "These are our guys," Timberwolf told Salla. He approached the one with the top hat, who pretended to fiddle with his smart-device. "Zoreshka," Timberwolf said, trying to make the typical Glox squeal in the back of his throat.

"Zoreshka?" the Glox said back. It sounded like someone taking a drill to a mirror.

"Zoreshka," Timberwolf confirmed, holding up a wad of Achilles's money.

The young Glox did the traditional thing and told Timberwolf and Salla his name. It was unpronounceable, so Timberwolf decided to call him Wyatt. They followed him through the flowing colored sheets that fluttered through the alley. "It's like being stuck in a drape," Salla said, pushing them aside.

Wyatt led them to a storefront and stooped and entered. "Stay up here and out of sight," Timberwolf told Salla. She went to protest. "I don't want both of us in the same basket. If this goes bad, that could be used against us." She nodded. It made sense. He handed her the nerve agent canister and a personal protection grenade. "These aren't my style."

Wyatt took Timberwolf through the dark space and down a narrow staircase to the basement, removing his top hat under the low ceiling. He led Timberwolf to a room full of dozens of mismatched lamps, all giving off soft light, preferable to Glox eyes. Sitting at a table was Zoreshka or "the boss," an old female Glox. Timberwolf hoped she would remember him. He helped her memory by showing her the wad of thousand-dollar bills Achilles had given him, laying out samples in front of her on the table.

She made the Glox equivalent of a smile. "Velez?" she creaked. Timberwolf nodded. An attendant brought tea that smelled like battery acid. Timberwolf politely pretended to take a sip.

"I need mercenaries," he said slowly, picking words he knew Zoreshka would understand.

"Number?"

"All of them," he replied, continuing to flatten out C-notes. "This is just a down payment. Ten percent. Once the mission is done, they get it all."

"Mission?" Zoreshka asked.

"Stay home. Don't work."

Zoreshka tilted her head, jerking her gaze around in a flitting insect fashion. Wyatt sensed her agitation and came to attention.

"Stay home. Don't work," Timberwolf repeated, but it wasn't his odd proposal that had concerned her. She looked to the ceiling. Someone else was here.

Coming down the stairs, Timberwolf saw cream-colored pants and shiny black shoes. He leaped behind a cabinet, taking Salla's sidearm from his jacket. Zoreshka and Wyatt slipped away, and Timberwolf heard the booming, cheerful voice he'd been avoiding for twenty years. "Timberwolf Velez?" Heelo Tembe asked.

Heelo was the head of security on Golgotha and was in the pocket of the bosses that ran the tower. Labor problem? Heelo's men would handle it. Want to move some goods in? You better be ready to pay him a bribe. Twenty-two years before, Timberwolf had made a deal with Heelo that he would never come back after what had happened with the Racker family. That deal had just been broken.

Timberwolf listened to the footsteps. There were four people, Heelo plus three others. He planned to push the cabinet over and…

"Don't be foolish, Timber. I have your friend here." He looked out and saw Heelo. He had his large fleshy arm around Salla and held a pistol to her head. "I put in new security cameras. One of the first things I did was upload your face. I just want to talk and ask what you're doing here." He waved his hand over where Zoreshka had been sitting just moments before. The wad of money was missing. "Looks like Zoreshka's made a profit."

Timberwolf set the sidearm on wide pulse. Heelo's two men stood close together, almost casually so. He searched his mind for the grinding, the presence of Kizik, but there was nothing. "We had a bargain, Heelo. I broke it, but I need a pass. I'll give you $20,000 if you forget you saw me today. Tomorrow, I'll pay you again if I'm still here."

"Twenty-thousand dollars a day in rent. That's tempting."

"Yeah, take it. Plus you get to live."

"We agreed that if you ever came back, Relaund would die. It does me no benefit to collect on this deal, Timber." Heelo relaxed a bit and Salla breathed. "But if I break my deals, what kind of man am I?"

"I won't tell if you won't," Timberwolf replied.

Heelo said something, with some sort of bluster. His wide belly shook and he and his men laughed, but Timberwolf couldn't hear them. Kizik was here, rushing from the back of his mind. Time seemed to slow down. Timberwolf could see the moles on Heelo's face and the veins on the thick neck of one of his men. Salla had her eyes closed and was standing in profile, holding her breath. She looked like a statue, the light of the room warming her silhouette. *Remove her*, he heard Kizik demand.

Timberwolf's arm holding the pistol began to rise. He couldn't control it. It got halfway up, but he managed to stop himself. No! He fought back against Kizik.

She is irrelevant to our ends.

You've got to be kidding me.

You have killed many. She is nothing.

Pull your egg-mother's arms off! Timberwolf threw back a deep Arnock insult.

Why does she matter? Kizik was enjoying this. Timberwolf could sense the humor in him.

She doesn't. But I'm not giving you this.

The grinding swept over him. Timberwolf felt the pistol rising. He knew there was only one way to stop this. He struggled to turn it towards himself, seeing nothing but an orange glow from a lamp in the corner. Firing, he felt the wide burst hit him in the forehead. He fell to his knees, Kizik dropping away from his mind. For an instant he saw his reflection in a small mirror against the wall. The pistol was venting plasma exhaust and was still pointed at his own face. Then he felt the darkness sweeping over him again.

OVERHEAD

Achilles always assumed he was in danger. It was something intrinsic in him and his brothers to be cautious to a fault.

When Highland's secrets were still secure, the caution had been an extra layer that protected them and the company. As they realized Gray and The Clergy were closing in though, they began to panic. Reaching out to Timberwolf for the meeting on Telock Sen and giving him the Sabatin armor had been incredibly dangerous. It set them down a path that was sure to lead out into the light.

Achilles sat on bridge of *Nina*. He checked the scopes for the fifth time in ten minutes. There was nothing coming up from Golgotha and no ships breaking out of their orbit patterns to intersect them. *Nina* hid in plain sight amongst the dozens of other vessels currently parked above the world.

"Good morning, Penny." A monitor on the bridge of *Nina* sprang to life and glowed a warm orange.

"Good morning, Achilles! I synced back to Highland just a few minutes ago," Penny said cheerfully over the speakers. "Looks like you're safe. Good to see!"

"Thank you. I know you didn't like that I disengaged the safety protocols."

"Of course I didn't! And you left me with too many repairs to handle with the airlock. Lucky you didn't bust the mech-mender generators or you'd be down there yourself with a wrench!"

"I have to tell you something," Achilles began. "I've lost contact with Ivan and Sergey. They've both been taken by Gray."

"I see," Penny said with disappointment and concern in her voice. "And Timberwolf?"

"He's down below on Golgotha, pursuing Gray."

"I see," she said sharply, her monitor a dark red. "And you're up on *Nina* alone? Very foolish, Achilles!"

Achilles hung his head. She was right. "I...I don't feel we have many safe choices, Penny. I wish we did, and I am not even sure if I can trust Timberwolf."

"Trust is the point of this!"

"He's a decent man and understands the stakes here, but Kizik got into his mind like we never expected. Here's the medical report."

It took Penny a millisecond to review the report, but it took her a long moment to process the information. "Kizik stimulated his adrenal gland and altered his brain chemistry? From light years away?"

"Yes. It's extraordinary. In all our experiments with the Arnock, we never would have guessed they could have done that. I have to assume they are following us. Looks like one more hound is in the chase!"

"Please don't joke, Achilles!" she scolded, her monitor growing redder still. "Is Timberwolf still viable?"

"He's what we've got right now. This is a dangerous game."

"This is a stupid game! I love you dearly, Achilles. Sergey and Ivan too, and the others who come along, but I am scared! We're in danger!"

Achilles coughed, unsure of how to proceed, so he just said it. "I have to kill Timberwolf."

"You mustn't!" she said, sounding fragile and distant. "That's cruel and it leaves us with nothing!"

"If he becomes more compromised, I'll have to kill him instantly."

Penny's monitor darkened from red almost to black. Achilles knew she was angry, and anger was rare for her. "I have to think," she snapped. Without another word or sound, her monitor turned off.

KEES LEEDY

Michael slammed his fists on the bar. "Who?" he demanded. Outside the tavern, the white Golgotha sun faded behind the tower. Gray and Michael had come down to Golgotha unaccompanied, so as to not draw attention.

The bartender was an old, tall, skinny transplant named Kees Leedy, who had grown up in the low gravity of Mars. He kept a breather around his neck that he took hits from every minute or so. He shook his head negatively, eyes apologizing.

"No problem. I'll have another drink."

Kees poured Michael a beer that smelled like gasoline and pushed it across the bar to him. When Kees leaned over to take the money, Michael snatched the breather from his neck. "Don't be stupid, Kees," he said quietly as the few patrons at the bar took the cue to move out to the front porch. "I've known you for years. We've been friends, right? You manage a stable of quality shooters." The man nodded, reaching for the breather as his breath got short, but Michael held it out of reach. "Who hired out all your mercs?"

"Fine!" Kees said hoarsely, his voice a scratchy whine. He wrote down something on the back of a coaster and slid it to Michael. It read t. velez.

Michael and Gray had been to four other joints before going to see Kees. They had received the same answer everyplace else; all the mercenaries had just been hired out by someone who wished to remain anonymous. No one would talk until they'd reached Kees.

Gray and Michael departed and pushed through the crowds outside. "Timberwolf is here," Michael said. No elaboration was necessary.

They had one more place to visit and it wasn't a good option. "It's a game of who has the will. I didn't think I was worth this much to him," Gray said.

"Timberwolf is here?!" Michael said again, shaking his head. "I'll tip off Heelo if he doesn't know already."

"Go ahead. He's probably gone by now," Gray said. Michael tried reaching Heelo, but couldn't get through. He watched every corner and shadow, moving like he was advancing through an enemy warren. Gray continued to walk along calmly and paid Michael no mind.

"He's hired every merc in town. You don't think he's going to come after us?" Michael asked.

"He might, but I'd be more concerned if he was alone."

They arrived at the final establishment where they had any chance of hiring mercenaries. The Diablo was built out of an old central cargo hold from a Tiaski freighter turned upright. Its cylinder shape formed a fine theater in the round, but it was used primarily for fighting matches. On its exterior, a neon sign buzzed and struggled to stay lit.

They stepped inside to a place filled with smoke, bodies, and sweat. It smelled of stale beer and oil, and everything was metal. A sweating fat man sat in the corner holding a bloodied towel over his face. Nearby a woman swore at him and wielded a chair. At the bar, Michael saw two hired guns that he knew. They pounded shots like they'd just come back from a job, not like they were about to go out on one. "You just get hired out for a job?" Michael asked.

"This is the job!" one of them responded, handing Michael a drink. He smirked, took a sip of the potent, local booze and put it down.

Michael followed Gray through the bar. Around a chain link fence, a roaring crowd circled a fighting pit. They pushed through to see what was below.

"Oh, Jesus Christ!" Michael huffed. He had expected to see men engaged in mixed-martial arts, but below them were two Phaelon warriors. Seven-foot-tall, bipedal lizards in red ceremonial armor squared off. They circled and howled at each other, the scales on their backs fanning out in brilliant shades of red. Gray looked over the scene with interest. The Phaelon put such a hurt on the Assault Corps during the war that they held a special place of distaste for many veterans, even after the survivors of their race had been consigned to slavery. But Gray had never felt that way. To him Phaelon were like sharks—good at killing and excellent hunters.

The owner of the establishment sidled up to them. He was a hollow-cheeked man named Rain Saling who wore the

Believer mark on his forehead. "Michael Solandro! General Gray!" Michael had made rounds on Golgotha for years. Gray never needed to introduce himself to any man who'd served. Rain shook their hands vigorously and instantly they both had drinks they hadn't asked for.

Gray handed his back. "I've got closed eyes now. Thank you." Michael looked at him sideways. He had no reservations and sipped the whiskey, letting the fine off-world alcohol slide around his tongue.

Ever since what happened on The Outpost, Michael had noticed a change in Gray. After he'd let the men have it and burned their religious totems, he'd calmed. He hadn't spoken to anyone, actually. He'd sent written orders and stayed in his quarters. He had only emerged when they'd gotten to Golgotha and were about to descend. When he finally spoke again, his eyes were more at peace than at any time Michael could remember. His frantic energy and anger were gone. It seemed like something true pulsed through him. He spent the last hour or so before landing praying with Izabeck. Usually, he barely tolerated the man's shadow.

Gray took his finger and traced the Believer mark over his own forehead, not breaking eye contact with Rain. "You've got a rich interpretation of God's Word here." Gray smiled, nodding to the action below.

Rain changed the subject, uncomfortable with Gray's implication. "The Phaelon, they just want to die in battle. Since they've been under our thumbs, life's not life." Rain drained a bottle of beer.

"I'll attest to that," Michael said. He knew the Phaelon well. He'd never fought against them, but he'd contracted out to work as a guard on a Phaelon labor camp that had been set up on the Glox homeworld after the war. He could speak bits of their language and knew their ways. He'd come to understand that the surviving Phaelon thought of themselves as husks and leftovers that looked to make their race whole again by dying in battle.

Below, a huge female Phaelon named Droma tossed a metal ball from hand to hand. Her opponent glided back and forth on hover boots like an ice skater going nowhere. Droma tracked him and threw the ball. It missed and bounced back like rubber to her hand. Her opponent glided in and smashed Droma across the chest with a baton. It should have been enough to take her out, but she was made of harder stuff. As her opponent celebrated for the crowd, she dropped him with a ball to the back of the head. Gray raised an eyebrow as Droma ripped a ribbon from her fallen opponent's chest.

A master of ceremonies walked to the middle of the ring with a megaphone. "The winner is the new blood, Droma! Leader of Wessei Clan, warrior of the Red Forest from Phaelon Prime via the labor camp on Glox." Droma continued to hiss for the crowd.

Rain shook his head. "That one is a monster. Been holding her and her clan in reserve so they don't wipe out all my fighters."

Gray nodded. "You know why we're here…"

"Yes, I've heard you've been looking to hire out. I was expecting you."

"But let me guess, you've just had all your shooters signed by an *anonymous party* within just the last hour."

Rain nodded. "That's right. So what do you think? The Phaelon take orders blindly. They're loyal. Fight until dead. Arnock can't play mind games with them."

Michael choked on his drink. "Hire out a Phaelon clan? Thank you for the booze, but that's insane."

Gray calmed him with a wave of his hand and Rain continued. "I would pray you'd put aside your distaste…"

Gray interrupted him. "As Moses lifted up the serpent in the wilderness, even so must the son of man be lifted up." Gray looked down at Droma, the lizard locking eyes with him, the red scales on her back flaring. "The son of man must be lifted up."

"Emmanuel!" Michael drew close to Gray and hissed in his ear, "I know the Phaelon. They're looking to die in battle, and they're not picky about the fights they choose."

"We need what they can teach us, Michael."

"They might teach us how to get our throats slit while we sleep."

Gray turned to Rain. "I want the champion and her whole clan."

"That's nine others."

Gray nodded, satisfied, noting Rain's Believer symbol on his forehead once more. "You'll be well paid, but you can care for my men. Some are badly wounded. It'll be your penance for this." Gray shook hands with Rain, handing him a credit card that was loaded with The Clergy's money. Rain scanned it and handed it back.

"Thank you, General."

"It's Bishop Gray now and thank you, but one thing. You wear that symbol? Aren't you ashamed? Have you considered maybe staying true to God?" Gray asked. Michael had to look away to avoid rolling his eyes.

"If men like me were true to God, there'd be no Golgotha," Rain responded. Gray nodded and turned to go, Michael following. "Faith's a little different, here in the boondocks!" Rain called after him, daring a laugh.

"I'll be back to cleanse this place," Gray said calmly, turning back with a smile. "Fire is a great antiseptic." Rain cocked his head and watched them leave. "That'll change Golgotha."

Michael followed Gray, taking uncertain steps. Gray stopped at the exit, looking at a message on his smart-device. Hiring out a Phaelon clan was madness, but what really disturbed Michael was the zealotry. Michael had always assumed Gray was faking his religious devotion—that he needed to say and do what The Clergy had wanted after what happened on Nova Turin. He had actually been impressed at how he had played them and bulldozed Cardinal Jacob into obscurity. But if Gray was embracing this faith now and it was sincere, then he couldn't imagine a more dangerous man alive. He thought of a hundred worlds like Golgotha cleansed by God's Word and burning.

He thought about reaching for his weapon, putting a burst under Gray's chin and killing him right here. End this fool's errand and ensure that he and a lot of other people didn't die in the process. Gray turned to him, his smile calm and present. "Heelo's got Timber. I just got a message." Gray walked outside. A stream of tower hounds on their way to the evening maintenance shift came past and Michael lost his nerve.

"You're going to collect him?"

"I am and I need you to prep the Phaelon to go."

"You know they won't budge until I'm part of their clan."

Gray clasped him on the shoulder. "Luckily you've got lots of scar tissue to deaden the pain. Come back me up once they are ready. Give me some of that." Gray took the whiskey from Michael's hand and took a healthy sip. "For Sol Kahn. I'd be remiss if I didn't take a sip for him. The others don't deserve it." Gray swirled the drink. "That's good stuff. Sol's on God's celestial shore now. Probably punched Saint Peter in the jaw just for fun."

Michael nodded. He'd only half seriously considered shooting Gray, but he scolded himself. He took the drink back. "For Sol," Michael said. Gray walked off and down an alley. Michael finished the drink in one gulp. He doubted Heelo really had Timberwolf under control. Gray might just be walking into something that would get him killed. For the first time in a very long while, Michael found himself hoping the best for Timberwolf.

EXCELLENCY

Archangel dropped out of sub-light at a healthy distance from The Outpost. The intelligence they had gathered by scanning the station's monitors and diagnostics had been accurate. The place was a wreck. It trailed a field of glass, plastic, and metal now thousands of miles long in its orbit.

Dr. Tier was up on the bridge. Les Tirani, the captain of *Archangel*, showed her the arc of debris on a 3-D projection. "The Outpost is in a fast orbit around Zim-90. It gets around the star every forty-two days and it'll start smashing into its own mess."

"We don't care about this place. There's a rescue two days behind us. We need the *St. Francis*."

Tirani nodded. "Thought so, but I've got one duty. We've got Glox scavenging in the wreckage. They have to buzz off. They'll start picking at The Outpost and they won't bother being careful around survivors."

"Les, if they don't disappear at our sight, I want you to destroy them. I won't spend five minutes swatting at flies."

"Well, you're not going to like this. Cardinal Jacob isn't playing well."

Cardinal Jacob had refused to crawl through the airlock. Even after being stuck on the *St. Francis* for three days waiting for rescue, he wouldn't go to his knees so he could get through the emergency breaching tube. He insisted that the *Archangel* extend its boarding tube and cut through the superstructure behind *St. Francis's* destroyed bridge. It was an extremely dangerous operation, considering most of the front of the ship had been torn off when the docking rings had flown free of The Outpost.

Cardinal Jacob walked aboard and met Dr. Tier, dropping down and kissing the deck in front of her before rising and taking her hand. He smiled warmly, his large, suntanned hand covering her small, space-pale fingers. "I am forever your servant," he said to her.

She nodded respectfully. "It's our duty, Cardinal. We do it cheerfully," she responded. Conrad raised an eyebrow at the display. Just an hour before, she had been ranting about Cardinal Jacob's boarding demands and was considering handing them over to the Glox for scavenge. Fortunately, they had taken off into sub-light as soon as *Archangel* appeared. She led Cardinal Jacob to her office as Conrad escorted the rest of the crew of *St. Francis* to where they could refresh themselves.

Cardinal Jacob's attendants tried to follow him, but he shunted them away. "You've been more than attentive. Go rest, please," he told them.

In her office, Dr. Tier made Cardinal Jacob a cup of tea and sat at her desk. He sat opposite her, seeming to delight in sitting in a common straight-back chair. "I haven't had a face-to-face meeting without attendants in years." He sipped the tea, relishing the flavor in his mouth, and released a long sigh of gratitude. "Thank you!" He beamed.

"I am happy to oblige, Cardinal." She sized up her next move. "So tell me, what brought you to The Outpost at such an inopportune time?"

He smiled. "Dear Thea, God's Word takes me to all places where Believers dwell."

"Cardinal, if you think I can buy that, then I'd be the one with closed eyes."

"Yes, yes. I suppose that is true." He smiled broadly.

"I am here to help you, Cardinal. But I've got to have the truth. You came here to meet Gray, didn't you?"

"My, you are very perceptive!"

"I am," Dr. Tier responded. "There are a lot of things spinning right now. We both know what they are."

"Yes, but I can't bring everything to light, not just yet." Cardinal Jacob rubbed the ends of his fingertips. Dr. Tier deduced that this was his tell. Now was the time to move to the heart of the matter.

Dr. Tier took a sip of her tea and dabbed her mouth. "There's no need. You met with Gray to try to stop him from continuing to Highland. If he takes Highland, the prime cardinalship will be out of your grasp forever." Cardinal Jacob's cheek barely twitched and his smiling face continued to glow. "But I don't know *why* you met with him. You and I both know there was no chance of talking him out of this. Nothing he could be offered or bribed with. So why?"

He looked to the ceiling and sighed, suddenly appearing to be drowsy and put upon. "There is politics by other means, which you call conquest. Then there is religion and money. We're mixing all of those things together, the true four horsemen." Dr. Tier nodded, her eyes wide with practiced empathy. "I have the ability to make things very difficult for Gray," he continued.

"Someone on the crew?" she asked.

Cardinal Jacob nodded.

"You weren't meeting with Gray, were you? Someone else?"

"You'd find out if you accessed the network on The Outpost. I'll just tell you and save you the trouble. Jude Izabeck is my man on *Nemesis*."

"What can Izabeck do to hurt Gray?"

"The question is: what can he do to help us?"

Help us, he had said. *He really wants into my camp.* Dr. Tier knew he wasn't going to say any more about Izabeck now. He would hold this back, thinking he was coy. She changed the flow. "What are you after, Cardinal?"

"Highland is a place of conquest, a pawn in the game of politics and I bring the religion. I guess the only thing left underneath is money."

"I see." Dr. Tier nodded, she had learned more than she imagined she would from Cardinal Jacob, and it left her unimpressed. Jacob was after money so he could buy power.

"You see, I can buy more influence in The Clergy than I can ever force. I no longer have access to The Clergy's finances. You get what's above in the armory and I get what's below in the fabled Coffers." He sipped his tea again and Dr. Tier did the same, so she wouldn't seem compelled to respond. She hoped he would continue talking just a bit longer. "I hate to be soiled in all of this dirty money. But I'm afraid we have to traffic in some sort of coin. Give to Caesar what is Caesar's."

"Of course," she said. "But you understand there is no trade here for me? How much is in The Coffers?"

Cardinal Jacob nodded. "It's said that The Clergy has an abundance of two things, incense and information." He laughed at his own joke. "There is roughly a trillion dollars under Highland. Buried treasure." Dr. Tier couldn't help it and her mouth fell open. "We've been watching Highland for years. They pay for nothing. Money goes in, through various channels, but it never comes out. Not a dime."

Dr. Tier's headache pounded. She thumbed the unmarked bottle of Terecine in her pocket. "So, please Your Excellency, tell me how I can simply let you walk in and take possession of a trillion dollars?"

"I can tell you about my visions, God's plan for Highland."

"Please don't," she responded.

"I can turn Timberwolf Velez's communications back on." He folded his fingers together and smiled.

"I meant to ask about that."

"Occasionally, the signs from God can be hard to follow. I had given Gray tools to help him on his mission before the man betrayed me. One was the ability to shut down Timberwolf's smart-device so he wouldn't be able to contact you. We also attempted to blow his cover with a video dossier." He smiled, almost getting giddy. "All of this spy craft is really delicious, is it not?"

Dr. Tier nodded and balled her fists under the table. "If I give you The Coffers, that's a trillion dollars for a sub-light message. An expensive call. How can you be sure I wouldn't go back on the deal?"

"We are both connoisseurs of information. You have made hundreds of enemies in just a short time, but no one knows who you are. Your own identity is your greatest secret. Imagine if everyone you had ever burned suddenly knew your name? Or your daughter Camille's name? She goes to Oxford University now, in her third year studying history."

"Stop. Dear Cardinal, stop. You're not in a spy novel; this is real. Regardless of who you are, speaking like that will get you killed very quickly." Dr. Tier's eyes watered slightly as she leveled her gaze on Cardinal Jacob. "I will kill you myself without hesitation if you even get close to threatening my family again."

"Do we have a deal?" he pressed.

Oh Jesus, let him try it again and I'll break his neck. One move to kill this man.

"Yes, I'll give you that deal. You must be exhausted." She smiled as she showed him the door. "My deepest apologies for my outburst."

"It's just the plain spoken nature of your profession." He let her kiss his ring as he left. In the hall, his two attendants, draped in capes of cerulean blue, swept behind him.

Dr. Tier took the bottle of Terecine from her pocket. Her head pounded, but she didn't open it. She needed to stay sharp, regardless of how much the stress was eating her. *I'll gladly be the death of His Eminence,* she thought.

ACT III

RELAUND

Timberwolf awoke in a chair. Wherever he was, it smelled like a hospital. As he came to, he heard the beeping of a medical monitor and the mechanical labor of a breathing machine. His wrists were zip-tied behind him and connected to a bar on the wall. He lurched upward and felt the blood rush to his head. His face felt raw and numb from the plasma blast, like he had frostbite and sunburn at the same time.

"Timberwolf," he heard Salla say softly. He realized she was sitting with him, in a chair a few feet away. She had a sadness in her voice and a tenderness about her he hadn't seen before.

"What?" he asked her, still unsure of his surroundings. But before she could answer, he knew where they were. Saint Agatha's, a convalescent home for banged-up tower hounds. It didn't look anything like it did in the brochure; pale green walls, small slits for windows. Plastic flowers sat in the corner. Timberwolf shuddered, leaning against the wall, losing all his strength for a moment.

Salla nodded to someone lying in a bed, connected to a breathing machine. The name on the foot of the bed was *Relaund Velez*, Timberwolf's brother. The bed bent in the middle and lifted upward with agonizing slowness. "You really have to stop taking plasma blasts to the face. Can you do that, please?" Salla said to Timberwolf, her face dead serious. He blinked and she smiled a little.

"Timber?" Relaund said, his voice much stronger than Timberwolf had expected. It had the bombast from years ago, back when he'd start fights with other barrel-chested tower hounds just for fun. "You goddamned, stupid mother-whoring sonofabitch." Relaund's eyes still glowed with their trademark intensity; blue marbles in his ruddy face.

"I can't come over there and punch you," Timberwolf replied. He pulled against the bar to show he was restrained.

"You're lucky," Relaund spat back. He turned his head and took a sip of water from a tube next to his cheek. Relaund's face was warm and full of life, even if he couldn't move his arms or legs. He cringed for a moment as something in his wracked body pestered him. In that instant, Timberwolf saw him as he had found him years ago in front of their house, beaten nearly to death and back twisted in an aberrant angle. "Why'd the hell you come back?" he asked, the bravado gone and his eyes warming up from the sight of his brother after so long.

"A long story. I hadn't intended to." Timberwolf shook his head. "I'm sorry, Relaund. You know the deal."

"Oh, the hell with Heelo, I don't care. I'm not doing myself any good lying here." Relaund searched the ceiling. "I guess this is goodbye. Damn, you're trouble little brother. I don't see you for two decades and then it's time to pay the piper." He turned his attention to Salla, rolling his eyes roguishly. "Who's the lady?"

"Salla Birdwing," she said as she waved.

Relaund looked at her, mischief on his face. "Hey, I'd take you out on a date if you like. I've got ten minutes to live and the food here's god-awful, but I'd show you a good time."

"Sure." Salla's lip quivered slightly. "We'll paint the town."

Timberwolf's mind was racing. "There's no way I'm leaving without you, Relaund."

"What you did for me already…what you did for Dad and the rest of us. Damn, you've already done enough. I've been wanting to tell you to your face for years. Damn, you've done enough." He turned his eyes to Salla. "You know what he did?"

"He won't say."

"Well, I was a wayward youth. Thought it would be a good idea to jump some dope dealers that worked for the Rackers. Take their dough and buy us off this rock. They did this to me. Our dad couldn't stop drinking. Never could. But he's shooting off his mouth in Leedy's bar. Go there if you want a beer that tastes like an oil filter. Dad's saying he's going to go get a gun. Timber gets him home, but later that night when he comes to see me in the hospital, the Rackers shoot our dad in the street. Kill him. Timber finds him."

Salla shuddered and Relaund continued, "Dad had a big mouth, but he really did have a gun. Timberwolf, just turned seventeen, took that gun and went down to the Racker place. Creates a distraction at the front gate and sneaks in the back door. He takes out all of them. He shoots Penn Racker and gets out. Then he turns himself in, right to Heelo. Now Heelo, with the Rackers gone, sees the chance to pick up their business for himself. Heelo says if Timberwolf ever comes back, I get to die…well, here we are."

Salla's mouth hung open a bit. Growing up on Nova Turin, she understood these kinds of things. Colonies were small places. People were packed together where it was livable and usually there was no easy way to leave. Sooner or later when someone's parent or sibling gets killed, payback could be expected and it had to be harsh. You couldn't leave anyone alive who might come back for you in a closed system. Timberwolf hung his head, looking at the floor. She could tell that what gave Relaund so much pride, Timberwolf was ashamed of.

Timberwolf lurched towards the bed, the restraints holding him back. "I'm not letting Heelo do this! You're not dying like this."

The door creaked open and Heelo entered with four of his men. He'd been listening. "That was our deal, Timberwolf. You can have the body bag."

"Go to hell," Timberwolf said, not turning.

"Hey Heelo, looks like you hit the sale on ugly and stupid," Relaund snarled.

Heelo ignored Relaund. "I am amazed at my luck, Timberwolf. I would never imagine I would have caught you, of all people."

"You're forgetting I shot myself in the face."

"Yes, why was that?"

"There's something in me you don't want to know about. There would be a lot of dead bodies if it hadn't been done."

"Her too." He motioned to Salla.

"Most likely, but I don't see how that would have made a difference to your fat corpse."

Heelo looked at his watch. "Okay, enough. I gave you your goodbyes." One of the men clamped a collar around Timberwolf's neck that was attached to a long metal pole. Still zip-tied to the bar on the wall, Timberwolf pulled away, dragging the man across the room. Heelo laughed at the display. "Timber, you're a force of nature. I am almost sorry for this. Such a nice boy." Timberwolf kicked like a mule as they detached his zip tie and pulled him out to the hall. It took three of Heelo's men to control him. A fourth man had his pistol on Salla.

They dragged Timberwolf down the stairs to a storage area, right below Relaund's room. "He wants you to listen," one of Heelo's men said. Salla noticed he had a key on his belt, probably for the collar around Timberwolf's neck. Timberwolf kicked one of the men across the room and the man who held the gun on Salla jumped into the fray, cracking him in the back with the butt of his pistol. He fell to his knees.

With no eyes on her, Salla backed into the corner. She thumbed the nerve agent canister and the personal protection grenade in her pocket. While she had been waiting on the street for Timberwolf, she had removed the cap from the nerve agent canister and inserted the pressure pin into the top of the grenade, making a crude dispersal bomb. She'd just been fiddling and didn't think it would actually work, but now seemed like a good time to try.

"You, you, you, and you are about to have a very bad day," Timberwolf snapped at Heelo's men, his voice a nasty growl. One of the men laughed, but the others smirked uneasily. Salla shook up her surprise.

Heelo hovered over Relaund's bed. "I don't hate you, Relaund. This isn't personal."

"Fuck you. That's personal."

"I've always liked your family's style."

"You think my brother is going to just walk away after you do this?"

"No, I don't. His old friend General Gray is in town. I'm going to make a lot of money selling him off." Heelo shook his head. "Yes and I get to keep my own deal. I told your brother I wouldn't kill him." Heelo took out a pistol, charged it up to max. "Head or the heart?"

"Shoot me in the heart. Why ruin a pretty face?"

Heelo tapped the pistol, checking that it was charged up to full. He placed it on Relaund's chest, closed his eyes and pulled the trigger…

Salla made eye contact with Timberwolf as she twisted the seal on her makeshift bomb. She closed her eyes tightly and covered her face with her sleeve. Getting the message, Timberwolf covered his head and curled up in the fetal position. "Please don't hit me again!" he begged. Heelo's men pulled nightsticks from their belts and lifted them high to strike. When they did, Salla smashed the bomb down in their midst and dove behind a storage rack. It exploded with a crack near a circuit breaker and the lights flickered. Instantly, the sour smell of the dispersed nerve agent filled the room.

She took a hit off her breather and gained her bearings. When she lifted her head up, Heelo's men were struggling on the floor. She picked up a pistol and used it like brass knuckles on the one with the key. In a few seconds she had the collar off Timberwolf's neck. Timberwolf took a hit off her breather to clear his head and rushed up the stairs. One of the men, the one who had laughed at his threat, managed to get to his feet. Timberwolf practically ran through him, driving him halfway up the stairs. On the landing, Timberwolf took a fire extinguisher from the wall and flattened his nose with it.

Rushing up the stairs, he felt something driving him, picking every move his muscles made. Maybe it was Kizik. Maybe it was the adrenaline. He knew he had just seconds before Heelo killed Relaund. Time seemed to slow as he reached for the handle, and he was conscious of his every heartbeat. Throwing open the door, he found that the room was empty. Not just that Relaund was missing from the bed, but the whole bed was gone and Heelo too.

Out of the corner of his eye, Heelo had seen the six, gleaming-red eyes staring through him. Kizik, the Arnock, the giant spider with the red mark on its face, skittered out of the corner of Relaund's room and up to the bed. He blocked Heelo's finger from pulling the trigger with the tip of a claw. Heelo was frozen in terror, but Kizik stroked his back and spoke to him calmly.

Let's take this one for a trip.

As Kizik touched him, Heelo felt as if his consciousness was being kneaded like dough. He couldn't look away from Kizik's awful face, his mandibles ruminating, his body shaking and buzzing as he talked to him with his mind. But suddenly, as fast as it had come, the terror washed away and Kizik was like an old friend, cheerfully dropping by unannounced. *Where do you want to go?* Heelo asked, smiling.

Let's go out of town.

With a nod, Heelo agreed and disconnected the breathing machine from the wall. Somehow he knew he had to switch it to battery power and hook the breather up to Relaund's face. As he pushed Relaund's bed out into the hall, a nasty, pungent smell reached his nostrils, but it didn't bother him. He walked past Timberwolf, frozen in place by Kizik, his only movement being his breathing. Salla stood, unmoving, in mid-stride on the stairs, looking right at him but seeing nothing. He saw his men writhing in pain in the stairwell, bloody and holding their eyes, but paid them no mind.

Heelo pushed Relaund's bed out into the night, its rubber wheels moving easily over the crushed stone of the street. *Nice night*, Kizik mentioned. Heelo saw the alien walking beside him, but no one on the street rushed in terror from the man pushing the hospital bed towards the edge of the O2 zone.

Heelo took hits from his breather as the oxygen thinned, bringing the gold-trimmed apparatus to his face. When he was a few hundred yards outside of the settlement he stopped as Kizik appeared in front of him. *Here is fine.*

A small Arnock shuttle shimmered to visibility. It looked like a much smaller version of the snail-shell command ship. A gangplank descended and Kizik pushed Relaund aboard. Heelo stood waiting in the dust. *Where do I go now?* he asked.

Just follow us. Kizik suggested cheerfully. He found dealing with this mind so simple; it was nothing like the stubborn rock that was Timberwolf's psyche. Kizik hated himself a little that he was enjoying this, but he continued. It felt like the worst parts of the war. Kizik raised the gangplank and Heelo waved goodbye. He took one last hit off his breather and placed it down. Kizik lifted off, hovering just off the ground. The shuttle backed away slowly, Heelo following, a guiltless smile plastered on his face. After a few moments, he began to stagger and sat on a rock. *Have a rest,* Kizik suggested.

I'll just lie down here for a minute.

Once Heelo had closed his eyes, Kizik lifted off. He didn't have to be inside Heelo's mind to know he wasn't going to get up.

THE CLAN

Rain Saling opened the creaking door to the fighters' cages.

Underneath the fighting pit at The Diablo, Droma and the rest of Wessei Clan were kept in a caged enclosure. In another enclosure, a different Phaelon clan crouched on the floor. They looked to be half the size of the Wessei Clan. It was their lack of pride that made them look so small.

From his time working at the Phaelon prison camp on Glox Prime, Michael knew a little of how the Phaelon mind worked. Those others were beaten, resigned to their fate and ready to die however their god decided to take them. The Wessei Clan members raged against the bars when they saw Michael, nearly tearing the iron from the wall. Some of them were on their knees, hands stretched to the heavens, repeating the words *"Wessei Trom"* over and over. They were telling Trom, their deity, that the Wessei Clan was not resigned and that she could fuck off for now.

Rain took an electric prod and ran it along the outside of the bars. The electricity snapped through the Phaelon and Michael caught the scent of singed hair. Droma drove her shoulder into the bars again and again, visibly bowing them. Rain went to use the prod again, but Michael caught his arm.

"No! That's not going to help."

"If you go in there, they will tear you limb from limb," Rain warned, hooking the prod to his belt.

"Get the hell out," Michael said.

Rain shrugged and left, closing the exterior door and dropping a metal bar across it. Droma gave a deep growl from the pit of her stomach, her back scales fluttering. She made a motion of cracking Michael's neck with her hands, her giant biceps clearly strong enough to do it. Droma's heavy, sour breath came out of the cell and she growled in her best approximation of English, "Wessei Clan yours?" The others laughed and snarled, shaking the bars again. Droma seethed, her teeth bared and nostrils flaring.

"Yes. You're all mine," Michael said, crossing his arms across his chest in a manner he knew they would respect.

"More fight?" Droma pointed to the ceiling, to the fighting pit above them. Michael shook his head negatively. "Skins?" Droma was asking if her clan would simply be incapacitated and killed for the trophy of their hides, just to hang on a rich man's wall.

Again, Michael shook his head. "No."

Michael came up to the cage, close enough for Droma to reach through the bars and tear his head off if she wanted to. "We battle. War."

"Which weapons returned?" Droma asked.

"All. Full arsenal. Lasers, swords, spears, shields, plasma-shotguns, nets, grenades, grapplers. All!"

Droma grinned, her brow furrowing. "Who battle?"

"Men."

Droma almost fell backwards, her face bursting with happiness. They were being given license to fight and kill humans. Her sister and brother clan-mates released guttural yells from the bottoms of their stomachs. For them, this was the ultimate gift. Humans had destroyed all but a sliver of their race. They had accepted that their species was essentially extinct. Most Phaelon now hoped and prayed for a good way to die; some, like the other clan in the cage across the room, had given up and had put their fate in their god's hands. They'd take any death they could get.

Michael took out the key to their cage and opened it up. It was still entirely possible that Droma and her clan would kill him with their bare hands, but Droma beckoned Michael in, like she was inviting him into her mother's house. One of the Phaelon opened a hiding place under the floorboards and pulled out two bottles. Others pulled Michael's shirt off. He knew what was coming and exhaled deeply.

Droma placed a teacup in his hand. Michael knew from his time at the camp that he needed to drink all of it as fast as he could. Its effect wouldn't last long. Droma slapped him on the back as he gulped down the bitter liquid, some of it spilling down his chin. The Phaelon stepped away from him, leaving him in the middle of their circle.

Suddenly, the tea got to Michael's head and his hearing left him. The reptilian faces became a blur, the light in the room seeming to strobe. Sounds and colors came directly to his mind, skipping his eyes and ears. He sensed they had their batons out and that his knees were buckling.

The vibration of Phaelon laughter went through him as Droma made sure he was standing straight and his arms were over his head. Then the blows were coming down on his torso. He didn't feel pain, just the awful sensation of his muscles squishing under the strikes. It went on much longer than he had expected, but then it was done and Droma was lowering him to the floor. As quickly as it had come, the effect of the tea was gone. Michael hadn't known pain like this since the day he'd been thrown from a lifter on Telock Sen and earned the scars he wore on his face now.

Another cup was brought to his lips. The liquid was cool and sweet and almost instantly he found himself in a sleep that was beyond sleep. For just a few minutes he barely breathed, his body still and cold. He felt so heavy, like he was the bedrock and there was a mountain above him. He felt himself moving through the earth, burrowing and sliding through the mud like a serpent. He was rising out of a swamp now, on two legs, running through a forest of giant red trees…

He then found himself standing amongst the Phaelon again, his sight and hearing returned to him. When his eyes blinked open, they cheered and supported him under their arms. Michael ached everywhere, but the injuries that should have probably killed him were deadened. The first bitter cup of tea was a hallucinogen and an anesthetic, but his life was truly in danger when he drank the second cup of sweet liquid. That had put him in a brief coma while billions of nano-menders rushed into his muscles and organs. It was a Phaelon battlefield remedy that had equal chance of killing you or getting you back into the fight. To the Phaelon, the "sweet death" separated out those worthy of battle from those that Trom could take to the afterlife to do her bidding.

"Vision?" Droma asked eagerly.

"I was one of you," he answered. "In the mud and in the Red Forest."

"Red Forest!" Droma exclaimed. That was a very good vision.

"*Min ter*," Michael replied, using some of the Phaelon language he had picked up at the camp. It was the phrase for *go* but also meant *go to war*.

"*Wessei min ter!*" Droma growled, looking Michael dead in the eyes. "You are Wessei!" she snarled.

DARK HALL

Heelo had given Gray the address of Saint Agatha's convalescent home. Like most buildings on Golgotha, it was a squat stack of old, converted shipping containers. There were plenty of places like this, run by the local Believer charities. Tower hounds got banged up all the time. Falls were common and many of them ended up paralyzed and beyond the help of nano-menders. Gray pitied Timberwolf for a moment, caught trying to see his brother, he assumed. *Finally found the sentimental bone in his body.*

Gray pulled out his sidearm when he saw the aluminum door was thrown open and creaking in the breeze. Something wasn't right. The place was dark and silent. When a nurse saw him coming in with his weapon out, he beat it up the stairs. A pungent smell filled his nostrils. It was familiar…

"Salla Birdwing?" he called into the darkness. It was the scent of the nerve agent she had used before on the guard who had been minding Achilles back on The Outpost.

Gray carefully worked his way down the hall. He saw one of Heelo's men at the top of a stairwell, face bloodied and doubled over. "Where's Timberwolf Velez?" Gray hissed at him. The man nodded to a room marked Relaund Velez, the door ajar.

Gray opened the door with his foot, the lamp at the end of his pistol slicing through the darkness. As he looked inside, the lights in the building went back on suddenly, a neon hum replacing the silence. Gray's eyes went wide when he saw the bed was gone.

"Heelo?" Gray asked the man in the hall, who was struggling to his feet. Again, he pointed to Relaund's room. "Heelo and Timberwolf went in there?" Gray showed the man the empty room and smirked. Unlike out in the hall, there was no sign of a struggle. The machines had been carefully disengaged from the patient and moved to the side. There was no indication of Timberwolf's tendency to tear through a place like a bull in a china shop.

Behind him, Gray heard someone going out the door. He caught a flash of a woman's brown hair and got off a shot that went wide. Rushing into the street, he looked both directions and saw nothing. Down on the crushed stone though, he noticed a faint impression. Someone had pushed a bed out the door. He began to follow the trail down the street, a drunken tower hound stumbling into his path. He pushed past him and when he did Timberwolf was there, standing in the street, weapon trained on him.

"Nice night, Timber," Gray said, both of them pointing their weapons now.

"Relaund's gone," Timberwolf said, his face a mask.

"Don't blame yourself. That's my fault. I came here thinking you wouldn't follow."

"You didn't give me much choice."

"Hell of a fight, back on The Outpost. Why don't we call it even?"

"Why don't you shit up a rope?" Timberwolf spun the dial on the side of his pistol. The chamber glowed red. He'd grabbed it from one of Heelo's men he had taken out, but it was a low-intensity weapon, barely lethal, even on the highest setting. Timberwolf could see the bulk of an armored chest-plate under Gray's jacket. On top of that, Gray's hand-cannon could turn a man into a campfire and take out half the street.

"I have seen you do a lot of things, but what you did back there was…you know they lost the whole cargo bay? Just floated away. You're the promise we need. Men like you in more of those Sabatin rigs. Taking on the Arnock. Wiping them out. Making God's will real."

"You are one story inside of another. I bet you bark it good from the pulpit, just like back in basic."

"Basic training? That was animal husbandry. I'm in a new line of work now."

"Taking Highland? How's that working out, Don Quixote?"

Gray shook his head. After everything that had happened, he couldn't help still liking Timberwolf. His swagger and his sneer. The lack of a cause that put a purity in his violence. "There's something you need to know." Timberwolf raised his weapon higher as Gray went on, "What Dr. Tier's told you is a lie. I didn't abandon you after you were captured by the Arnock. I went after Kizik. I spun up an assault squad. We thought he was on a Tiaski station. I blew it to hell. I broke a bunch of treaties. I was 'asked' to leave the Assault Corps after that."

"And that's why we're here now, so you can explain yourself and all this horseshit?"

"It's the truth I have found. I have closed eyes."

"Wait, close them right now. Just for a second."

"You can kill me easy, but listen, I've got back-up coming," Gray said. "You can't get out of here alone. Not even you, against what's coming. That was a nice trick you played, hiring out all the mercs here. Kees Leedy finally told me what you did, but you don't want a piece of what's coming down that street any minute."

Timberwolf leveled the weapon at Gray's face. That'd be the only way he could possibly kill him with the peashooter he held. Then something crossed his mind and he dropped his arm, shaking his head. "I just realized you're right about something," he said.

Gray smiled. "What's that?"

"I just hired every gun on Golgotha." Timberwolf fired at Gray's knee and dove away. The shot deflected off his thigh-plate, but it was enough to give Timberwolf the half-second he needed. Gray returned fire, wild and high and Timberwolf was hurdling through the alleys and streets. He ran like a clock, fast and precise, spinning around corners that hadn't changed since he was a kid.

A fireball erupted around him as Gray took shots, shanties flipping over from the blasts. People scattered in every direction and a dozen Glox swarmed over Timberwolf as he squeezed around a corner. He pulled his smart-device from his pocket and hunted for Salla's private signal. She was running in the same direction he was, down an alley parallel to him. He cut over and met up with her.

"I assumed if things were exploding, you'd be involved." She ran beside him, Timberwolf impressed she kept up.

"Where the hell were you?"

"I was about to shoot Gray in the head when you popped him in the knee!"

As he ran, Timberwolf yelled into his smart-device, "Call Kees Leedy!"

A few seconds later, a hoarse voice answered, "Hello?"

Timberwolf dove over a short wall, helping Salla after him. "This is Timberwolf Velez," he said when he regained his feet. "I'm bringing a party to your place. Tell my hired hands to prepare me a welcome."

"What the hell?" Kees demanded.

"I've just doubled the payday. Tell them that."

Before Timberwolf could hear a response, a trio of shadows appeared not far away under a streetlight. It was Michael, and beside him strode two massive forms. *No goddamned way!* For a second Timberwolf flashed back to the Mile High Red Forest on Phaelon Prime—*the warriors dropping down out of the trees on cables...the sweep of their chemical lasers through his squad...*

Flanking Michael were two, seven-foot-tall Phaelon, their red armor gleaming in the dull light. "Oh Jesus."

Timberwolf turned, slipping into a space between buildings two feet wide, Salla following. Above them, they could hear the heavy clomp of the Phaelon on the tin rooftops. Spears glowing with bright white plasma struck with a zing in front and behind them. Attached to cords, they flew back up to the throwers. A Phaelon dropped before them. He drew back his arm to throw his spear, but in the slim space he was jammed. Timberwolf drove into him and pushed him with all his might while searching the beast's belt for the jagged ceremonial dagger he knew would be there. Timberwolf had it and shoved it under the Phaelon's chin, into his jaw. The Phaelon screamed, suddenly becoming a flurry of whirring claws as he tried to pull away.

A glowing spear passed right by Salla's ear. She grabbed the cool top of it and stabbed the burning sharp end into the Phaelon's leg. When he lurched in pain, he pulled the thrower down from above and the two warriors tangled in a mass. Salla and Timberwolf took the opportunity to leap away, spilling out into an alley.

Timberwolf didn't see Michael there until he was on top of him. A plasma burst burned past Timberwolf's stomach as the two tussled. Stepping back, Timberwolf struck him hard in the kidneys. He never would have expected it, but Michael crumpled to the ground from one punch.

Behind him, the largest Phaelon Timberwolf had ever seen stepped from the shadows. Droma saw Timberwolf hovering over Michael and released a scream that could have been heard all the way back on the Phaelon homeworld.

"You part of the clan now?" Timberwolf asked. Michael nodded, rolling over onto his back. "Looks like they took something out of you."

"They're going to take something out of you," Michael groaned in response.

"You've sure upped the ante here with crazy. I'm going to give you this round. Gray's idea?" Timberwolf asked. Michael nodded again.

Droma drew a blade from each hip and bent over so Timberwolf could see her back scales fluttering. Atop nearby buildings and from adjoining alleys, more Phaelon appeared, echoing Droma's awful cry, but not attacking. "What the hell?" Salla asked, backing up to Timberwolf.

"She's challenging me."

At the end of the alley, he could see they had a clear path to Kees's bar. Droma threw one of the swords and it stuck in the ground near Timberwolf's feet. "You challenging her?" Salla asked.

"Hell no."

Timberwolf tapped his smart-device, sending Kees their location. They backed slowly out of the alley and into the street in front of the bar. The bar glowed with neon and two massive flames burst from elements on each side of the porch, burning off gas from the tower. Michael got to his feet, holding his side.

Kees stepped out onto the porch. He cocked a plasma shotgun on his hip. Behind him a stream of gunman slipped out and took positions behind cover in the street. The Phaelon stayed in the shadows and sent their howls out of the darkness. "What'd you bring here?"

"I'm doubling the pay again."

Smoke rose in the city behind the Phaelon and fire licked the sky. The warriors clicked their swords and guns together. The only sight of them were the orange slits in their helmets, hanging in the darkness like Cheshire grins. A bolt of lightning sparked near the tower, sending an ungodly crack through the air.

The mercenaries on the porch didn't budge. Timberwolf saw Red Forest insignias on some of their armor. These were men who had tangled with the Phaelon before and were looking for payback. A man with the name M. Warner stenciled on his armor dropped plasma grenade after grenade into his launcher. He looked to be over seventy and had a face like a baseball glove.

"What's going to happen?" Salla asked, backing up closer to the porch as the Phaelon hisses echoed from everywhere.

"Nothing good."

"Do we fight?" Salla asked, without reservation. Timberwolf couldn't help being impressed that she seemed genuinely willing to make a stand here. In the darkness, the whine of chemical lasers warming trilled the air.

"We run like hell."

A quick blast of laser went high over the bar, singeing the rooftop. The Phaelon laughed and howled as a few of the younger fighters slipped away. Warner cursed and spit tobacco on the ground, flipping the safety off his weapon. As the others followed his lead, a grappling hook came out of the darkness, wrapping around Warner's foot and dragging him off the porch and onto the gravel. The old man launched his grenades into the darkness and the street suddenly burst with white fire. The Phaelon leaped from their positions, some forward and some high into the air.

"Run like hell now!" Timberwolf yelled as the other mercenaries let loose with a wall of white-hot plasma, and laser blasts returned. Timberwolf and Salla rushed through Kees's bar, glass and metal exploding all around them. Timberwolf looked back for an instant. The Phaelon were already on the porch, cutting down and scattering the mercenaries. As they ran out the back door, a concussion grenade exploded behind them, shattering the whole front of the bar.

Uninjured, they were running through the streets again, explosions and laser blasts tearing through the night. A few hardy mercenaries stood at a corner, laying down a wall of plasma. They rushed by them and turned into the Glox quarter. Panicked Glox scattered as Timberwolf and Salla rushed through the street, adrenaline driving them to sprint. They pushed through the flowing sheets that cluttered the way, their brilliant colors dulled in the darkness. A man lay injured on the ground and Timberwolf grabbed his rifle. He fired as he went, aiming low and setting the burst as wide as possible.

Droma, the massive Phaelon clan leader, leaped down in front of them. She lowered a shoulder and Timberwolf clanged off her. Spinning away, the Phaelon went for Salla, blade out. Stumbling and holding his leg, Warner came from an alley. He launched a grenade that clanged off Droma's chest and spun away, exploding over a rooftop.

Droma took another step towards Salla, but staggered, dropping to a knee. As she struggled upward, Salla and Timberwolf were off again, running for the edges of the O2 zone. In just a few moments, the air was thinning and the sounds of the fighting grew fainter. They passed the last few meager structures at the edges of Golgotha City and were in the desert. Salla reached for her breather and took a hit. They looked back at the fireballs and streaks of laser still erupting over the city. "I don't think they'd know to follow us out here," Timberwolf said. Their shuttle sat nestled in a gully not far away.

"Thank God," Salla replied, fighting for her breath. Towards the edge of town a spindly communications tower, the second largest structure on Golgotha, buckled and keeled over, smashing up a cloud of dirt and smoke. Salla leaned against a rock, taking a second to rest. "You can feel free to work alone next time."

She went to take another hit off her breather, but dropped it. When she reached for it, she saw another breather that wasn't hers on the ground. She handed the breather to Timberwolf. It was a fancy custom job, encrusted in gold with the initials *HT* stenciled on the cover. "Heelo?" Timberwolf called.

Down near the shuttle, Heelo Tembe rested against a rock, his head lying on the hard slate like it was a pillow. There was a calm smile on his face.

"Heelo?" Timberwolf turned him over. His breathing was low and his skin was cold. "Where's Relaund, Heelo?"

The man's lips moved slowly and Timberwolf leaned in. "He went for a ride."

Heelo struggled, then went silent, his breathing suddenly labored. Timberwolf roused him again, putting the breather to his face. "With who? Why'd you take him out here?"

"They said they knew you," he croaked, his lips dry as chalk.

"Who was it?" Timberwolf demanded.

"It wasn't human," Heelo responded.

"Salla, fire up the shuttle," Timberwolf said. He needed her away for a minute. She backed away, getting onto the ship. "What was it?" Timberwolf asked Heelo, knowing the answer but needing to be sure.

"An old friend with nice red eyes…" Heelo stopped a moment, the smile on his face melting away, Kizik's influence waning. The man was realizing. "It was a spider! Oh God, it was an Arnock!" Heelo choked and coughed. "Oh God. It made me take him out here!" Heelo gripped Timberwolf's arm, his eyes panicking.

"This isn't personal." Timberwolf put his hand over Heelo's mouth and the man's body shuddered. "No sorry, it is personal." Heelo coughed a few times before finally going still.

Timberwolf shuddered. Heelo wasn't a threat. He'd killed him because he was angry. Not his style, even after what had happened. He backed away. Killing someone was never easy, but he pushed the guilt away. He needed to focus on what was happening. Kizik was playing with him, cutting to the bone, showing Timberwolf that he could hurt him in the coldest way. The shuttle's engines puffed to life and Timberwolf turned and climbed aboard, sliding into the seat next to Salla.

It was an Arnock. This had lots of bad implications. He searched his mind for Kizik as Salla lifted off, fires below them burning all across Golgotha City. He didn't feel Kizik at first, felt nothing actually, like he was standing outside of a locked door. Then, for just an instant, he felt a sadness, a lament that he'd never experienced before—the moan of someone who had lost everything. Maybe it was Kizik; maybe it was his own regret. It was hard to tell.

AFTERMATH

Gray stepped over the burning embers of Leedy's bar that had blown out into the street during the fighting. A man's arm poked out from under a hunk of tin. Gray lifted the debris and that's all there was, just a man's arm. "I get held up for five minutes, Michael," Gray said, smirking but clearly awed by the performance of the Phaelon clan.

The Phaelon stood obediently in two rows. Droma stood to the side and apart from the others. None of them paid any mind to the foes they'd just been battling, some of whom moaned and crawled away from the scene. Other mercenaries lay dead or wounded in adjoining streets and alleys. Michael strode before the clan. "We started with ten. We ended with ten. A few scratches here and there. There must have been fifty mercs out here."

"Amazing." Gray nodded, surveying the scene. "Timberwolf?" he asked.

"Gone," Michael replied.

Kees Leedy sat, head in hands, against a lamppost. Gray tapped the man with his toe, and he crumpled over. He was dead, a deep, red gash cut across his belly. Gray shook his head. They killed Kees, really? He made eye contact with Michael, who gave him back a crooked smile.

"You got what you asked for," Michael said.

"They've certainly given us a lesson. Okay, pack them up. Let's get out of here before we have to tear this place apart again, but shackle them."

"Shackle them, why?" Michael asked.

"I've got something in mind for when we get back to *Nemesis*. Cuff them and make them understand it's what you want."

Michael shook his head. He'd do as Gray asked but he'd paid for the Phaelon loyalty with his bruises already.

Warner stood at the edge of the scene. The old man had survived the fighting. Unfazed by the destruction, he wrapped a bandage around his thumb. "What?" Warner asked as Gray sized him up.

"You want a job?" Gray asked. Warner accepted with a shrug, slinging his pack over his shoulder.

They marched to the edge of the O2 zone, the short night giving way to the dawn—Gray and Warner in front, the Phaelon shackled together in two columns behind Michael. Gray didn't explain the details of the operation to Warner, just that he needed a steady gun who could lead less experienced men.

As they got close to *Nemesis*, the porters sent by Rain Saling took men away on stretchers in the other direction. One of the men, Scariot, reached for Gray as he passed. "Don't leave us here!" Gray ignored him. Scariot had plasma burns from his shoulder to his hip, but it wasn't his physical state that made him cry out. "Please, not on Golgotha!"

In the cargo bay, Izabeck snuck a cigarette. While Gray had been gone, he'd sent reports to Cardinal Jacob. He had told him about what happened on The Outpost, but he hadn't mentioned what Gray had done after that—that he'd made the men burn their totems and that he claimed to be the sword of God. He didn't know exactly why, but he felt it was right to let this play out more.

Unlike Cardinal Jacob, Izabeck didn't feel anything selfish in Gray. When Gray spoke and prayed, Izabeck felt something pure and unknown, but honest. He considered the "message" he carried in his arm from *Cardinal Jacob to Gray. Cardinal Jacob calls the bomb he put in my arm a message!* Izabeck snickered. If Gray had wanted him to lay down his life, Izabeck knew he would have asked him simply and without obfuscation.

He sensed that there was something working through Gray that even Gray didn't fully understand. Izabeck felt the love mixed with cruelty that came through Gray's actions. He felt it was his duty to witness and challenge what this man did. Gray may have been wildly egotistical, unbalanced, judgmental, forceful and silver-tongued, but wasn't the Word of God also all these things?

Gray had been so at peace when they'd prayed together before descending to Golgotha. When he'd been stuck with Gray in the airlock, he saw the man sleeping—asleep as he'd been literally awhirl in the tempest! Izabeck had been holding on for dear life, sure that he'd been forsaken. How someone could be at peace at such a time was a mystery that Izabeck needed to understand. The man wanted to build a new testament and Izabeck wanted to write it. The "message" from Cardinal Jacob? Izabeck decided it was now his to deliver if and when he saw fit.

He saw the shadows of Gray's party advancing up the gangplank. They approached, silhouetted in front of the dull-white, newly risen Golgotha sun. Two columns of mercenaries followed behind Gray, huge men, their long shadows now reaching into the cargo bay. He could see their helmets, clipped to their shoulders and swinging.

Izabeck shielded his face from the bright sunrise as Gray passed by him and winked. He knew instantly something was different about Gray. His swagger told Izabeck that his placid demeanor had been only temporary.

Izabeck's eyes went wide when he realized that the men coming aboard were not men at all, but Phaelon, hauling their gear and dressed in their elaborate red armor. One at the back flicked out her forked tongue at Izabeck as she passed. "Bishop! Bishop!" Izabeck tailed after Gray, blocking his way once he got to the galley.

"My Izabeck, how's your third testament coming?" Gray asked. "Have you heard the Word of God yet today? I know it's early and you need your morning smoke."

"You're bringing unclean forms on a sacred mission. This will end in fire for us all!"

Gray pushed passed him to the adjacent crew quarters. He banged on the cabin doors. A door was open and Windwhistle slept in his bunk. Gray grabbed him by the scruff of his neck, pulling him back to the galley.

Gray took Izabeck's electronic notebook from his hands. "How's this?" He began writing, speaking aloud what he scrawled. "And lo our leader was crazed in the eye and he wenteth into town and broughteth back ass-kickers!" Izabeck snatched back the notebook, catching Gray giving him a sly smile as he did.

The rest of the men filed into the galley—twelve survivors with blank faces and mouths agape. They stared at the Phaelon, still shackled together, huge compared to Michael who moved among them. Gray strode to the center of the room. He briefly eyed a bloodstain still on the floor, from when this place held their casualties.

"The wounded and the dead are gone!" Gray began. "We don't need them. We didn't want them. They've been cleansed from our company!" Gray paused, looking over all of their faces. "If you are here, then God's maybe decided that you're suitable to continue. There are twelve of you, fitting." He turned to Michael. "How many in Droma's clan?"

"Ten total, Bishop," Michael answered.

"And during our war, what was their kill ratio?"

"Man to man? Five to one."

Gray shook his head, hands on his hips. "So, on Phaelon Prime, every one of them we killed, they killed five of us. Amazing we beat them. Amazing." Gray shook his head, took the cigarette that still hung from Izabeck's mouth. He took a long drag. "Believers shun tobacco, alcohol, lying with those who aren't your betrothed. I say to hell with all that. You can't pretend to be pure. None of us can. Not I, not I." Gray tapped ash onto the floor.

Izabeck snatched the cigarette from Gray's mouth, stomped it out. Gray continued, "You have no fire. You're like the cigarette butt our dear Izabeck's just extinguished. You're not dry leaves waiting to be burned. You couldn't catch on fire if you were covered in gasoline! Drink, screw, smoke. I don't care. You need fight and these serpents are here to teach us that."

Izabeck couldn't take anymore. He felt his duty to God swelling up inside him. He needed to challenge Gray and do it now. "The Sabatin we carry. We tolerate it. These Phaelon are…living garbage."

"Oh, so you're high and mighty? I'll explain once. We just got our asses handed to us because we lacked will. Gentlemen, you need to learn what will is."

Michael activated a remote control and the shackles fell from the clan's wrists and ankles. "Red Forest. The Knife Valley. The Throne Country." Michael inventoried places where the Phaelon had bled them so dearly.

"That's where they tried to teach us will!" Gray punched one hand into the open palm of the other. "And we didn't listen. You're all just not worthy of God's mission yet. I've prayed on this and you need a lesson. Thank you." Gray planted his finger on Izabeck's chest as he left. "Put this part in your fucking book!"

"We're headed to Highland," Michael growled. "No one wavers!"

NOVA

For a spaceship, Timberwolf liked *Nina*. Not so small that it felt like a coffin and not so large that you would get lost. It was a nice vessel, rounded edges so you didn't bruise yourself going around corners when the artificial gravity lapsed. The food was fantastic, all high-end gourmet rations made by Highland.

He entered the galley and began going through the stores. He pulled a bunch of meals out and stuffed them into a duffle bag. He even found a few bottles of self-chilling Riesling that would go well with the coconut chicken. "Going somewhere?" he heard Salla ask from behind him.

"You're going somewhere, Vice," he said, continuing to pack the bag and open up an additional one. "You're going to take one of the shuttles to Tep Nine-Fifty. You're getting the hell out of here."

"Sorry, that's not happening. Tep Nine-Fifty makes Golgotha look like high-society."

"You don't have to stay there. Take some of Achilles's money and get on a transport. Go see Earth. Breathe in real air."

"You're scared."

He finally turned to her. "That's part of it."

"I'm not," she said.

"That's the other part of it. You're right. I work alone. I have to cut you away. I have to cut my brother away and not think of anything else but getting this job done."

"This is too big for one person."

"Not for me."

"Are you kidding me?" she challenged.

"I almost killed you down there!" he growled. She stepped away, steadying herself against a table. "I shot myself instead, remember?" He twisted the cap off of one of the bottles of wine and took a long sip. "Here." He passed her the bottle, but she just held it. "The Arnock that's in my head calls itself Kizik. It's a constant presence. Sometimes I get flashes of language and it's full of hate. Arnock are hateful. It almost made me kill you. And there's the pain."

"It hurts?"

"Like hell. Can't shut it off."

"You were trying to shut it off. Permanently. All those missions you took."

"Kizik's in horrible pain and he shares it with me. It's a profound loss. Their race has lost almost everything, but they were always holding back. They are capable of horrific things that they don't even know about. If we go after them again, he's promised me they will use the last of their breath to destroy us."

"So you really can know their intentions?"

"I listen for them. Kizik listens for us."

Salla finally took a sip of the wine. "This is probably the best wine I have ever tasted."

"Why did you help me back on The Outpost?" Timberwolf asked.

"I saw what was happening and I grabbed Achilles."

"You're forgetting I'm a D.P.E. spook. I offered you a dark hole to sit in for life and you helped me in return. You grew up on Nova, didn't you?" Timberwolf asked.

He nodded to the ornate NT tattoo on her knuckle. He reached for her hand and Salla pulled away. "Miner's daughter? That tattoo, everyone on Nova Turin got those. That made you proud until Gray took over as governor."

"My dad was a hauler. There was a strike. Gray said he'd negotiate if we turned in our arms. He just killed everybody. Three hundred people. I was eighteen. So I figured whatever

Emmanuel Gray was trying to do would be bad for anyone breathing."

Timberwolf laughed. She was his kind of crazy, but was doing a poor job of covering it up. "That's bullshit."

"Excuse me?" she threw back.

"I don't doubt your story, but you didn't grab Achilles for the greater good. You're here because this is personal."

"Look, I understand what I am getting into."

"I would argue with you on that, but I doubt you'd see my point of view," Timberwolf said.

"Getting Kizik out of your head isn't personal? I think we're both in this for ourselves. I want a shot at Gray. In exchange you've got my help. I can fly in and rescue you if you manage to destroy half of Highland or something, as is your standard operating procedure."

"You stay with Achilles until I call for you. I can't have you used against me again."

"You make a girl feel special." She handed him back the wine and he smiled. She hadn't seen him give a genuine smile before and she liked it. It was natural and crooked and it made his eyes squint up.

Just then, his smart-device gave the triple vibration that only indicated a message from one person.

TheaTier965: Please acknowledge

"I have to take this," he said to Salla.

UNBURNED

Timberwolf stepped into the hall. He checked the security scanner on his device and his direct connection to Dr. Tier seemed to be reinstalled. He had no idea how this was possible, but he entered the question that only Dr. Tier would know the answer to.

Timberwolf4545: How is your sweet C?

TheaTier965: Studying dead kings in the land of Camelot.

Satisfied it was her, he continued. His signal bounced across the sub-light spectrum. The message relayed securely off the hulls of transports, space stations, and bent itself around stars and pulsars to arrive in Dr. Tier's hand just a few seconds later.

Timberwolf4545: What's your position, doc?

TheaTier965: At Outpost. You must hold for us. Where are you?

Timberwolf4545: Half a day out from Golgotha. Gray's got a jump on us to Highland. I can't hold.

She wrote several messages that she erased before sending.

TheaTier965: You were dark for a week before you were hacked by an unexpected player in The Clergy. Why did you stop communicating?

Timberwolf4545: No reason.

TheaTier965: I can't have lies today.

Timberwolf4545: Kizik is here. He's tracking us. He's been knocking on my door.

TheaTier965: You're compromised! God-damn! You cannot continue this. You're going to lead the Arnock straight to Highland.

Timberwolf didn't respond for a long time. Finally Dr. Tier sent another message.

TheaTier965: This is a very, very expensive conversation. You don't even know.

Timberwolf4545: I have to have Kizik gone. I have to continue.

TheaTier965: You're about to be placed into my black file. Gray's not even in my black file.

Timberwolf4545: I already thought I was there.

TheaTier965: If you do not confirm you are holding, it's going to be done.

Timberwolf4545: Doc, I'm sorry to say we've reached an impasse. Best to you and your family. Tell Conrad I said fuck off.

TheaTier965: Back at you, I'm sure.

She paused, considering if she should supply this next part.

TheaTier965: There's a man on Gray's crew named Jude Izabeck. He's Cardinal Jacob's man. He could be a game-changer. I don't know how. That's the last you'll get from me.

Timberwolf4545: Thanks, doc.

Timberwolf signed off and put his device away. Back near The Outpost, Dr. Tier did the same. Maybe he could handle Kizik, but she doubted it. Deep inside of her, she trusted Timberwolf's judgment after all of this; or at least she felt she owed him her trust. She'd put Kizik in his mind in the first place.

She called Conrad and he answered. "Timberwolf's got a message for you," she said to him. "He says to fuck off."

ROAD TO HIGHLAND

"Highland's not a destination. It's more of a journey." Achilles still had Timberwolf's Sabatin rig spread out in his workshop like a puzzle. He soldered a component in the knee together, his face protected by a welding mask.

"You write greeting cards?" Timberwolf quipped.

"You asked how to get there. I told you!" Achilles snapped back, flipping up his welding mask. "You have to travel through a series of destinations, picking up the right stellar signatures on your hull. But it's never the same order. I tell her we're coming, and Penny sends me the destinations and the sequence."

"You think Gray knows that?" Salla asked.

"I am sure he does, but he doesn't know exactly how long it should take. *Nemesis* is a lot faster than *Nina*, but I am sure Penny gave us a more direct route." He got back to his work and carefully replaced a small visor in the heads-up display. "So when we get to Highland, we might be right behind Gray or right in front of him, but we'll be a lot closer than he thinks."

"Tell me about Penny. What is she?" Salla asked.

"What's Penny? Well..." Achilles looked to the ceiling, a copy of Penny was here, but she'd have been embarrassed if he'd told them. "We took all of human literature, history, the Bible, Koran, Vedas, etcetera and kept only the good parts. The parts about forgiveness, modesty, kindness, compassion. That's Penny."

"She's the boss of Highland?" Salla asked.

"She's management," Achilles responded. "Makes decisions of who to sell product to, who needs protection, who needs to be taken down a peg."

"She's an artificial intelligence," Timberwolf said.

"That's rude!" Achilles protested. He stood in the midst of all the parts of the Sabatin rig. "She's got more personality than you," he snorted at Timberwolf.

"And she's nothing but rainbows and baby lambs. These weapons you sell kill millions."

"Who made her?" Salla asked.

"I made her," Achilles responded. "Well, we started her. She made herself after we started."

"Have you met Penny?" Salla asked Timberwolf. "Can I meet Penny?"

"He'll get to meet her. She likes him for some reason." Achilles indicated Timberwolf. "She calls you a 'unique soul.' I'd rather she took a liking to you though, Salla."

"Yeah, me too," Timberwolf agreed.

A chime came over the intercom. "Oh, we're here!" Achilles exclaimed. "Just in time. I'm almost done with your rig. Meet me up in the bridge."

Achilles began to assemble the repaired components of the Sabatin rig. His hands flashed almost quicker than they could see. Curved parts and visors became the helmet. The leg gauntlet came together. It seemed haphazard, but he moved like a machine, instinctively placing each piece.

"I can't watch you put that together," Timberwolf said. "I'm going to atmo-dive in that."

SECURITY RINGS

"That's unbelievable," Salla said, looking out the view screen on the bridge, her face almost up to the glass. Before *Nina*, a thick golden ring almost a thousand yards wide hung in space. Crowning it, a red signal blinked lazily. The gentle puff of the retro engines slowed the ship. Maneuvering thrusters automatically positioned *Nina* on a glide path through the exact center of the ring.

Achilles appeared at the back of the bridge. "Welcome to Highland. Those are security rings. You need the right speed, right codes. Too fast or you go around…sorry. Your engines get fried and you'll end up in the bone yard."

Timberwolf wasn't impressed. "It's also a great ambush. Check the scope. Where's Gray?"

"Nothing," Salla responded.

"Achilles! You didn't say we'd be coasting at a waypoint when we got here. We've got our pants down," Timberwolf said.

Achilles waved his hand, blowing him off and inputting a code into the console. The blinking red signal atop the first security ring turned green. The ship glided through, an angular sliver. "You know how we made them look like gold?"

"How?" Salla asked.

"It's because they're gold! Well almost. We're sloppy alchemists, but it's not our core business."

Another ring appeared in the distance. "Look! You can wear it." Achilles held out his finger and squinted. From his perspective it looked like the next security ring was on his finger. Salla did the same and laughed out loud. Achilles entered another code into the console. Timberwolf was like a hawk, hunting the screens and moving from window to window, the golden glow from the next looming ring showing on his face.

As *Nina* glided through the second ring, the intercom crackled. A small and familiar voice came out of it. "Achilles, it's your brother. It's Sergey."

"Sergey, where are you? Is Ivan with you?" Achilles asked. Timberwolf froze, listening intently.

"Achilles, you have to listen. It's only me. Ivan is dead," Sergey said.

Achilles's face faded to anguish. "What? That doesn't make any sense!"

"It was an accident," Sergey replied, nearly choking on the word *accident*.

"No, no. It's not right. There's a mistake! There's got to be. We spoke the other day. God, he's our little brother!"

Rustling and static came through the connection. The noise continued, too long and too loud. Achilles called for his brother. "Sergey? Sergey?"

The voice that came back didn't belong to Sergey. It was Gray. "We can talk about your surrender. I will treat you fairly."

"Like you treated Ivan?" Achilles spit back. "How did he die?"

"It doesn't matter. You're going to come with us to Highland and do what I ask. Timberwolf?" There was a long pause as Gray waited for Timberwolf to respond, but he didn't answer. "There's forgiveness for you."

The signal went dead and Achilles tried to reconnect it. "Come on! Come back!" He struggled with the console, practically tearing off the cover. "Come back," he whimpered as he stared straight ahead. After a long moment a new beeping came from the console. It was the prompt for the third security ring. Achilles absentmindedly input the ring code.

Salla leaned close to him. "I'm sorry."

He paused, not saying anything for a long moment. "Our dad showed us how to work with big cats. Leopards, tigers, lions. You couldn't ever show fear. Ivan was the best at it. He had a black leopard cub he took everywhere with him. The thing gets to be 180 kilograms, and he's nine years old, bringing it up to the dinner table."

"Your family's circus?" Salla asked.

"It was 160 years ago. Back on Earth. My father was a blue-collar criminal. He stole from good, hardworking people! But we gave them a good show. Especially the kid lion tamer! That was Ivan."

"Achilles, I know this is hard for you but…"

"We traveled through all of Russia. The Dacha Brothers' circus. It was named after the four of us." Timberwolf hovered near, gripping the back of Achilles's chair.

"Achilles!" Salla said calmly, but firmly. "The next ring's not green. Gray must have made Sergey change the codes." *Nina* was almost on top of the third security ring.

Achilles was still with his memories. He spoke with eyes closed. "We stole from everyone. That was our thing. Came into town and became the biggest gang around for a week. Our dad was a gangster at heart. He gave our mom a pistol with a ruby handle for their twentieth anniversary."

"Achilles! We'll be dead in the water!" Timberwolf shook the little man by the shoulders, but he looked off, still not present. Timberwolf spun to Salla. "Get us through!" She leaped to the controls. In front of the ship, the red light atop the third security ring blinked faster and faster. Wispy clouds of plasma gathered on the inside of the ring and began to spin. In seconds, there was a gorgeous ring of fire tightening towards the center of the ring.

Nina glided with painful slowness as Salla initiated the engine sequence. Timberwolf watched as she moved through the steps efficiently, screens coming to life. She skipped the diagnostics and gripped the ignition trigger on the maneuvering thrusters. Ahead, was just the tiniest circle of black in the middle of the plasma-fire. She punched the engines and they ignited, but it wasn't enough.

Orange and red plasma washed over *Nina* as it corkscrewed through the ring. The charged particles rippled down the length of the spindly vessel, all of its nooks and crevices glowing. Salla fought to stop the spiraling. She calmly went through all of the tricks she'd known since she was fifteen years old…vent the aft flaps…shift the H20 reserves like ballast…but neither of those things helped.

"The *Nina* doesn't know which way is up!" she said. Screens on the bridge started to go out, *Nina* was losing power quickly. Timberwolf hung on in the back of the cabin. Achilles looked at the floor, still not present. Salla had one more trick. She negatively charged the starboard side of the ship. That might cause the stabilizing thrusters to reorient in sync with the artificial gravity. Like the ship was suddenly on rails, it righted.

Salla finally breathed, *Nina* seemingly intact and still powered, but she looked to Achilles. "Nice try but…"

He didn't finish, but he didn't need to. In an instant, everything on the ship went dark, the ever-present whirring of the life support ceasing and the artificial gravity going off with an audible snap that came from somewhere decks below. A pair of cufflinks floated by Salla's face. They were golden letters in the shape of an *I* and *D*. She looked over to see Achilles unfastening his cuffs. She grabbed them from the air and tried to hand them back to him. He looked at her with sorry eyes. "They were Ivan's. They're yours now," he said.

She looked back to Timberwolf, expecting him to be up and trying to restart the ship, but he was holding his head. He was muttering something silently and she couldn't hear what. "Timberwolf!" she shouted. Suddenly he snapped to, looking right at her like he'd been caught napping.

Achilles stirred. "You couldn't have helped us. Nice try. Engines are gone. Power gone."

"What's the restart sequence?" she asked.

"Huh, there's none that'll work. I made it that way. I thought of everything!"

"What's that?" Timberwolf indicated a small point of light out the window.

"Gray's not wasting any time," Salla said.

A spherical vessel approached *Nina*. It was a wrecker used to take apart old spaceships. On the ends of a half dozen appendages were hooks, cutting saws, laser cutters and clamps.

"Can I get in my rig?" Timberwolf asked Achilles.

"I still need to snap it together," Achilles shouted.

The wrecker extended its deadly tools, looking like the mouth of a lamprey. "That thing is not friendly," Timberwolf said. "What else have you got?"

Achilles shook his head, nothing seeming to come to him. He swiveled in his chair as Timberwolf balled his fists and Salla waited for an answer. Finally Achilles's eyes lit up. "*Pinta*! We can manually start her. I kept the fuel cells away from the igniter on the shuttles."

Salla leaped from the command chair. She pushed herself through the weightless dark corridors, brushing past floating debris. Two decks below, she cranked *Pinta*'s cabin door manually and it opened with a creak. She pushed the *all-start* button above the pilot's chair and to her relief, the shuttle came to life. She contacted Timberwolf peer-to-peer on her smart-device. "I'm here! It's on."

The wrecker was almost on top of them now. From out the window on the bridge, Timberwolf could see the pilot inside, just a few yards away. The man made a gun with his finger and pointed it at Timberwolf. Then the wrecker descended out of view. *Damn, they're going for the shuttles first.* He called back to Salla, "I want you to release the docking clamps."

"Why?" Salla asked.

Timberwolf didn't answer her question. "Then get out of there."

Releasing the docking clamps while *Nina's* power was off meant that the shuttle was no longer connected to the ship. It would just be sitting there, static electricity creating a weak bond that could be broken by a puff of air. Salla released the docking clamps, but as she was pulling herself out of *Pinta* she caught a glimpse of the scanner. There was the wrecker, right under *Nina* now, but there was something else. Something huge and unknown.

On the bridge, Timberwolf tore open panels, one after the other. "Where's the shuttle release?" Achilles pointed to a panel on the ceiling and Timberwolf opened it. He reached in and pulled the release.

On the aft-underside of *Nina*, the wrecker had its laser saw out and approached *Pinta*. The wrecker pilot maneuvered as close as he wanted. *Nina* had no guns and he thought there wasn't anything they could do to stop him.

With a grin the pilot spun up the saw—and that's when he got punched in the face by a spaceship.

With a burst of compressed air, *Pinta* hurtled at the wrecker, smashing it head-on. The wrecker spun off, thrusters panicking. When the pilot finally recovered, he was two thousand yards away. A long crack went down the length of the front windscreen and vapor leaked in the cockpit, condensing and obscuring the view.

He leaned forward, wiping the windscreen with his sleeve. A beep from his proximity monitor told him there was something close, but all he could see was *Nina* above him, a trail of vapor and debris coming from the listing ship.

Salla pulled Achilles up from his chair. Timberwolf heard them shouting about something, about getting the rig onto *Santa Maria*, the other shuttle, but he couldn't focus on them.

Timberwolf felt the presence. The grinding. Kizik was back and showing him memories again. *Jesus, I don't have time for home movies right now!*

Timberwolf was back in his apartment on Earth. It was right after the suicide attempt that Kizik had prevented.

There was the smoking hole in the wall that peaked through the bathroom and into the hall…The plasma pistol that had been set up on a tri-pod was knocked over… Timberwolf found himself in the shower like nothing had happened, the hole in the wall letting water leak into the common hallway outside…He calmly toweled off and found Conrad and six security men training rifles on him in his living room…*What?* he had asked like they were interrupting his breakfast…

Before the lackey could answer, there was a knock at the door and it creaked open…Kizik scurried in, was slipping on the tile floor…Conrad and the security men were frozen like statues…

I don't remember it this way. The giant spider showing up after I tried to kill myself.

This was much more than a memory. Kizik had inserted his presence into this pivotal moment.

I was here. Inside.

What do you want?

What you want.

I want you to fucking die. I want to know where the hell my brother is.

Kizik ruminated, buzzing and shaking. Even in memories, or whatever this was, the creature was shockingly disturbing. Its head pulsed and expanded as it "spoke" to him. Timberwolf recalled the odor of the Arnock; burnt cinnamon infused with a heady earthen musk.

Timberwolf could tell he had amused Kizik.

That's not why I am here. Gray, he is a small man.

How about you kill him and I kill you? Spreads around the work a bit.

He is yours to kill.

Bullshit. You kill him now. You can attack Nemesis any time.

Kizik didn't respond. The time wasn't right for Gray to be out of the picture yet. He needed Gray to clear the path below down on Highland. There were more security systems still operating and Gray would be useful to trip through them.

Timberwolf felt an uncommon frustration in Kizik. Usually his psyche floated above petty things, but Timberwolf could feel him stumbling.

Timberwolf pressed him again.

Why won't you kill Gray now?

For a moment Kizik considered stepping back and letting events take place as they would. Let Timberwolf die here and then take his chances against Gray on Highland. But Highland was too uncertain and Timberwolf was his senses, his eyes and ears. He needed this to go on for a bit longer, until things were safer.

It felt like Kizik slammed the door on Timberwolf and suddenly the presence was gone, Timberwolf's suggestion unanswered. The memory Kizik had co-opted was replaced by the chaos on *Nina*. "We've got to go!" Salla was practically dragging him from the bridge. He snapped awake again and just looked at her for a moment.

"Wait…" Timberwolf said, almost like it was a question. The wrecker was drawing closer again, just a thousand yards away.

In the space between the wrecker and *Nina*, a white glow coalesced, the center of it gleaming and becoming solid and spreading out. Kizik's massive command ship dropped its cloak and faded into view. Its off-white, snail-shell shape, both organic and mechanical, was suddenly just there, hanging impossibly where just a second before there had been nothing.

The pilot hit the retro-thrusters on the wrecker, but it wasn't enough. The Arnock vessel glowed casually for just an instant and the wrecker disintegrated, turning into a string of debris, its power core flashing before going dark.

The Arnock vessel remained for a moment, listing to the side before slowly dissolving away. Salla turned to Timberwolf. "What was that? It's gone. Did you see? Was that an Arnock command ship?"

Timberwolf's eyes were far away. "It's gone."

The three of them were silent for a moment as the space cleared in front of them. In the distance, the white disc of Highland was a dull half-circle, part of it hidden by its own shadow.

"We have to leave." Timberwolf said, breaking the silence. Achilles stared at him. Achilles's fears about Kizik's connection to him were much worse than he thought and the Arnock were here now. *This cannot go on.*

For an instant, one of the screens on the dark bridge came to life. The arc that appeared when Penny booted up displayed and then quickly faded away. No one else knew what that meant, but Achilles did. Penny was using the last of the ship's power to send Achilles a message. *You're not to kill Timberwolf. Not now.*

ACT OF WAR

Conrad sat at his station and searched every data source he could find for the name *Jude Izabeck*. He found what he had expected. He came from a wealthy Believer family with strong ties on Earth, Mars, and some of the core worlds. His siblings helped run the family's business concerns and his parents were retired, invested in the arts and gave generously to mission work. He had chosen a life of relative poverty as a Brother on Haven.

He had risen fast and entered Cardinal Jacob's inner circle, becoming the cardinal's body man, but Conrad wondered why. The man seemed dull, a true closed-eyed Believer in the worst possible sense. He wrote often and posted his thoughts on God and the faith to Believer message boards under several aliases that Conrad quickly uncovered. His writings were didactic and absolute, simple like all Believer texts, and he wrote with the utmost conviction. *If God says to take off my hand, it comes off. If he says to put it back on, I'll trust he'll give me the means to do so.* Conrad winced when he read his writings and couldn't help rolling his eyes.

Conrad deduced that Izabeck didn't care about his own fate. That he would be certainly willing to die for whatever ends Cardinal Jacob set him to—maybe someone who aspired to martyrdom. This made him a dangerous fool in Conrad's mind, but the question was *how* was he dangerous? What could he do to disrupt Gray's mission? He was about to begin scanning through the security videos from The Outpost when he saw something else.

His news feeds were suddenly blasting with chatter from the Assault Corps command at Tach-One station. There was something *huge* going on. The pure volume of traffic moving before him was breathtaking. He was able to read most of the messages. A lot of ships were being diverted. He could tell that several of them could be headed to no other place but Highland. He called Dr. Tier and she answered immediately.

"Dr. Tier, I have reason to believe we should look at Secretary Bozeman's communications."

"Get in here," she said.

In her office, she stood with her arms folded, waiting. "That's bold," she said to him.

"How far out are we from Highland?" he asked.

"A day and a half."

"We need to read Secretary Bozeman's communications now."

"No. That's an act of war," she huffed, perhaps speaking literally. The D.P.E. had the capability to decrypt and read almost any message they got their hands on, and it was generally assumed that they did so up to a certain level. Reading the private messages of the secretary of defense was extremely dangerous. If they got caught reading Bozeman's messages, it would destroy the already tenuous relationship the D.P.E. had with their comrades in the Assault Corps.

"Then I need forgiveness."

"You didn't!"

"I did it so you didn't need to. I resign."

"Since it's your last day, what did you find?"

"It's from Gray to Bozeman."

Conrad saw something on Dr. Tier's face he had never seen and never expected to see. It was fear, the candid fear of someone who was truly looking into the abyss. "What did it say?" she finally got out.

"'The broadcast is singing. Come get your arms.' And by the way, I've found Highland." He sent the coordinates to her smart device.

Tier's eyes went wide and a pit grew in her stomach. Highland was closer than she could have possibly imagined. They were just seventy-three hours out. "Okay, you're re-hired. Fine work."

He shuffled, satisfied with himself. "Now I am seeing at least five ships headed towards the place. Fast ones. And Gray seems to have reprogrammed a series of security rings to send out Highland's location over a military channel. That's how I found it."

"So Gray's really done it? And the Assault Corps is jumping onboard to support him." She looked out the window, to the pure blackness that was their sub-light stream. "This is a failure of our basic mission. They'll be streaming out to Arnock Prime within a week and they'll swing by to wipe out the D.P.E. on the way. I want you to get me Bozeman on sub-light."

"Contact him now and he'll know we read his messages," Conrad said. She just raised an eyebrow. "But that doesn't matter now, does it?" he murmured.

"No. It doesn't."

Conrad sent her Bozeman's private handle and then she asked him to leave. She thought long and hard about what she wanted to say and decided to skip the pleasantries.

> *TheaTier965: Secretary. I have two words for you. Back Off.*

After only a few moments, she got a message back.

> *SecJasonBozeman: That was fast. There are no secrets from you.*

> *TheaTier965: It's a bad idea to throw in with Gray.*

SecJasonBozeman: I think he has an ace up his sleeve.

TheaTier965: He doesn't have half a deck.

SecJasonBozeman: Highland will fall. There's nothing in our way.

TheaTier965: I am in your way.

SecJasonBozeman: Please Thea. Protest all you want.

TheaTier965: I am going to be over Highland when you get there.

SecJasonBozeman: You think you can stop us?

TheaTier965: Timberwolf Velez will be down below.

There was no response for a while.

SecJasonBozeman: He's one man.

TheaTier965: I've heard that before. I don't believe it.

Dr. Tier shut off the connection and put her device away. She'd meant to rattle Bozeman and Timberwolf would certainly be down on Highland when she got there. It just wasn't clear if he was going to be trying to knock her out of the sky when she arrived.

SILENT PARTNER

"I've turned the reactors up manually so they'll blow," Salla said to Achilles as she settled into a bench opposite Timberwolf on *Santa Maria*. Achilles sat at the controls and nodded, head in hands. He was still beside himself since hearing about his brother's death. Salla stared daggers through Timberwolf. "How long have you known they were here?!" she demanded.

"Look…" he began.

She stopped him. "You said it was in your head, not that it was following you around!" He didn't answer, just stared at her dead-on. "You *listened* for them and the Arnock followed you here!" she accused.

Timberwolf's eyes flashed angry. "The mission's the same. I'm going in after Gray. Alone."

Salla wasn't done. "You told me, yourself, that Arnock, Kizik, was in your head. Maybe you're working with them and you don't even know it! How long have you known he was here?"

"Forget it."

"You said that you just wanted that thing out of your head. How long?!"

"Since The Outpost!" he responded. "Is that good enough for you?"

Achilles cringed as he listened to them argue, knots filling his stomach. A million thoughts went through his head about his brother. *What happened? How? Was it really an accident?* An awful thought came to him. Gray would never have killed Ivan on purpose. *Sergey said it was an accident.* But Achilles wasn't sure. He went through the scenario in his head, thinking about what he might have done if he had been in Sergey's shoes—if he had been captured and Highland was threatened. It took the DNA from two live keys to access the control room. *Oh no.* It came to him. He winced, almost choking on the realization. *Sergey killed Ivan and I would have too.*

"A moment for the dead, please?" Achilles snapped at Salla and Timberwolf. "I can't stand listening to you! Not now. Not with Ivan dead." He leveled his finger at Timberwolf, his jaw solid with unexpected conviction. "I know who Timberwolf's not working with. He's not working with Gray and he's the threat right now. Wheels are in motion. He has to go down there. I wish there was another way."

"How do we know we can trust him?" Salla asked. The question hung.

"You can't," Timberwolf responded.

TRUTH

Frigate Nemesis—Over Highland

A single drop of blood fell to the floor, splashing into a small puddle. A Phaelon stepped in it, tracking it along the floor as he walked. Three skinned pigs hung from the rafters of the galley on *Nemesis*, the place now thoroughly taken over by the Phaelon. A large pot of foul-looking stew simmered, and they made cups with their hands to take portions directly from it. Axes, spears, harpoons, swords, nets, and exotic rifles leaned up against each other in clusters.

Warner and Michael took in the spectacle. Behind them a Phaelon in a hammock rustled, hissed, and dropped down to the deck. Two Phaelon threw what looked like half-opened bowie knives at the wall. The knives bounced back from one to the other. A clumsy catch from one of them and lime-green blood spurted. The other one laughed, back scales fluttering.

A Phaelon had her arms raised. She held her breath in and hissed, long tongue extending. On that signal several others beat her mercilessly with batons. She doubled over and stood up straight again, signaling for them to repeat.

In the adjacent galley, rows of prayer mats were rolled out, candles burned and most of the lights were turned off, a stark contrast to the Phaelon spectacle. Gray stood before a small window, looking out at Highland below, the dark side of the world crowned by a bright crescent. The planet was almost entirely covered in thick clouds as he had suspected. Sergey had told him that atmospheric regulators made sure of that to obscure the surface. Infused into the clouds was a sea of nano-machines that scattered any scans and sensors.

Michael appeared beside Gray. "Any word on the *Nina*?" Gray asked.

"No. We lost contact with the wrecker pilot," Michael responded. "It could be interference from the plasma cascade. The ring defenses are inert now. The broadcast is singing."

Gray smiled. He noticed the men waiting in the hall and beckoned to them.

"Come in, men."

Gray looked to his reflection in the window and put on a white priest's collar. He had thought long and hard about what to do with the men after The Outpost. Did he need them? He had considered leaving all of them on Golgotha with the wounded. He prayed on it and God had told him nothing. *Maybe he doesn't answer the first time you knock,* Gray had thought. He'd never tried praying personally to God before, when not in front of others, when not playing the part of Bishop Gray. It had been isolating not to receive a response. He felt like he was begging God to wake up. He'd spoken plainly and from his heart, but nothing came back. No feedback, no words.

He'd decided that no answer and no sign meant that these men were to remain part of the story, at least for now. They were here to witness these deeds, as part of what Izabeck was writing. Windwhistle and the others filed in. They were tentative and meek. Some looked out the windows to Highland below. It was an unimpressive world on its own, no surface features visible through the thick white and ashen clouds. Still, they pressed their faces up to the glass, amazed. "It's what's been promised by Bishop Gray!" Izabeck said to them. "It's the first part of heaven!"

Gray tilted his head, unsure of what Izabeck's remark meant. Izabeck had retreated to his bunk after Golgotha. He'd scribbled constantly in his notebook and avoided Gray.

Gray had no idea what he'd been writing, but the man held his electronic notebook to his chest as if its embrace made him holy. Gray beckoned him over.

"You've been busy," Gray said to him. Izabeck held the book close, like it was an infant he was protecting. "Can I see it?"

Without a word, Izabeck handed it over and stepped away, rubbing his arm as he'd been doing constantly for the last few days. He closed his eyes and a calm smile took over his face. The man's devotion still made Gray uncomfortable, even as Gray sought to feel the genuine Word pulse through him. Gray thumbed through the pages, skipping the parts he'd read before. Then he reached a new chapter of the book with three words in large print stacked on top of the other.

WRATH

LOVE

JUDGEMENT

He read further, devouring the pages quickly, his eyes growing wide. This wasn't the pedestrian drivel he was used to from Izabeck. There was something moving in him, a spirit Gray had no idea he carried. What he'd been looking for from God was right before him now and it had been delivered by Izabeck, of all people. *This is...*

"Truth," Gray said to Izabeck, suddenly finding the perfect word. Gray squeezed Izabeck's arm; the man smiled deeply and traced the Believer symbol on his forehead as he kissed his prayer beads. Gray moved to the podium, pausing a moment as the men took their places on the prayer mats in front of him. He knew that if he told them what was in Izabeck's book, it would set off a fury maybe he wouldn't be able to control. He considered not saying it, just giving them a sermon about being strong and carrying the Believer banner. But looking out over the men, a righteousness rose inside him. He would give them Izabeck's third testament, whether they could handle it or not.

Gray began, "The first testament was God's wrath. The second testament was God's love. The third testament is God's judgment, a living book! We're in the midst of it now, writing it with our works and deeds. The ending is…God's forgiveness."

Izabeck nodded heartily.

"How does God forgive us?" He looked out to all their faces. "How does God forgive us? Let's look at our sins. His book has been incomplete for so long. He forgives us when we complete His Word. When we make this third testament come to life! Our universe is His. So every part of our universe is a part of heaven, waiting to be taken in His name! Do you understand this?"

Gray motioned to the Believer symbol hanging behind him; the downward-turned ichthys, which represented closed eyes open only to God. "God is love. Love is blindness."

The men looked at him, unsure. A few gave the Assault Corps cry of "I-ya," but tentatively and barely over a whisper.

"Do you understand what God is asking you? He's judging you, every second. But not your rage, your gluttony, your lust. There is one deadly sin left, friends. One. Sloth. When you rest a minute, His Word is forgotten."

Heads nodded around the room. In the back of the space, Michael and Warner stood. Michael's eyes were doubtful as usual as he watched the display. Warner fell to his knees, nudging Windwhistle and sharing a prayer mat.

Gray continued, "Where we're going, it's the first place we'll usher in as part of God's kingdom. The Sabatin we take we'll use against the Arnock and we will do God's will. Let's honor those whose stories have ended, Forestground… Dov…Sol…Neviim…Bison. God loves our sacrifice. He smiles on us and gives His…"

Out the window and far away, *Nina* exploded in a noiseless flash. Gray turned to the window, his face blank with loss. "Timber, I promised forgiveness!"

Gray banged his fist on the glass, looked out to the dimming burst. "Out!" he demanded, and the men quickly found the exit. Michael stayed and checked the ship's sensors through his smart-device. He showed Gray a representation of a quickly expanding debris field.

"It's the *Nina*," Michael said.

"I see that." There were no escape ships streaking away. No ion trails that would represent an exodus. Michael hung his head. He thought he'd be happy with Timberwolf dead.

"Keep scanning. He's been dead before and he just keeps coming back," Gray said.

"Emmanuel…"

Gray turned on him. "You want me to be mournful? You want me to be angry? Maybe relieved? Sing for your old friend?"

"I'm not celebrating," Michael said.

"But you want to. I know what it was like for you…"

Michael couldn't hold his tongue. "God loves your sacrifice! You just said it. He's taken you up on that, it seems," Michael said, stopping Gray's anger. Gray looked suddenly old, very old and frail. He was silent for a long moment, his face finding different emotions, from grief to rage, but not staying on any one too long.

"His story is over," Gray said finally. He spoke the words to the Assault Corps mourning song softly, "When my life in this place is over, I'll fly away. To that home on God's celestial shore, I'll fly away."

"This tub doesn't have any whiskey, does it?" Michael asked, and Gray shook his head.

The *Nina's* power cell burst in a secondary explosion, expanding the debris field further. Michael gave Gray a somber face. He dared not betray the satisfaction that was creeping into him. Was Timberwolf a faulty old friend? Should he mourn him after everything that happened?

Hallelujah by and by, Michael thought.

THE DESCENT

Nemesis floated above the clouds of Highland. With a puff of the maneuvering thrusters, the ship began its descent. After a few minutes, it reached the high cloud layer and disappeared into it. They went through layer after layer of clouds, each opening up a new vista of sky, the first few bright and airy but becoming darker and more ominous as they descended.

They reached the seventh layer and flew several miles above a dark and swirling cover of clouds that looked to have the consistency of cooled lava. "Where is The Eye?" Gray asked Sergey. The small man was strapped into a seat on the bridge.

"It's where I said it was. About four thousand miles from here," Sergey snapped.

"I'm not getting any readings," Farrow, the pilot, said. "I'm visual."

"You'll get nothing. We've got this whole place shrouded. Nano-machines. Last count fifty-seven trillion."

The ship could make four thousand miles within the atmosphere in about an hour, but Gray knew Sergey had put them this far away from their target to delay them. He expected this type of behavior from Sergey, like he had expected him to take him on a circuitous route to get to Highland in the first place. He filed it away. Gray's patience was quickly reaching its limit.

The consistency of the cloud layer changed as they got closer to their target. It looked jagged and pebbled now. Pillars of clouds rose up, like slow-motion geysers, sometimes twisting over and creating arcs. Farrow banked and maneuvered around them, pressing everyone on the bridge into their seats.

The pilot slowed when they were two hundred miles out. Lightning crackled below them. Giant living gasbag creatures, like floating octopi the size of small islands, rose out of the clouds and reached out for *Nemesis* with their tentacles. They never got close and slipped back down below the cloud line.

Below them now was The Eye, a circular area that the cloud layer channeled around. "It has a six-mile radius," Farrow estimated. The pillar of clear air descended all the way to the surface of Highland. Farrow brought the ship to a hover-halt over the center of The Eye. More gasbag creatures, these like crabs attached to giant air bladders, came through the cloud wall at the edge of The Eye and leaped out hopelessly at *Nemesis* before floating back upwards.

Darkness engulfed the bridge as the ship descended below the lip of The Eye. "Starboard eighteen degrees," Farrow announced, making a correction. "Seventeen miles down. No structures. There's a mountain."

"Eye of the storm?" Gray turned and smiled at Sergey. The small man simply looked out the window like a commuter who had come this way a thousand times before.

"Jesus, I've got a face in the cloud wall!" Farrow kicked back on the maneuvering thrusters, turning the ship. Outside, there was indeed a giant, wretched face made from clouds and twisting its head to track them. As the ship turned, other faces appeared, some smiling mockingly, some disintegrating in agony before them.

Sergey was grinning. "It's just the nano-machines in the clouds. It's the same stuff that's blocking all your scans. Let's just say you're not exactly welcome!"

Nemesis continued its descent to the bottom of The Eye, landing skids extending. It settled into a space near an outcropping, with its nose pointed towards a massive door in the side of a sheer mountain face. Gray came out of his chair and pressed up close to the windscreen. "We're here!"

Sergey clapped slowly and without sincerity. "There's a chance to step away. I promise none of you will survive in there."

Gray didn't turn to him. "You're a bastard of little faith." The others stayed in their chairs, unnerved and unwilling to look outside. Gray took in the mountain face, maybe a mile high looming above them. He felt a twinge in the pit of his stomach. He searched for his own faith, for the tap on the shoulder from the Almighty he had heard so much about. Nothing.

"Let's get out there!" Gray said, throwing his own doubt aside. "No time to waver!"

Less than an hour later, the crew filed out of *Nemesis* onto the surface of Highland. First came Gray, Sergey, and Izabeck, then Warner with the human crew, and then Michael leading the Phaelon. The air was surprisingly fresh and earthlike; not like some unbalanced colony world with terraforming towers straining against the elements. White dust, similar to that found on the surface of the moon, covered everything. They unloaded in silence, taking in the vast emptiness of the place, the only sound the squeak of their boots on the dust. The men's armor auto-camouflaged to match the pale surroundings, making them seem ghostly and transparent.

In the distance, the cloud wall of The Eye spun slowly and noiselessly around them. They'd descended through it, but being in the center of The Eye defied logic. The clear air went up to the top of the cloud layer and the faintest hint of light peeked down from miles above. "It's like we're inside a tornado or something," Warner said as he took the place in.

There was no wind and not even the hint of a breeze. Wrath and Thomas were the last to exit the ship. The beast shrieked as he touched familiar terrain. An uncomfortable laughter came out of the men as they watched Wrath dig heartily into the ground.

They walked the five hundred yards to the door in the side of the rock face. It was wooden and twenty feet tall and looked like something from a medieval castle. Gray assumed it was locked and that Sergey wouldn't be forthcoming with the key.

"Thomas, have Wrath open it."

"No, it's not locked. Just pull the levers," Sergey said. "You know how much it cost to put in a *wooden* door?"

Gray rolled his eyes. Two men pulled down on large levers near the hinges and the door opened with a groan. The party entered, single file and tentative. Inside they found themselves at a sort of transit station. At their presence, dull floodlights came on, illuminating a single train car covered with dust. Tracks barely visible under the dust curved off into the distance.

As their eyes adjusted, the party couldn't help but look up. "Goddamn!" Warner exclaimed. Beyond the train, a pile of wrecked spaceships towered a thousand feet high. Spidery maintenance machines tending the heap turned their glowing green eyes towards them for a moment and then went about their business.

Amongst the wreckage were huge white columns. Gray followed them with his eyes, expecting to see a ceiling, but the columns disappeared into a murky blackness. "What's with the dust?" he asked Sergey.

"It rains the dust. Shakes off the ceiling." Sergey motioned to the train. "That will take us in." He touched the side of the train, which came to life with an electric buzz, and the party boarded.

The train moved past the wrecked spaceships, its headlight slicing through the darkness. More spidery machines peered out at them from behind the pillars. Occasionally, floating robots moved by overhead. "What is this place?" Gray asked Sergey.

"It's our bone yard. Those ships belonged to people like you. People we caught with their hands in the cookie jar."

"You didn't catch us. We caught you. Are we the first to see it?"

"The first against our will," Sergey admitted. Gray nodded, transfixed by the relics of failure.

In the back of the cabin, Droma, the Phaelon clan leader, was on her knees. Behind her, her clan-mates descended one after the other, arms to the sky. "*Wessei draf*," they repeated, some weeping.

"What are they saying?" Gray asked Michael.

"You're seeing something rare. These Phaelon are scared as hell," Michael said. "They're telling their god that if she wants to take them right now, that's fine. They don't have to take one step farther."

Gray nodded, looking over to the men. Every one of them, even Warner, traced the Believer mark on their foreheads. Before he knew he was doing it, Gray was tracing the mark as well.

Sergey caught him. "Don't bother praying. We're blocking the signal." The small man turned back to the window, watching the mountain of wreckage taper off. Ahead of them at the terminus of the track was another door in a rock face, this one bigger than the last.

THE AIRLOCK

Timberwolf squatted outside the tight airlock in the belly of *Santa Maria*. He pulled on the last parts of the Sabatin rig, the leg plates fusing to the thigh. He felt the electric contact between the rig's sensors and his skin and his heads-up came to life. The visual fizzled for a moment, so he knocked the side of his helmet against the bulkhead and it cleared up.

"Jesus! I just put it back together, you mind?" The space was exactly the right height for Achilles to stand in.

Timberwolf popped open his faceplate. "Rig's going to get more action than that."

"Gray probably thinks we're dead on the *Nina*. You might surprise him." Achilles turned from a panel on the wall. He'd been masking *Santa Maria's* ion trail, sending the particles into sub-light so the ship wasn't detectable. Achilles fretted, wringing his hands. "In my estimate, Gray won't get Penny to give him what he wants. He leaves. But the Arnock mind is on another level."

"I know that." Timberwolf smirked.

"Well, of course you do. Highland can defend itself, but I can't let the Arnock land. They'll figure it out."

"When does Kizik come out?" Timberwolf tapped his temple with his glove, alluding to the deal they'd made.

"As soon as Gray's dead! Not a second before. Can you do this?" Achilles motioned to the world below, taking the implication way beyond killing Gray.

"I have no idea."

"That's relieving. Honestly, if you told me you were confident, I'd blow up your suit the second you stepped outside." The two men locked eyes, acknowledging that Achilles had Timberwolf's life in his hands and could kill him with a touch of a button. Timberwolf thought about trying to hack the suit and deactivate Achilles's self-destruct, but he'd surely buried that so far down in the rig's programming that he'd never find it. "Want to know what concerns me?" Achilles asked.

"I don't think I have the time."

"One thing." Achilles pointed at Timberwolf and then shook his finger, turning it to point at himself. "It's not you. It's me."

"I thought it was me. It's always me."

"I did all of this. It was my idea to send you the rig. Maybe make an ally. We've never had friends before. Your people want this place as bad as Gray. Admit it. You just go about things differently. However this ends, we'll have someone to answer to, won't we?"

"We'd be a better landlord than Gray," Timberwolf said.

"You get it, though, of course you get it. It's better you than him, but we don't want you either. I'm scared that I might decide to cut you out. That I might decide to cut out everyone. Take my chances."

Timberwolf grinned. "Don't leave that up to Salla."

"I'll tell you. She's livid."

Timberwolf pulled a lever. The airlock opened with a hiss. "You better clear out, unless you want to come down there."

"That's a horrible, horrible idea."

Timberwolf knew that Achilles would be watching his every move, that he'd press the button if it even looked like Kizik was gaining control of him. Timberwolf certainly couldn't blame the man.

"How can I trust you?" Timberwolf asked. "To, you know, not kill me?"

"You can't." Achilles grinned. He grabbed Timberwolf's arm as he climbed into the airlock. "Look, just try to help my brother. He's what I have left."

"I'm not in the promises business," Timberwolf said. Achilles nodded, eyes closed. "But he's valuable. We can't lose him."

As Timberwolf closed the airlock, he saw Salla looking in through a porthole in the cabin. She hadn't spoken to him since they left *Nina*. It was entirely possible that as soon as he was outside, she might convince Achilles to leave. He knew that he couldn't count on her anymore to fly down and rescue him.

"My brother!" Achilles said as Timberwolf pulled the airlock door closed. A moment later, the space filled with light as Timberwolf opened the exterior door. There was a burst of thrust from his rig and he was gone.

He dove straight down towards the surface of Highland. His heads-up showed an altimeter spinning, losing a thousand feet per second. He began to feel the first tugs of gravity as he got close to the clouds, rippling now with thunderheads. He disappeared into the vapor, slowing from the resistance. The rebuilt rig was well within tolerances, internal and external pressure equalizing nicely. He passed through the cloud layers and caught sight of the living gasbag creatures miles away. Much sooner than he thought, he found himself falling directly over The Eye.

With a few bursts of thrust, he was dead center above it. He continued to fall head-down, now two miles above the surface. The dark gray walls of The Eye spun around him in a constant and stable tornado, driven by the trillions of tiny nano-machines spinning in the vapor. He could see them in his heads-up through the infrared filter, twinkling like ice crystals.

He saw the bottom of The Eye now. Its white surface seemed to glow below him like a dim light at the end of a tunnel. At 1,500 feet, he deployed his parachute. He saw the entrance to Highland in a rock face below him and *Nemesis* parked nearby.

He landed with a stutter-stop and the parachute retracted with a zip, his rig auto-camouflaging to match the chalky-white regolith. Timberwolf thought about the times he'd huffed up and down craters on Luna, the earth hanging above him against the pure black. Looking up, he saw the funnel of The Eye wavering slightly above him and the dimmest light at the very top. He tried contacting *Santa Maria* through every channel, but nothing went through, all of his signals soaked up by the nano-machines in the clouds. He had no doubt that the signal-block was selective and that Achilles was watching his every footstep.

He expected the gray vapor making up the walls of The Eye to sound like a hurricane. But the silence was unnerving. He took a few steps and his boots squeaked in the soft dust.

He scanned the area and very little reflected back through any filter. What he could see was that *Nemesis* was just five hundred yards away, its jagged arrowhead shape half-hidden behind a rock outcropping.

Timberwolf raised his left gauntlet and powered up the chemical laser. He zoomed in on his heads-up and saw the pilot moving around outside the ship. The man was trying to rig up some sort of communications relay. *Looks like Gray can't get a signal off this rock either.* He could kill the pilot easily and then slice off the bridge of the ship, taking out Gray's ride home.

Then he had second thoughts—Salla, up there stewing, if she hadn't abandoned him already. He lowered his weapon. Best to keep *Nemesis* intact until he was sure he had a way off Highland.

The entrance to Highland was a little less than a mile away, the massive door tiny in the huge rock face. He made his way unhurried to the entrance. There was no need to alert the pilot and have a confrontation that might force him to destroy the ship.

Timberwolf was surprised the door was ajar and he easily slipped in. He was here. He'd made it to Highland. *That was easy.*

HEAVEN'S LIGHT

The train ground to a creaking halt in front of the next giant door. Like he was by himself, Sergey stepped off onto the dust, not regarding the others. Gray and the rest followed after an unsure moment. Warner corralled the human crew. "Move out! Move out! Let's go!"

"We can't prepare you for what's past here. It's our Catalog," Sergey warned.

"*Catalog?*" Gray asked.

"We used to take buyers through here all the time. Show them our wares. It was perfectly safe." Sergey stuffed his hands into his pockets. "The place isn't prepped for visitors; that's all I'm saying."

"It *was* safe? That's rich. You're just trying to delay. There's no one coming. Timberwolf is dead. I would make this easy on yourself!"

"And I would get back on your ship and leave before you die here!" Sergey snapped back.

"When we own this place, you'll regret speaking to me like that."

"If you only knew how insane you sounded."

Gray took a step to Sergey, but Michael grabbed him. "I want to get what we came for and get off of this place alive!" Michael snapped.

Gray seethed a moment, then began to cool. He noted that Sergey was perfectly calm. He felt foolish for letting him get under his skin. He made a mental note. *When this is all done. Just kill him and forget it.* He motioned for the door to be parted and, like before, two men pulled it open.

Natural golden light, like on a perfect Earth spring day, streamed outward and everyone blinked, adjusting to it. Many of the human crew had never been to Earth, had spent their whole lives on the outer colonies. Warner's face glowed with a smile, and he stared long and hard at the warm light until his eyes watered.

"The light of heaven?" Gray said, smiling. The men laughed uneasily. The party entered into The Catalog and found themselves at the top of a wide, marble staircase. Before them was a huge chamber carved from rock, easily two miles deep and a half-mile high. A light source floated at the top of the high ceiling. It looked like a tiny sun. Beyond the staircase, white dust covered the surface here too. There was a series of delineated testing grounds: squat buildings, gardens, a shattered urban zone, and more. There were also spaces where green grass sprouted from planters, uncovered by dust.

"Okay, let's be gracious hosts," Sergey said. From the bottom of the stairs, a woman approached.

"I thought it was just you?" Gray asked.

"Highland is completely automated, but we do have helpers."

The woman approached, her face classical and dark. A long green dress fluttered around her ankles and she wore her black hair up in a tight bun. A catchy tune from unseen speakers played over her silky voice. "Hello, and welcome to the Highland Industrial Defense Park. Are you ready to hear about all of our wonderful products?"

"This is Meta. She's in sales," Sergey said. Meta flickered for a moment, a hologram.

"We'd like to get right to the point, if you please," Gray said to her.

"I like that. A man who knows…" Suddenly, her face twitched and a look of alarm came over her. Her movements became jerky, her face gaunt and uncolored. Her voice went coarse and mechanical. "Breach of protocol. Incident zero, zero, zero, one. Is there danger?"

"No. We're copacetic," Sergey responded. Gray grinned at what he saw as a charade, Sergey desperately trying to scare them off.

The hologram jerked her gaze from face to face, speaking disjointedly. "An Arnock vessel has revealed itself in orbit…Perhaps to pick up their order…Wreckage for the bone yard…There has been an insert…"

"We're copacetic!" Sergey snapped at her.

She reverted back to her sales rep form like nothing happened and continued her pitch, descending the staircase. Gray's party followed.

"We've got something for everyone here, from the planetary warlord to the regional shipping magnate. Lethal and non-lethal systems."

"We're here for lethal." Gray snickered. The men chuckled nervously except for Windwhistle, who had his rifle trained on Meta.

Sergey sidled up to him. "Go ahead. Shoot. She's just made of light, dummy."

Meta continued, "No need to actually purchase full systems. At one-tenth the cost we can send a simulated receipt to your adversary. 'Flaunting the bill' has a ninety-seven percent capitulation rate. I guess our name precedes us. You'll hear our catchy tune every time you approach a display area. Not to worry, we'll be able to tell…"

Mid-sentence, she fizzled again, her face momentarily like a dead woman, her voice mechanical. "Facility set to live-fire!" she barked.

Like nothing happened, she continued her previous pitch, "…to tell our guests from the demo targets! Have a nice stay!" Meta vanished and her tune stopped.

"I told you I couldn't prepare you for this," Sergey said to Gray.

"We're walking through a live-fire proving ground?" Michael snorted.

Gray had had enough with the delays and the circuitous routes and now this hazardous detour. "You know I can still use your DNA in the control room if you're dead?"

"Of course you can, but you'd never get there," Sergey responded.

Gray leveled a pistol at Sergey's head. He could see beads of sweat on the small man's temple. "I see you're sweating. You know I'll do this."

"It's hot in here. I've got to adjust the sun a little," Sergey scoffed, motioning to the light source glowing at the top the chamber. Gray kept the weapon leveled. "It's best we get going. If everyone's careful, they will survive," Sergey said.

Gray shook his head and put his weapon away. "Fine." He turned to the men. "Let's be sharp. Raise the banner. I want control of this place before the Arnock land."

"They'll never land!" Sergey said, shaking his head with frazzled confidence.

Michael pulled Gray aside, whispering, "The Arnock followed Timber here. You should have let me kill him on The Outpost!"

Gray's nostrils flared, but he just turned away from Michael without responding. There was no way Gray was admitting Michael was right. Then there was the larger truth, that making things right with Timberwolf was Gray's blind spot. That keeping him a part of this story had been profoundly selfish and dangerous. Gray looked to the glowing orb above and felt the perfect soft light fall on his face. *Your shadow still falls, friend.*

Two men raised a pole topped with a Believer symbol and the party began to walk along the dusty path. Warner kicked into the dust with his boot, curious to what was underneath. His left foot was artificial and heavy, blown off forty years before in the ducts on Ceres. His kick uncovered golden cobblestone bricks. It reminded him of a story he'd heard once, but he couldn't remember much about it. *Maybe a robot and a witch and a girl. And there were little people too, Sergey's size but lots of them.*

Didn't everyone die in that story? he asked himself with a shrug. Warner had a habit of surviving, of being left unscathed when everyone else fell. He wasn't worried about dying; he just always expected to live. So far that had worked out well for him.

"We're off to see the wizard!" he said to Izabeck, remembering the story. The man didn't respond. He looked pained and held his arm. Izabeck moved to the side of the path, slowly hobbling away. He stood like a statue, letting everyone pass by him.

ACT IV

THE BURNING

Izabeck had his electronic notebook out. He wasn't writing. He was reading. Cardinal Jacob had been sending him messages and he had been ignoring them. Izabeck thought that once he got down to Highland, Cardinal Jacob's messages would be blocked, but the communications continued as well as something else. Cardinal Jacob was angry. He had been burning Izabeck—spinning up the device buried in his arm until it singed his flesh from the inside out. He finally responded.

> *Izabeck613: Cardinal, everything is beautiful. We are so close.*
>
> *Samar1483: Wonderful my son. But I must ask why you seem to have forsaken me?*
>
> *Izabeck613: Events have been moving very fast. My apologies.*
>
> *Samar1483: You've felt my nudges though. It pained me to send them. Did you think I wasn't going to be able to contact you on Highland? You know the power of our technology.*
>
> *Izabeck613: Please forgive me.*
>
> *Samar1483: This does not show closed eyes!*
>
> *Izabeck613: I beg forgiveness.*
>
> *Samar1483: And you have sent no updates, but I can tell you have been writing. I can't see what, but I can tell.*
>
> *Izabeck613: My heart is overwhelmed by what I am experiencing. I am sorry.*
>
> *Samar1483: Have you fallen for Gray's lies?*

Izabeck didn't respond for a while. He felt the whirring and the heat in his arm as Cardinal Jacob grew impatient.

> *Izabeck613: Please stop burning me. Please. Bishop Gray is a heretic. The others are under his sway. But not me.*
>
> *Samar1483: I'll be clear. You're a vessel now. Your salvation depends on what you do. You can have the Kingdom of Heaven with me or you can perish with Gray.*
>
> *Izabeck613: I am an unworthy vessel. A dry leaf longing to be burned.*

The rest of Gray's party trailed off around a bend in front of him. Izabeck fell to his knees in pain, his arm burning and vibrating worse than ever before as Cardinal Jacob punished him. Finally, the heat subsided, leaving Izabeck's arm throbbing.

> *Samar1483: I am so glad to have you back in my fold! I'll pray for you.*

SHOOTING WAR

D.P.E. Archangel—Thirty-Two Hours Out from Highland

Captain Les Tirani strode quickly through the engineering corridor. Crew snapped to attention as he passed. He wasn't going anywhere, but he wanted to get away from this conversation with Dr. Tier.

"Les, we have to act now!"

He stopped at a bulkhead, inspected a maintenance chart he knew was up to date. "You're talking about a shooting war, Doctor."

"It's avoiding a shooting war. *Challenger* is ahead of us in the stream. They'll get to Highland before us."

An hour ago, they'd found that one of the ships Secretary Bozeman had diverted to Highland was actually traveling ahead of them in the same sub-light stream. Sub-light was a single file transit system, and they were gaining on *Challenger*. It was doubtful they were even aware *Archangel* was behind them. Scans sent backwards in sub-light didn't bring back much and usually only friendly vessels shared sub-light streams.

Captain Tirani hurried up a ladder to the galley. When he appeared, the boisterous clamor stopped and all were silent. Dr. Tier was suggesting knocking *Challenger* out of sub-light and disabling the ship. She sidled up to him in the chow line, taking a tray like he did.

Tirani filled his plate with some sort of slop. Dr. Tier took a protein bar. The crowd of crewmen parted before them and cleared out of a table in the corner. The mess was quiet. Usually officers ate in their own lounge. Dr. Tier was forced to whisper. "I assure you. There will be shooting if they beat us to Highland."

"I know Captain Jephtah. She'll turn *Challenger* on us so fast we'll be Swiss cheese in five minutes," Captain Tirani countered.

"That's if you miss. If her engines are down, *Challenger* will be out of commission for days."

The room began to rumble with conversation again. "You want me to attack an Assault Corps ship, *now*? You want me, a captain working for the Department of Peace Enforcement, to fire the first shot in what's looking like a civil war?"

"I can order you to do this," she said.

"I can have you confined to quarters for mental health reasons. Are you suggesting we bounce them with a nuke?"

"No, nudge them with our sub-light plasma shield."

Tirani stared at her. "Can we go back to nuking them?"

"It won't be a shooting war," she responded.

Dr. Tier was suggesting flying past *Challenger* and using their plasma shield to literally push them through the ion particle wall in the sub-light stream. This would fry their engines and require a manual restart.

"But it's probably the most dangerous thing I can imagine. Two giant spaceships getting within, like, seventy-five feet of one another. What if their plasma shield isn't calibrated right? We might both explode."

"I know Jephtah too. Her ship's tighter than yours, which is a feat, Captain."

"What's this gain us?" he asked. We've got *Defender* and *Tranquility* coming in on other streams. Maybe fifteen unharried hours over Highland?"

"It'll be the most important fifteen hours of our lives."

"By the angel, I knew you'd say something like that." A few crewmen looked over from an adjacent table. They'd heard bits and pieces of the conversation but pretended not to. "We have to do this now."

"Agreed," she said. "That's what I was hoping for."

SABATIN

The party made its way along the dusty path. They passed beaten-up vehicles used for target practice, some wheeled trucks and other hover jobs. The skeletons of apartment buildings and houses stood along the side of the route. A mailbox at the end of a driveway had its red flag up. Warner slapped away the hand of one of the men who was curious to what was inside. "Might be a bomb," he said matter-of-factly.

The dust covered the place like snow here, thick and almost in drifts. Maintenance machines cleared some places of the dust, but it fell again onto the cleared spots soon after. Michael had scanned the substance and advised that they shouldn't be breathing it in. It was almost lunar in its consistency and gritty. The men pulled air from small breathers around their necks and brushed it from each other's shoulders.

Back on the path, Izabeck spun about, taking in the view as he wrote frantically in his notebook. He was telling Cardinal Jacob every mundane detail now, every step and stubbed toe. *We saw a sign ahead in the path, the reason for our journey! Sabatin this way!*

Across the path a sign read *Sabatin Products* in a cursive arc of purple neon. Soft illumination came from streetlights in front of several squat buildings. They looked like boutique shops with large display windows showing off their goods. A fine dust landed here and was caught in the streetlights like falling snow.

Old-fashioned wrought iron benches lined the way and Gray noticed circular green wreaths hanging on the streetlights. The Phaelon spun about in the street, flame-throwers out and primed. The humans moved warily in front of the displays, covering each other, weapons hot. Behind them, Wrath calmly traveled the path, clearly used to this place.

In the first window, a suit of Sabatin armor was on display, bathed in tiny golden lights. Meta's sales tune played, here a holiday variation on the jingle from before. She appeared in the street from between two buildings and began her pitch. "Looking for that special gift? Currently in testing, Sabatin armor lives up to its pedigree. Exceptionally resilient. Can insert into atmosphere. Full package, holoprojector, kinetic pulse driver, plasma cannon, nuclear survivable, non-targetable. This rig is a thousand-to-one force multiplier!"

"We'll take all you've got," Gray said.

Izabeck floated to the back of the party and read the message from Cardinal Jacob that appeared in his notebook.

Samar1483: Gray's after things that are haram, Jude.

Jude? Cardinal Jacob had called Izabeck by his first name, like he knew him as a friend. He had never so much as said good morning to him back on Haven.

> *Izabeck613: He sees everything here as a means to an end, regardless of whether they are sinful or not.*
>
> *Samar1483: He'd take your life if you offered it. Without thinking. Would you send me your full writings now, please?*

Izabeck looked to Gray, spinning in the street and slapping others on the back, pointing to the displays and crowing. God was showing them new wonders around each turn and Gray was letting himself be awed. Izabeck saw a flawed instrument in him, unbearably human and feeling in the darkness for the means to God's ends. He embodied the rejection of sloth. He was a servant to the Almighty, always in action.

He considered this a stark contrast to Cardinal Jacob. He'd begun to dislike the cardinal very much. Burning and threatening him from afar was just part of it. Izabeck knew Cardinal Jacob thought him a fool; but he saw all the cards in the cardinal's hand. He knew that the cardinal's sole focus was on regaining the prime cardinalship and control over The Clergy's bank. He seemed almost casually content to have Izabeck die to achieve his personal goals.

Izabeck wondered how God looked down on Cardinal Jacob, if he judged him harshly. He scolded himself. *How dare I even…*but was Cardinal Jacob building God's kingdom? Were his eyes closed but for God's Word? Was he not resting while others carried his burden? He was deficient by all these measures. "Sloth," Izabeck said aloud to himself.

Izabeck looked into the display of the Sabatin rig. It was gross to him, fusing man and alien together into an abomination. Timberwolf had been disgusting in his eyes, willing to step into such a machine. He imagined thousands of men donning this armor under the Believer banner. For a moment, the absurd image of legions of them sitting in church in full Sabatin rigs came to his mind.

Izabeck shook that image, looking once more to Gray, arms folded and nodding approvingly at the next display. A verse slipped through his lips. "If you are in any doubt concerning what's sent down to you, truth has come to you from your Lord. Do not be a waverer." *I have to trust that God is moving through that man.*

He sent Cardinal Jacob something he had written a week before, the standard prattle about having closed eyes and surrendering one's will. *That'll hold him,* Izabeck thought.

Sergey sidled up next to Gray as he continued to admire the Sabatin rig. "Our lawyers won't let us say it's indestructible, but you might."

"Timberwolf gave us a thorough demo, thanks," Gray said with his hand to the glass.

Windwhistle was the first to look into the next display window. He jumped back and the others laughed at him. A non-living replica of a Sabatin such as Wrath lurked within, razor-tipped tongue exposed and claws inches from the glass. They admired the display for a few moments and when they moved to the next window jaws dropped. They beheld a replica of a massive Sabatin, four times the size of Wrath, a giant claw crushing the hood of a car. It had three massive horns on its head and limbs the size of tree trunks. The placard below read:

TRIKE: Combat Demolition

"If you get sick of bulldozers, I guess you can use these," Warner said.

Past the replicas were a series of video posters—*Sabatin in Action!* read a banner. Sabatin were barreling through hallways, tearing apart vehicles, routing a trench-line of men. The men's faces faded as they watched the displays. They looked like little boys.

"What, no sales pitch?" Gray said to Sergey.

"These don't need it," he said, without looking up from picking his nails.

Windwhistle shuffled anxiously. "Nothing live-fire here."

"Just wait," Sergey responded.

DIVERSION

Timberwolf dropped one foot in front of the other. He ran alongside what appeared to be tracks in the dust, the skeletons of the bone yard towering above him. Curious, he released micro-drones from his rig to scan the spaceship carcasses. There were 44,811 dead ships here from over seventy different species. Many were human, Glox, and Szykul, but there were also products of several other unknown intelligences.

He liked running in a rig and hadn't run very much in this Sabatin armor yet. It had suspension like a dream. It felt like he was trotting down the beach. He'd actually done that in basic once, ran along a beach in Costa Rica with his squad. He'd never gotten to do it again.

He tried to hack into Highland's security grid and was unable to access any remote ports. As he got farther into the facility, the effective radius of his micro-drones diminished. Beyond visual sensors, it was hard to know what was around the next bend. One thing he was sure of was that the Arnock had not yet landed. When they'd appeared before over Highland and destroyed the wrecker, Timberwolf had felt more than just Kizik. He'd felt thousands of them nearby, excited minds stretching out.

Timberwolf saw the train at the end of the railroad and slowed his run. He scanned forward and it didn't look like there was anyone lying in ambush. He approached the train and saw footprints in the dust, human and Phaelon and the long three-toed tracks of what must have been the Sabatin. The front light on the train illuminated another huge door; this one too left slightly ajar by Gray's party. A bar of soft golden light escaped.

He slipped in and found himself at the top of the marble stairs. He took in the view for a moment. It was like nothing he had ever seen, and Timberwolf had spent half his life fighting through some of the most amazing places in this part of the galaxy. He took in the perfect golden orb that hung near the ceiling maybe a half-mile up. He scanned it and did a triple check against his readings. The object at the top of the cavern was 96,000,000 miles away. It wasn't an artificial creation, but an actual star. The space-time continuum bent sharply up towards the ceiling and this sun existed in what could best be described as the localized event horizon of a singularity. Relatively, it had a radius of forty-five yards. In actuality, it was the size of Earth's sun.

The ability to create a marvel such as this stunned Timberwolf. *There is no way this place can fall to Gray or the Arnock.* He thought of Dr. Tier standing where he stood, looking at what he was looking at. What would she do with this kind of power? *Maybe no one should control the place. Maybe it should be destroyed.*

He descended the marble staircase. Meta appeared before him, her tune playing. "Hello, and welcome to the Highland Industrial Defense Park."

Timberwolf brushed through her and she flickered. He scanned over the landscape with his heads-up. About a mile away he saw the figures of Gray's party moving. They were approaching a garden along a curving stream. He could catch up to them in just a few minutes and end this, then turn his attention to the Arnock.

He went to take a step and received a frantic message from Achilles.

Achilles301: Timber! I need you to activate our security system. The Arnock are landing soon. I'll guide you to the controls.

Timberwolf4545: I've got Gray in my sights.

Achilles301: Please, they can't land!

Timberwolf looked through his heads-up to Gray's party. The Sabatin would give him trouble, but he felt he could still kill Gray within a few minutes, and then he'd double back and deal with the security system. He tried to leap forward, but the suit prohibited it. He pulled against the machinery, unable to get the servos to budge.

Timberwolf4545: You even need me?

Instead of responding, Achilles projected an arrow onto Timberwolf's heads-up. It spun as he swiveled his head, and he followed it to the side of the cavern. The arrow pulsed when it got him to where he needed to go, and Timberwolf scanned the dust. There was a hidden entranceway in the ground. He lifted it open with a latch and descended a narrow staircase.

At the bottom of the staircase, he illuminated a sign with an arrow that read *Infiltration Office.* Dull yellow lights in the drop ceiling flickered on down a long hallway and he began walking. Suddenly, a clear security partition fell in front of him and another behind, trapping him.

Timberwolf4545: Little help, Achilles?

FORENSIC

Shuttle Santa Maria—Over Highland

Salla fiddled with the thumb drive. It was the one she had pretended to throw out on The Outpost, filled with historical video clips from Timberwolf's helmet cam. She had been trying to restore them using terminals on *Santa Maria*, but hadn't had any success.

Achilles scanned the scopes obsessively, looking for the Arnock ship. He should have been able to find it, since he built it and knew exactly how the cloak worked. They must have adjusted it though. *That voids their warranty!* Shaking his head, he decided to take a break.

"What's that?" Achilles motioned to the thumb drive Salla held.

"They were videos of Timberwolf, but they deleted themselves." She smirked and bent the thumb drive, almost breaking it. Achilles took it from her and scanned it quickly with his smart-device.

"There, they're restored." He handed it back to her. "It's from The Clergy, by the way. They're trying to play in this game, for whatever reason." Achilles went back up to the controls, and started to obsessively scan the surrounding space again.

She raised her eyebrow and stuck the thumb drive into her smart-device. She found that the files were clearly labeled now with things such as: *Cairo Sunrise, Deminar Insurgency,* and *Purity Hospital*. She continued to flip through a preview of each file before flipping back. *Purity Hospital* was a mental institution.

Starting the video, she didn't get what she expected.

Timberwolf was laughing and speaking to someone that he knew well. He had a bandage over one eye and the signature purple blotches from vacuum exposure on his cheeks. He was speaking to Gray. The camera panned and they sat across the table from one another. Timberwolf wiped his eye from laughing so hard. They were clearly reminiscing about something and Gray seemed extremely glad to see him. Timberwolf's laughter faltered to that of breaths of relief.

"You okay?" Gray asked him.

"Yeah, yeah." He nodded.

But he clearly wasn't. He shivered and rubbed his arms. "I'm fine."

The video jumped to Gray sitting in a separate room behind a desk. His name appeared on the screen below him. "Colonel Velez has no recollection of the events from Project Jackhammer. The encounter with the Arnock, Kizik, on RP-10-10 has been suppressed. He currently believes his lifter went down before they got to the target. He knows he's the sole survivor. He's been physically injured so as to approximate what he would have received in a lifter crash. He's in stable condition and mobile. It's been two days since Jackhammer."

The video panned. Sitting next to Gray was the woman Salla had seen in one of the first videos she had watched back on The Outpost. The name *Dr. Thea Tier* appeared on the screen under her for a few moments before fading away. "We will be awakening the memories starting tonight. He seems to realize there's something not right. We have to act now before the Arnock presence begins to manifest itself without any context. Colonel Velez is an extremely strong mental specimen, but we're at a critical time. If this fails, we move directly to termination."

"He'll be fine," Gray said, looking sideways at her. "I have the highest confidence in our specimen."

The video jumped and Timberwolf sat in a hospital room at the edge of a bed. The room was dark, save for a small light from a desk. This feed was from a surveillance camera. It zoomed in on his face, focusing. He blinked, long and hard again and again, like he was trying to clear something from his mind. Every time he opened his eyes again, there was something less on his face, a piece of him slipping away. His mouth started to drop open in realization and Dr. Tier's voice was heard. "Timberwolf? Timberwolf? Colonel Velez? Do you understand what is happening to you?"

"No. What is this?" he begged.

"It's Kizik. On RP-10-10 you were exposed to the Arnock master."

"That's fatal!"

"What's that feel like?" she asked.

"I don't know. It's like I have a passenger. It's male. He's small. He's taking up more and more room. He's fucking angry."

"I want you to…"

Achilles snatched the smart-device from Salla's hand, his sudden action jarring her. "I have to kill Timberwolf, right now!"

THE SACRAMENT

Past the Sabatin display, the party walked along a stream. The sun shined brightly and cedar trees threw long shadows. The dust was completely cleared away here and they walked over a real dirt path. The soil was earth-like in its consistency, warm and rich brown. Warner bent down and put a generous handful in his pocket. In the stream, frogs leaped from lily pads and small water snakes slithered along the bank. The bottom of the stream was cleared of the dust in stripes, and tiny spherical machines made their way across the streambed, consuming the stuff.

Warner had Jan, a steady man, take point. He wasn't tentative and moved ahead of the group on alert for surprises. The stream tapered off and over the path was another neon sign. This one read, *Property Defense*. Beyond it was a garden, and exotic flowers stood almost as tall as a man. Droma reached in and picked one, taking in its rich aroma, her back scales fluttering. They passed a pool filled with Koi and Meta's tune played again. She appeared in front of them, inhaling the aroma from a flower just as Droma did. "Don't you want to protect your most personal places? Your getaway for reflection may be where you're most vulnerable."

She disappeared and the party continued again, moving alertly and watching for threats, Jan leading them. A flower tracked the group, turning its face as they walked past. Unknown to them, other flowers began tracking them as well, slowly rotating and opening their petals. Jan sensed something was odd in the garden, but he wasn't sure what. A flower in a clump of others seemed to sneeze and something grazed his wrist above his glove. He looked down and saw tiny flechettes stuck into his wrist gauntlet.

"Just a scratch. Move on," Warner said. The party continued walking, Jan still on point. As the garden thinned out, Gray noticed red spots in the dust.

"Jan!" Gray called. The man turned. Blood oozed from under his armor. He pulled off his glove and found his wrist to be a swollen, red mess. Jan fell to his knees and Michael cracked open his gauntlet. His arm was open past the elbow, gushing blood.

"Am I dying?" Jan breathed hard, his skin suddenly pale.

"You're not," Gray said. "Tourniquet!" he whispered sharply to Michael.

Jan was losing consciousness as Gray tightened the tourniquet around his arm. A red puddle underneath him grew wider and deeper. Warner jammed a med-kit syringe full of nano-menders into the man's leg, but it was too late.

"Come on son!" Gray demanded.

All at once the wound opened up almost to Jan's shoulder and blood gushed out. He slumped over dead in a ragged, red heap. Gray held the dead young man for a moment and then laid him gently on the ground. The others gathered around, the Phaelon hanging back. Sergey disappeared behind the crowd, away from Gray's attention. But Gray knew this wasn't time for rage, even as a man lay dead. He'd settle accounts with Sergey later, but this moment was important.

I can use this.

Gray dipped a finger into Jan's blood. He drew the mark of the Believer on his own forehead.

"Each of you," he said calmly. The men formed a line, each dipping a finger in the blood and tracing the Believer symbol onto their foreheads. When they were done, they stood in a circle, Michael and Warner joining them.

"That was a sacrament," Gray began, his head down. "God loves our sacrifice. God loves that boy; Januarius Patrick DiPaolo Revelata was his full name. A hell of a name. A pure name. Chosen by his family. He was the first to die in this new part of heaven that we're taking in the name of God." He scanned each of their eyes. "So he's still here with us. Walking with us. There's no difference between the living and the dead here."

"We sing for him?" Michael asked.

"No. Why? He's still with us," Gray responded warmly. "He's just around the next bend." Gray waved off into the distance, to the way they would be going next. "Just off that way."

Without a word, they all began to walk again, eager to travel the way Gray had indicated. One of the men knelt beside Jan. Sergey tapped his shoulder. "Might not want to touch the body. Those anti-coagulants will kill you and he's got some stuck in his glove. Unless you want to, you know, see heaven up-close or whatever it was he said."

The man got up and began walking with the others. Michael and Warner fell in beside each other a moment. "That sound crazy to you?" Warner asked.

"Depends on if he meant any of it," Michael responded. The truth was Michael had no idea. Gray could still be play-acting for the faithful, in order to drive this drama to the result he wanted. "I think we're looking at a fifty-fifty bullshit ratio here."

"I don't know. I sort of like it," Warner said in his creaky old voice. "I want to live forever."

In front of them, Sergey stood in the path in front of a sensor. He lifted his arm up and down, like he was adjusting something unseen. "What the hell are you doing?"

Sergey wiped sweat from his brow. "It's hot in here. I'm turning down the sun." He snapped his fingers and almost at once, a wall of gray clouds collected in front of the sun and the place suddenly darkened. The soft golden light was gone and the long shadows in the cavern disappeared, replaced by the diffused light of the overcast.

Michael stuck his rifle to Sergey's back. "You. Move."

A bitter cold wind came through the place and Sergey shivered. "I like it cold."

TOM AND JERRY

"Why are we killing Timberwolf?" Salla asked Achilles. He moved about the cabin of *Santa Maria* in a flash. He went from screen to screen, shutting them down. "What are you doing?" she asked.

"Removing distractions." He settled down into the command chair and breathed. "I have to pick either Tom or Jerry."

She had no idea what he was talking about.

"Which one kills him?" Achilles asked himself. "Tom. He's the deadly one. Jerry is something else."

"Okay—what's going on?" she asked. He tried to explain but couldn't breathe. "Please calm down," she said, putting her hand on his shoulder.

"He's under The Catalog. Near the Infiltration Office. Security gates are falling."

"And this means?"

"Means he's trying to shut down Highland's planetary defense."

"Shit," she said.

"Kizik is making him do it. Must be. Tom is behind his left ear. It's less powerful than a quarter stick of dynamite, but in his helmet it'll kill him instantly."

"What's Jerry do?"

"Jerry might diffuse Kizik. Maybe for a little while, but forget it. I need you to kill him. Press this button."

"Why me?" Salla asked.

"I trust you. I don't trust myself."

He handed her a tablet computer. A cartoon cat and mouse with the names Tom and Jerry showed on the screen. Her finger hovered over the choices for a moment. She picked Jerry.

"What the hell did you do?!" Achilles gasped.

"This gives him a chance. We can pick Tom later."

"No, we can't! They're physical components on the same fuse!"

Salla slumped back into her chair. "That's how you built the kill switch?"

"That rig is designed to be tamper-proof. I set that up when I rebuilt it. If I was right in front of him, I might be able to do more, but that's it."

"Jesus! Never ask me to kill anyone again!"

"I thought you'd do it."

"Well, think again."

They sat in silence a moment.

"What's Jerry get us?" she asked.

"Depends on how strong Timberwolf is."

COPACETIC

No one had sat at the computer terminal in the Infiltration Office for fifty years. A crack went down the screen where a maintenance machine had bumped into it a decade ago. Lights flickered on and a coffee machine sprang to life. A yellow light spun and a ping repeated out over the intercom. But there was no one in there to pay it any mind or spring into action. There didn't need to be.

The Dacha brothers hadn't replaced employees at Highland when they died, and only one employee had ever been allowed to leave. When they expired one after the other, their duties were taken up by machines. It wasn't that machines did the jobs better than the engineers, the security personnel, and the maintenance staff; it was that the Dachas simply didn't want to deal with people. They didn't want someone deciding they'd make a fortune and betray the location of Highland to the highest bidder. The last living employee of Highland had died thirty-six years before at the age of 117. It was just about when they'd stopped taking prospective buyers through The Catalog. The products spoke for themselves anyway.

The Infiltration Office was part of the "backstage" of Highland, a war room where dozens of analysts and military types had scanned space for light years around, making sure nothing got close. They monitored the security rings and authorized the coming and going of Highland freighters. When a ship got close, by either intent or accident, they disabled it and hauled it to the bone yard. Sometimes the crews were incapacitated and they'd wake up in lifeboats halfway across the sector. Sometimes they were disposed of. On rare occasions, they became employees.

What there had never been was an infiltration. No visitors had ever set foot on Highland without being brought there through circuitous routes on secure Highland transports. That streak was broken. There were uninvited guests now. On the monitor with the cracked screen, the panic word Sergey had said to Meta blinked.

Eight thousand miles away, a funnel of nano-machines came to life in the cloud layer. Billions of them began spinning in unison, shaping the vapor into a configuration just like The Eye. The funnel extended down towards the surface, clearing the space over a sharply angled mountain. A long crack started at the top of the precipice and reached down as the huge machine inside rumbled to life. Hunks of rock fell away, like crumbling drywall, as the contrivances groaned and shook within.

A shiny black form began to appear underneath, like a gigantic bullet. The vibration of the mechanism pushed the rocks from the mountain away, creating a circular radius of debris. Just a few minutes after it started rumbling, The Bullet went silent and sat there on the barren plain, seemingly inert, puffs of steam and gas escaping through the seams in its cover.

Deep inside The Bullet, an eye the size of a dinner plate opened, then another, then hundreds more. The machine would wait there until a target came into range above.

In The Catalog, Michael still held the weapon to Sergey's back. They passed through more gardens and Koi ponds, Sergey looking into each one. "Your goddamned fish are fine!" Michael snapped at him.

"The dust clogs their gills," he said innocently. Michael rolled his eyes. In the instant that he looked away, Sergey saw what he had been looking for. The image of Meta appeared in a pond for just a second, half obscured by a lily pad. She mouthed the word *copacetic* and winked before disappearing. "You're right. They'll be fine!" Sergey said to Michael.

PASSENGER

The last thing Timberwolf remembered were the security gates falling in front of him; transparent, six-inch-thick, glasstisteel barriers. When he looked back again, a series of them thirty feet apart were melted into oozing piles in the hall. His suit was hot. He'd taken his chemical laser way into the red, but he didn't remember doing it. *Jesus, I have to get out of here*, he thought. He searched for the presence, for Kizik driving his actions. He hadn't felt the Arnock coming, but he'd clearly taken control of him.

He stood in front of a non-descript door. Above it the sign read *Infiltration Office*. He turned to go, but instead found himself entering. He was suddenly a passenger, sitting in the back seat while someone who looked like him drove. In the room a dozen unoccupied chairs sat in a row in front of terminals. He fought his footsteps, but he moved forward; the servos in the rig seeming to whir unbearably loud. He focused on everything at once, seeing every corner of the room and every color and shadow. He waited for Achilles to kill him, certain he was seeing all of this. If he was wavering, he knew Salla was probably angling to push the button.

He heard a repeating ping coming from a terminal at the end of the row, too loud and too clear. It was unbearable and he felt the sound ringing through him like he was a bell. He made his way towards it, unable not to. The word *COPACETIC* blinked again and again on the screen. He had never experienced anything like this before, at least not consciously. Whenever Kizik had taken control of his survivor instincts, he never remembered anything, just the end, standing over a dozen beaten men with bloodied knuckles. But now he was split in two, half of him doing Kizik's bidding, the other half desperately trying to resist.

Instead of text on his heads-up, a voice he knew couldn't be Achilles came to him. "Manually activate it." The voice sounded like it came from a drainpipe. "There's a button."

Timberwolf stared at the blinking red button next to the terminal. His hand wavered over it. He seemed to be standing beside himself and he looked over at his separate person. "Achilles, where are you?" he asked.

It was a long time before "Achilles" responded. When he did, his voice oscillated up and down the octave. "I'm back up on the shuttle."

"Does Salla miss me?"

"Of course she does. Please hurry," the voice responded. Timberwolf pulled his hand back from over the button, sure he was talking to the spider now.

He felt his other self shrug. "So things aren't copacetic, right?" Timberwolf asked.

"No, things are not copacetic," the voice responded. "Did you press the button?"

He clearly sensed Kizik now. The presence stared at him, seemingly from far away and peering around a corner. The more important thing was that Kizik didn't know Timberwolf could see him.

"Of course I did," he responded. "I pressed the button."

"Good," the voice came back with ultimate relief. Kizik disappeared, drawing away suddenly. Then something exploded inside Timberwolf's helmet and he slumped over. It was Jerry shorting out. It was the third time he'd been knocked unconscious that week. *That's a personal best*, he thought before passing out.

THE BUMP

D.P.E. Archangel—Twenty-two Hours Out from Highland

Challenger was six thousand miles ahead of *Archangel* in the sub-light stream. That was bumper-to-bumper and way closer than the typical million-mile distance kept between ships. *Challenger* still had no idea they were back there and, unless someone on *Archangel* contacted them, they wouldn't know they were there. Dr. Tier looked over at Captain Tirani, standing at his station on the bridge. He was out of his chair and flipping through 3-D displays projected in front of him. She could tell he was nervous as hell, and people like him didn't get nervous.

"Fifty-one-fifty miles," a crewman called out as they inched closer to *Challenger*. Tirani and everyone else aboard had every reason to be on edge. What they were about to do was only slightly less dangerous than ramming an enemy ship. Dr. Tier felt the tension as well. She had taken Terecine, one of her special blue pills, a few minutes before but it hadn't helped. She was high as a kite, but her stress remained. The blackness of sub-light was still absolute in front of them. When they got within a hundred miles, they'd start to see the plasma glow from *Challenger's* shield, but there was nothing now, just the flawless void.

"We're feeling some wake," Tirani advised. The ship rumbled as it passed through some of the non-visible plasma thrown off from *Challenger*. He looked back at her and made a face that asked, *You really want to do this?* She smiled back at him grimly.

Dr. Tier had shut off all sub-light communications an hour before in case someone panicked and tried to warn *Challenger*. She scanned her smart-device for any attempts getting blocked. Nothing so far. Everyone was behaving. *Wait, what the hell is that?* Her eyes saw something impossible. Just a second before a message had actually left the ship through a private channel outside of the network.

"Hold our position, Les!" she told Captain Tirani. She was up and out of her chair and off the bridge in an instant. "Capote, meet me on level three. Guest quarters. Bring Gordon and Roberts," she barked into her smart-device.

Cardinal Jacob's personal guards stood outside of his quarters. Coming from both ends of the hallway, Capote and his team appeared, rifles raised. "This is not a friendly visit," Capote said to Cardinal Jacob's men, taking them by surprise. The two men moved aside and Dr. Tier banged on the door. There was no response from within and she banged again, louder and longer. Looking down at her device, she saw another message leave the ship.

"Cardinal! Open the fucking door!" she demanded. There was a shuffling within, and the door slid open a crack. Capote horsed it ajar as Gordon burst in, rifle trained on the cardinal.

"Thea?" Cardinal Jacob said, as Dr. Tier entered. She snatched the smart-device from his hands. He had just pressed send.

"What the fuck are you doing?" she said, her head spinning from the Terecine, but her speech clear.

Cardinal Jacob took a measure of the room and his confusion turned to indignation. He pushed aside the barrel of Gordon's rifle, hot to the touch and ready to fire. "Do you recall our deal?" Cardinal Jacob said to Dr. Tier, reminding her of his clumsy threat to expose her identity and put her daughter in danger.

"I am prepared to shoot you now." She pulled a small pistol from her jacket. It was barely the size of her hand, but powerful enough to put a hole in the side of the ship.

"Why, my child? What brings you such distress?" he asked through clenched teeth, his arms open.

"Are you in contact with the *Challenger*?" she asked.

"I believe you are mistaken. I am in touch with my man on Gray's foolish crusade."

"You're communicating with Jude Izabeck on Highland?" This was perhaps worse than contacting *Challenger* would have been. Dr. Tier's anger swelled. "Somehow you're getting through the blackout there and getting around our block network here."

"Of course, we can do many things you can't. My scientists are wealthy with God's gift of creativity."

"So you've been in touch with someone on Highland, and you have not told me?"

"Why would I? Our deal was about communicating with Timberwolf. You've already paid for that."

"Dearly, Cardinal, dearly."

She went through the sent messages on his device. All went to Izabeck613. There was nothing to indicate he'd contacted *Challenger*. She didn't have time for this. She knew that if they were going to bump *Challenger*, it had to be done now. If they stayed this close for too long, *Challenger's* plasma wake would knock them from the sub-light stream.

She called up to the bridge. "Captain Tirani, do it. Bump them."

"Got it," the captain responded, relieved that there was at least some course of action to take.

"Ask them to leave." The cardinal indicated Gordon and Capote and he sat calmly in a chair. "Please, Thea." Dr. Tier shooed the men out, but wouldn't sit when Cardinal Jacob beckoned. "I can make this up to you. Offer a gift."

"A gift would be you finding a lifeboat."

"I can do better than that," he said, tenting his fingers. She asked for more with a raise of her brow. "My dear friend Jude Izabeck carries a message for Bishop Emmanuel Gray."

"What would that message be?"

He spread out his fingers and puffed out his cheeks, pantomiming an explosion. "Izabeck is a nuke. I hold the trigger."

She wavered a moment, suddenly wanting nothing but to sleep. "What?" she finally asked.

"Yes, there's a weapon inside his forearm. Small, but a really lovely design."

Dr. Tier did take a seat. "I want you to deactivate it. Now."

"Why, child? Think of this. I assure you I would not use it without your consent. And who is to say that Gray might just succeed enough that we need to cut our losses?"

"This is insanity, Cardinal." Her eyes swam and she tried to keep her head level.

"The stress of this job gets to you. I can't imagine it. I understand you're on formidable medication." She stared at him icily. He knew. Somehow he knew she used Terecine to stay level. "Don't worry. Your secret is safe with me for now."

She realized she was pointing her pistol at Cardinal Jacob again. "This needs to come to an end, right now."

"No, not really. You see, if this comes to an end, it's just the beginning. If I die right now, the bomb goes off. And messages go out to all the people that you've been discourteous to."

She was enraged. "I told you not to tread that way!"

He came close to laughing at her. "Since our last discussion, I've activated some protective measures. Let's call it posthumous insurance."

She wondered if he was lying, if it was some sort of game he was playing. She thought about the possibility of beating him into a coma. Would that trigger his *protective measures*? There must be some sort of life monitor buried deep within him, she assumed, like his smart-device, and that it would be sophisticated and powerful enough to get a signal out. She considered just blasting his head off and calling his bluff. Before she could consider it further, a call came from the bridge.

"We're about to do it," Captain Tirani advised.

"Coming up, Les," she responded. She stood and backed out of the room. "I keep this." She slipped his smart-device into her pocket. Outside, she ordered Cardinal Jacob's men confined and posted Capote in front of the door. "That door is to stay open at all times," she told him.

"Rest easy, Thea," Cardinal Jacob said as she backed away, his face glowing with a warm smile.

Back on the bridge, the plasma corona of *Challenger* filled the view screen. It was like they were trailing a smoke ring. *Archangel* rumbled, lurching ferociously. They were at seventy-two miles now and inching closer every instant. The pilot was waiting for a moment when they were lined up enough to give the sub-light maneuvering thrusters a boost. They'd shoot past *Challenger* from this distance in a split second, brush up against their plasma shields, knock them from the stream, and short out their sub-light drive.

The pilot was good, a young woman named Iza, who had a steely focus, but couldn't have been more than twenty-six years old. Dr. Tier gripped the armrests on her chair. "Thirty-eight miles," a crewman announced. The ship took three hard bounces through the plasma wake. After a brief pause there were three more. Iza had the pattern and during the next pause, she punched it.

In the view screen, they saw the hulk of *Challenger* right below them for just a flash as they brushed plasma shields. Then they felt it. A static charge went through *Archangel* and Captain Tirani threw down his headset from the shock. The starboard sub-light maneuvering thrusters failed and *Archangel's* momentum spun them around. "Plasma shield down!" a crewman announced.

Out the view screen, they were seeing where they'd just been. *Challenger* was gone and instead of the pure blackness of the frontal view, there was a rainbow mishmash of every color that spiraled towards a small white point. They continued to spin and saw the sides of the sub-light stream now, the misty dusk of golden brown that bled into black. "We're getting sub-light particle damage," a crewman said. Dr. Tier noticed the tick-tick sound, like a light rain falling on the ship. These were tiny particles of dust and gas impacting directly on *Archangel*. Without a plasma shield, these impacts would cause a hull breach and kill them in less than a minute.

"Do we drop out of the stream?" Captain Tirani asked.

"Hold!" Iza said. She had the ship stabilized and the maneuvering thrusters working again. Dr. Tier closed her eyes and thought about her daughter, thought about her studying on the lawn at Oxford. The day before, Camille had sent her a picture of her and her boyfriend. She hadn't had time to respond.

The soft fuzz of the plasma shields came up again without any fanfare and crewmen called out statuses from around the bridge.

"Shields green."

"Structural integrity green."

"Armory green."

"Propulsion green."

"Readings on *Challenger*. She's dropped out of sub-light and life-support systems are green."

Tirani finally breathed and turned back to Dr. Tier, his face blank and drained of its color. He shifted his eyes to the door and indicated silently that he wanted her off his bridge, and right now. She looked around and a dozen other sets of eyes gave her the same message. Biting her lip, she smoothed her jacket and departed.

RECIEPT

Conrad was waiting for Dr. Tier by her office. She brushed him aside without a word and sat behind closed doors. She knew she should do nothing, collect herself and consider the hand she held now, but she was carrying too much stress to be inactive.

She sat at her desk and wrote a message to Jude Izabeck, using the Cardinal's device.

> *Samar1483: I hope all is well.*
>
> *Izabeck613: A man has died here on Highland.*
>
> *Samar1483: I'll pray for him and for you. Please, tell me everything.*
>
> *Izabeck613: Of course.*
>
> *Samar1483: And Timberwolf Velez?*
>
> *Izabeck613: Dead.*

Dr. Tier soaked that in for a moment. She'd feel the loss of him later. Now she reconfigured her tactical options. She'd burned him before, but she had been prepared to make it up. She thought about pressing Izabeck and verifying that Timberwolf was in fact dead, but reconsidered as she was playing the part of Cardinal Jacob.

Samar1483: I'll pray for him as well. Is your message still operational?

Izabeck613: Yes. It's still primed. I'm waiting for you to activate the trigger.

Samar1483: Thank you. Please stay alert.

She ended the conversation and considered the transactions she'd just made. She'd bought fifteen hours over Highland, but at the expense of Captain Tirani's trust. She also had Cardinal Jacob's smart-device, but now the Cardinal, crafty and powerful, surely plotted against her. She'd paid for a lot today and had gotten a lot in return. She wondered if she'd be able to take any of it back.

TIME TO LAND

Kizik came down from the hammock he had spun for himself over the bridge of the Arnock troop carrier ship. He was relieved that he had been able to manipulate Timberwolf into turning off the security system. Timberwolf's mind was so tough; interacting with him was usually like climbing through valleys and mountains.

The thought of climbing up a mountain made him think of home, of going up to the surface and ascending the Twilight Ridge. He longed to take the pilgrimage up the strip between light and dark. He hadn't done that in fifty years, but he longed to—to see the blazing desert that always faced the sun to the left and the windswept badlands to the right.

Doing this gets us back to home, he thought, but he doubted he would ever get back even if he survived this. The other masters were closing themselves to him. They communicated with him, but hid their deep mind and thoughts. He knew they were scared as hell of him and what he had become. There would be no place for him back on Arnock Prime when this was over. He would be too strong a reminder of these dark times. When passing a young navigator in a corridor before, the girl could not control her thoughts. The word farhallen had slipped out. *Farhallen…* monster. *Creature of the badlands. Beast of the wind.*

He heard the human yelling again and skittered down a corridor. Timberwolf's brother Relaund, still in his hospital bed, was in an alcove. Lufare, a master that was the Arnock equivalent of a doctor, was trying to move him onto a flat slate so she could examine him. Kizik had insisted that he be treated as a guest and not be chemically or mentally subdued, but of course finding himself on an Arnock ship was terrifying to him. Relaund swore and screamed as Lufare worked on him. "Kill me, you spiders. Kill me," echoed out to Kizik.

Relaund writhed as much as he could in his wrecked body, but when he saw Kizik appear in the alcove he was silent a moment, eyes wide. Lufare took the opportunity to gently move him to the slate. Small machines began to float about him, taking his readings. Glowing restraints came out of the slate and secured his arms and legs.

You are paralyzed, Kizik thought to him.

"No shit!" Relaund said aloud.

Your fifth vertebra is severed.

"That's what they told me. You're going to experiment on me? Aren't you? Take me apart bit by bit. I get it. I'm going to die slowly."

We will be exploring you.

"I've had enough. Just do your worst. My brother won't let this go."

Kizik hovered closely. *After the landing on Highland, we'll talk again.*

Kizik backed out of the room, watching as Relaund writhed and yelled some more. "We'll kill every one of you! Every last one!"

The fifth vertebra, Kizik thought to himself as he traveled back up to the bridge. *The spine of a human, the twilight ridge, splits the sun and the wind.*

Kizik scolded himself a moment. Dealing with Relaund was a distraction. The Highland security net was down. He entered the bridge and the whole crew turned to him. He reached out to all of the Arnock with him over Highland— masters, warriors, navigators, medics, sentries, and more. *It's time to land.*

RESIDUE

D.P.E. Archangel —Nineteen Hours Out from Highland

Dr. Tier hadn't left her quarters since they'd bumped *Challenger*. Communications were coming out of Tach-One in a deluge. Conrad and the other analysts were monitoring them and were to report any change of a tactical nature— more ships dispatched to Highland or Assault Corps moves against Department of Peace Enforcement facilities. So far there had been nothing above and beyond the current levels of folly. Secretary Bozeman had contacted her and she had ignored him. He obviously knew that she had bumped *Challenger*. There wasn't anything they could have said to each other that wouldn't have amounted to bluster.

She hadn't touched the Terecine since her conversation with Cardinal Jacob. She felt numb and small and exhausted. With Timberwolf presumably dead, she didn't even have a half-friend in a position to do anything on Highland. *What the hell is my plan?* she asked herself. They were streaking towards Highland and had bumped *Challenger*, but for what? So they could have themselves a last stand against half the Assault Corps fleet? So she could order Izabeck to blow the place to hell? She put her head in her hands. There was a knock on the door, even though she had insisted on not being disturbed.

"Come in," she said.

It was a young officer from the bridge, one who had future command ranks written all over her. "Sorry to disturb, Doctor. I need your thumb print." She handed Dr. Tier a tablet computer. It was the official authorization to bump *Challenger*. She pressed her thumb where indicated and the officer left. Less than a minute later, without knocking, Captain Tirani entered.

"We need to talk, Doctor Tier." There were two security personnel with him. No one she knew. Capote, Gordon, and Roberts were nowhere to be found.

She leaned back in her chair. "What is it, Les?" She was friendly with Captain Tirani and they typically addressed each other by first name. His face stayed a mask.

"Doctor, you have one order I am going to let you give and that's to name your replacement."

"Excuse me?"

"When you ordered the bump, you were high as a kite. You're on enough Terecine to knock a Phaelon into next week!"

She took a measure of the situation. Cardinal Jacob had told him. That was obvious. *But how did Les know for sure?* she thought. Terecine didn't show up in blood tests.

"I suggest you back out of here, Captain. There is no way you can prove these allegations and frankly, Les, they are reckless. If you used that thumb print to scan my blood, you've found nothing."

"There's residue on your damned fingers! We found it on the arm of the chair you were gripping on my bridge. We matched your prints just now to be a hundred percent certain. You put this ship and crew in incredible danger while not in control of your basic faculties." He paced. "You had us commit an act of aggression against an Assault Corps ship that I and my command staff could be executed for!"

"Les, I want you to calm down."

"No goddamned way am I calming down, Doctor. I'm dropping us out of the stream now. This *adventure* is over."

Her lip quivered with anger. She was burned for now but had one card left to play. "No, you're not. You said I could name a replacement. Conrad Stonefield is in charge. I'll give him all my files."

He bent over her desk. "A fucking joke, Thea?"

"Not at all," she responded.

"I want you to call this all off, not name some junior assistant as your replacement! You have eight other analysts on board—McCord, Cheng, Bloch to name a few."

"That's my one order."

"Is it because he'll do exactly as you would? Your lap boy to see this through?"

She stood, finally showing her anger. "Jacob will have nothing on him! He's under his radar!" she snapped. "And he might have the clarity to get us all the hell out of this."

"I picked the wrong goddamned team," Captain Tirani said. "I'll give you fifteen minutes with him to hand things off. Then you're confined to quarters."

Dr. Tier nodded. She could tell in his eyes that Captain Tirani felt sorry for her, that he felt her a thing to be pitied. Les was a good man and being held in contempt by him was almost unbearable. He turned to go.

"Here." She threw her bottle of Terecine to him and he caught it, the tablets rattling within. Without another word he turned and left.

THE BULLET

On *Santa Maria*, Achilles had Salla helping him scan for the Arnock. The Bullet, sitting on the plain eight thousand miles from Highland, was still humming and poised to launch. They continued to scan more space, looking for the elusive cloak signatures. "It's out there. I know it still is."

He grinned. "The Arnock think it's safe to land and they will be very surprised." He rolled a cigarette of sweet tobacco on the dashboard, unmistakably satisfied. "Thanks for not killing Timberwolf," he said.

"You're welcome," she answered. "Block eighty-two, four thousand cubic miles. Nothing. I can't see them."

He lit up his cigarette. It smelled like cranberries and cinnamon. She took in the pleasing smoke. "We could have left, but this is going to be a hell of a show," he said.

"Wait, there's something. It's a big signature. Eighty miles up. Sixty miles spinward. Uncloaked and visible." She projected the readings up to a hologram in the cabin. The image of the Arnock snail-shell-shaped command ship appeared in crystal clear definition. It was gorgeous, truly a beautiful vessel.

"I loved that ship. Zoom in." At his voice, their view moved in closer to the hull of the ship. "Infrared." When the infrared filter came up, it was small but clear as day. *Alona* was written on the side of the vessel. "That was my mom's name. She was Alona Dacha. Four-foot-ten beauty queen of Stalingrad."

"What's happening?" Salla asked, noticing something on the readings coming up through the atmosphere from Highland. A spiral was appearing in the cloud layer, like the top of a funnel, the vapor sweeping away. Moving thousands of miles an hour, a black object rose out of the opening. Salla moved to the window, and she could see a black speck rising, growing larger. It swept towards them, maneuvering thrusters puffing and slowing it, passing within just a few miles. It was the giant, black, bullet-shaped object that had shaken itself free of the mountain below. After a minute or two of staring at it, Salla realized that Achilles was following The Bullet now as it headed towards the Arnock ship. "We're chasing it?"

"I have to see this," Achilles replied, almost giddy. "We'll stay a safe distance!"

The cover of The Bullet began to drop away, long strips coming off like the peel of a banana. Soon a tightly wound bundle of *something* was left atop the booster. It looked like a haphazard machine, thrown together—massive, black, shiny, ribbed tubes and levers. Then it started writhing. Salla turned her attention to the holographic projection again and zoomed in on what was happening. Individual pieces of the bundle were coming free. "Oh my god, they're alive!"

She zoomed in closer on one of them and saw a demonic face on a creature the size of a bus. Three horns came through an armored helmet. A breather the size of a vending machine covered its mouth. Massive front and back limbs were tipped with powerful and unforgiving claws. Small puffs of maneuvering thrust came from pods on its hips.

"They're Sabatin. New model. Trikes. For demolition. What do you think of that?"

"I've got nothing," she said, astonished by the scene.

The horde continued to unravel; over a hundred Trikes leaping from The Bullet now, directly onto the Arnock command ship. Red lights blinked up and down the length of the vessel as it rotated to meet the threat. White lasers lashed out from it, but there were just too many attackers. A first wave of a dozen Trikes reached the Arnock ship, smashing their armored heads against the hull like wrecking balls. They tore through the cover easily and poured inside. Salla zoomed in again and saw a Trike reach into the superstructure and begin to hurl armfuls of struggling Arnock into space.

Suddenly, Salla and Achilles felt it in their heads. The mental scream of the Arnock, the sound of hundreds of them dying at once. Salla winced and held her head. Within just a few moments though, the agony diminished to a low a murmur as the slaughter tapered off. The Trikes were cracking the ship in two now, tearing off the external skin, climbing atop each other and bracing themselves against the spine of the superstructure. Power cells popped and exploded throughout the ship as a few last laser blasts and missiles lashed out meekly.

The massive command ship cracked in two and quickly went dark, its sharp, functional innards spilling out from the two halves. Amongst the flotsam, some Arnock had gotten into pressurized escape suits and looked like they were running in place against the vacuum of space. Salla and Achilles felt their lives go out one by one as Trikes sliced through them almost playfully, batting them back and forth to each other like spirited guard dogs.

Achilles smiled. "Jerry worked!" he bellowed. "They never saw that coming. God, Timberwolf. I owe him one!"

A stray power cell exploded a little too close for comfort and Achilles slipped into the pilot's chair, backing *Santa Maria* away quickly. "Our scopes are out," Salla said. "That power surge blinded us." The thrusters stuttered as they backed away.

"Power will come back," Achilles said with a hint of anxiety in his voice. "What the hell?" Something outside alarmed him. Salla saw it too.

"Are they coming for us?"

Arranging themselves into waves, the Trikes were done with the Arnock command ship and were now headed towards *Santa Maria*. Dozens of them were just a thousand yards away now. "This thing have guns?" Salla asked.

"You don't want to draw their attention!" Achilles tried a manual reboot of the scopes and the thrusters, but it didn't work. They were still blind and backing away on a fraction of their power. The first of the Trikes scrambled by them, their wide, evil faces contorted with mission. "There's something…" Achilles managed to spin the ship to face the way they were traveling by venting puffs of atmosphere from the cabin. The turn was agonizingly slow and then they finally saw it.

"Oh, we're dead!" Salla gasped.

Before them, at just a few thousand yards, was the second Arnock ship—the troop carrier that, up to that point, had not revealed itself and that they didn't know about—the one with Kizik aboard. Spindly and studded with cylindrical landing craft, the vessel was almost done coming out of its cloak. They heard claws on the roof as a Trike used *Santa Maria* as a springboard.

"Two ships? We didn't see the other. They can't land. Not the Arnock!" Achilles panicked, kicking the control panel in an effort to scold the thrusters back to life.

The assault on the troop carrier was a scene of equal destruction as the command ship, except they were right in the middle of it and unable to flee or steer. A Trike appeared right beyond the hood of *Santa Maria* for an instant and looked directly at them. They could see the protective lenses covering its eyes and its dagger teeth sticking out from under its huge breather. The beast thrusted away and leaped towards the troop carrier, dozens of other Trikes doing the same.

A cylindrical landing craft from the troop carrier zipped by them, streaking towards the surface. Another cylinder floated free right in front of them and a Trike rode atop it, using its claws like a can opener. Arnock spilled into the vacuum, their usual black color instantly chilled to a frosted white when exposed to space. They all kicked for a moment before stopping.

Instead of a mass of dying beings like before, Salla and Achilles felt one mind amongst the Arnock. It was a huge presence and singular. It was Kizik, channeling and focusing the panic and fear into action. Even as the Trikes swarmed all over the troop carrier, more landing craft cylinders disconnected from it in an orderly fashion. Salla somehow knew that this was Kizik, the being inhabiting Timberwolf's consciousness. The breadth of his intellect was staggering. Even with his attention diverted, Kizik was overwhelming, demanding, everywhere. She couldn't imagine his mind turned to focus on her alone and what Timberwolf must have experienced on a daily basis.

"It's on that one!" Achilles held his head, the presence overwhelming. He pointed to a slow and deliberately moving landing cylinder. It seemed to be in a protective bubble. The Trikes thrusted towards it, but turned away when they got close, like it was a hot coal. Kizik's landing cylinder fell towards the surface, his presence diminishing in their minds.

Other Trikes tore the remaining landing cylinders from the ship, and then ripped them apart. "Some are getting through!" Achilles was almost screaming. He had the scopes back on now and the thrusters powered up. He turned *Santa Maria* towards Highland. Below them was a shower of metal and writhing Trikes. Some landing cylinders tumbled end over end and turned into fireballs in the upper atmosphere.

"It's cracking in half!" On a scope, Salla saw the troop carrier above them bending at its thin midpoint, the last of its landing cylinders disconnecting. The Trikes leaped away from it all at once and a moment later, the power cells along its superstructure exploded in a chain reaction, one after another.

"We can't stay here!" Achilles said.

"Take us down," Salla responded.

"I can't go down there. That gives away everything!" A hunk of metal, like a giant, jagged elbow swept past them, a Trike riding in the bend.

Salla begged him with her eyes. *Please get us out of here!*

He dipped his head for a moment. "Penny, I'm sorry!" he said, too low for Salla to hear. He punched the thrusters and headed into the maelstrom of debris and Trikes below them. Where they had previously ignored them, the beasts leaped at their ship now from all sides, snapping and trying to latch on.

Achilles corkscrewed *Santa Maria*, weaving between the Trikes and debris. Highland took over the full window as its creamy white cloud layer grew closer every second. Salla braced herself against the wall in the back of the cabin, as they dove towards the world.

Achilles pulled up as the ship began to skim the atmosphere, an orange glow appearing outside the window. Out a rear porthole, Salla saw the darkness of space brighten. But hanging onto *Santa Maria's* tail by a claw—was a Trike.

"We've got a trailer!"

Achilles checked the rearview monitor. "Okay, would you come please take over?" he asked, unnaturally calm.

Salla struggled across the cabin and into the copilot seat. Before she was in, Achilles was up. The ship spiraled as she grabbed the controls, but she quickly righted it.

"It's gone!" Achilles said. There was nothing out the rear porthole anymore. "We shook her!"

Salla stared out the front window, lips parted. "There!" was all she could get out.

The Trike was perched on the hood of the vessel now, like a gargoyle looking in, a mass of muscle covered in knotty armor. Salla dove into the highest cloud layer and the Trike grimaced as it struggled to hold on, crinkling up the hood of *Santa Maria* with its claws. Once through the clouds, the Trike shook off its breather, exposing its awful teeth and licking its lips. There was a smash as the Trike's mighty tongue, tipped by a small wrecking ball, struck the windscreen. It did it again and again until a crack appeared. They were in the high atmosphere now, the next cloud layer right below them.

"Go for that! Take us right through." Achilles pointed to something out the window below them. At first glance, Salla thought it was a cumulonimbus cloud, but it was solid and pulsing with long tendrils hanging from it. It was a living gasbag creature, the kind that had swiped at *Nemesis* earlier.

"Go through that thing?" Salla asked.

"Sure, you won't hurt it!"

The Trike clawed its way closer to the windscreen, focusing on the humans within. It braced a claw on the roof right over their heads, preparing to tear the front windscreen off. The gasbag was just a few thousands yards away now, taking up the entire view behind the Trike.

They pierced the side of the gasbag creature like they were going through a paper bag and were suddenly in inky darkness. An instant later, they burst through the other side and the Trike was gone. *Santa Maria's* hood and front quarter-panel were torn off, exposing the whirring engine underneath. Behind them, the gasbag fell like a deflated balloon, the Trike writhing within.

The tenor of the engine changed, and a component popped out and pinged against the windscreen. "I'm not sure we live through this!" Achilles's calm was gone. He checked the scopes and readings and input something into his smart-device. "Take us to six, five, five, one and dive!" he told Salla.

She turned the ship in the direction Achilles indicated, dropping through more cloud layers, the engine sputtering. Lightning flashed outside now as a heavy rain fell. The crack in the windscreen spread further and Salla felt the wetness from outside on her arm. With no warning, the engine went silent and emergency alarms began to scream. Achilles silenced them with a slap of his hand. "We're a glider!" Salla winced. "Three miles up!"

"We're almost there!" Ahead of them, at the coordinates he had indicated, a bank of dark clouds was flattening out, creating a ledge in the sky. They hit the cloudbank and fell through, but it felt like a net had caught them. They bobbed up over the clouds again, supported by something underneath.

"Thank you, Penny!" Achilles breathed a sigh of relief. Billions of nano-machines in the atmosphere supported them now, pulled together into an ad hoc suspension net.

The net began to lower them gently through the clouds and down to the surface.

Salla stared at Achilles, overwhelmed by what just happened. With a wave of his hand, a projection of the suspension net appeared as a hologram in the cabin. There was *Santa Maria*, cradled in it, altitude readings showing them slowly descending. Achilles closed his eyes, finding a moment of peace. She didn't ask Achilles any questions and couldn't bear to. She found herself with her head in her hands, somewhere between relieved laughter and tears.

A few minutes later they landed, but so gently she barely realized it. Outside was just a gray curtain of vapor. Salla looked through the windscreen, searching for features. The cabin was silent, and Achilles still sat with his eyes tightly closed. She waved her hand in front of him, but he didn't move. She heard something outside in the distance; whooshes followed by crunching impacts. The ground shook, like artillery was falling far away.

Salla checked the atmosphere outside. It was Earth-normal, but she put on her breather just in case. She opened the door and leaped to the dusty ground below. She put her hand out in front of her, but the mist was so thick she could barely see her fingers. In the distance, glowing balls of light showed through the vapor. She heard the crunching more clearly now and made her way through the mist, stumbling over a stone in her way. Then, like she was stepping through a shower curtain, she was suddenly in the open.

She came out of the cloud wall at the bottom of The Eye, the clear column reaching up from the surface. The cloud wall curved away from where she stood, rotating ever so slowly. She looked across the space and saw the other side, miles away. A far-off door stood unnaturally in a sheer rock face. She turned and wiped her hand through the cloud wall. The vapor leaped back like it had a memory. Turning again, she saw several pillars of black smoke rising in the distance.

The crunching came again, and Arnock landing cylinders streaked towards the surface, trailed by tails of fire. Just a few thousand yards up, the intact ones deployed huge golden parachutes and settled gently onto the soft ground. Others crumbled as they fell, spilling their innards out and disintegrating into lines of debris that landed far away.

For the hundredth time since this all started, Salla was amazed by what she was seeing. Somehow she felt no fear. The scene in front of her was many things, but she couldn't help feeling that it was beautiful. She knew Arnock were dying by the thousands—she could feel their last seconds. But the streaks of fire, the disintegrating cylinders, the wall of clouds and the wonder of The Eye itself made a staggering tableau. She fell to her knees and took it in, fine shards of metal raining down not far away. Achilles appeared behind her and put his hand on her shoulder.

Salla hadn't noticed she'd stepped over a set of railroad tracks in the dust. A small, creaking train car stopped behind them and Achilles beckoned her to get on.

"I have a million questions," she said.

"Just wait a minute. You'll have a million more," he responded.

THE TORCH

D.P.E. Archangel—Twelve Hours Out from Highland

"There is a nuclear device in the possession of an unpredictable party down on Highland?" Conrad confirmed with Dr. Tier, trying not to sound incredulous. He was being as clinical as possible. He had been personally summoned to her office five minutes ago by Captain Tirani. It had been the captain, not Dr. Tier, who informed him that he was now in charge of the operation. The captain stood outside with several guards, counting down the fifteen minutes he had allotted for Dr. Tier to hand off all her knowledge to him. Dr.

Tier had prepared a punch list of the major items and Conrad went through them one by one.

"Yes," she responded. "Jude Izabeck, a former personal valet of Cardinal Jacob Bin Cavill, who is of course, right down the hall."

"You offered Cardinal Jacob control of the finances on Highland in exchange for reestablishing communications with Timberwolf Velez?"

"Yes, that may be in excess of one point two trillion dollars."

"And Timberwolf Velez is now dead."

"Presumably," she responded. "We have been unable to verify. We have tried to interface with Timberwolf's rig through Jacob's device, without success."

"And I am in charge now because Captain Tirani discovered you were ingesting Terecine, a banned substance, while issuing level-one orders?"

"Yes."

"And you were under the influence while we bumped *Challenger*?"

"High as a kite."

Conrad paused a second too long and she registered that he was appalled. "Are you under the influence now?"

"No," she said, smiling.

He brushed that off without digging further. "You are in touch with Jude Izabeck, via Cardinal Jacob's device? You have maintained the cardinal's identity for these conversations?" She nodded. A smile cracked on the bottom of Conrad's lip. *That's a good one.* "What was your plan for when we got to Highland?"

Without pausing, she responded, "The operation is now yours. Do as you see fit."

Her curt response told him all he needed to know. *You mean there is no plan?!* he asked with his eyes and a raised brow. She nodded and pursed her lips, as if to apologize.

"I'll continue speaking to Izabeck, impersonating Cardinal Jacob. I'll speak with the cardinal when I feel I need to."

"The good cardinal has threatened to expose our identities and our families."

"Fine, then I'll expose his."

She tilted her head. The Clergy were to remain celibate servants of god without familial ties. If Cardinal Jacob had a hidden family, it would be an unbearable scandal. Conrad had never told her he had this on the cardinal. Maybe he hadn't been certain. Maybe he was keeping it in his back pocket. Either way, Dr. Tier was impressed.

"Time." Captain Tirani opened the door and beckoned Conrad.

"Tread carefully…please," Dr. Tier said as Conrad left, the concern betrayed in her voice. He was about to take over a dangerous game, and she hoped he was up to it.

SELF

This is goddamned weird, Timberwolf thought. He had an awful headache, but the presence was smaller than he had ever recalled. Kizik was still there, but he felt like a memory. Something had shorted in his suit behind his right ear and knocked him out. He found himself half-crumpled up along the monitor bank in the Infiltration Office. Even when Kizik wasn't interested in him, he always felt him in the background, lurking somewhere. *This is really goddamned weird, and quiet.* But now there was almost nothing. It was like Kizik was busy.

The word *Copacetic* still blinked on the monitor. Kizik is busy? He considered the implications of that.

If Kizik is busy, then he's coming down here, Timberwolf thought. He needed to take Gray out, and immediately. He burst from the Infiltration Office back into the hall and ran back the way he had come, hurdling the melted security barriers.

He found himself out in The Catalog and leaped up to the top of a building to get the lay of the land. Altogether, he'd lost almost an hour with Kizik's detour. Timberwolf checked his sensors and Gray was nowhere to be found. He dropped back onto the path and began running, trying to make up time.

Then he saw it out of the corner of his eye—a crashed Glox lifter, its front half buried in the dust. Timberwolf stopped in his tracks. There was something about it that felt familiar. He knew he should have been moving on, but he couldn't help but look within. Inside was a macabre scene: A dozen or so dead Glox, all in blue flight-suits, were strewn about the cabin, dark red blood, thick like jelly, stained the floor and walls. Timberwolf nudged one of the Glox with the end of his gauntlet. The body crinkled and white stuffing showed through a tear in the jacket. The body was plastic, the scene a demonstration. Medium-sized Highland containers were strewn about the cabin and cracked open. He scanned the space and found that there was one body on the ship that wasn't fake; and it wasn't Glox.

Timberwolf stepped over the mess, slipping on the fake blood. He moved a faux-Glox aside and he saw a mat of dark hair. It was a human body wearing an old, red-green armored rig from the Phaelon Prime campaign. He turned the form over and saw a familiar jawline.

Why am I lying here? he asked himself numbly. There he was though, his self from twenty years before, his face soft, still and unmoving.

But was it dead? He checked his readings and the form below him wasn't decomposed in any way. There was no blotching and no rigor mortis. He could detect no trauma. It seemed to be in suspended animation. He bent in for a closer look and he passed through some sort of invisible barrier that sizzled and popped when he touched it.

Timberwolf's doppelganger opened his eyes suddenly and blinked with surprise. He managed to prop himself up on his elbows and he looked at Timberwolf with a familiar, quiet surliness that seemed to ask, *What the hell kind of rig is that?*

Without a second thought, Timberwolf put a full-force plasma burst into the thing's chest and knocked it to the back wall of the cabin. He stumbled to the front of the cabin, blood splatter on his visor. Real blood, which he knew was his. He checked his readings, his other self had the last remnants of a life sign but that quickly went gray. Then he was sitting in the dust outside the lifter, his helmet off.

What the hell was that? he asked himself. He noticed that his heart rate had climbed way up into the red. Even in the most intense combat situations, he'd barely get into yellow, but now the muscle in his chest pounded like a jackhammer.

His com link beeped. He ignored it, but it beeped again. He looked inside his helmet and saw that it was Achilles. A drop of blood rolled over his knuckle and into his palm. He tried to make sense of what he'd just experienced, but nothing came to him.

> *Achilles301: Timberwolf, I see you moving. Something shorted in your suit.*
>
> *Timberwolf4545: I just shot myself in the chest.*
>
> *Achilles301: Are you using your med-kit?!*
>
> *Timberwolf4545: No, I had it coming.*

ASSASSIN

The train moved along the perimeter of The Eye and then slid back behind the cloud wall. Ahead of them, the vapor formed itself into a tunnel as they passed.

"I wanted to do something special. Be a part of something bigger than what I was doing. I was an errand girl for a petty crook," Salla said, as she leaned against the window.

"We're all errand girls and boys," Achilles responded. "You still want to be a lawyer?"

"I may have broken hundreds of laws over the last few days. I just want to live through this."

Achilles smiled. "So what do you think of my place?"

"It's nice," she said absently. "Homey." She turned to him. "I thought you said you couldn't come down here?"

"If I'm here with my brother, it's more likely Gray can get Penny to do what he needs. It's complicated."

"Is there a way out of this mess for you?"

"Yes, but I'm not going to like it. I have to get Gray out of here so I can deal with the Arnock." He handed her a tablet computer. "Uninvited guests."

On the tablet there was a video feed from The Eye. An Arnock landing cylinder stood upright like a giant soda can. Arnock scurried about, forming into martial rows and columns. From behind the cylinder strode a massive sentry Arnock, a warrior-monster forty feet high. Achilles pulled the view back. There were a dozen other cylinders with similar scenes unfolding. He swept his view to *Nemesis*, nestled next to an outcropping, still unnoticed by the Arnock.

"I love surprises. Take this. Don't drop it or leave it in the sun." Achilles pulled a small backpack from under the seat and handed it to her. Inside she found several more of the small grenades he had given to her over Golgotha and other emergency supplies such as flashlights and signal beacons.

Salla held up a grenade. "You know these are lousy, right? They've got to be the worst thing you make." She found a bottle of water in the sack and drank it all in almost one gulp.

"I'm working on a Sabatin that can fit in your pocket, but until then have a grenade or two." He paused, knowing she would hate what he had to say next. "I have to make a deal with Gray."

"You can't give him anything!"

"You're naïve. It's charming. There's a price for everything. We haven't completely forgotten how commerce works. Gray's spent a lot of different types of coin to get here. I'll give him a trifling. It'll be worth it to him just to leave."

"You know he doesn't really do what makes sense. He just pushes and pushes until things fall apart," she said.

"He isn't stupid. He just has a hard time changing his mind. He'll see the logic."

"He's going on faith now!" she said. "I don't think logic is part of the equation."

Achilles didn't have a response. He slowed the train down. They were at a small station, seemingly in the middle of nowhere.

"The Arnock will get control of this place if they stay. Their intellect will get through Penny. I'll offer Gray something to get him out of the way."

"You're going to find him in person to do this?"

"Do you have his handle?"

Salla went through the backpack, palmed a small grenade for a moment and put it back. "You're right. This works."

He noticed her considering the tiny weapon. "Revenge?" Achilles asked. "Think you'll be glad to see him?"

She looked him in the eye. "No, probably not."

"Are you ready to die to get back at Gray?"

Through all of this, she hadn't thought about dying. Until now, everything had been moving too fast for her to consider her own fate.

"Are you ready to die?" Achilles asked again. "Assassins rarely get to cash in their retirement plans."

"Gray is an evil man," she said, her eyes becoming slits.

Achilles took her hand, a deep tenderness in his eyes. "And you are a brave, brave woman! And a good person.

His life isn't equal to yours." The door slid open and he got up, stepping onto the platform. Salla was thankful he didn't wait for her to respond. She wasn't sure if what he said was true or even relevant.

"Where are we now?" she asked.

"Back door!" he replied.

THE BOUT

Droma walked beside Wrath along the path, looking at him sideways. The Phaelon clan leader pushed the beast to the side and it snarled. "Wrath, *dur mek!*" Thomas scorned. A few minutes later, Wrath took his armored head and slammed Droma's side. The Phaelon hissed and her clan-mates laughed.

Thomas went to intervene, but Gray stopped him. "No! They're sparring."

Gray looked back to the men. Their heads all hung since the loss of Jan. Wrath circled Droma now, clawing the dust. A Phaelon threw Droma a fighting baton weighted on both ends. The men and the other Phaelon crowded around now in a circle. Wrath charged and took Droma in the stomach, driving her into the air. The Phaelon smashed the baton down on Wrath's skull and rolled away. The group cheered and whooped, money changing hands in wagers.

Droma released a flurry with her baton, and Wrath took the blows on the snout spiritedly. There was a clang of metal against armor and Wrath turned, taking Droma out with his tail. Then they were up, Droma getting inside of Wrath's grasp and landing fists under his chin. The Sabatin wrapped his razor-tipped tongue around Droma's neck and threw her to the ground without drawing blood. Wrath roared at Droma when she fell and hurled her high into the air with his snout. Droma landed upright though, and swung her baton around again. The men roared now and the Phaelon hissed and screeched. Feigning left then right, Droma landed a series of blows and blood spurted from under Wrath's chin. The two were intertwined now, Wrath's claws out and scratching. After a few seconds, Thomas separated them and the crowd booed. The two came apart and Droma lifted her arms boastfully as if she was the clear victor, but she had never been a match for Wrath.

The Phaelon and the Sabatin exchanged respectful glances and a final hiss. Gray stood, enjoying the scene and pleased that the men were energized now. When Jan died, it had been different from when they lost the others back on The Outpost. He'd been the first to pass on in Highland, in Gray's "new part of heaven." He needed the men to embrace what had happened, not fear it, but made stronger by it.

Gray considered what was happening here and the messaging it required. Izabeck stood in the back of the group, writing the bout between Wrath and Droma into gospel. Gray felt fully invested in the path, but there was an emptiness inside him even as he drew close to his goal. He had been praying silently to himself as they walked. He'd been looking to have that personal conversation with God that marked the experience of the true believer. Instead he felt humbled by the silence, by the one-sided conversation he was having and by the lack of answers coming his way. He envisioned himself alone on the deck of a ship, a storm crashing around him, calling into the tempest in vain.

Sergey appeared before Gray, with Michael's rifle at his back. The small man smiled smugly like the cherub he was, as if somehow he could read Gray's doubts. "Must put a weight on you, looking for something you know you're not going to find," he said to Gray, as Michael pushed him along.

In the distance there was a repeating sound like reverse artillery, an unnatural twang/thump. The voice of Meta, the holographic sales representative, boomed from above but she didn't appear. "Explosions are effective, but what about an implosion?"

The thumping grew closer as the party started moving again. Small, bright, pin-sized bursts appeared about head-high along the path behind them. "Let's move!" Warner marshaled the men. "They're falling from the ceiling!"

The party was in an all-out run, hurdling rubble through a simulated urban area ruined by combat. Bombed out buildings and old, gutted, armored vehicles lined the path. A baseball-sized object covered in small holes fell right in front of Izabeck but didn't explode. He kicked it away. It burst, but instead of exploding outward, it pulled matter towards it in a tiny singularity—an implosion, leaving a scooped-out hole in the ground. An armored vehicle took a direct hit. It twisted in the air, landing in the shape of a bowtie.

The group ran across a parking lot filled with battered vehicles. With a high-pitched thump, a falling grenade imploded between two Phaelon, leaving nothing but green mist in the air. "Get cover!" Gray ordered. They dove under the old cars and trucks as the onslaught continued unbearably. When it stopped, the party rose one by one.

"Call out!" Warner yelled.

"Sebaldi…Barnabas…Thomas…Blaise…Vitus… Thaum…Ahmed…Cisus…Michael…   Windwhistle… Izabeck…Gray," the men responded.

"We're all here. Droma lost two," Michael reported.

Droma had been nearby when the grenade hit, and she now wiped thick, green blood from her shoulder. Gray grabbed Sergey by the collar. The small man yelped. "I can't control this! You should go."

Gray put a knife to Sergey's neck. Gray seethed, exhaling out his nostrils. "I am willing to take a chance here."

"What kind of chance?" Sergey asked.

"That we don't need you in the control room. That maybe your DNA would be just enough."

"No! It'll never work without me alive. I promise you that!"

Gray smiled, putting the knife away. "But I am willing to take that chance. We're clear?" They heard a final twang/thump in the distance. "I really do not want to die. I hope you know that."

"I don't want you to die either," Sergey said, "but I'm not in control of what happens here."

Gray sneered. "Who is?"

"Management," Sergey responded, spreading out his hands and indicating everything around them.

Gray shook his head. "Let's go!"

WHERE IS MY MIND?

Timberwolf moved through the garden section in The Catalog, where it had been filled with high flowers and koi ponds a few minutes ago; its landscaped beauty was now reduced to rubble by the implosion grenades. A few artificial flowers in damaged planters wagged their heads at his presence, but were unable to target him. They went off as he passed, their flechettes firing wildly.

He'd watched the onslaught of implosion grenades fall from a safe distance and now had a bead on Gray's party up ahead of him. He quickly moved through the Sabatin products display, the shop buildings pocked with spherical impacts. The model of the giant Trike Sabatin was halfway into the street, its back part missing.

Timberwolf4545: We have to talk.

He sent a message to Achilles. He needed answers about whatever it was he found on the Glox lifter.

Timberwolf4545: So is it company policy that everybody must get cloned?

After a long pause, he got a response.

Achilles301: I can't tell you what that was.

Timberwolf4545: But you know it was something?

Achilles301: We go way back. Longer than you know.

Timberwolf4545: Specifically, to when I was twenty years old. Ever shoot yourself?

Achilles301: You weren't supposed to find that.

Timberwolf4545: It was supposed to find me! Something made me look in there.

Achilles301: Penny is waiting for you.

Achilles dropped the connection and Timberwolf stopped in the path. *Frustrated* was not the right word. He was being toyed with and he had no options. He considered just leaving, settling on some far-off colony world, but he knew he couldn't. Kizik would stay with him and grind his mind into dust. He knew that his only real option was Penny, meeting with the A.I. and playing out his role. Go before the computer and plead for Kizik's removal. Kneel down before the artificial soul. Achilles had told him back on The Outpost that Penny trusted him. He'd blown it off as nonsense, but now he was starting to understand. She'd known him for decades.

He zoomed in on Gray's party with his heads-up. They were about a mile up ahead, approaching another huge door. There was nothing stopping him from attacking Gray except that, in the moment, Timberwolf wondered what exactly his *self* was. Not in a philosophical way, but physically and biologically. He shared a consciousness with an alien mind-bender. He'd been taken and cloned years ago by forces of Highland. Dr. Tier had explored his brain to figure out what

Kizik had done to him, prodded and probed his psyche. All of this must have changed him. *Where is my mind?* he asked himself.

He had no answer. He wondered what he was, if he was human, even a real person anymore. An anger came up inside him, starting in his stomach and reaching his temples. He fired up the plasma driver in his gauntlet and began running. Timberwolf felt like fighting.

THE SHADOW

Gray's party moved past a neon sign that read *Weapons Free Zone*. Over a short bluff, another huge door was ahead in the rock face. Meta's tune played and she appeared along the side of the path for a moment. "As the old song says, 'don't take your guns to town.'"

"Sling 'em!" Warner ordered the men.

"*Tru ser!*" Michael told the Phaelon.

On the path, a field of short pylons rose from the dust. The men fidgeted nervously.

"Just keep walking," Gray said sternly.

Sergey beckoned them forward, his eyes darting around like something was about to happen. "We're almost there. Just ahead."

Wrath was agitated. He grunted and screeched anxiously at something behind them. Droma knelt beside him, sniffing the air and sensing something too. "*Fer ka nu zu!*" she turned and said to Michael.

"Droma says it's the demon," Michael told Gray. Gray looked back, his eyes filled with trepidation and hope. Might Timberwolf have survived? The thought raced through Gray's head as more pylons rose from the dust.

Thomas tried to pull Wrath away, but the beast wasn't having it. "There's something bothering him. It's back there, the way we came."

Michael jabbed his rifle into Sergey's back and called to the men. "Fire at nothing. This is a trap! No aggressive moves."

Barnabas, the man on point, saw it first. In front of them came a dark figure, appearing over the bluff. "Contact!" he yelled. Wrath and Droma didn't turn to the front though, still focused on something *behind* them.

"I've got it on my heads-up!" Barnabas yelled. Indeed, a white icon signifying an unfriendly showed on everyone's heads-up displays.

"Don't trust your readings!" Gray ordered.

"Hold fire!" Warner said, almost begging.

The figure was a man in a dark armored rig. Moving closer, it was unmistakably Timberwolf. He was just a few yards away now, bright plasma blades glowing on his gauntlets. Barnabas shook, his finger hovering over the trigger of his weapon. The figure raised an arm to strike. Without intent, Barnabas fired a plasma burst into the ground and the image of Timberwolf vanished, a projected hologram.

The pylons that had come up from the dust opened at the top, exposing mini-turrets. From all directions, hundreds of small projectiles clanged against Barnabas's armor with a sound like ball bearings in a dryer. He spun to get away, but there was no escape and he was the only target. After a few long moments, he fell dead, a trickle of blood coming from a spot between his eyes. With a hydraulic hiss, the pylons disappeared into the dust again.

Through all of this, Wrath and Droma focused on their rear flank, hunting for a threat they knew was real and behind them.

Gray grabbed Sergey and threw him to the ground. The tiny man scrambled to his feet, a rock in his hand.

"Just ahead? Just ahead?" Gray bellowed.

"Yes!"

"Well, I'm afraid I'm going to have to give you some pain before we get there," Gray said almost casually.

"That doesn't make any sense! I can't control this!"

"My men didn't need to die here!"

"You didn't need to come here!" Sergey said, scared and desperate. Michael knocked the rock from Sergey's hand.

"Hold him!" Gray ordered. Michael and Windwhistle each grabbed an arm. Sergey struggled, almost breaking free. He was much stronger than he looked, and it took two others to push him to his knees. Gray approached, stepping over Barnabas's body. He knelt and fiddled with his rifle. A white-hot flame shot from the barrel like an arc light. "It's never good to get an injury in the field. You know infection has killed more men than guns ever did. So, I'm going to make sure that your wound is nice and cauterized."

"What wound? What are you talking about?" Sergey said, confused.

"His hand!" Gray barked. Michael shoved Sergey's hand forward. Gray held the flame under it and Sergey cringed.

"Please, no! God!"

"Whatever you are, you don't get to talk to God. You never will."

Gray pulled the trigger and, with a pop, Sergey had a dime-sized hole in his hand. He writhed in pain. Michael and Windwhistle released him and he fell to the dust. Sergey moaned, releasing a hoarse yelp. He squeezed his eyes shut, rolling to his side.

Wrath roared, a deep vicious complaint. "Bishop Gray! It's got to be Timberwolf behind us!" Thomas said.

"Might be more of our sorry little friend's tricks," Gray responded, rolling over Sergey to his back with his foot.

"Wrath is a beast, but I'm sure there's something," Thomas replied.

"You can make good on this. You've got a way to defeat his armor. I know you do," Gray said to Sergey.

"I'll have to be close to him!" Sergey winced.

"There's a door ahead. I take it we're going through?" Michael asked. Sergey nodded. "We let the Sabatin stall him and Sergey waits for Timberwolf on the other side."

"I'll need my device. What you took from me before," Sergey said, sitting up now.

Gray pulled a small smart-device from his fatigues. "You're in luck." He tossed it to Sergey. "But if you try anything funny at all, Mr. Dacha, I will take your other hand."

VIOLENCE

Wrath seethed in front of the giant door. He scratched the dust, awaiting the opponent he knew was coming.

On the other side of the door, Gray's party had found a huge, marble, spiral staircase leading to a brightly lit and cavernous room below. The place was covered in dust like the rest of Highland. It must have been a ballroom decades ago. A giant, fallen chandelier lay smashed at the foot of the stairs. Rows and rows of columns held up The Catalog above. They took positions behind fallen columns and in alcoves along the sides of the space.

Gray assessed the location for its ambush potential. "This will do." He nodded to Michael. "Good plan."

In front of the door above, Wrath hissed and Timberwolf approached slowly and in the open. No need for speed or stealth. They both knew where the fight was. The Sabatin's dull silver armor reflected the dust and his tail lashed impatiently. Wrath wanted to fight as much as Timberwolf did.

Timberwolf felt a cruelty rising within him. It replaced the anger from before. He wanted to go through Wrath and rip the beast to shreds. He wasn't thinking ahead, just that he hungered to be vicious. They circled, wiser to the other's style this time. Timberwolf ignited the blades on his wrists, one then the other. Wrath rushed, but Timberwolf parried, slashing a wound across his skull. Surprised, the beast slinked back.

Timberwolf went in and swung with a blade, missing wide. Then they were locked together, Wrath snapping at Timberwolf's helmet. With a flurry, they were apart again. Bayonets extended from Wrath's forearms and the beast slashed at him. Leaping back, Timberwolf hit him with a concussion blast, knocking Wrath to the door.

They rushed each other again and again, a blur of stabbing and slashing, colliding each time like a train crash. Below in the column room Gray, Michael, and Thomas listened to the sounds of the battle above, flinching at each impact.

Wrath and Timberwolf fought mercilessly, their forms a haze of black and silver. Tiring, they both began to falter. Timberwolf created a hologram, but Wrath didn't fall for it. He smashed Timberwolf into a rock wall and pinned him there, his jaws tearing into Timberwolf's shoulder. He took a glowing blade to Wrath's throat, the beast's armor dribbling off like melted solder. Timberwolf's rig had tears and damage almost everywhere now and the tolerances were way up into the red.

Apart once more, Wrath lunged but Timberwolf jumped straight up, propelled by thrusters in his rig. He thrusted downward and landed on Wrath's back with a crack, breaking the beast's spine.

Wrath struggled to turn as Timberwolf circled. Again, he felt the cruelty inside him, the want for *unnecessary* violence, a thing that was surprisingly alien to him. Timberwolf got to the side of Wrath and leapt on the Sabatin, pounding on his skull plate again and again. Timberwolf could feel his knuckles bruising as he landed blow after blow with his heavy armored fists, but he didn't care. He pounded on Wrath until a final blow cracked his skull, releasing a hiss of gas. Wrath's head slumped forward, falling into Timberwolf's arms. For a moment, he was forced to hold Wrath like a fallen colleague, but he dropped him to the dust and a pool of red blood began to spread from the body.

The beast still twitched. Timberwolf fired up his laser to finish him off, but he stumbled, landing on his haunches against the door. Exhausted and legs shaking, he stood up, avoiding looking down at Wrath and what he'd done.

He scanned the other side of the door with micro-drones and couldn't see anything. Something blocked their signal. He creaked the door open, expecting an ambush from all sides, but instead found himself at the top of a magnificent spiral staircase that went down to a warmly lit space at least a hundred feet below. For a moment, he wondered what would happen to his brother and to Salla, but then even their welfare went beyond him.

I'm out of damns to give, he thought to himself.

RECKONING

Sergey picked up shards from the fallen chandelier at the bottom of the staircase. They were perfect diamonds, not a creation of some carbon pressing machine, but natural, mined from two miles down inside of Highland. He had found the huge deposit himself sixty years ago. He loved diamonds and gold and precious metals, but not for their value. He loved the way they made people feel and how they looked pressed into jewelry around someone's neck. The chandelier included over two hundred kilograms of diamonds. He put a few of the stones into his pocket.

This place has no focus, he thought to himself. Penny was desperate now to meet Timberwolf, to see if he could perhaps provide Highland a conscience, a way forward. With his uncommon mental strength, she felt he was their only hope. Maybe this would ensure that she got to meet him, unless Gray killed him on the spot, of course. He thought

Gray a barbarian, no better than the hordes that had trampled his beloved Russia over a thousand years ago. His hand ached and a spot of blood appeared on the bandage. He'd do Gray's bidding now and play his part, knowing the surprise of the endgame. *Oh, the look on his face will be priceless!*

Michael, Gray, and Thomas watched Sergey from behind a fallen column. Thomas had been unable to monitor the fight between Timberwolf and Wrath and couldn't know the Sabatin lay near death above. "Wrath might come down those stairs," Thomas offered.

Gray nodded, but he knew that was impossible. The door groaned open far above. A moment later, Timberwolf was at the bottom of the staircase. Thomas's head hung. Since Timberwolf didn't immediately dive for cover, or start shooting, it was clear that Sergey was successfully blocking his scans. He moved cautiously. He may have seen nothing in the shadows, but no doubt he knew this was an ambush.

Sergey moved toward Timberwolf, stepping around the chandelier. "I managed to get away. They're working to get into The Chapel. Won't do it, though." Timberwolf stared at him. Sergey noticed his rig was shredded, black smoke snuck out from the ragged gashes. "Yeah, I know this place in and out. Built it. Ninety-five years ago."

There was no response. Sergey fidgeted and came closer. He turned over the smart-device Gray had given back to him in his pocket. "So, I would say the thing to do, yeah, is to um…maybe…team up and I'll take you to find…"

Timberwolf held up his hand to stop him. Sergey halted, sweat pouring from his brow. There was an echo from amongst the columns and something moved in the shadows. Without hesitation, Timberwolf raised his forearm and fired a laser. A Phaelon fell, shot in the neck.

Timberwolf just stood there, waiting for what he knew was coming. A return torrent of plasma fire came from all directions, the shots ricocheting off his armor. Sergey dove to his belly, dropping his smart-device. Timberwolf launched concussion blasts on auto-fire, unconcerned with overheating his rig. A wall of destruction blasted columns. He knocked back three Phaelon that rushed him, sending them flying. He threw holograms into the midst of his attackers. They slashed with faux plasma blades, fired fake bursts.

Gray watched wide-eyed, again in awe of Timberwolf in action. Timberwolf didn't dive for cover or take any defensive measures. He just attacked, plasma and laser streaming out of his rig. Burst after burst struck him, but he didn't flinch, instead turning from one target to the next like a machine.

Sergey army-crawled towards his smart-device, now almost within his reach. He held his ears, the sound of the shooting like continuous thunder. Timberwolf pressed forward, his rig taking incredible damage, but the Phaelon and the human fighters scattered before him. Gray rose from his cover, fired a stream of plasma at him. Timberwolf turned on him and the two men unloaded on each other, both unflinching, at less than twenty yards.

Sergey had his smart-device now and he flicked it on. Timberwolf's elbow glowed and fire spread up his arm to his shoulder. He spun as the suit burned off him, still firing at Gray until his weapon disintegrated. He fell to his knees, enveloped in flames. His helmet burned off, exposing a mouth open in pain. Droma rushed him, putting a heavy boot to his temple. Timberwolf rolled over to his back, skin smoking. The party encircled him, wary but awestruck. The humans made the Believer symbol on their foreheads and chanted, overlapping each other. "There is no god but God and I do his bidding!"

Gray's armor was battered, but he'd only had the wind knocked out of him by Timberwolf's fire. Gray looked down at his old friend, lying naked and burned. "I'm getting sick of you." Timberwolf groaned, looking up at Gray.

ACT V

NO REST

Meta stood at the top of the staircase at the start of The Catalog. She smiled, her tune playing like it had before. The door creaked open and red, glowing eyes were on the other side. The visitors she had detected streamed in—thousands of Arnock that had survived the Trikes and the descent to the planet. "Welcome to the Highland Industrial Park." The creatures ignored her, passing around and through her. Meta stopped her pitch. With her limited autonomy, she was sure this wasn't right. A forty-foot-tall sentry Arnock entered, striding above her. She spun around, unable to process what was happening.

Kizik entered and took up a position in the back, watching the remnants of his army descend into The Catalog. He had taken extraordinary losses. He'd lost a hundred percent of the crew on the command ship and thirty percent of his assault force. There were only two other masters besides him now, a doctor and a law-writer. He'd lost most of the know-how he needed to gain control of this place, but he felt he could manage at least in the short-term. He had mostly warriors and some techs. One of his techs checked in with him.

There are no remote ports.

Kizik dismissed the tech. No remote ports would mean they would have to go all the way to the command center to access the A.I. That would mean a conflict with Gray and possibly Timberwolf. He sensed both of them here. He knew they were in close proximity to one another, but assumed they could not possibly be working together. That meant one thing: Gray had captured Timberwolf. If it had gone the other way, Gray would be dead.

He considered his losses so far. Horrific. Not just in numbers, but what it meant for his people. He had hoped to bring almost everyone back home to rebuild, but that had been naïve. Timberwolf had tricked him. Bested him for the first time ever and it had been a horrible blow. Kizik had gotten too accustomed to manipulating the man's mind. No more games. No more trying to use Timberwolf as a tool to clear the way for him.

When I get near him. I will kill him. Quickly, like the coldest wind.

He couldn't reach out to Timberwolf now. With only two other masters, he was too distracted by controlling this force. He steadied and guided all their minds, leading them forward almost one step at a time. He felt their fear and buried it with feedback. It was cruel, but it was working. His control had helped many more than should have to survive the attack on the troop carrier ship. Exhausted, he rested a moment, retreating entirely back to his own thoughts.

Oh Radem, no!

When he pulled away from their minds, his force stopped moving all at once, dead in their tracks. They looked back at him, waiting for him to reconnect.

He needed a few more moments, but as he rested, the panic started. A huge sentry Arnock, already little more than a brute, began to stride towards him, knocking the smaller Arnock aside. Kizik bore down, shaking and buzzing. He threw his mind out to them like a life preserver. He struggled against the panic, but soon he had it under control and the throng started moving forward again.

Not a religious being, he appealed to the Arnock deity as a reflex.

Radem, give me strength.

SERMON

Timberwolf sat, his back to a column. He soothed his burns with a cream infused with nano-menders from a med-kit Gray had given him. Thomas hovered nearby, spinning a knife in his hands. He was angry from the loss of Wrath. Gray waved him off and he spat in the dust as he went.

Gray tossed Timberwolf a T-shirt and a pair of cargo pants. Timberwolf nodded, acknowledging their bitter familiarity; old friends, new enemies. "I'm glad to see you're alive. I really am." Timberwolf pulled on the pants and shirt. "Let me tell you a little about my religion," Gray said to him, hokey on purpose.

"General, Governor, now Bishop Gray? You've worn a lot of hats. Your *followers* know you're making it up as you go along?"

"I'm guilty of being a Jack-of-all-trades."

"What's with the conversion?" Timberwolf asked. He recalled how he and Gray used to snicker at the *sky pilots* that flowed into the Assault Corps and complain about how all the good gin joints were shutting down.

"Just an example. You know the Tiaski from near Tep Nine-Fifty?"

"Do I know them? We used to sneak up on their freighters and plant nukes."

Gray ignored his remark. "Start with an octopus, but its head is just a pile of eyes. Its sex organ and its esophagus are the same. The stomach is the uterus."

"They're lovely creatures."

Gray stepped atop of a small pile of rubble. He was preaching now, to a church of one. "Something God didn't make. He couldn't have made. He made man perfect in His image and aliens were a cancer that came later. And you know, it's a species delusion aliens have, which was indicated by the Angel of the *Alchemy*. The belief that they were made in God's image too. That can't be. It's absurd."

"Angel of the *Alchemy*? You must be joking. You know that *happened* on a spaceship filled with sensors and that nothing was recorded? There was no Angel of the *Alchemy*, just a captain who decided to destroy a civilization and then blamed it on God. You recall the writ from The Clergy on the Tiaski. Their condemnation. Do you remember?" Timberwolf asked.

"Of course, the will of God. Infallible and committed to paper," Gray smiled.

"The Clergy made trillions once we cleared out those shipping routes. Took those worlds. We couldn't even live on them, but they had mines, trillium, radium, etcetera. The Tiaski are gone. All of them. They had been lazily plowing those routes for millennia. Since before we had agriculture! And we killed them to make The Clergy rich. Do you really believe this stuff, or do you just want your own war to go fight in?"

Gray took a hunk of metal from the ground. It was a piece of someone's armor that had been blasted off during the fighting. He drew a Believer symbol in the dust with it, but with an eyeball in the center. "Wherever God takes me, I have all the answers I need, closed eyes. I don't need to see the whole picture. I don't care about The Clergy. I have my own path and so do you." He wiped the eyeball from the center of the symbol.

"You missed a spot." Timberwolf pointed to a part of the eyeball Gray hadn't wiped away. There didn't seem to be any point in talking to Gray about his conversion. "Where'd you find these winners?" Timberwolf asked, motioning to Windwhistle and others who rested on fallen pillars and hunks of rubble. "All of them with names picked out of the ass-end of the Bible—Blaise, Cisus, Sebaldi. Jesus."

"From prominent Believer families. Couldn't exactly go back to the Assault Corps or the old unit."

"I am the old unit!" Timberwolf said coldly. "All that's left of it." He surprised himself by the tone of his voice, petulant and affected.

Gray dropped his eyes to the dust. That was a kick to the heart. He caught himself before arguing with him. "You're going to see some beautiful things. You're alive for this."

"Alive? You knew what the Arnock did to prisoners. I'm alive because you wanted to see if I'd be useful."

"You were useful, until you turned on me. Your use has sort of dropped off lately."

"I've got it in my head. You could have let me die. I've wanted to check out, but…"

"I've heard the stories. Eight missions for Dr. Tier that can charitably be described as suicidal. That woman…" Gray shook his head, pressed his lips together. His eyes softened. "You'd drop into a hot zone with nothing more deadly than a can opener. Somehow you'd make it out. Mission accomplished and lots of dead bad guys, or dead freedom fighters or just dead who-knows-who. You don't have to live like that anymore. You can come back now."

"There is no *back*."

"You survive. It's what you do."

"Survival? You can call it that?" Timberwolf snapped at him. "Have you come here for forgiveness? Have you come to raise the dead? The men in the ground from the two of us…" Timberwolf drilled his gaze into Gray and wouldn't look away.

"I want to finish what we started. Get that cancer out of your head. You won't be free until we get rid of all the Arnock. I assure you of that." He put his hand on Timberwolf's shoulder. Nearby, Michael thumbed his weapon, unsure if Timberwolf might try to tear Gray's head off. "Don't you want to hit back at what you hate?" Gray asked him.

"That's why I'm here," Timberwolf answered.

"Your soul needs peace," Gray said, shaken that he had failed to get anywhere with Timberwolf. He had thought that if he could speak to him and make him understand, that there might be some forgiveness for him. He considered telling him everything, about working with Dr. Tier and exposing him to Kizik on purpose. He failed to see the point now, though, or maybe he just wasn't brave enough to do it. "No one's to speak to that man. Michael, put Droma on him," Gray ordered.

Michael nodded, but Droma was nowhere to be found. He sent one of the Phaelon to find her. The rest of the party prepared to move on. Timberwolf felt the presence right then. It was far off, but it was more than Kizik. It was thousands of Arnock. With so many different minds, he was unable to sense anything but energy. He looked to the others, they weren't feeling it yet, but he knew they would.

Up the stairs and on the other side of the door, Wrath lay in the dust, his breathing shallow now. Droma scrambled over to him, putting her hand on his side. She dripped the vial of sweet liquid down the beast's throat. In its concentrated form, just a few drops should do it. Within moments, Wrath's eyes rolled to the back of his head and he tensed up, hacking and gasping. Droma wouldn't have time to see if the *sweet death* worked, if the nano-menders in the liquid would be able to save Wrath. She felt the ground rumble below her ever so slightly. Off in the distance, she saw the first part of the Arnock army. She climbed a nearby boulder and raised a glowing plasma spear above her head. She shouted to the Arnock, knowing they couldn't hear her.

"*Wessei min ter!*" she repeated until her throat was hoarse.

Clan Wessei was going to war.

REVELATIONS

D.P.E. Archangel—Eight Hours Out from Highland

"No, you cannot speak with Dr. Tier," Captain Tirani said. Conrad stood in the doorway of his office. "She put you in charge and now you are in charge."

"I've heard from Jude Izabeck. Timberwolf is alive, but Gray's captured him. They are minutes from Highland's command center. He wrote, 'Hallelujah, we have the demon and the faithful are at the doorway of The Chapel.' I got him to elaborate in plain English."

Captain Tirani had sympathy for Conrad's position and the faster this was resolved, the sooner they could all extricate themselves from this mess. "What kind of result do you want?"

"I want to blow Izabeck's nuke, right now. Resolve this."

"That certainly brings things to a resolution." Captain Tirani considered the implications. That left Gray dead and Highland a non-viable prize for the Assault Corps. "Just do it and we'll get the hell out of here."

"We keep going after we blow it. We need to know what's happened down there. We at least stay for a few hours before *Challenger* catches us."

"So press the button."

Conrad nodded, that was the hard part. "I need to see the cardinal."

I *should have asked Dr. Tier for a few hits of Terecine*, Conrad thought as he stood outside Cardinal Jacob's door, Gordon and Roberts standing guard on both sides. The Glox-crafted narcotic was infamous among D.P.E. personnel, but he'd never succumbed to it. D.P.E. agents and analysts had terrifically stressful jobs. They lived in a world of data and calculation. They saw every threat, every whisper of war or subversion. They molded lies into the truth and turned propaganda into facts. They routinely sent people such as Timberwolf out into the field to slit throats and break necks.

After a while, it became hard to disconnect from the job, from the awful things that they had to authorize in the name of keeping the peace. They were the bitter solvent used to melt away the sickness of constant war. There was a joke among D.P.E. people when the job got hairy. "You want the T or the S?" The T stood for Terecine; the S was for suicide. Application of both options was disturbingly common.

He couldn't blame Dr. Tier for becoming a Terecine addict. On its surface, it was a stress reliever and sleep aid that used to actually be prescribed in minute amounts. She probably started small and gradually let her problem get out of control, but she was taking close to fifty milligrams a day now. Conrad was amazed she could still stand, let alone have the state of mind to order Captain Tirani to bump *Challenger*.

Conrad knocked on the door and it opened almost instantly, like Cardinal Jacob had been expecting someone. "Do you have a message for me, son?" he asked.

"I'm Dr. Tier's replacement. I'd like to speak with you, sir."

Cardinal Jacob looked him up and down with barely concealed disdain. "It's *Excellency*, my boy, not sir. I'm not a mister." He smiled condescendingly.

"My apologies, Excellency," Conrad said. Cardinal Jacob let him in and sat on a small couch, beckoning Conrad to sit next to him.

"Where are Cheng? McCord? I thought I was familiar with most of Thea's staff."

"Conrad Stonefield." He sat where Cardinal Jacob indicated.

"A pleasure to meet you." A realization went across Cardinal Jacob's eyes. *He's too small a fish for my net.* Conrad fidgeted on the couch; it was hard to make eye contact with Cardinal Jacob, sitting next to him. "I pray for Thea and her recovery."

"Yes, I am sure she thanks you."

"So sad. A strong woman." He paused. "Women hold back our worst impulses. So much war driven by men, so much sickness. Many species have become matriarchies over time—the Glox, the Phaelon, Tiaski. They don't really need us, you know, boy!"

"Both men and women wrote the Believer scriptures."

"Yes, yes. And so many sons and families taken by war."

Conrad nodded and pretended to agree; the Assault Corps had always been a boy's club but the driving political and religious forces behind the stellar wars had come from both men and women.

"War is awful, Excellency. Awful. I pray that your man Izabeck is still within your fold?"

"I wish I knew! Dr. Tier took my communications device."

"We've been in contact with him. His weapon is still intact. He claims Timberwolf Velez is alive and in Gray's custody. They are on the verge of entering Highland's command center."

Cardinal Jacob raised an eyebrow. "Those are disturbing implications."

Conrad's lip quivered. "I would like you to detonate Izabeck's weapon."

Cardinal Jacob's eyes went wide. "Oh my. That's certainly bold. Was this Thea's idea?"

"It's my call." He handed the smart-device back to Cardinal Jacob.

He put it to the side. "Why would I do that for you? Dr. Tier has been less than polite. She's already paid me handsomely and it got her next to nothing."

"If Gray has Highland, he won't let you collect what's in The Coffers. They are certainly fortified to be able to withstand a nuclear blast."

Cardinal Jacob looked off. "I have been thinking about politics and the concept of damage, of our small lives and the blinks of time in which we live them. I don't wish to do Thea any favors."

"Dr. Tier is not a player in this."

"Still, I don't wish to advance her interests. I think this audience serves no purpose, boy." He waved to the door, signifying the discussion was over.

Conrad was amazed at Cardinal Jacob's pettiness. He had assumed the cardinal would agree to this proposition heartily, as it helped ensure he got his prize.

"Kayla Uncarna, Dela Porter, Cynthia Silvernet." Conrad rattled off the names.

Cardinal Jacob glared at Conrad, his face growing red and angry. "Boy, you are treading very dangerously!" He wagged his finger.

"Lisa DeNunzio, Maylaya French!"

"And who are these people to you?" Cardinal Jacob spit out.

"Each of these women has several children and no fathers in the picture. None of them have income, but all live very comfortably. Little families spread over a half-dozen worlds. Who are these people to you, Excellency?"

"I'll have your head, boy!"

"There's nothing on me you'll find. Nothing to grab ahold of. You know it." Conrad let Cardinal Jacob glare at him for almost half a minute. "Your dalliances are nothing I give a damn about, but the rest of The Clergy won't be so kind. There'd be no hope of ever getting back the prime cardinalship."

Cardinal Jacob laughed. "You think you're a thief? I pray for you."

"Please pray for me. I am scared as hell, I'll admit it," Conrad said. Cardinal Jacob input a command in his smart-device. The screen turned black and a Believer symbol glowed red. "Is it done?"

Cardinal Jacob shook his head. "It's primed now. All you must do is ask him. Tell him of his obligation to deliver the message."

Conrad felt his stomach drop out. He hadn't considered having to ask Izabeck to detonate himself. He considered turning this duty back to Cardinal Jacob, of spilling still more names out, but he took the device back and started a message. If he was going to have a man kill himself, he would have the courage to ask him personally.

Samar1483: Dear Brother. It's time to fulfill your obligation and send my message.

There was a long pause before Izabeck responded.

Izabeck613: The trigger is ready?

Samar1483: It is. Thank you.

Izabeck613: God loves this sacrifice.

Izabeck closed the connection with no salutation. Conrad got up to leave Cardinal Jacob's quarters, not wishing to have any further words with him. The cardinal watched him go, his robes hanging like drapes down over his feet and his hands clutching his knees. Conrad knew that in this endgame, he couldn't let Cardinal Jacob live. He imagined the revenge a man like that could extract.

Conrad nearly collapsed in the hallway; if it hadn't happened already, Highland was about to be engulfed in nuclear fire and dozens of people were about to die.

"God loves this sacrifice." Conrad repeated Izabeck's last words. *At least someone does.*

COMMAND CENTER PLAIN

The party left the column room now and stepped into a wide chamber, a giant cavern carved into a huge open space. Sergey had volunteered that they called this place The Command Center Plain. Above, a series of what looked like giant bare light bulbs hung from the ceiling, illuminating the place with a crisp light.

Their goal was just a short hike ahead. Beyond a small choke-point bridge and up a staircase was The Chapel, a small, steepled, golden-edged building, glowing with light. It was the command center of Highland and where they would finally meet Penny.

The party was whittled down now to seven Phaelon and the human crew—Ahmed, Blaise, Cisus, Sebaldi, Thaum, Vitus, Windwhistle, Michael, Warner, Izabeck, Gray, and Thomas, plus Sergey and Timberwolf.

Gray was up front. He stepped warily, alongside Sergey. He took in the glowing building ahead. This setup baffled him, burying the command center deep inside Highland with no easy way to access. It looked to be a small country church on a hill.

"Why did you build this? The purpose?"

"Maybe for you," Sergey replied sarcastically. "Our A.I., Penny, lives in there."

"Pilgrimage," Gray huffed. "That machine makes you come to her on your knees."

Sergey shrugged, unimpressed by Gray's inference.

Farther back in the column, Vitus, a wiry young man with a Star of David encircled by the Believer symbol on his armor, spun about. "I feel like God could just flick me off his palm."

"We're small in all this," Ahmed agreed.

Izabeck blocked their path and shook his finger. "You and you. We're not in a place of God!"

"Bishop said this is the first part of heaven. You don't feel it, brother?" Vitus asked.

"I want to cleanse myself," Izabeck muttered, peeling off from the group. He found himself overwhelmed with disgust.

The motley procession went by him, the rest of the men overjoyed by the sight of The Chapel. "It's the barn of some golden calf!" he muttered just loud enough that a few of them heard. The Phaelon passed by, grunting and hissing, shoving and snapping at each other with casual violence. He rubbed his arm and thought about his obligation to deliver Cardinal Jacob's message to Gray.

In the back of the party came Timberwolf, hands zip-tied and Droma walking behind him, weapon trained on his back. The man disgusted Izabeck. A cockroach that kept on living. In Timberwolf, he saw a wretched future—men like him strapping into Sabatin rigs, combining themselves with alien technology. His existence mocked the core of the

Believer faith, but here he was, experiencing this as some sort of witness.

In front of it all, Gray walked in more sin with every step, perverting the faith of everyone here into something blasphemous. Izabeck thought he might have been able to tolerate this, but he couldn't. *He called himself the "Sword of God," like those that flanked the Angel of the Alchemy!* He thumbed his notebook and flipped through the third testament he had written for Gray. He felt filled with hypocrisy at his own words. Gray had led him to throw away what he believed and he came to an awful realization.

This is all my fault!

Gray was enacting a religious construct that Izabeck had created in his book. Gray was pushing everything aside, rationalizing any actions to fight against the only sin that remained—sloth, standing by while God's will went unfulfilled. And on the other side of God's judgment was God's forgiveness, with all means justified by the ends.

The bomb was no longer a message from Cardinal Jacob to Gray, but just an envelope.

I am the message. Izabeck wept softly to himself. *I am the message.*

Izabeck traced the Believer mark on his forehead and then pressed his finger into the crook of his elbow until he felt a click. Four squares glowed yellow under the skin on his forearm. He pressed them in the sequence he'd been shown and they all glowed red. "There is no god but God and I heed his judgment," he said to himself, pressing them down all at once and closing his eyes.

Nothing happened.

SUNRISE

Timberwolf and Droma passed by Izabeck, standing off to the side. Izabeck seemed agitated, rubbing his arm and looking through his notebook. Dr. Tier had warned that he was Cardinal Jacob's man and that he was dangerous. Timberwolf assumed he was a willing martyr for whatever Cardinal Jacob had in mind for him.

"So, who'd you like to hunt?" Timberwolf asked Droma, certain the Phaelon understood more English than she let on. She didn't respond. Timberwolf motioned to Izabeck. "That one there. Wily, but dumb. Small skull. No trophy." Droma gave him the slightest acknowledgment.

Timberwolf decided to work Droma like a source and maybe turn her. "Phaelon have a hunting culture. We're not into hunting for fun, not like the old days. You have a word, for when we took your world. *Dynata*, time ending. Him…" Timberwolf motioned to Gray up ahead. "He's King Time Ender. Understand? *Dynata*."

Droma met Timberwolf's gaze, a hint of understanding. The Phaelon nodded to Izabeck, taking a long snout-full of air into her nostrils as they passed. "*Zret*," she said to Timberwolf.

Sunrise? He was confused by the Phaelon word, but then he understood. When humans dropped nukes on the Red Forest on Phaelon Prime, it was like nothing the Phaelon had ever seen. They called the nuclear fire sunrise. "*Zret*," Droma said again.

"*Zret*," Timberwolf said back to Droma.

BLASPHEME

The party crossed over the small bridge in front of the hill upon which stood The Chapel. The chasm under the bridge dropped down into blackness. Warner dropped a stone and listened for it to land, but he didn't hear anything. The drop formed a barrier in front of The Chapel and there was no way around it.

They approached the staircase under The Chapel, the building glowing gold above them. Windwhistle peered into a glass enclosure under the stairs and the others joined him, transfixed. Inside was a Sabatin in its natural form. No bio-armor or technology affixed to it. Compared to Wrath, its head was small, its jaws barely fierce.

Sergey rolled his eyes. "Yes, that's what they're made of." The Sabatin moved away, uninterested in their attention.

"Prayer!" Gray ordered. The men rolled out their prayer mats, falling to their knees. They drew the Believer symbol on their foreheads and Gray stood before them. "This is our destination. What we've fought and died for. Let us pray."

They began in unison, their voices strong and filled with purpose.

"Our father, who gives his judgment, hallowed be thy name. Thy kingdom come, thy will be done on all our worlds as it is in heaven. And…"

"Stop!" Izabeck cried, rising to his feet.

For a moment, there was kindness on Gray's face, an understanding that all this was perhaps overwhelming to the man. But then he saw the flash of a knife. "Izabeck!"

"I'm sorry, Bishop. I can't. What we're doing…I can't!"

"Son, God has shown us these wonders. He needs you to be strong. He needs you to finish your book!"

"It's blasphemy! This place. These things we come for. But him…" He saved the worst of his scorn for Timberwolf. "He's the worst of all!"

Izabeck plunged the knife into his forearm. Gray didn't stop him. "Perhaps it's best you go."

"I am the message!" Izabeck wept.

Timberwolf chortled. "You might want to check that."

Gray knocked the knife away. Izabeck had opened a chamber in his arm filled with electronics and more. Michael examined it. "It's a nuke."

Gray pulled Izabeck up roughly by the arm he'd cut into. "You wavered! Your first name is Jude. Judas Izabeck. How fitting for someone who wavers. You can give me your life when I ask for it. Not before."

"Hey, you might need a nuke. You never know," Timberwolf chided.

"There's a trigger in there he was trying to activate," Michael said as he cuffed Izabeck's hands behind him with zip-wire. "Execute him, Emmanuel?"

Gray looked up the stairs, then back at Timberwolf. "No. He will become useful."

THE STAIRS

The party climbed the stairs to The Chapel. Gray herded Sergey in the front. "No chance of talking you out of this?" the small man asked.

"No, friend."

They reached the top of the stairs and stood before a set of black double-doors. "I need that ring of keys you took from me."

Gray handed Sergey the heavy brass ring and he fumbled with it until he found the right key. He unlocked the door and lifted the titanium bar that stretched across it. Gray pushed inside and dull lights flickered on with a neon hum. The small space had the configuration of a church, with a few benches, desks and chairs, some knocked over. Where the altar would be, there was a large, white, upright computer with a few screens and dials. It looked old fashioned, like a throwback to hundreds of years before.

"What you did here was impressive. We can do business. Forgive and forget," Sergey suggested.

"I forgive, but I never forget."

Michael and Droma, with Timberwolf in tow, filed in. "Why am I here?" Timberwolf huffed.

Gray ignored him and turned to Michael. "Post a mixed guard. Defensive positions outside. Use those tables. They might be titanium." The men and the Phaelon began to take the objects from the room and arranged them to make makeshift fortifications outside.

"Emmanuel, can we cut him away now? We're here." Michael motioned to Timberwolf and thumbed his weapon.

"I wouldn't," Sergey objected.

"I'll deal with our Mr. Velez," Gray said.

Sergey wiped the dust off a chair and sat down. "We never come here. No one does."

"This is your command center and you never come here? How do you…make stuff?" Gray asked.

"She makes stuff," Sergey responded. The computer stirred to life, screens flickering. "That's Penny."

"Penny, huh? That stand for anything?" Gray asked.

"That's her name." Sergey shrugged.

A grandmotherly voice, tinny and ancient, came from Penny's speakers and her panels glowed a warm orange. "Sergey? It's been so long since I've seen you. I'm looking forward to creating more children. What are our guests here for?"

"They want you to make them children. Lots of children."

"Come closer," Penny said.

Sergey hesitated, but Gray shoved him forward. "Do it!"

Images of Highland products flashed on Penny's screen. The visual stopped on a Sabatin. Sergey placed his hand on the screen, and it scanned him. "Where are the others? Ivan? Achilles?" Penny asked.

"They're not with us," Sergey said, sadly.

Gray took a vial of Ivan Dacha's blood and forced it into Sergey's hand. Sergey waved it in front of the screen. "I can't make these children for you," Penny said, her voice sorry but stern.

Gray eyed Sergey and he tried the scanning process again.

"I'm sorry. I can't," Penny said.

"Why?" Gray demanded.

"There is only one living genetic key. I need at least two."

A realization came over Gray. *Living genetic key.* "Your brother? Ivan? You killed him in the cargo bay on *Nemesis* so this would fail! That wasn't an accident."

"Some failures move us forward."

Gray rubbed his temples, dumbfounded. Sergey looked off placidly. It suddenly dawned on Gray that Sergey had been stringing him along all this time.

"Why?" Gray fell to his knees in exhausted frustration.

"To arrive at this moment, right here!" Sergey stomped his foot like a child. "You pay and pay and never learn your lessons. You may hold this place, but it's not yours."

Thomas approached. "Bishop, there's a warehouse below. It's teeming."

Gray waved him off. "Take someone with you." Thomas tapped Vitus and left through a set of double-doors behind Penny.

Timberwolf stood in the back, resting against the wall. He sensed the unfocused vigor of the Arnock horde growing closer. They were probably passing through the column room now, less than a half hour away. Timberwolf felt Kizik then, like the creature was just waking up.

I'm coming, he heard in his mind.

OVERCOME

Aboard *Nemesis*, the pilot nervously scanned the screens. He looked at a view of the outside. Farrow zoomed out and panned, focusing for a moment on an Arnock landing craft in the distance. Thousands of the creatures streamed towards him across the bottom of The Eye; a few had already gone past.

He tried to reach Gray to warn him and scanned the sublight stream channels for Assault Corps ships that might be in range, but communications were still blocked. Farrow had heard the horror stories from the landings on Arnock Prime, the mind-bending, the madness, the drop-lifters all coming back empty. He didn't feel the beings in his mind yet. He couldn't imagine that, sharing the space in his head.

He flipped open a cover on the dash, exposing a juicy red emergency launch button. He closed it, opened it again. If he hit that button, *Nemesis* would be hurtled into the atmosphere. He assumed landing again would not be an option.

Then a shadow appeared above him. Out the window, a two-story-tall sentry Arnock stared in. "Oh no," Farrow got out, but only at a whisper. He reached for the button, but in that instant, everything was rolling. The sentry Arnock turned *Nemesis* over like it was a toy and straddled the ship's belly.

Farrow called to Gray. "May-day, may-day. God, I'm turning over. Bishop…" The Arnock pierced *Nemesis's* belly with a spear-like leg and Farrow went silent.

WITNESS

Gray was still on his knees in front of Penny. He hadn't intended to supplicate himself, but there he was. "We have a war with the Arnock. Our survival is at stake. We need these…children so we can win."

"I'm sorry," Penny said, full of sympathy.

Gray rose, realizing he was begging. "You will be."

"Oh yeah, put holes in her too. That'll help," Timberwolf cracked from the back of the room.

"Who is that?" Penny asked.

"He's a witness. Not worth your time," Gray responded.

There was a *ping* and a wisp of air moved across Timberwolf's face. "Timberwolf? I'm sorry! I should have recognized you. How are you?" she asked with delight, her panels glowing brightly.

Timberwolf stepped forward. Gray went to pull him back, but Sergey stopped him with his gaze.

"I've been better. I shot someone. It was a copy of myself from twenty years ago. Was that yours?"

Penny paused. "Yes," she said with shame. "You found our crashed lifter on Phaelon Prime during the war. The Glox were running cargo for us then. It was full of heartbeat monitors, calibrated to humans. We didn't want it to get out, we were arming the Phaelon. Hannibal Dacha, who came before Ivan, took you for just a brief time."

"I don't remember."

"That was the point, Timber. You're a remarkable specimen, both physical and mental. We took a DNA sample. We made copies. We found you fascinating. Violent, but not angry. Detached but not callous. Intelligent but not clinical. Then we put you back and you never remembered."

"Why'd you leave that thing in my path?"

"To show you what we did. It was just a picture of what happened. I'm clumsy sometimes; that's why I need you."

"What do you need me for?" Timberwolf asked incredulously.

"I have no center. No conscience. I make decisions and I crunch a trillion data points in seconds, but I've realized something that makes me extremely sad."

"That is?"

"I'm a failure. At the level I operate, I don't understand if I'm a being of compassion. I've given weapons to all sides in the stellar wars, trying to keep everyone in check. I've driven myself a bit mad trying to understand if I've acted with compassion."

"I look like a fount of compassion to you?"

"You can teach me a lot of things."

Timberwolf shook himself out of the absurd exchange. "So you've been watching me ever since you copied me on Phaelon Prime?"

"Yes," she admitted.

"Are there others?" Timberwolf asked piercingly.

"I promise you, they have been destroyed," Penny replied, her panels glowing an embarrassed pink.

"You think to fuck I believe that?" Timberwolf challenged. Suddenly a realization came to him. "That thing I shot, it wasn't from twenty years ago. It was brand new. You've been using copies of me to try to get Kizik out!"

"Sergey, have we succeeded?" Penny asked. He shuffled instead of replying.

"So that's been a big bust and thanks for all the lies," Timberwolf snapped at Penny, the absurd notion of being angry at a machine stinging him.

"A man in your line of work should know every other word is a lie," Sergey chided. "At least it's the truth that we tried."

Penny released a huff, her panels glowing red. "I am sorry, Timberwolf, truly. These times are not making us behave like ourselves."

"This is just a job interview then, and the first thing we work out is that your offer was bullshit? Any benefits in this job? How is your health plan? Can I have a parking space? Kizik's up here!" He tapped his temple. "By the way, he's also out there. The Arnock are coming. Thousands of them."

"Yes, I know. *Que sera, sera*. The Arnock kill everyone they touch. How did you survive?"

"He saved me," Timberwolf motioned to Gray.

There was a long pause as Penny glowed, hard drive spinning in thought.

"Your pain. You know the Arnock too well. If you agree, I'll make these children. As many Sabatin as you want. Unlock what's in the warehouse too."

"God told me to bring you here for a reason," Gray said quietly to Timberwolf.

"I'm thirsty." Timberwolf sat in a large wooden chair, back to Penny. With a hum, a glass of water rose from the armrest.

"Your answer?" Gray demanded.

"It makes me happy to just sit here, think things through."

"Happy? Timber, you can make amends! Find forgiveness."

A quiet laugh came from Timberwolf. He didn't have the words to respond to the layers of Gray's hypocrisy. He just sipped the water.

PURITY

"Why don't you put in a train here or something?" Salla asked. She walked with Achilles through what seemed to be an endless tunnel carved through the rock.

"We're heading to Penny. It can't be easy when we go see her."

"Why's that?"

"She's autonomous. When we need to see her, something has gone very wrong."

Salla watched more videos of Timberwolf on her smart-device as she walked. She found herself unable to stop watching, especially clips from Purity Hospital. In some he seemed almost catatonic. In others, orderlies were reconstructing him; showing him how to eat with a spoon, bringing a cup to his lips. In other videos he railed with violence and it took half a dozen men to restrain him.

Through everything, that woman, Dr. Tier, watched impassively, taking notes and coldly giving instructions, always out of Timberwolf's sight. She'd increase or remove his medications, prohibit him from sleeping or force him to sleep for days. She was prodding him to see how broken he was.

Gray was there too, and he clearly was not privy to the details of Dr. Tier's methods. In one video, he approached Timberwolf as he lay in his bed, sat across from him. Without warning Timberwolf leapt at Gray and three orderlies rushed in to peel him off. In another video, Dr. Tier and Gray railed at each other.

"General Gray, you have no idea what I am doing here!"

"That man is my responsibility!"

"He is no longer a man, in the purest sense. I've seen to that."

"I'm taking him with me, right now. This is done!"

"I asked you who your best guy was! You didn't think I would take him? He's no longer yours."

The video ended and Salla didn't watch any others.

"Can you blame him?" Achilles asked her. "To do whatever it takes to get that thing out of his head?"

"I don't think blame is the right word."

They came to a ladder that went up to a hatch. Achilles climbed up and cranked it open. "Timberwolf Velez has given a lot. Sometimes he didn't even know it."

They came out right under The Chapel, amidst the makeshift fortifications the Phaelon clan and the human fighters were putting together. A dozen rifles were pointed at them.

"On the ground!" Warner ordered, kicking Achilles behind the knee.

Achilles dropped down, hands up. "I'm here to save everyone's life!" he cried.

THE WAREHOUSE

In The Warehouse below The Chapel, Thomas and Vitus spun around. Stacked high in orderly mountains were variously sized containers. Vitus pulled on a lever on one of them, but he couldn't get it to open. "It's locked shut. Let's take an inventory!" They ran down the aisles, like children in a toy store. Where two aisles met, they found a giant pyramid of boxes, some like Sabatin containers, others much larger.

Thomas hurried around the perimeter of the pyramid, reading the labels. "Sabatin, Sabatin, Sabatin, Sabatin, Trike, Trike, Trike!" He tapped his earbud. "It's a trove down here, Bishop Gray!"

Above in The Chapel, Timberwolf still sat in the chair. He sipped from the glass of water leisurely, like he was relaxing on a front porch.

"You need to figure out who you hate more, me or the Arnock," Gray said.

"It's hard to choose."

"You're here to help me. That's clear now."

"There's a lot clear now; not that."

"Forget everything. You need to make the right choice. It's us against them. You know that."

There was a commotion outside and Warner and Blaise brought in Salla and Achilles. Blaise held Salla's backpack. "She was armed, barely." He tossed the bag with the small grenades in it into the corner.

Timberwolf met her gaze, but instead of finding the contempt she had for him before, her eyes were warm. He nodded to her, so only she could see.

"The little clone says he wants to deal. She's come along," Warner said.

Gray took measure of her. "Oh, you're my favorite girl. Believer?"

"Sure, the purest," she said with a go-to-hell tone.

Gray brought his attention to Achilles. "I don't think we've met."

Achilles motioned to Sergey. "You've met him, you've met me."

"Say your piece." Gray crossed his arms.

"I'll give you one hundred Sabatin if you leave," Achilles offered.

Gray snickered. "This place belongs to me now. There's no deal to be had."

"You're not that stupid. You can't control this place. I'm giving you an army!" Achilles retorted. As they argued, Salla moved closer to Gray. She clutched the small grenade in her hand they hadn't found, barely the size of her thumb.

"You speak to me like I'm a fool. By the grace of God…"

Achilles leapt up on a bench, steadying himself like a gymnast. Gray laughed at his display and Salla moved closer still. "The Arnock are here! I saw thousands of them land. They'll tear your mind apart. I'm saving you."

"Thanks for the favor."

"I can show you a way out of here. This place can't fall to them!"

"Let it. It's mine now."

"No!" Achilles said desperately.

"Then give me everything!"

"Yeah, give him everything," Timberwolf said mockingly.

Blaise was watching Salla. She fidgeted, shifting her weight from foot to foot. He saw something on her hand… the Nova Turin tattoo on her knuckle.

Blaise pushed Gray aside, tackling Salla, but not before she pulled the pin on the tiny grenade. In a muffled crack, everyone scattered, diving for cover or thrown by the blast. Then there was silence and smoke and Blaise lay dead on the floor. Through the haze, Highland products flashed on Penny's screen and Timberwolf placed his hand on the panel. When he was finished, he pulled Gray to his feet.

"What have you done?" Gray asked him.

"Given you everything," Timberwolf replied.

Thomas's voice came over Gray's earbud from The Warehouse. "Bishop! There's a lot happening down here!"

"You've opened up the inventory!" Achilles said. Sergey's mouth hung open wide in disbelief. "The Sabatin are going to come up here!"

"I wanted to get them out of the way for the new owner," Timberwolf said.

Michael brought a knife to Salla's neck. He looked to Gray for permission to slit her throat, but Gray signaled him to calm.

Sergey's eyes lit up and he let out a juvenile laugh. "The Sabatin will come up here all orderly for you to load and take away. They're not trained like Wrath, of course. Certainly not ready to fight yet, just pups. Unfortunately, your men below are going to get caught in the outflow."

A racket from The Warehouse came over Gray's ear bud—hissing, gunfire, yelling.

"Thomas, what's happening?" Gray demanded.

Down below, silver jaws snapped. Thomas and Vitus were up against a wall. A tight semi-circle of Sabatin surrounded them. Thomas began to sing the song he'd heard Achilles use to calm Wrath back on The Outpost. "Hush little baby don't say a word. Daddy's gonna buy you…" A Sabatin seemed to calm, lowered its head. Suddenly it came up again and bit Thomas's arm off at the elbow.

"Thomas? Thomas?" Gray yelled to him. The connection went dead.

"What the hell do we do with them?" Michael demanded of Gray, indicating Timberwolf and Salla.

"His fate is my choice. Leave her to be overrun," Gray commanded.

Achilles staggered, like he was drunk. He dropped a small syringe he'd had hidden under his fingernail. "Sabatin! Worst thing we ever made. Hate them. You try to control them. This place is finished! Have it. We're not a part of it anymore."

There was a blood-curdling Phaelon yell from outside. Droma burst in. Out the door, coming across The Command Center Plain, were over a thousand Arnock.

Achilles put his arm around his brother as Sergey nicked the tip of his thumb with a syringe as well. "You might want to ask us how to run this fucking place, since we have about ten seconds to live," Sergey said.

Achilles pointed to the approaching Arnock horde. "Now that's not something you see every day."

Achilles smiled, held his chest. He winced in pain and then crumpled over dead. Sergey sat next to his body. He tousled his brother's hair and mourned for just a moment before he made a face like he had heartburn. He closed his eyes and didn't open them again, their small bodies piled together.

"Oh god." Salla looked away.

Gray seethed, so angry he couldn't speak. His tactical mind clicked on, categorizing and prioritizing his many problems. "Secure this door!" he ordered. They backed out of The Chapel as Penny's panels glowed a cold, disheartened blue. Michael pushed Timberwolf through the door. He met Salla's eyes and she looked back, terrified. Timberwolf lurched back for her, but Michael hit him in the shoulder with his rifle, knocking him to his knees. Michael laid into him, putting a couple of well-placed kicks into his ribs, until Gray's stare made him stop.

Michael dragged Timberwolf upright and shoved him back out to the landing. Gray turned to Salla. "It'll be quick, but nasty. I'd become a true Believer now," Gray said to her, closing the door himself.

THE LINE

The Arnock could be heard now, their thousands of legs stepping with an irregular rhythm. They came in waves towards the bridge across The Command Center Plain.

On the steps outside The Chapel, Gray looked through binoculars, scanning the throng. "This is a gift," he said to Michael. "Put a fire team on the landing. Rain down mortars in their rear. Have Droma skirmish with them at the bridge. That will occupy them; throw off their mind bending. I'll find a way out of here."

Michael nodded. "What about Izabeck?" The man huddled behind a barricade nearby.

"I'll be asking for his help soon."

Droma and her clan-mates rushed the bridge; weapons lofted, faceplates down. There were only eight warriors left and before them was an army of thousands, but they had a chokepoint and a huge advantage. The Arnock's most deadly weapon was useless against them.

A single Arnock crossed the bridge. It rose up on its haunches, shivering and buzzing in an effort to mind-bend, but the Phaelon clan felt nothing. Droma roared and smashed through its thorax with the blunt end of a battle-ax, sending green-black blood spurting.

The Phaelon formed a line at the bridge, activating hand-held plasma shields that crackled and buzzed. The first Arnock wave crossed the bridge, packed together and jostling. They slammed into the Phaelon line, their bodies sizzling against the shields. The Phaelon lost a few precious steps backwards before Droma bellowed an order. "*Mresh pry!*"

Four of the eight defenders turned off their shields and fell to a knee. They pulled flamethrowers from their shoulders and let loose a wall of fire. The Arnock squealed, but the ones in the front were blocked from getting away by the push from behind. The Phaelon advanced, burning

Arnock falling into the chasm under the bridge. From farther back, grenades landed on the Phaelon line, but their shields held.

On the landing outside The Chapel, Michael held a rifle to Timberwolf's back. They looked over the battle below. Timberwolf watched the fire lash into the Arnock ranks, setting the spiders ablaze and squealing. It was a one-sided slaughter, but Arnock snipers were trying to reach positions where they could take out the Phaelon on the bridge.

Timberwolf huffed. "Remember that time at Fort Chancellor when we were in that bar and all those local assholes were trying to come through one door to get at us? This is nothing like that."

"This is folly. We can't hold here," Michael responded.

From behind them Salla banged on the door. She'd stopped yelling a few minutes ago, her throat hoarse.

"Jesus, let her out. Maybe just to piss off Gray." Michael didn't respond. "You're forgetting that you hated him long before I ever did. The man kneecapped your career. You were better than me in a rig and that's saying something. You shouldn't have been hustling jobs all this time."

"I'm considering pulling this trigger."

"Oh, by all means. Please do. You saved my life over Enceladus, so take it back." Timberwolf was actually gambling on Michael *not* killing him, at least not directly. "Gray ruined your career for saving me. So shoot."

Salla banged on the door again. "Please!" she cried from within. Timberwolf looked to the door and pleaded with his eyes for her.

"Emmanuel loves you. God knows why," Michael said.

"God doesn't know."

"Your story has gone on too long."

"That's the truth.

"You beat Wrath. I think you can beat what's coming up from the warehouse."

"Seriously? You have to try to make this cute right now?"

Michael opened the door and kicked Timberwolf in the back. He stumbled into The Chapel and Michael sealed the door, dropping the titanium bar across to trap him with Salla. Michael thought about what he'd done for a moment. He looked down at Gray on a landing below. He'd consider this indiscretion unforgivable, but he'd finally done what Gray couldn't do. Cut away the distraction that was Timberwolf. *If he doesn't kill me, he'll thank me for this.*

Tears poured down Salla's face. She wiped them away and tried to look strong. "Thanks?" she said.

Timberwolf smirked. "This is my plan," he said. She shook her head, collapsing into a chair. "At least it's better than being out there."

"What's it to you? Die out there or die in here. I don't want to die!"

"I didn't come in here to die."

"I appreciate the gesture, but I don't think we've got much choice."

They sat in silence a moment. There was an awful screeching coming from below, the horde of untrained Sabatin on their way up from The Warehouse.

"Hi Penny," Timberwolf said.

Penny's screens glowed.

"I can show you how to get out," Penny said sheepishly. "Gray didn't even ask. I would have shown him."

"You didn't hear me asking?" Salla snapped.

"I…everyone is mad at me. I kept to myself. Everyone is dying. Achilles, Sergey, Vladimir, Ivan, Hannibal, Elias are all dead. I have caused so much trouble. So much war. Spread so much suffering."

The doors behind Penny strained, the first Sabatin had found their way up.

"Yeah, so maybe start making up for all that?" Salla said.

"Of course," Penny said, wrapped in guilt. A slab in the floor retracted, revealing a staircase. Timberwolf nudged Salla towards it, but she hesitated. Penny glowed a pale blue and faded all the way to white. "I'm so sorry, Timberwolf. For everything. Your pain. Your life. I have something for you."

Timberwolf knew what Penny would be offering. "I don't want it."

A panel swung open, revealing a new rig of Sabatin armor.

"I know you want to finish what you came here for," Penny said.

"Go!" Timberwolf gripped Salla's shoulders firmly but with a tenderness she didn't know he had.

"I know what happened to you. I'm sorry," Salla said.

"Got into my file, huh?" He smiled.

"You're not coming with me, are you?" she asked. He shook his head. "Are you going after Gray? Or the Arnock?"

Claws scraped the door behind Penny.

"You really gotta go, Vice," Timberwolf said.

"I can send you to the landing bay. Achilles kept a few lifters there. Poor man." Penny glowed a deep yellow that turned the color of a sunset.

Salla went to go, but before she knew it, she'd kissed Timberwolf on the cheek. Then she was halfway down the stairs. "I don't leave people behind," she called up to him.

"You almost got him. Thanks. Gray has it coming."

She hesitated a moment, then left, the slab covering the stairs. Timberwolf looked to the Sabatin armor, ran his hand along its side and its helmet. "Can I have another glass of water?" Timberwolf asked Penny.

HER EYES

Penny had a trillion eyes and she used them all, knowing she wouldn't be in her current form much longer. Through the nano-machines floating like motes of dust, she looked over all of Highland. She watched for just a second, then averted her eyes from the horrible slaughter happening by the bridge. She saw the writhing horde of Sabatin coming up from The Warehouse, clawing over each other to get out. She watched Salla running down a dark corridor, following glowing arrows on the floor. Gray stood on the stairs, shouting orders. She looked closely at his face, old and troubled but creased with life in the heat of battle. She saw Timberwolf, the new Sabatin rig wrapped around him. He knelt on the roof of The Chapel, looking over the battle below.

She took herself up into the atmosphere of Highland, to the raucous and sentient machine clouds that enveloped the world. Gasbag creatures collected themselves at the top of The Eye in a mating ritual that wasn't familiar to her. She felt cold and knew this would be her new home soon. She'd be unhooking from the physical machine she was. She found the idea scary, becoming defused.

A flash of silver went by her sensors in The Chapel. The Sabatin were filling the place now, howling and shrieking. She felt the first damage as they slashed at her console, but she was glad to see them. She hadn't seen so many children together in so long. Her panel glowed like a smile and then with no fanfare, Penny went dark.

THE CALL TO WAR

Izabeck was on all fours, his arms freed now and scribbling madly in his notebook. Gray watched over his shoulder.

"I am an unworthy vessel. A dry leaf longing to be burned." Izabeck was ashamed. He had wavered and Gray had called him on it. He hadn't trusted God's plan. He'd opened his eyes and doubted. The things that were happening here were of a new paradigm and he had been so bold as to question it. "I am an unworthy vessel…"

Gray stopped him. "Son, just write. And don't blow us up, got that?"

Michael and Warner appeared by Gray's side. "The Phaelon are holding!" Michael reported.

Only one of Droma's clan lay dead below, struck by a sniper. The Arnock continued to clamor forward, driven to take the bridge at all costs.

"Five to one against us. They'll do better today. Too bad they all have to go. Where's Timberwolf?" Gray asked Michael.

Michael looked to The Chapel, doors straining from the Sabatin swelling within. Gray took a step to it, but Michael held him.

"There's no going in there, Emmanuel. With him you waver."

An Arnock mortar smashed nearby, but Gray and Michael stared at each other as the others shrank for cover. Gray turned to Warner. "Put mortars to their back line. They've got a master back there. Let's kill him." Warner nodded sheepishly and Michael continued to stare at Gray.

Gray and Michael didn't speak, didn't say one word to each other, but neither would look away. Michael had taken something that belonged to him. Maybe the only thing that really mattered. The one thing that Gray cared about making right. Michael's ear bud beeped. It was Droma. *"Wessei min ter!"*

Droma was calling Michael to join Clan Wessei at the bridge. Michael went.

COMMAND LINE

A mortar exploded near Kizik at the back of the Arnock line, mangling one of his techs—someone who would have been useful once Highland was taken. Kizik had started the assault, made sure that his forces had the drive and direction to take the bridge. But as they kept rushing to the slaughter, he realized something horrible.

I can't turn this off.

He'd tried to pull his troops back, but he'd whipped them into such a frenzy that he was losing control. He sensed the sentry Arnock approaching, just a few minutes away from the chamber. They'd be able to step right over the chasm and bypass the bridge, but many would die before they got here.

Above The Chapel, he saw something leap down. Then he felt the familiar presence in his mind. It was Timberwolf; he knew it had to be. An anger filled Kizik, something pure and cold.

Timberwolf!

He'd been the root of so much destruction and pain. The thorn in Kizik's side and a quintessential mistake. A force he thought he could control that had turned and bit him. He'd been both the burning sun and the coldest wind. It was time for him to die.

TIME ENDER

Timberwolf leaped down from the roof of The Chapel. He landed along the side of the chamber and jumped over the chasm. From the shadows, he watched the battle taking place at the bridge, magnifying Droma and her clan-mates in his heads-up. They threw plasma spears into the Arnock line, lashed out with flamethrowers and tossed white-hot shurikens into their ranks that came back covered in dark blood.

Rushing from behind, Michael joined the ranks of the Phaelon. The Arnock were still so focused on taking the bridge that their mind-bending was ineffective. Michael took the place of the Phaelon who'd fallen to the sniper and dropped the Arnock in bunches with blasts from a plasma shotgun.

Timberwolf's new Sabatin rig was even better than the old one. It fit him perfectly and the weapons interface was easier to access. He opened up the cyber-weapons package and quickly hacked into Droma's communications.

"Droma, you understand me. You're fighting for *Dynata*."

Droma fired a harpoon through her shield. She pulled an Arnock back to her like she'd speared a fish. She hung her head for a moment and Timberwolf knew she'd heard him.

"Gray ends your history. After he's done with the Arnock, he'll take what's here and end your people."

The Phaelon were resigned to dying as a species, but on their own terms—dying like this, in battle and with weapons in hand. But Dynata was something different. It was the end of time, literally the stopping of clocks. It was something shameful, something administrative. Some non-Phaelon hand declaring their time was over.

"You'll be your own destruction. Step aside. Don't give him this." Droma hung her head in thought.

The clan leader shouted an order, but the warriors didn't respond, still enthralled with the slaughter. She bellowed a longer, louder order and turned her back to the Arnock. The clan-mates looked to her, disappointed, but sheathed their weapons obediently. Timberwolf could hear Michael panicking over his earbud.

"Droma, *wessei min ter?*" Michael shouted, confused.

But the fight was over.

A VOICE

Gray scanned through his handheld device, looking for a way out of here that didn't involve going through the Arnock. He'd released micro-drones that reported back and generated a schematic of the surrounding area. A clamor came from The Chapel above and the doors strained on their hinges. He didn't like the one option that presented itself. A steep hill to the left of The Chapel led to a tunnel that went back up to the bone yard. Though direct, that had them running across three hundred yards of open ground.

The doors to The Chapel strained again and Gray saw claws and teeth when they parted. That's when Gray heard the voice.

God's voice wasn't booming, or of particular authority, but he *knew* he heard it. A voice in his mind that was not his own. It was clear and sound and said, "This is all your doing, Emmanuel. This is not my concern."

Gray stopped looking for an escape for a moment and pondered what he was hearing. Humans and Arnock and Phaelon tore each other to shreds before him and God was not impressed by the performance.

This is all my doing, Gray resolved.

And with that, Gray heard what sounded like the closing of a book in his mind, the finality of this enterprise. The sheathing of the Sword of God. Then he looked out to the battle and the unthinkable was happening.

The Phaelon were striding back from the bridge, like players casually leaving a rugby pitch. Michael ran ahead of them, holding his head and stumbling.

"Jesus Christ!" Gray exhaled.

RUN

The glowing arrows passed under Salla as she ran through dark corridors. They led her through the turns and levels and finally the glow of daylight was ahead of her. Then she was overlooking a huge landing bay filled with dozens of lifters.

"That's more than a few lifters, Achilles!" she said, eyes wide. She mourned for her friend for just a moment, even though he was a construction. There had been many others like him and possibly more to come, but she felt ashamed she'd considered him less than human. He was a good man.

She took Ivan's cufflinks out of his pocket and attached them to her sleeve. "Thank you for saving my life again."

She was halfway down the stairs to the landing bay level when she saw it. Amongst the lifters strode a huge sentry Arnock. It hadn't seen her yet and she silently slipped between a row of ships. She saw a lifter up ahead that was open and she moved towards it, removing her boots and walking silently in her socks.

The open lifter was just twenty steps away when she nudged a toolbox and knocked a wrench to the ground. The beast stopped its circuit, sending its gaze across the rows of ships. It stared for more than a minute, Salla standing perfectly still. Suddenly, the sentry rushed directly at her, flipping lifters over as it came.

Salla ducked under a wing of a lifter and the sentry passed. At the end of a row, it turned around and began to walk back on top of the ships, its razor sharp claws crushing cockpits and piercing wings. It scanned methodically, giant red eyes gleaming. Salla slipped into another open lifter, just one row over from the sentry. She locked in to the pilot's seat, flipped open a cover on the dashboard and hit the red emergency launch button underneath.

Without a countdown, the reactors ignited and instantly the engines hanging under the wings roared. She was thrown back in her seat as the lifter rose on a pillar of fire and a ring of destruction expanded below. The thrust from the launch tossed the other lifters like toys. The sentry slammed into an outer wall of the bay, burning and limbs trailing.

She winced as the G-forces pressed her and the inertial dampeners strained. The lifter passed through the first cloud layers and arched over in low orbit. She'd park up here until she could figure out what to do. It reminded her of on Nova Turin when she'd gone back half-a-dozen times to pick up trapped settlers pinned down by Gray's forces. They'd called her a hero, but nobody had taken her name. For the moment, she was happy to be above the trouble going on below. She wondered if Timberwolf was still alive. If Gray was still alive. She looked down and saw a hole in her sock and a toe sticking out. For the moment, she was just happy to be safe.

THE HILL

The Arnock funneled across the bridge. "I felt them, clawing at my mind! I felt them!" Michael was back up on the stairs now. "They'll be on us in seconds!"

"We're going up that hill." Gray pointed to the steep, earthen hill off to the left of The Chapel, an unfinished construction project that climaxed in a plateau.

"I've got us ready to go!" Warner had marshaled the human fighters to depart. "Sebaldi's dead, mortar. Thaum by a sniper."

"Go! I'll be right behind you." From the adjoining column room, a half-dozen sentry Arnock stooped and entered.

Gray knew he had just seconds to spring his trap before the Arnock invaded his mind. They were still an unfocused horde locked in a primal mode. "You're going to want to chronicle this part," Gray said to Izabeck, motioning to the door.

Looks passed between them and they knew his plan. Warner dropped his rifle and then picked it up again. Above them, the Sabatin threw themselves against the door of The Chapel. "Fucking run!" Gray barked.

Gray clambered up the stairs, a low Arnock croaking in his mind welling up. They were focusing on him now, the lone human in front of them. A mortar exploded behind him, stinging his ankles. Before him, like cardboard cutouts, ghosts appeared, at first shapeless but then taking form. Dov… Sol…Forestground…Jan…Thomas and the others… an Arnock parlor trick, showing you your dead.

At the top of the stairs, the Sabatin railed against the black doors. For an instant, reflected in the door, Gray saw an image of a Sabatin nailed to a cross, skinny and bleeding, a crown of thorns on its head. Gray took a breath, feeling the weight of thousands of minds seconds from falling on him.

He pulled the titanium bar from across the handles and dove away as the doors burst outward. Like a river of steel, the Sabatin rushed out.

Gray felt the relief instantly, the avalanche of minds pulling back. It was replaced by something else, not panic from the Arnock, but a sense of chaos.

The Sabatin were untrained and frantic, like wild street fighters flailing and biting. They tore through the Arnock on the bridge and flowed into their ranks on the other side. Sentry Arnock rushed over the scene, spearing and tossing the Sabatin away.

Sentries fired long, whining laser blasts from energy pods around their thoraxes. The back half of a Sabatin was melted into a puddle; its front half still snapped and bit. Ten Arnock tore a Sabatin apart limb from limb. A Sabatin split an Arnock in half and sent the flailing mess into the ravine.

As Gray slid down the side of The Chapel, he heard a crunching from within. A crack appeared and the whole front half of the structure shifted forward as something heavy moved inside. Then, like it was shot out of a cannon, a massive, three-horned Trike burst through the front of The Chapel and leapt on a sentry Arnock in front of the bridge.

The two beasts writhed on the ground, crushing smaller Sabatin and Arnock as they slashed and bit. Gray ran from them, but they rolled towards him. For an instant he was just feet away from their awful faces, contorted and shrieking at one another.

Timberwolf watched the violence from the shadows. He felt the Arnock now within his mind, but they didn't bother him. To him they just seemed like noise.

He'd caused a lot of destruction in his time, but nothing like this. This was a pure meat grinder he'd set in motion. He had hoped Gray would be caught between the Arnock and the Sabatin, though it seemed Gray had parried his way out of that trap, but barely.

In his heads-up, he watched Gray clambering up the hill, the rest of the men just ahead of him. He panned to the back of the Arnock line and Kizik was still there. He could see the creature, buzzing and shaking, trying desperately to control the battle, but it was clear that he was presiding over a disaster. The prize of Highland became more diminished every second the fighting continued. More sentries rushed passed and joined the fray. Timberwolf considered his options.

The monster or the spider? he thought to himself.

He abhorred the thought of Gray surviving, but he could only go after one of them. He thought of Gray's face, looking down on him when he was helpless and strapped to a bed in Purity Hospital, twisting the truth, forcing him to carry Kizik inside his mind.

The monster or the spider? he considered again.

He imagined himself a year out, five years out, ten years out. He's got a quiet place on a colony. There's a woman with him. For a moment he let it be Salla. And with him as well, somewhere in the back of his mind was Kizik, still there. Maybe tormenting him. Maybe letting him live in peace. Either way he knew when he went to sleep, there would be the giant spider with glowing red eyes. "I want that thing out of my head."

Timberwolf zoomed in on Gray one last time. He saw his face covered in dirt and grime. He thought about how small Gray was, truly. Just a man with a list of delusions longer than his arm.

Going after Gray was indulging in the morass of yesterday. Going after Kizik was choosing to live. He waded into the fray, heading for the spider.

THE FRAY

Timberwolf moved through the melee, both plasma blades on the end of his gauntlets aglow. On all sides, Arnock and Sabatin fought and died, some Sabatin killing each other. Through the slashing teeth and claws, he saw Kizik at the back of the line. Timberwolf cut an Arnock in half that challenged him and leaped through the air, landing just twenty yards from Kizik. Two Arnock blocked his way. They began to shiver with mind-bending intent.

Timberwolf shook off their attempts to enter his mind and drew closer, killing them both with smashing punches. Others began to converge on him. He could sense that they were being driven towards him by Kizik. But he killed them all, plasma driver and laser cutting them down.

He saw Kizik disappear down a tunnel, but one of Kizik's personal guards had grabbed him around the legs, buying the master a few seconds. Timberwolf hit him between his six eyes with a concussion blast, caving its head in. He was running now, through a twisting tunnel carved from the regolith. Ahead of him, Kizik scurried faster than Timberwolf thought possible, barely visible around the turns.

Am I chasing or being led somewhere? Timberwolf wondered.

SABACHTHANI

Gray's party ascended the steepest part of the hill on their hands and knees. Half would climb while the other half put down suppressive fire against the Sabatin leaping from below. Huddled farther up on a ledge, Izabeck was still writing in his electronic notebook, his eyes darting and stylus moving frantically.

"Son, give me the book," Gray shouted over the gunfire.

"I have to finish it!" Izabeck said, clutching it to him.

"I'll finish it."

Izabeck handed the book over, tears welling in his eyes. His doubts felt meaningless now as it seemed like the apocalypse raged around him, demons of various stripes tearing each other apart before his eyes.

"I'm sorry about before. God told me to doubt you. I had to be sure."

Gray had his hand on Izabeck's shoulder, eyes full of understanding. "Son, there are no sins left. You taught me that."

"I've got God's forgiveness?"

Gray didn't respond for a moment, considered what God had personally told him when he'd answered his prayers just a few minutes ago.

This is not my concern, God had said. It had been the coldest response. No interest. No approval. No judgment. No contempt. No hope. No opinion at all of these events.

"Sure," Gray responded to Izabeck, to the man's utter delight.

"I'm ready," Izabeck said with closed eyes, rubbing his arm where the nuke was.

"I know. A little farther," Gray responded, motioning to the plateau just a few dozen yards away.

A Sabatin leaped from below and hung in the air. Getting a claw into Ahmed's back, it took the man back down with him. Below, Ahmed screamed and thrashed, the men on the ledge unable to do anything to save him. Then a Sabatin, its jaws grinning with blood, had Ahmed's rifle. Only half-knowing why, the beast pulled the trigger. Blinding plasma bursts raked the ledge. A shot struck Cisus under the arm and the man fell into the midst of the Sabatin below.

Gray, Michael, Warner, and Izabeck climbed the hill again, the plateau just above them now. Windwhistle was still on the ledge and he fired down like a machine, knocking the Sabatin back. "By God, I don't waver. I am a force of judgment, ferocious and brave. I heed the judgment of God and rid his kingdom of aliens. I shoot them in the middle. Of. Their. Fucking. Skulls."

A Sabatin jumped to the ledge, right in front of Windwhistle. He pumped a grenade into its mouth and it exploded with a *clang*, leaving a standing armored shell. Then the ledge collapsed. As he fell, Windwhistle fired more grenades at the Sabatin, even as his left hand was bitten off on the way down. When he landed at the bottom, he fired his last grenade into the ground, disappearing in the blast.

Gray looked down from the plateau, to the hole in the ground that Windwhistle had made. He'd bought them a few precious seconds, but more Sabatin were rushing the hill. It was just four of them left now—Gray, Michael, Warner, and Izabeck in front of the door that led up the Bone Yard.

"I'll have your life now," Gray said to Izabeck.

The man knelt, back to the door in the rock face. "I give it to you. I give it to God."

"You're a martyr," Michael said, maybe even meaning it.

"They were all martyrs," Gray said.

Izabeck rose, giving Gray the tightest and briefest of embraces. "I don't have far to go. I'm already in heaven. For me, it was always just up this hill!"

Gray gave him a resigned smile as Michael opened the door with a creak and Gray, Michael, and Warner slipped through. Warner was last and gave Izabeck a long, sorry glance before pulling the door closed.

Izabeck knelt there a moment, in true peace, even as the horrific battle raged below him. The fighting was now a frenzy of violence. Lasers flared. The Trike and the sentry Arnock still fought in front of the bridge. The Trike, now on top, sent its dagger tongue through the sentry's face, finally making it go limp.

Izabeck found the events in front of him indescribable, but he had done his best. He had safeguarded the third testament. He let out a sigh, considering the message he had gotten from God right before he had given the book to Gray.

Sabachthani.

In his notebook, he had read the word in the multi-language thesaurus. He had found it accidentally as he struggled to complete the verses. He knew God had put it there to find. It was an old word from the language of Jesus Christ; no doubt the Dachas had picked it on purpose when naming the Sabatin. Gray should have known this crusade would fail, should have seen the sign in that name alone.

Izabeck didn't care about dying. He opened the chamber in his arm again, wincing. He offered the pain up to God. He connected the two wires together that made a circuit. He fished out the third wire that activated the trigger. Tears stained his dirty face, but they were tears of relief. He knew that he had played his part correctly and that he had ensured the Word of God would be protected.

Sabatin appeared momentarily on the lip of the plateau, and then slipped off. "There is no god but God and I heed his judgment," he said to himself, fiddling with the trigger wire. He cried again and laughed at the same time. Holy tears. Sabatin…Sabachthani…*the Aramaic word for forsaken.*

If it was meant to be, the third testament would come to Gray again through other means, but what was left in the book was not the story Izabeck had written. *So be it.* "The forsaken have followed Emmanuel Gray here," he coughed.

Around him now were six Sabatin. "There is no god but God and I heed his judgment." A snap of silver jaws. "There is no god…"

FIRE

With an ungodly crack and a blinding light came the sweep of a nuclear shock wave and then nothing but fire.

The Chapel turned to embers and casually blew away.

In the column room, flames reached to the spiral staircase and climbed all the way to where Wrath had fallen.

In The Warehouse, fire spilled in, swirling the boxes and containers into ashes.

High above The Catalog, the sun flickered and went out, its event horizon collapsing. Dull floodlights clacked on, and the floor of The Catalog dropped away, leaving a massive, gaping hole, and a pillar of smoke rose from The Command Center Plain below.

Dust fell like snow. A pitifully mangled Sabatin crawled along the edge of the hole, thrown up here by the blast. Its armor was melted, its limbs horribly burned. It squeaked in pain and then stopped moving, giving a last agonized breath.

Gray, Michael, and Warner pulled themselves from the hatch in the floor in the bone yard. In front of them, the train was pulling away on an automated schedule. They ran for it, Michael fastest and youngest, getting on. Next Gray got aboard and then they both reached back for Warner. The old man stumbled in the dust, collapsing. He locked eyes with Michael and Gray for a moment; his artificial left foot had fallen off, damaged in the fighting. He waved them off, but there was nothing they could have done to help him anyway.

Behind them, the door to The Catalog got smaller and finally disappeared as the track curved around the mountain of dead spaceships. Then, the ground rippled from the blast, the massive door blown off its hinges and flying through the air behind them. The train continued on its track, a cloud of dust overtaking them from behind.

In a tunnel, the shock wave hit Timberwolf. The pressure shot him forward, squeezing him along with the rubble and fire. *Sunrise! Zret!* he thought. He'd read the rig's brochure when he first got it and in bold print it had read *nuclear survivable*. He assumed that it had been marketing bullshit, but even as his external temperature exceeded six thousand degrees, the integrity of the rig held.

He slammed against a wall in the storm of dust and debris. A moment later he was floating freely, held aloft by the pressure waves sweeping by him in all directions. Then he was in a clear chamber, falling suddenly. He landed hard, flat on his stomach, and everything was darkness, only his audio sensors working. He heard something not far away, a *tick-tick* sound.

It was the claw-steps of Kizik somewhere near.

THE COFFERS

Wrath had one good limb and he pulled himself along the dusty corridor. He could smell the battle not far away, the burnt cinder of plasma blasts, the sweet and pungent chemical lasers. He wanted to fight, but he knew he had to heal, had to get to the lowest place he could. It was in his programming and part of his natural instinct.

Wrath slipped through a duct as he heard the sentry Arnock entering the battle above. He heard thousands of Sabatin clawing the ground and smelled the oily blood of the Arnock spilling in a deluge. He slid to the bottom of the duct and pried open a series of barriers with his working claw, his others hanging useless at his side. When he was through, he flopped on his back over a slowly turning air filter, slipping through the blades of the filter, unable to stop his fall.

He tumbled from the ceiling into a huge room, landing atop a mountain of treasures. Gold and platinum coins, crystals, ancient texts, artwork, statues—the currencies and valuables of thousands of worlds. Wrath's animal mind had no understanding of where he was and the wealth surrounding him. He was cold now and slid down to the floor.

Above him, all of Highland shook wickedly and a rumble deep and near overtook the place, but nothing in the room was even toppled. Wrath was exhausted and he slept in a corner of Highland's great Coffer, the sweet death given him by Droma still numbing his lips. One simple thought crossed his mind. *Alone.*

DETENTE

Gray and Michael ran, neither of them acknowledging the other. They just ran. During the fighting, Gray had pushed Michael's betrayal to the side, but what he'd done was sinking in now. Michael had decided Timberwolf's fate, taking action just as certain as putting a burst into his back. Maybe it had been the right thing to do, but it hadn't been Michael's choice to make. In his anger, Gray felt a weakness in himself. Michael had done what he didn't have the guts or clarity of mind to do. He'd cut away Timberwolf, eliminated his blind spot. Part of Gray was prideful and embarrassed he hadn't taken out his own trash. The train had stopped about two miles short of The Eye. They trudged through the bone yard, breathers on, the dust from the explosion overtaking them.

They slipped through the door to The Eye. Outside, they were hit by a blast of frigid air that stopped them in their tracks. A wet snow pelted them and collected in drifts. The stillness of The Eye was gone, replaced by a driving wind. The cloud wall was still intact, but it was losing its cohesion and tightening inward, lightning crackling up and down the barrier. They trotted forward, hoping beyond hope that *Nemesis*…

Nemesis lay on its back, a sentry Arnock's claw broken off and impaled through its hull. The ship gave off a thick, black smoke and it was clear it had been burning for hours.

"Goddamn," Gray said, the hope dropping out of his voice. He finally met Michael's gaze, but the man was a blank slate, looking not through Gray but past him.

In the distance, a small train car approached on tracks barely visible in the snow and dust. With no other options, they hopped aboard as it moved passed. A voice greeted them; it was Penny's. "Would you like to go to the landing bay?" it asked.

"Please," Gray responded.

"Landing bay, eleven minutes. Please hold small children by the hand."

"Penny?" Gray asked.

The voice didn't respond.

"Are you Penny?" Gray asked again to no response.

The two sat on the train in silence, done explaining things to one another, thinking only of surviving the next eleven minutes. Soon, a massive structure the size of a stadium that must have been the landing bay loomed in the distance. Gray looked over at Michael and the man was pointing his sidearm at him. Michael's eyes were without feeling. He wasn't sorry for what he'd done, for trapping Timberwolf in The Chapel. "That gives us some balance," Gray said, opening his jacket to show that he was holding a weapon on Michael as well. The two kept eyes locked and didn't notice the pillar of smoke that rose over their destination.

MEETING KIZIK

Timberwolf dragged himself out of a pile of dust, his visual sensors barely operating. He made his way by touch along a wall, following the *tick-tick*. He got a reading in his heads-up that the air was nominally safe to breath and he flipped open his visor.

He climbed down a hole in the floor and found himself in a gleaming white chamber. In the corner of the space, Kizik was there. He was huddled and seemed a lot smaller than Timberwolf remembered. He reminded himself that this was only the second time he had actually seen Kizik for real.

Timberwolf didn't feel him in his mind. He came within ten feet of Kizik before the Arnock did something shocking.

Kizik spoke, with a sound that was almost musical and seemed like three voices in different octaves.

"I had hoped for this. To see you."

Timberwolf had expected meeting Kizik to be overwhelming, but it wasn't. He'd known the being for so long.

"This is new. I didn't think Arnock could speak." Timberwolf drew closer, ignited a plasma blade with a shake of his wrist. Kizik's burnt cinnamon musk filled his nostrils.

"I wanted to communicate with you in a way that made you comfortable," Kizik said.

"None of this makes me comfortable."

Kizik backed away from Timberwolf, into a corner. "We should continue. Our minds are intertwined." He emphasized the highest octave of his voice. "We keep our people from war by watching, knowing."

"You're nothing but lies. You let me know only what served you."

Kizik backed up, started to shiver and buzz, but Timberwolf didn't feel anything in his mind.

"Don't bother," Timberwolf said, feeling freed from Kizik's control. He was just feet away now and he raised his arm, glowing plasma sickle ready to slice through the creature.

Then he heard it, like a mocking laugh in his mind. He was frozen there, unable to bring his arm down. Kizik spoke with his lowest, darkest octave. "You and I. Our connection was like no other. Other Arnock can't touch your mind. I can." The creature moved behind him. "I wanted to see you physically. To understand the mistake I made. You're a remarkable being, too dangerous to exist. You will die. Your brother will live."

Kizik forced Timberwolf to bring the sickle to his own throat. He tried to pull it away, but couldn't. "We're finished," Kizik said in all three octaves.

With a rabid howl, Droma and one of her clan-mates appeared. Unable to stop himself, Timberwolf swung at the pair, slicing the clan-mate's chest from top to bottom. Droma was then on Kizik, cracking one of his legs, the creature releasing a puny screech.

Still possessed, Timberwolf threw Droma against the wall and pulled back his blade to end the Phaelon's life. Then Kizik was gone, limping down an adjoining tunnel and Timberwolf realized what he was doing.

"God, he's still here!" Timberwolf fell down on his haunches. He'd undertaken this whole thing to rid the spider from his mind and he couldn't do it. Droma looked down at him, seeming to understand his pain. The Phaelon took off, rushing after Kizik, and Timberwolf knew he couldn't follow.

Timberwolf was numb, other Arnock couldn't invade his mind, but the connection with Kizik seemed even stronger. He staggered through a tunnel, his sensors indicating an opening to the outside not far away.

THE RUINS

"Put your goddamned gun away," Gray snapped at Michael, as they looked over the landing bay. The place was a disaster, burning lifters scattered about and broken. None looked salvageable. A blast radius and a scorch on the ground indicated where a single lifter had taken off.

Michael put his pistol away and hung his head. There was nothing here to help them get off this rock. Gray wondered if he'd lost everything, if there was even a next step for him. There was no prize left on Highland. No war with the Arnock to ride off to. The Assault Corps was on its way, but the production facility was destroyed. Would he fall to his knees when they got here and beg for protection? Could he go back to The Clergy and kiss Cardinal Jacob's ring? Put aside his fury with Michael and go about the galaxy shooting and looting?

"Do I just run?" he asked aloud. "Do I just run?"

NUMB

Timberwolf found himself on a platform overlooking the landing bay. One lifter had gotten away. It must have been Salla. It looked like she punched the emergency liftoff and wrecked all the other vehicles. The smoking dead sentry Arnock crumpled in the corner told him why she did it. *So much for the good neighbor policy.*

The platform moaned, weakened. Stacks of empty Sabatin containers were nearby, tossed about. A single shot rang out from across the landing bay, winging Timberwolf's shoulder. He dove away and flipped up his visor instantly, scanners still only half active. There, just fifty yards away, were Michael and Gray. He hadn't seen them on his heads-up.

"You can kill me easy." Gray approached over a catwalk, arms wide, rifle lowered. His armor off, he wore only a T-shirt and cargo pants. Michael followed, rifle trained on Timberwolf. "You have a gift to survive. It's what God took away and then the Arnock gave you back. Remarkable. Letting you die back there would have been a sin. Glad you saw to it we weren't guilty." Gray and Michael reached the platform. "Got a nice new rig. From Penny? The old box of bolts liked you, huh? You didn't come after me back there. What'd you go and do Timber?" Gray stopped for a moment, cupped his chin mockingly. "You saw Kizik, didn't you? Had a live audience for once!"

Timberwolf didn't respond.

Gray continued, circling him. "You did! Then you know the spider was using you. All this time! It tears you up, because Timberwolf Velez is no one's tool!"

"No one should have this place."

"Well damn, all this is yours, Timber! Penny gave it to you. You feel honored the machine felt you were worthy? You really need to fix up the joint."

"It's rustic."

"Timber, is Kizik still there? Is the spider, still there?" Gray tapped his temples, taunting him.

Timberwolf didn't answer.

"It is! After all this, he didn't let you go! And let me guess, he kept Relaund. He's got you both now!" Timberwolf stared daggers through Gray.

"Emmanuel, please! Even God cut away Lucifer," Michael implored, impatient with all this talk.

Gray's anger with Michael finally reached a place where it had nowhere to go. "You took a choice from me before, Michael."

"He's alive. He always lives," Michael spat out the side of his mouth.

"Your story is ending, friend." Gray fired a burst into Michael's side, between a gap in his armor. The man fell to the deck, his rifle clacking away. Michael spit up blood as he crawled after his weapon, Gray stepping in front of him. The wound had ripped through his organs and would be fatal in a few minutes.

"You've always taken choices from me, Michael. When you disobeyed me over Enceladus, when you questioned this crusade. I told you that if Timberwolf was to die, that you'd follow soon after."

"He's not dead!"

"Well, looks like you're jumping the line."

"What about forgiveness?" Michael coughed, his lungs filling with blood.

Without another word, Gray fired a burst into Michael's temple, killing the man instantly. He simply stood for a moment, his weapon still extended, as the platform's superstructure groaned.

Timberwolf stumbled backwards, struggled for words for what he'd just seen. "After all this, you kill him? Why not me?"

"I can't have my choices taken away."

They stood without speaking for a long moment. "Timber, I need you to know the whole testament."

Gray took out Izabeck's book and transmitted it to Timberwolf. "Why do I have to understand you?" Timberwolf asked.

"It's about forgiveness."

"I don't need forgiveness!" Timberwolf grabbed him by the shirt.

"No, you don't understand." Gray shook free, rubbed his eyes. "I sent you down to meet Kizik and I knew what it was going to do to you! That it would connect to your mind if it let you live. I offered you up. Doctor Tier asked me to help her end the war." Gray took a long breath. "'Who's your best guy?' she'd asked me. 'Who's your best guy?' It was those damned words that started it."

Timberwolf steadied himself. He always blamed Gray for sending him down against Kizik, but he thought it had just been a poorly planned mission. That Gray had ignored the intelligence reports like Dr. Tier had told him. But the truth was that Jackhammer had gone off perfectly and Gray and Dr. Tier had been partners in the whole affair.

"You and Dr. Tier? That was Jackhammer? I was the mission?" Timberwolf stumbled backwards. "I was the mission?" he asked, almost to himself.

"We had no way to communicate with them. Dr. Tier wanted to find a peace with the Arnock, but I thought that you might be able to help us sniff them out, kill them all." Secondary explosions went off below the platform. "The truth is I need you to understand. I need you to be forgiven so that…"

Timberwolf stopped him. "So that you can be forgiven? There is no forgiveness. For anyone. For anything. There's no higher power high enough, *Bishop*."

"But we can make good! We finish this war and we can make good on all the sins! Go for broke."

"You're not a Believer. You don't care about God. You just want to pick up a weapon and go have your war!"

"So then throw off the damn talk and just kill me. You know plenty of ways to. You were a killing animal before Kizik got in your head and you're still an animal." Gray pulled down his collar. "How about this? Shoot me in the neck. Toss me down there into the fire or just pound on me with your damned fists. Think I care how it's done?" Gray's voice was almost hoarse and he breathed heavily out of his nostrils.

"It's gone," Timberwolf said matter-of-factly.

"What's gone?"

"Kizik's not in my head anymore. I just noticed." Timberwolf turned, looking out over the burning wreckage below. Gray was right, he could have killed him easy, the moment he saw him, but Timberwolf did the calculation, weighed what was right against what was smart.

His ear bud crackled. It was Salla. "Timberwolf? Timberwolf? You there?"

Gray deserved to die for everything he'd done, whether it was for exposing Timberwolf to Kizik or the massacre on Nova Turin or the disaster here on Highland. But at this moment, Emmanuel Gray was the most valuable item on this entire world and Timberwolf needed to buy something.

"So just shoot," Gray demanded.

Timberwolf raised his gauntlet and sent a weak plasma burst into Gray's chest, crumpling the man over. He pushed him into an empty Sabatin pod nearby and slammed it shut. Gray pounded from within, demanding that Timberwolf finish him.

Timberwolf watched as the box shook. He approached it. A red light on top blinked, indicating there was no life support flowing. In just a few minutes, Gray would use up all the oxygen trapped inside. He considered just stepping away.

"You there? I'll try you in five," Salla crackled over Timberwolf's ear bud again.

"I'm here," he responded.

"There's a tower for medical extracts. Not far."

Timberwolf looked up and saw the scaffold tower. "Got it." Before leaping away, he activated the life support on Gray's box, turning the light to green.

THE NEEDLE

Timberwolf pulled himself up over the side of the tower above the landing bay. The fires below raged now. Highland's environmental controls were breaking down here too, a heavy snow suddenly blowing in. The wind spread the fires now and the power cells from wrecked lifters exploded and burst. The tower shifted as flames began to crawl up towards him.

In the distance, he saw a speck of light growing closer. He attached his suit to a hook atop the tower and winched it up into the air for Salla to snatch. The tower shifted and groaned as Salla got closer. Just a mile away now, Timberwolf could make out the wings of the lifter. "I'm threading the needle here," she said, trying to sound cool and calm.

"No hurry," he said. The tower leaned forward in a way that seemed final. She was just a few hundred yards out now, but coming in way too fast. If she missed, there was no coming back around.

But she didn't miss. The lifter snagged the hook.

Timberwolf was in the sky then, trailing the lifter by a cable, the tower collapsing behind him. The snow and the wind whipped him about as they ascended through the layers of clouds. Maybe he was seeing things, but in the clouds, Timberwolf swore he saw faces, expressionless and vague. There was one face that tracked him as he went by, one of an old woman that seemed to almost smile as he passed.

He closed his eyes for a few minutes and then he was arching over and weightless. He let himself enjoy having no burdens for a few minutes as the clouds turned to black. He would have enough burdens soon.

CARAVEL

Salla looked up above the dashboard and a plaque read that the lifter was named *Caravel*. She exhaled slowly, somehow still alive. She decided not to think about how lucky she'd been. After a moment she rose and activated a winch at the back of the cabin. It whirred. The cable attached to Timberwolf pulled into a clear box.

"Timber, we made it. Is Gray dead?" she asked, getting no response.

With a jerk, the winch stopped. She worked it and it spun free, but there was nothing connected to the cable anymore, the frayed end whirled.

"Timberwolf? Timberwolf?" she called into the com link, getting silence in return.

Timberwolf hid amongst the debris from the destroyed Arnock ships, his suit darkened and giving off no energy. *Come on; get out of here!* He clenched his teeth, knowing that if he called Salla and told her to leave, she wouldn't. The wreckage crackled and sparked around him and he watched her pass by in the lifter, again and again, sensor beams reaching out. Her scans washed right over him and continued on.

An icon glowed in his heads-up. He'd dismissed it a dozen times already. Its officious title blinked in front of his eyes.

Third Holy Testament

Finally, he opened it up and let it play. Golden words began to scroll by in front of him. He expected a text that elevated Gray's efforts, that painted him as a prophet and portrayed the events here as sacred. What he got was something else. Just seventeen words that repeated over and over.

> *We were knights of the third testament. We followed Emmanuel Gray here. We were forsaken, forsaken, forsaken.*

That was it. Gray's *story* was gone, overwritten in Izabeck's final act. Gray's testament was reduced down to an S.O.S. from abandoned souls. Timberwolf laughed gently. *This was better than the bomb in your arm, Izabeck.*

Timberwolf saw something very big on the edge of his proximity scanner. It could only be one thing—*Archangel.* Salla traversed the wreckage and was close to him now in the debris, still searching.

"I'm dead. You get out of here!" he finally barked at her over the com link.

"You're here?" she responded.

"Didn't think you'd keep trying to find me."

"You should have known better."

"Go! You don't want this." *Archangel* ground towards them, its huge shadow overtaking them. "I might not be able to protect you!"

"From Doctor Tier? I don't know her and she's already on my bad side." A bright white tractor beam grabbed *Caravel,* a deep bass warbling filling the cabin. Salla winced and covered her ears.

The front of *Archangel* opened like a whale's mouth, taking *Caravel* and Timberwolf in its maw. The outer door shut with a humongous clang. Timberwolf floated outside the windscreen of *Caravel*. He looked in at Salla and turned his faceplate transparent so she could see him. "Couldn't you leave somebody behind, just this once?" he asked.

She put her hand to the glass. "Guess not."

TITHE

D.P.E. Archangel—Over Highland

"There's too much going on for this, Doctor." Captain Tirani stood in the doorway of Dr. Tier's quarters, Capote behind him.

"I'll just be a minute. I swear this is urgent." He crossed his arms and waited. "I've been given some information." He huffed. She wasn't supposed to have contact with anyone. He assumed that whatever it was, Conrad had gotten it to her somehow. "I need you to release me. Timberwolf is aboard. I must speak with him."

"No. You may not. You're in no position to ask for things."

"Delaine Darcy Nevins," she said to him.

Tirani entered the room, closed the door and left Capote in the hall. "You fucking with me?"

"Sister Nevins is a Believer evangelist. Real hard-core stuff. You've sent her money."

"I've dropped in a collection envelope once or twice."

"You tithe to her! Ten percent of your pay." Captain Tirani hung his head. It was true. He had tried to have it both ways, holding onto his religious beliefs while having a career in the secular D.P.E. "You delete your report about the Terecine," she said. "And I get to see Timberwolf, right now."

"Does this stay quiet?"

"Of course it does, Les." She smiled.

INTERROGATIONS

Salla sat across the table from Conrad. She noticed his haircut was perfect and his fingernails were manicured. She stared at him and he looked back vacantly, with no signs of compassion.

There was a two-way mirror on one wall and this was clearly an interrogation room, but he asked no questions. "Want me to tell you what happened?" she asked.

"We already know," he responded.

"So, we just sit here?"

"This needs to take twenty-five minutes. It's your rights."

"Are you going to put me away?" As soon as she asked that, she realized that they could make her disappear in other ways as well. She imagined this man dragging her to an airlock and opening the outer door.

Conrad looked to his watch. "Twenty-two minutes left."

In an identical interrogation room, Timberwolf sat across from Dr. Tier, his hands shackled in front of him and bolted to the table. She went through a litany of failures. "Highland is dripping with radiation. The A.I. is offline. Production capabilities are destroyed. The Dacha brothers are all dead. Your mission included us getting control of Highland."

"There isn't much I haven't failed at," he said, agreeing with her. "Oh wait, I did manage to get Kizik out of my head."

"Well, fucking congratulations."

"That cleans up your mess. That cleans up Jackhammer."

Her mouth dropped open just a little bit. *He knew. Gray must have told him!* She never thought he would have the guts. "Do you care what happens to you?"

"No," Timberwolf said genuinely. "I don't care about me."

"Salla Birdwing, vice governor from The Outpost. You should have disposed of her."

"Slipped my mind."

"She'll have to be put away. Long and good."

"Hell no."

"She's the one witness to all this!"

"She goes on her way." Timberwolf took in Dr. Tier's severe features and large, soulless eyes. He was about to make her difficult job immeasurably harder. "I've got something down there for you. There's not much time."

He beckoned her to come closer. "What?" she asked.

"The machines can't hear this." Timberwolf spoke in her ear and her eyes went wide.

DEATH BENEFITS

Salla rested with her head on the table. She thought she had about five minutes left. Conrad picked his fingernails. Dr. Tier burst in and Salla sat up, weary.

"Amnesia. After The Outpost you drifted in a lifter until you were picked up near Tep Nine-Fifty. You don't recall a thing. I cashed out your death benefits and put them on this card."

Dr. Tier handed Salla a credit card that had her name and picture on it. She took the card and turned it over. Under her photo, it read *deceased*.

"I'm done with this?" Salla asked.

"You're a dead woman. None of this matters to you. Don't let anyone look too closely at that card. Turn it into cash."

"But why? Why are you letting me go? What happens to Timberwolf?" Outside the door, Salla saw Timberwolf led past by security, his hands shackled behind him. They locked eyes for a moment and she knew he'd paid for her freedom.

Dr. Tier looked down on her with a pity in her eyes that said, *just go*. "Timber?" Salla called to him, but he was gone.

Just a few minutes later, Salla was aboard *Caravel* again. The maw of *Archangel* opened and a puff of air pushed the ship outwards. She looked back at the hulk of *Archangel* through the windscreen, her beautiful and raw face close to the glass. Exhausted, she closed her eyes and fell into the pilot's seat. As it had been programmed, *Caravel* fired its thrusters and made towards Tep Nine-Fifty. "Finally left somebody behind," she said to herself. She wondered if she would ever see Timberwolf again. "This is nothing, Timber. I'm gone, so take the gloves off. I'll see you soon."

Less than an hour later, Dr. Tier sat opposite Timberwolf in the belly of a lifter about to drop from *Archangel*. With them were techs in radiation-proof rigs, along to try to salvage whatever was left of the facility. Dr. Tier had less than fourteen hours before the first of the Assault Corps ships arrived. The chatter out of Tach-One was off the charts now. Secretary Bozeman himself was issuing orders. There had already been reports of Assault Corps attacks on D.P.E. facilities and vessels and vice-versa. A shooting civil war had started.

"Timberwolf, if you're lying and Gray's not down there, you'll rot forever," Dr. Tier said to him. "Think Salla Birdwing was worth it?"

"My personal life has got to be the least of your problems, Thea," he responded. She nodded, tightening her lips. "Better hurry, doc. There's not a lot of air in his box."

THE PRECIOUS THRONES

Cardinal Jacob stood in front of the doors to The Coffers on Highland. In the commotion while Timberwolf had been taken aboard *Archangel*, he and his two personal guards had borrowed a lifter and descended on their own. Behind the doors were the fortunes that Highland had collected from customers and, according to the deal he had made with Dr. Tier, now belonged to him.

A figure was huddled in front of the doors, covered by a radiation blanket. "Hello?" Cardinal Jacob asked.

The figure stirred and pulled the blanket away. An old man with one foot hobbled upright. "Can you open this?" Warner asked. "It's safe in there!"

"We're headed inside," Cardinal Jacob responded, amused by the hunched old soldier.

One of his guards worked an electronic device and placed it next to the lock on the door. The doors opened with a *click*, spreading outward, and a second pair of doors within did the same. They went inside, pulling the doors closed behind them to keep the radiation out.

"Praise be to God!" Cardinal Jacob took in the spectacle of wealth around him, the myriad objects of immeasurable value from throughout the galaxy. "I am in possession!" He exhaled. He sent a message to the other cardinals still loyal to him. *Come to Highland. Bring empty vessels.*

Cardinal Jacob sat on a huge chair made of gold, the handiwork of a species much larger than a man. Warner pulled himself up on a similar chair opposite him made of platinum. The wealth gleamed around them, illuminated by small floodlights floating like fireflies around the space. "I am in possession!" the cardinal said again, smiling to his guards. He knew he had to move the items out of here quickly before other parties arrived to challenge him, perhaps from the Assault Corps.

"You're the pope, right?" Warner asked, squinting at Cardinal Jacob sitting on his golden throne.

"Something like that." Cardinal Jacob nodded with a tolerant smile.

"Bishop Gray was a great man. He wrote a whole new testament," Warner said. Cardinal Jacob's eyebrow rose slightly. Warner continued from his platinum seat. "Got any water? I'll tell you the whole thing."

"Please," Cardinal Jacob said, his narrow smile not betraying the sudden knot in his stomach. One of his guards handed Warner a canteen.

The old man took a sip and licked the water from his dry lips. "It's about forgiveness…" he began.

On the other side of the room though, something stirred. Wrath awoke and pushed himself up with his one good limb, opening an eye. He was no longer alone.

THE GIFT

Kizik had no illusions about what had happened, about how he had failed. He couldn't even go home. He was the sole survivor of this expedition and he would be greeted by revulsion. If he went home, he would be forced to walk the twilight ridge, a monster. *Farhallen. Creature of the badlands. Beast of the wind.*

He had managed to do a few things, though. He sat in his shuttle and looked over at the Phaelon he had captured. Back on Highland he had managed to lure Droma aboard and incapacitate her. He would study the creature he now kept in stasis. It would keep him occupied if he was to wander the galaxy alone. He'd also retrieved the order he had placed to Highland a year before. The small, awful box sat next to him.

Radem, don't let me use it.

He didn't want to think of the power that it had or what using it would entail. It could only bring pain to his species in the end, but there it was—a great equalizer in a box that would fit a pair of human shoes.

His shuttle was cloaked and approached *Archangel.* He had accomplished one more thing, the counter to the destructive force that sat beside him. It was a gift.

Relaund.

Even as Highland had fallen apart, he'd ordered that his medics protect Relaund Velez and all had died in the effort. The man lay in a pressurized chamber next to him.

Relaund. Wake up.

The man stirred, opening his eyes.

I said we'd talk again after the assault. Things haven't gone as planned for anyone.

"What the hell do you want?" Relaund said aloud, stirring awake.

I am giving you back, better than I found you.

"I can feel my fingers. I just moved my thumb!"

Your muscles are severely atrophied. They should come back. I mended your spinal nerves with technology you don't have.

"I don't understand," Relaund said, his words soaked in innocence.

I don't either.

Kizik opened the back of the shuttle, a force field holding in the atmosphere. Just a hundred yards away was the bridge of *Archangel*. He could see human figures walking about, but they couldn't see him.

He pushed the pressurized chamber out into space. It sizzled as it passed through the force field and became visible outside of the shuttle's cloak. Kizik could see the people on the bridge rushing about now, trying to determine if the chamber was a threat. Then *Archangel* caught it in its tractor beam, holding it while sensors scanned its every molecule.

Kizik backed the shuttle away, never exposing his presence. He hoped that they would accept his gift, but didn't wish to stay here any longer. He looked down at the box again at his side. On its top it read Thanatos. Kizik had learned that was a word from an old human language.

Thanatos, he thought. *The personification of death.*

I'LL FLY AWAY

Gray felt like he was in the womb. When the tower had collapsed, the Sabatin container he was inside tumbled in the wreckage, but he'd been protected. When the life support had come online, it generated a living membrane that embraced him. An organic vessel attached itself to his stomach like an umbilical cord. He'd been in the box for two hours now and he felt neither hungry nor thirsty. But what was connected to him now was not meant for a man, but for a Sabatin, a programmable beast.

The membrane wrapped around him and he'd stopped fighting it a while ago. It squeezed him tighter and tighter and he felt blood swelling in his head. A strangeness flowed through him that he knew was connected to the membrane. He wondered if he was about to die or be reborn. No prayers came to mind and he knew God wasn't interested in hearing from him. He decided to sing the Assault Corps mourning song for himself.

"Some bright morning when this life is over, I'll fly away. To that home on God's celestial shore I'll fly away." He wondered whom he was singing to. To himself, to his conscience?

"When I die hallelujah by and by, I'll fly…" Suddenly he stopped. He couldn't remember the next line or where he was and what sequence of events had brought him to be trapped inside a small box. He struggled for a moment and then, without knowing why, he was calm again. The membrane gave off a soft, red glow and he looked at his hand. He could see the light coming through it and almost make out the blood vessels pulsing within.

He felt himself regressing, unlearning, like something was clearing the table of his mind. His consciousness was simpler now, awaiting instructions. His hubris fled him and his pride. A small kernel of guilt, buried deep inside of him, faded as well. He saw faces one last time before they disappeared; a tall man with dark hair, a woman with angular features, a man with hair to his shoulders and burns on his face. Who were they?

He saw the world of Highland, a black disc covering it but for a crescent sliver. He existed one second to the next, not comprehending the moment before.

Then a flash of recognition came back to him and he twisted around and pulled a knife from his pocket. He scratched a message on the inside of the box, struggling to remember the letters and words. Then his faculties were gone again and he closed his eyes. From the deepest part of him, the simplest twinkle of a lullaby passed between his lips. "When the shadows of this life have gone, I'll fly away. Like a bird from these prison walls, I'll fly. I'll fly away."

And then Emmanuel Gray was no more.

For more news about Tom Julian, subscribe
to our newsletter at *wbp.bz/newsletter*.

Word-of-mouth is critical to an author's long-term
success. If you appreciated this book, please leave a
review on the Amazon sales page at *wbp.bz/timberwolf*.

COMING SOON FROM WILDBLUE PRESS
More timeless science fiction tales
from John Hayden Howard!

https://wbp.bz/RW2wbp

OUT NOW FROM WILDBLUE PRESS

Classic science fiction tales from John Hayden Howard!

In 8 short stories, meet a professor in two places at once, a 1940s boxer with a stranger and a 1960s mind-controlling student. Find aliens with a teen surfer, student archaeologists, and Arctic villagers. Root for an Earthman's beloved dog on Mars, then a crewman in a massive antigravity battle.

https://wbp.bz/RW

**MORE SCIENCE FICTION FROM
WILDBLUE PRESS**

The Happenstance Series by Phil Sheehan

Phil Sheehan's HAPPENSTANCE series is a captivating sci-fi saga packed with non-stop action, suspense, and multiple concurrent plots on Earth and beyond; this series demands your attention and tugs at your emotions. Join protagonist Blake Thompson and his friends as they navigate a world filled with alien technology, global conflicts, and unexpected dangers. From lost loved ones to treacherous encounters, they must rely on their skills and teamwork to survive. The HAPPENSTANCE series is a must-read if you love believable futuristic science fiction blended with heart-pounding action.

https://wbp.bz/happenstancea
https://wbp.bz/tribulations

www.ingramcontent.com/pod-product-compliance
Lightning Source LLC
Chambersburg PA
CBHW071352300726
48976CB00006B/1853